Critical acclaim for
RUMORS OF SPRING

"A WONDER OF A BOOK . . . BEAUTIFULLY WRITTEN, ORIGINAL AND A GREAT DEAL OF FUN. IT WILL LIVE."
—R. A. MacAvoy

"READERS WHO CARE ABOUT GOOD, THOUGHTFUL WRITING WILL DELIGHT IN *RUMORS OF SPRING*. RICHARD GRANT'S PROSE IS SUCH THAT I KEPT STOPPING TO THINK OVER AN IDEA, OR REREAD A CERTAIN TURN OF PHRASE OR BIT OF DESCRIPTION, SIMPLY BECAUSE IT WAS SO GOOD. IF YOU ENJOYED THE WAY JOHN CROWLEY PULLED SO MANY DIVERSE ELEMENTS SO SEAMLESSLY TOGETHER IN *LITTLE, BIG* THEN THIS BOOK IS FOR YOU."
—*Fantasy Review*

"A FASCINATING LOOK AT THE FUTURE. THIS BOOK HAS A WARM AND WONDERFUL CHARM."
—*The Stamford Advocate*

"A FUN, HEARTWARMING EXPERIENCE. GRANT'S CHARACTERS GROW AND DEVELOP AND HIS DESCRIPTIONS OF THE FOREST ARE WONDERFUL."
—*Rocky Mountain News*

"A LITERATE, AMBITIOUS WORK."
—*Locus*

RUMORS

OF

SPRING

Richard Grant

BANTAM BOOKS

TORONTO · NEW YORK · LONDON · SYDNEY · AUCKLAND

RUMORS OF SPRING

A Bantam Spectra Book
Bantam hardcover and trade paperback edition / March 1987
Bantam paperback edition / May 1988

Excerpt by Randolph Stow from THE GIRL GREEN AS ELDERFLOWER.
Copyright © 1980 by Julian Randolph Stow. Reprinted by permission of Viking
Penguin Inc.
Excerpt by Edward O. Wilson from BIOPHILIA (1984), Harvard University Press.
Reprinted by permission.
Excerpt by James Merrill from "The Book of Ephraim" in Divine Comedies.
Copyright © 1976 James Merrill. Reprinted with the permission of Atheneum Publishers,
Inc.
Excerpt p. 199 reprinted by permission of The Putnam Publishing Group from PALE
FIRE by Vladimir Nabokov. Copyright © 1962 by G. P. Putnam Sons.

Library of Congress Cataloging-in-Publication Data

Grant, Richard, 1952–
    Rumors of spring.

    (A Bantam spectra book)
    I. Title.
PS3557.R268R8   1987   813'.54   86-22359
ISBN 0-553-26648-9

Published simultaneously in the United States and Canada

Bantam Books are published by Bantam Books, a division of Bantam Doubleday
Dell Publishing Group, Inc. Its trademark, consisting of the words "Bantam
Books" and the portrayal of a rooster, is Registered in U.S. Patent and
Trademark Office and in other countries. Marca Registrada. Bantam Books,
666 Fifth Avenue, New York, New York 10103.

Quercus robinia
(Classification attrib. to Hayata)

May not be a true oak. Its botanic and medical
   properties are not fully catalogued, but
appear widely variable. Merits further research.

Prelude

Nothing so foolish could be impossible:
whenever one looks twice, there is some mystery.
— ELIZABETH BOWEN

Rosa gallica 'officinalis'

Apothecary rose

One prolonged, magnificent, late-spring flowering.
The fruits, borne later, make a soothing
infusion.

One

TROVER GOODFELLOW, tired of traveling alone, decided to risk abandoning the safety of the woods for a small roadway that twisted through the Carbon Bank Forest toward the mountains in the north. He wasn't sure what kind of companion he wanted on this adventure, or whether he wanted a companion at all, or even an adventure. The old feeling had come upon him, these last few days, and it terrified him. He gave up napping in the afternoon, and sunning himself in crumbled parking lots. Still the feeling followed him. It nattered behind his ears like a cricket. It accompanied him on the harp. It drove him to spend his money on the soothing stuff of the city until there was nothing left for him but the highways and the woods, which were all there had ever been for Trover anyway. And soon he was walking alone through the forest, the last great forest in the world.

The roadway led him into deep spruce woods where the sun never touched the ground and his way was often blocked by fallen logs. In places the road was overgrown by saplings as tall and lank as Trover had been a decade ago, when aloneness never troubled him, nor companionship either. Well, times were easier then, he told himself.

And the honest part of his mind replied: Maybe.

One morning he paused by a streambed, trying to coax a memory to the surface. It was not a simple memory like a song or someone's birthday. It was more a kind of pattern, an interlocking of many things together, and trying to remember it was like trying to think about something that didn't fit in the mind all at once: not a song but the way you felt when you sang it; not a birthday but the whole year it belonged to.

And it was important.

Trover was sure it was important though he was sure of nothing else. He felt as though the act of having this memory was a long parturition, the seed of the thing having lain dormant in him for a time and then begun to swell and now to burst the seams of his brain if he didn't remember it, and *Mother Mab* was it important. But he couldn't remember why.

In time he decided the whole thing had to do with the streambed before him, which until he thought about it had seemed no more than the usual gurgling pebble-bedded moss-banked sort of thing you always find in woods like these. The roadway crossed it at a graveled ford. But the memory hadn't nagged him till he got here. And now—when he really *saw* the place—the streambed brought the memory even closer, as though it might leap from the water and land wet and wriggling in his hands.

Had he been here before, then? Years ago, maybe, when his life had been lived on roads like this?

Trover doubted it. He had lost nothing in these woods that he cared to find again. He had never reached that special destination, that place of rest and contentment that had seemed to be waiting around every turn. He sighed. And you're not (he told himself) going to find it now, old man.

Leaning out over the water, Trover dispensed a generous wad of spit, thinking, So much for *that*.

He wobbled and nearly fell after it.

Behind him, crunching up the roadway, boots were approaching at a rapid and noisy gait. There were two sets of them, it sounded like, and suddenly Trover's desire for companionship evaporated. The only people he could think of who would walk so loudly through a forest—in times like these, especially—were people he did not want to meet. In the few seconds remaining before the footsteps rounded the turn, Trover surveyed the undergrowth along the stream, found it adequate, and plunged in knee-deep. Something fell from his knapsack and landed with a tiny splash, but he did not stop to see what it was, did not stop for anything until he was safely behind the scrub pine at a bend.

The footsteps reached the ford. Trover gulped air and marveled at what he had come to: scared and breathless after fleeing what might, after all, have been a profitable encounter—drinks all around, maybe, and a chance to collect saleable gossip. Moreover his trousers were wet and would not dry for hours in this dampness. Peering through the bracken, he glimpsed two gray-green-clad figures tromping, carefree or merely uncaring, into the woods on the other bank. Black-barreled weapons, of the type favored by the Pure Force, lay across their backs.

A faint smile of vindication flickered over his face as Trover hoisted himself onto a boulder. The old instincts weren't *totally* lifeless, he thought.

That was before he started to wonder what he was going to do next.

In his days of professional wandering, it had been Trover's habit to travel by water when possible, or by paths beside the water when these presented themselves. Waterways led to people, he found, and were less carefully watched than roads, often affording the opportunity to slip into a village without the bother of presenting a work-card or signing the Registry of Pilgrims. He reckoned these advantages might be even more considerable now.

Unfortunately, the present stream, humble thing that it was, was not equipped with a path, and Trover was obliged to slog ankle-deep through the ooze left behind by several weeks of spring showers. The character of the forest changed, too, as he made his way upcurrent. Once flat, the landscape assumed bold contours, sloped steeply up from the streambed and cut off much of Trover's light. The spruce gave way to mixed oak—though near the stream there grew an unusual profusion of thorntrees, on account of which the sleeves of Trover's jacket were reduced to rags and his hands were striped with welts as red and sore as lash marks.

After two days of this, he reached a place where the stream flowed deep and quiet. The hush that lay on the water caused him to walk more slowly, with an affectation of reverence, like an atheist entering a temple. The breeze carried rumors of a waterfall, whispering then falling silent as the stream insinuated itself into the fabric of the land, and the unborn memory started to ache again. Trover wondered if it was really his own memory at all. Maybe it was some mood of the forest trying to force itself upon him. (This idea he dismissed as the sign of an oncoming cold. God knows it was chilly enough.)

The great oak tree, when at last he noticed it, startled him more than he could have expected.

It was as unmistakable as a lifelong enemy. An ancient thing, its bark pitted, its limbs too broad to encompass at a single gaze, it squatted so low beside the stream that the water over the years had dug a C-shaped course around it. Its leaves grew in dusty green clusters on limbs that were long past being fruitful. And yet the oak did not look ready for the slow retreat into the soil. Unlike other old trees, with their look of weary survivors, this one remained an aggressor, a devourer of sun and water, a patriarch unwilling to give place to its progeny.

Trover drew his knife and glanced around him. A path—he had known there was a path—led him up a hillside where mountain laurel bloomed, across a meadow, orange with afternoon and marigolds, and finally through an orchard of slender trees that grew from old, thrice-coppiced stumps. Trover remembered this detail, remembered everything about the place and yet remembered nothing. And then he came to the wall.

It was new, unweathered, its cedar planks twice as tall as Trover, with no gate in sight. He regarded it approvingly. Anyone scared enough to build a barricade like this had to be Trover's kind of folks. Stripping off his pack, he set about tumbling the wall in the time-honored fashion.

He released the fastenings of the harp, easing its dirty beige power-box into a mound of wild shamrock. His arms slid quickly, from a lifetime of practice, into the leather harness, and his fingers lay gently on the sounding board. He hummed a B-flat, punched POWER and closed his eyes.

The air around him began to stir and then to moan as the chthonian harp—his only possession of note, but worth his life several times over to the likes of those men on the trail—vibrated in resonance with the shimmering ganglia in Trover's spine. He let it go awhile, its undertones dipping below the edge of audibility and its upper register flushing bluejays from a tree. Then he squeezed the ball of sound into a semblance of a G-minor chord (his favorite) and hurled it blaring into the wall. The notes phosphoresced behind his eyes.

From the outside, unwitnessed by Trover (though he had seen it happen on scores of disks), his face glowed with a roseate aura of serenity. He opened his mouth; he shook his verbal brain awake and sent words shuttling downward to his vocal chords. This was the hardest part: his senses having turned inward, he could make out neither the pitch nor the meaning of his song. The trick succeeded, somehow; the disks had proved it. But it was astonishing, every time—as though the song came out of somewhere other than Trover's tattered and febrile mind.

It was his act, his bit of sideshow magic. He sang:

> From Oberon, in fairyland,
> The king of ghosts and shadows there,
> I Goodfellow, at his command,
> Am sent to view the nightsports here.
> There's not a hag
> Nor ghost shall brag,
> Nor cry, Ware goblin! where I go;
> Goodfellow I
> Their feats will spy,
> And fear them home with ho ho ho!

He paused a moment to force his eyes open and upward, seeking the top of the wall. It was futile. Whatever message the retinas tried to relay was lost in the whirlwind of his consciousness. He picked up his old abducted theme song.

> If any wanderers I meet
> That from their nightsports do trudge home,
> In counterfeiting guise I greet
> And cause them on with me to roam.
> Through woods, through lakes,

Through bogs and brakes,
Through brush and brier,
There I go.
I call upon them to come on,
And wend me laughing, ho ho ho!

Trover felt himself weaving. Something had disturbed his balance, some new center of gravity was pulling the bright ball of sound off its orbit. He plopped himself down on the power-box and tucked his feet into the shamrock.

Sometimes I greet them like a man,
Sometimes a bird, sometimes a flow'r.
Or to a horse I turn me can,
To trip and trot for half an hour.
But if to ride
My back they stride,
More swift than wind away I go,
'Cross hedge and fronds,
Through pools and ponds,
I whinny laughing—

The notes of the chthonian harp were sucked into an invisible maelstrom, vanishing with a last electric *plup*. Something caused Trover to tip backward; disconnectedly he managed to shield the sounding-board as he thumped onto the ground. He opened his mouth, expecting to groan, but a feeble titter emerged instead. The harp really took something out of you.

Above him, staring down from what to Trover seemed a vertiginous height, was a pale face with two very large dark eyes. Something about the eyes pressed down on him: something like heat, but no, that wasn't it, his senses were still tangled up. It occurred to Trover that the person connected to the eyes was a woman, some kind of woman. How many kinds were there? He tittered again.

"What brought *you* back here?" a voice said.

It was the woman's voice. Her lips moved. Soft wide lips.

"—You bastard."

To Trover's absolute astonishment, the woman kicked him. Right in the ribs; he could feel that pretty clearly.

"Oh, Trover, what are you *doing* here?" she said. And Trover thought he should say something now, for the woman was crying.

He sang softly,
"Ho ho ho."

Two

BALANCE ACT Reporting Station 12 was the only one of the series actually built—a fact that would have surprised and disappointed those who lobbied for its creation, most of whom died under the comforting misapprehension that the entire chain had been completed, that throughout the hemisphere teams of researchers held their fingers to the wind, cups to the rain, eyes to the logging roads, and computers to the kind and quantity of plant life that remained in the world's carbon reservoir.

Not so. The public law that created Station 12 (and lent it its name) provided authorization but not funding for the endeavor—the money having been expected to arrive by way of separate legislation, or not; in the event, things grew complicated very quickly and the lawmakers turned their attention to other concerns. Station 12, underwritten briefly as a "demonstration project" by an overextended university, had in fact received no money for the past forty years or so. But the place had taken root, as things will do in the fertile soil of a forest, albeit the last in the world. The name had taken root also, in an odd sort of way, for a refugee camp in the area had ripened into a town that called itself Balance Act, and for some decades afterward an occasional piece of mail would arrive for one of the researchers in care of Reporting Station, Balance Act. Then the town was abandoned and the world forgot Reporting Station 12, or perhaps the mails ceased to run; the researchers by then made little effort to keep abreast of current affairs, which they were powerless, they thought, to affect. The only thing yet remaining in this cul-de-sac of civic history was the name Balance Act, and the only person left to remember it—but one—was Amy Hayata.

Amy watched Trover pick through the bowl of stew she had given him, looking (she supposed) for meat. There was none.

"I'm sorry I can't offer you anything more elaborate," she said. "If I'd only known you were coming . . ."

"Hey, that's all right," he said cheerfully, then looked across the expanse of the table—barren except for a lone indigo iris in its handblown vase—and saw Amy's expression. "Oh," he said. "I see. Yeah, I'm sorry, Amy."

And he cast his eyes downward in an attitude of such dire dejection that Amy was almost—almost—drawn to sympathy.

He looked frightful, really. Much more . . . *abject* than he had looked nine years before. His red hair was thin and rangy, flying in wisps in all directions as though repelled from his skull by an electrical charge. The dozen pounds that had collected in the midregions of his body did nothing to diminish the thinness of his shoulders or the gauntness of his face. His eyes, though still bright, seemed to study the world in a series of furtive glances, as an animator assembles a story from flickering stills; it was a mannerism she did not remember. But what *did* she remember, really? It had all been so brief, and so long ago.

Amy herself had never looked better, and she knew it. Her blue-black hair fell to her waist as thick as sheaves; her round face and wide glowing eyes were like those of a porcelain doll. She supposed her enduring youthfulness was, in the present setting, a kind of revenge, then reflected that it was wrong to desire revenge upon someone, especially someone . . . Then she thought, What the hell.

Trover slurped while he ate.

"I never hear from *anyone*," she told him. "I'm still waiting for supplies I ordered two years ago. Isn't anybody out there anymore?"

"They're out there," said Trover. "Too many of them. You should see Riverrun these days."

Amy had no wish to see Riverrun, or any of the other places she had known. Her life was here, her work, everything. She nodded absently, but Trover was still talking.

"Things have gotten a little . . . disorganized, I guess you could say. And dangerous. But then, you know, I'm not much into politics or anything, so I don't worry too much. Money's tight, real money. The electronic stuff nobody trusts anymore. I was kind of stockpiling it there for a while, but then I got to spending it again. And there's this Pure Force business. . . ."

Remembering something, or responding to some subtle key-change at the table, Trover set this unpleasant topic aside. (Unpleasant, he guessed, at any rate, to a scientist probably discouraged enough already.) The quietness with which he laid down his spoon gave this simple act the weight of deliberation.

"Listen, Amy, how about you? Aren't you lonely way out here? Is it safe, do you think? I saw these two guys in the woods—"

Amy smiled. "Lonely," she repeated, aloud but to herself. "No, I'm not, really. And my research is going *wonderfully*, so much better than when you were here before. I'm almost . . . I feel as though any time now, any *day*, I might break the whole thing right open. Really any day."

"You're still doing the, ah, trees?"

"White oak." She gave him a magisterial smile. "*Quercus alba*, Evidence for the Activity of Morphogenetic Fields in the Development of. I keep sending out papers—actually it's the same paper I keep writing and rewriting because every time someone comes by to carry it, the work has gotten so much more advanced . . . but they never come back. What's going on out there, Trover? Aren't there journals anymore?"

Trover shrugged ambivalently, but Amy didn't wait for an answer.

"But I mean, the end of the project seems so near that I don't even feel excited about it anymore. Just . . . certain. I've been reading biographies lately, at night, and I've started to recognize the attitude. It's this sublime confidence that scientists have, sometimes, in the importance of their work.

You don't often sense it in their writing, but in interviews or TV appearances or whatever, you can just *feel* it. And this project—my project—could really turn the corner on the morphogenesis thing. And if I can demonstrate the activity of growth fields in a genus as, um, stolid as *Quercus*, then the whole evolution debate is wide open again."

She settled back in her chair, unsure of herself for rattling on like this. Did Trover understand any of it? Did he care? He looked up from his bowl, empty now, and nodded unhelpfully. "That's really nice, Amy," he said. "I'm glad things are going so well for you."

"Yes," she agreed, allowing herself a smidgen of smugness. "We've been doing just fine." And to herself she appended: Without you.

"What we?" said Trover, and from his tone Amy thought the aging *pícaro* might actually be a bit jealous. "I thought you were alone here."

"Well, almost." She looked upward, twisted her head to follow the planks of the stair where they spiraled through the rafters. "Come on down," she said softly. "He won't hurt you, I don't suppose."

Trover, by temperament unflappable, found himself amazed for the second time this afternoon. From the shadowy stairwell, one small leg at a time, appeared a boy whom Trover, inexpert in such matters, judged to be seven or eight. He had inherited all of Amy's beauty, but also a certain pallid wistfulness that Trover didn't recognize right away.

"Hi, mate," he greeted the child, and aside to Amy added: "Who's *this*, now?"

"You idiot," she said, "it's your son."

Robin followed them all over the station next morning: through the airy living quarters at the top of the dome, where he helped Amy water her flowers, between the rows of tables in the greenhouse, where all Trover saw of him (owing to his height) was a soft sun-gilded cowlick of brown hair, and out to the young forest that Amy called her orchard, where he popped like a wood-sprite in and out among the narrow trunks of the oaks.

"What the hell did you name him *that* for?" Trover

whispered, glancing uneasily through the limbs around him because you never knew where the kid was going to turn up.

"The way you disappeared," said Amy lightly, examining a broad leaf as though it were a child's frail hand, "I thought you might be some kind of supernatural being. So I naturally decided—"

She stopped herself when she saw Trover's look of puzzlement and, just possibly, pain. "Oh, look, I'm sorry," she said. "I shouldn't be ironic with you. It was just a private allusion. No, but I've always loved the name Robin, for a boy or girl either one. Maybe "—she pointed her pruning shears—"you could teach him to play the harp."

Trover brightened, looked a moment around for the boy, then said solemnly, "I don't know about that. It's not exactly something you can teach. It's a kind of, you know, *feeling*. Most people never . . ."

"Well he *is* your son. Maybe he's inherited it from you." She smiled. "He's got your eyes."

Trover turned upon her that look of yearning and affection she had always found so disturbing. "Really, does he? Where is he, anyway?"

"I don't think he knows what to make of you." *And*, Amy thought, *I don't either.*

From an outstretched limb above their heads, Robin climbed down then, perhaps recognizing some change in his father's mood. With feline adroitness he perched on Trover's back, wrapped four small limbs around his mount and allowed himself to be bounced along the path leading back to the compound. During this show of familial acceptance he did not cry out in delight as another child might have done, or tease his father by tugging on his hair or covering his eyes. Nonetheless, as the two of them gamboled through the trees, Amy could sense the gush of her son's emotion as though it were being beamed out on some secret, silent channel—beamed out to her and to the silent audience around them.

When Robin and Trover were gone she went back to her work, which she had pursued every day for the present half of her life and which, with Robin, sustained her.

* * *

Father and son, quick to take advantage of mother's occupation in the woods, did a little reconnoitering, for which there
had been no time that morning.

"What do you say, little man?" said Trover, maintaining
an intermittent monologue because the boy was not much
given to talking. "Let's just take a look up here in your
mother's library."

He was panting and trying to hide it by the time they
reached the top of the stair. The topmost triangular windows
of the dome were six feet over his head, and the floorboards,
prior to being sawed and sanded and shined with oil, had
been the trunks of the very trees among which Amy strolled,
prior to their most recent coppicing. Trover thought it was
funny. Tree-harvesting per se was not prohibited by the
Balance Act, so long as the resulting lumber was used in some
carbon-preserving manner. But it did seem, didn't it, to
violate the spirit of the place? Trover put the question to
Robin, but the boy just smiled and shrugged and traipsed
after him through the partitioned-off end of the loft, where
an awesome clutter of human knowledge was stored in several media in canisters and cabinets and the sunlight was
dyed citron and vermilion and mauve as it filtered through a
canopy of orchids.

"Your mom stays busy, doesn't she?"

Robin stared up at him, his thoughts unfathomable.

"Hmm, well, let's— What was that?" It had been some
kind of cooing, like . . . "It sounded like an owl," said
Trover.

"You talk so loud," said Robin unexpectedly, "you've
woken up the *owls*."

"Yeah!" There was a bit more cooing and Trover dashed
around the loft excitedly, getting lost and finding nothing.
"That's what I thought it sounded like. What the hell is she
doing with owls?"

Robin giggled, running after him. "They're *magic*," he
explained. "My family's *always* had owls."

"Your family . . . Oh, right, Amy's folks. Yeah, that
does ring a bell for some reason." Trover was trying to figure
out where he was. "What's this?" he asked the boy.

They had reached a kind of alcove, near the down-
sloping wall of the dome, where the floor ended in a low

vine-covered railing and, just at the edge, a little chair and writing desk of rough-hewn cherry commanded a view of the laboratory below. Trover paused to listen to the soft electric hum of the holoscopes transcribing whatever was going on down there. Not much, it didn't look like. Maybe you just had to be patient.

On the desk was a notebook, its pages off-white and crudely cut as if they had been hand-milled, which Trover guessed they had. Because this was just the sort of thing he had been hoping for, he sat down and without hesitation began reading what was written there in Amy's small meticulous hand. Robin watched him gravely.

"Look here," Trover said. "She writes the month and year at the top of every page, but not the day. Why would she do that?"

"Days don't count," declared Robin.

Trover eyed the boy skeptically.

"The *woods*," the boy explained. "They're slower than us. It only matters what year and season it is."

Trover thought the kid must have gotten his mother's brains and was not sure how happy he was about that. The notebook said:

a step further and demonstrate the possibility of direct, dynamic interaction with the fields, TWO-WAY. The capacity to get in there and pull the genetic trigger. No environmental pressure. Within one growth-cycle.

Examples. I don't know. What about phalanxes and guerrillas? We can get a species that normally uses one strategy to "borrow" the tricks of the other. Acorns, say—heavy, slow, and dense in the immediate vicinity of the tree. Classic phalanx approach. Tell root cells to un-differentiate, act like apical meristems for awhile. *Quercus* could put sappers fifty, eighty feet from the main trunk.

New species perhaps too ambitious at this point. Though McClintock thought it possible. (*Quercu robinia!*) Stress said to be necessary. New genus even. That would be a *real* hybrid—genes by God, body by

"So what's all this about?" Trover said, closing the note-book and arranging the desk as he had found it. "What's your mother up to?"

But Robin turned away and announced, "I've got to go now. It's time for Mommy's program."

"What?" called Trover after his scampering son. "Her what? Hey, wait, how do I get out of here?"

A momentary breeze fluttered the orchids overhead and then the library was silent.

The forest felt differently from where Amy sat, legs folded beneath her, beside the little stream. There was a depth of silence that was due partly, she supposed, to the enclosed feeling one naturally had in such a place, banked by boulders and sheltered by the overreaching arms of the oak. Also there were the faint incessant gurgle of moving water and the way the midday sun, so harsh in the meadow, was down here softened and diffused into a sort of permanent twilight. But Amy believed there was more to it than this—something about the quality of feeling here that all these things together did not explain.

The explanation, Amy's explanation, lay very close in fact to the heart of her work, her own contribution to whatever was left of the great tradition. And the problem had not been in discovering it, for the inner nature of this silence had been clear to her the first time she closed her eyes in the little grotto. Rather, the problem was one of translating into the measured cadences of science a kind of cognition that had owed nothing to logic, nothing to theory or induction or hypothesis. She had made a number of attempts, in her early years here, to give words to that cognition. How well she had succeeded was a matter for history to judge; Amy herself could not, and the community of her peers had, for all she knew, found sanctuary in places as remote as Balance Act. In the end she had returned to the laboratory, determined to demonstrate in the material world what she believed—what she knew from direct experience—was happening in a world one shade more subtle.

Hence her daily visits to the stream, and to the aged oak. For all things in Balance Act were threads of an intricate pattern. The seedlings in the dome had sprung from acorns of this mighty progenitor. Just so, Amy's work had begun the first time she nestled like a flower in this space between two rocks. And each day, as the sun eased itself down behind the trees, she returned, and the work continued.

Amy closed her eyes and methodically slowed her breathing. She would begin by meditating until the clamor of thoughts fell away, and then she would begin the crucial part of her program. Today it would take longer than usual; the unexpected advent of Trover had thrown her life, and her consciousness, out of balance. But in due time the silence—the Silence—would come.

Amy did not know how much time had passed when she heard the scuffle of footsteps coming down from the meadow. In her mind was an image of the great old oak—but a cartoon image, flattened and simplified, the tree's sinuous limbs made to look like human arms that flailed in agitation. Amy forgot the image as one forgets a dream, and she thought, Good, here's Robin. It was so much easier to relax, to settle back into herself, when her son was near her, playing among the rocks. The thought of him now released her, and she took up the first of the quiet rituals that would turn her nervous system into a channel for impulses finer than thought.

The footsteps were not Robin's, but Amy had ceased to listen. She did not hear the two sets separate, approaching her at wide angles along the moss-banked stream. Whether there were words to accompany the footsteps, whether one of the men glanced aside and said It's her or the two exchanged grim silent smiles and nodded, Amy did not know and likely would not have cared. By the time they reached her, nearly together, one set of callused hands arriving just a moment before the other, her consciousness was already lying blissfully at the bottom of the ocean of silence. She had thus no great distance left to travel, and the men took little time in sending her on her way.

The boy may have had his mother's intelligence, but he had also something of his father's mercurial emotions. When he left the foot of the trail and saw his mother, saw the just-recognizable bloody detritus of what his mother had been, he did not react as a smart boy might have, by stealing away to fetch one of the heatweapons hidden in the orchard. No.

He reacted instead by throwing all the emotional mass he had accumulated during his short lifetime into one great lung-rending shriek. Then, as if the very sound impelled him, he hurled himself toward the murderers with his arms outspread like the wings of a fledgling owl. All this served to startle the men into immobility for a moment, giving rise in Robin to a fantasy of reaching the black weapons propped against a boulder and avenging his mother on the spot.

The moment passed. When it was over, one of the men stood with a look of irritation which gave way to faint amusement, and raised his arms to tackle the onrushing boy. Robin saw this in time to scuttle sideways into the rocks. The man said something he had never heard before and moved forward a few steps to capture him.

But Robin was gone. It was something he was good at.

The men slipped off their gray-green cloaks, preparing to give chase. Methodically, with bloodstained hands, they lifted their weapons. We cannot know precisely what they had in mind for the boy—whether they meant to kill him, or to carry him off to be raised and schooled by their order— but to Robin at least the situation was clear. He must get back to the compound and tell Trover, who would kill these horrible people and take him far away from Balance Act.

This might have happened, at least in part. But Trover just then appeared from the path saying, as usual quite loudly, "Hey, kid, what's going on? I thought I heard—"

These were not very remarkable last words, but he was given no chance to amend them.

Robin was all alone now. He felt rather than knew this. And the enormity of that loss drew out of him a small squeaking wail, more the sound of an orphaned forest creature than that of a little boy. It was enough. The two men, neither more than a few feet away from him, turned to look down on Robin, who was suddenly as exposed and defenseless as if he were standing naked in the clearing. He darted his eyes one way and then another, but the only refuge left to him was the venerable oak. He clambered over its roots as the two men converged behind him. Hugging the pitted trunk he slipped around it and, for the moment, was invisible again.

The two men exchanged a look: they had had enough of this. Taking separate sides of the tree, they moved easily around it and prepared to pounce on their delicate prey.

They halted at the same instant. Instead of a small boy, they were each from opposite directions staring waist-high at an enormous and powerful-looking man. His unclad upper body was matted with hair and thick with muscles, and his dark eyes managed to glare at both renegades at the same time and with such ferocity that they found themselves mesmerized.

The man who had almost tackled Robin regained his presence of mind long enough to raise a fist. In the act of doing so, he noticed the small horns protruding from the stranger's thick mane of hair. Then the stranger extended his two mighty hands, and life flowed out of the two gray-green-clad men as quickly as he touched them. Not wishing, perhaps, to be troubled with their sagging bodies, he dispersed their molecules at once to the air and to the water, and shook his fingers clean of the last traces of them.

And then the great being turned to Robin. He had placed the boy out of danger, on a lower limb of the tree. There Robin sat trembling in a state of shock and horror. Now, as the being reached up and lifted him, cradling the boy in his arms and making soft, many-toned sounds like the flutter of wind through orchids, Robin began to sob loudly and heedlessly.

"Don't cry, little one," the great being murmured. His voice was like an alluring music of distant flutes or reeds. "Don't be afraid," he said. "You will be *my* son now."

Robin stopped crying and seemed to sleep. The being carried him lightly in his arms. The oak tree,

the silent witness,

received them.

Forest

When the green leaf starts to tell
the story of the yellow petal,
we have to be careful.
—MAHARISHI MAHESH YOGI

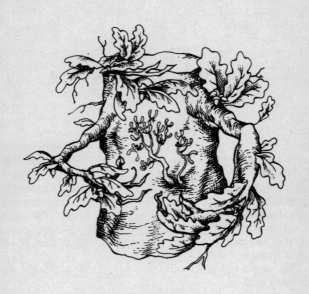

Quercus alba
White oak

Highly selective as to habitat. Where happy,
it is long-lived and eventually dominant.
A decoction of the bark closes wounds.

Three

HEAT AND DEATH, after a century-long courtship, were married on the winds that summer. Neither was a stranger to the forest.

The west wind, the very breath of spring, had through the decades grown hotter and drier, bringing fewer phero-chemical messages from the evergreen forest on the coast. The toxins which once that other forest had absorbed now filled the air at full potency. Yet a shifting of the breeze brought nothing better.

The east wind held rain that was gray with dust and bitter with acid.

The south wind, formerly welcomed for its warmth, was now a fetid exhalation of cities and failing farmlands.

Even the north wind was enfeebled. Its once-bracing gusts were no more than chilly and damp, as though the sickness had spread to the very pole.

Something was surely wrong. But the Carbon Bank Forest could not investigate, could not consider what lessons these things might hold for its own survival. It could only adapt in ways it understood.

So its trees, over the last hundred years, had begun to transpire more freely, drawing more moisture from the sub-soil to replace what they lost to the parching air. The taller ones retreated from their vulnerable upper branches, allowing second-tier species a greater share of light. As the canopy died, the sun gained admission to depths it had not penetrated for an eon. The temperature of the soil began to rise, enhancing the activity of the new acidic compounds and revising the lists of microbes that could survive there. Symbiotic unions that had formed over millennia dissolved in a single season. The great cycles of energy and food turned more slowly, more erratically. Decay outpaced production. The carbon ledger showed a growing deficit.

In the consequent period of retraction, animals enjoyed certain advantages in being short-lived and mobile. Their populations thinned, reducing pressure on the habitat, and their migratory patterns carried them farther north. The succession of observers at Reporting Station 12 marked the passing of a dozen species, and then a hundred, and then the observers themselves took their place on the roster.

If a tree falls in the forest when no one is around, who will mourn it?

The crucial point, the moment of genuine crisis, was reached during the summer when the oaks that grew from thrice-coppiced stumps outside the wall at Balance Act ceased to be well-tended. It was in that summer that the forest's ability to adapt seemed to falter. It had modified itself in all the ways of which it was capable. It could not change further without becoming something remarkably different—as had, in fact, occurred already to the other forests of the world. The land where those forests once stood was now reduced, at best, to patchy woodland; the fallen empires were overrun by cities and farms and browning lawns and dusty prairies and, more often now, deserts. The Carbon Bank Forest was the last of its kind in the world.

And it might have been that the forest sensed this, somehow, during that summer, and knew for the first time a kind of despair. The season was a bad one for several families of trees, and the worst in memory (were there anyone to remember) for Q. *alba*.

A thunderstorm, raging from the east, blew a dead treelimb through a window of the dome at Reporting Station 12, shattering it and allowing the rain to enter. In July a crop of purple mushrooms appeared on the floor of the laboratory. A few of the experimental seedlings—those whose planters sat under the broken window—survived that season untended, though by the end of it their roots were bent for lack of space. The winter was relatively mild, but a valve froze in the mechanism that directed water from the solar tanks to the heat-pipes, so the dome grew very cold and most of the remaining plants perished. Of the few that did not, one was knocked from the table by a young wildcat, a kitten whose family had discovered the broken window and made a cozy home of the owl-inhabited loft. There was quite a bit of dirt from other planters on the floor by this time, and leaves that had blown through the window, so this sapling lived out the second year. Its leaves were brown but still clinging to their stems when rainwater finished the job of corroding a cut-off switch, allowing electricity to flow from the cells on the roof to a holoscope machine on the table. The machine was set to PLAY. All the wild kittens—big ones by this time—were frightened, confused, and ultimately attracted by the sound of Amy Hayata's voice as it held forth intermittently in the empty lab. When the kittens arrived to investigate they were no less bewildered to see the form of a human female strolling up and down aisles that were crowded with small green plants.

"The trouble is," Amy told them, "we can *do* all these things, but we can't make the *trees* do them. Spontaneously, I mean. So ultimately it's no good. It's a problem of volition, really—of will or choice or something. A forest meets all the criteria for cognitive systems but that."

She sighed, and the kittens, mistaking the sound for a hiss of challenge, drew down on their haunches and stiffened their backs.

"Well," said Amy, "I guess there's nothing we can do about it. Evolution is either going to save them or it's not. All the big jumps are preceded by some major challenge to survival, so here it is. *Quercus robinia* or bust."

She turned away from her audience and retreated down the illusory aisle.

It is the nature of wildcats to perceive the world holistically—with all their perceptions at once, that is, and not through a filter of analysis, which isolates the aspects of reality for separate consideration. The kittens quickly realized that the sight and the sound of this woman were not accompanied by a human scent nor (as they drew daringly near) the warmth of a human body. Therefore the woman was not a human or, as far as the kittens were concerned, anything of interest at all. They drifted off singly, climbing to the loft or leaping gracefully through the shattered window to seek adventure in the bright world beyond. The recording went on for several hours and finally fell dark and quiet. The tiny blue light on the panel of the machine outlived three generations of wildcats.

The sapling died that winter.

If a change occurs in a forest when no one is around, who will understand it?

In the lifetime of an ecosystem one summer is insignificant: a moment, a memory: duly noted in growth rings and afterward in a layer of dead leaves, but otherwise quickly forgotten. Yet lives can turn upon moments that are in themselves trivially brief—the moment, for example, in which a terrorist's gunshell pierces, or misses, the victim's heart; or that in which a traveler, alone on the nightblack road, debates which path will lead him to his destiny.

The summer in which the window broke and the coppiced orchard grew wild must have marked some kind of turning point in the life of the Carbon Bank Forest, for none that came after it was quite so bad. To be sure, whatever change may have occurred was both subtle and slow. But this is the way of forests and should come as no surprise. Nonetheless, that there *had* been a change, and that it was an important one, seem certain.

The century of retreat ended in an unremarkable fashion. Trees stopped dying, was all. From somewhere—deep in the genome, perhaps—they found recipes for resins to toughen their leaves against heat and dryness. These recipes were passed from tree to tree, from parent to progeny, even shared with kindred species. It would have been a fascinating process, perhaps, had there been eyes or instruments to observe it. But those patient eyes were gone now; the instruments disused and rusted. The great drama was being played with no audience but its own cast. The director, if there was one, remained hidden behind the stage.

Slowly the broken canopy restored itself. The temperature in the heart of the forest fell slowly, about half a degree per decade, until it regained its normal range of fluctuation. Roots that had lost their old allies found new ones among the acid-hearty microbes that now dominated the soil. The secondary and herbaceous layers flourished. Migratory animals, their food stocks restored, returned from their northern exile, and ravaged populations grew numerous again. By the end of two hundred years things were something like the way they had been before.

But not quite. When a turning point is passed, both the path and the traveler are changed.

Early in the third century, as though driven by some new spirit akin to wanderlust, the forest began climbing the edges of its glacier-scooped bed. By yards and then by miles it extended itself onto mountainsides that had lately been held by ice. For a decade at a time it would pause, thickening its trunks along the high frontier, before again hurling pinecone grenades against ramparts of stone and resuming its slow advance. Finally—five hundred years after that summer of heat and death—it unfurled its green banners on the mountaintop. Its advance guard of eagles soared into the skies of an unaccustomed world.

Unlike the other great forests in that world, the Carbon Bank Forest had found a way to survive. But like the rest of them, it had become something remarkably different.

Crusaders

I believe the future is only the past again,
entered through another gate.
— SIR ARTHUR WING PINERO

Cyprepedium pubescens

Lady's slipper orchid

The Law of Affinities holds this to be
an effective woman's tonic, especially helpful in
balancing the turbulent humors of youth.

Four

IN LATER YEARS, Vesica
would remember the coming of the sunglider as a change in
the air above the vineyard.

First there was the buzzing. Not an ordinary, teeth
together, bee-buzzing. No, a rounder sound, a rubbing in
the ear, noises like a fever makes or maybe like you've
swallowed a cocoon and the butterfly is humming inside
there. Vesica liked it but chiefly it bothered her, so she left
off pruning the roses on the gazebo to climb up fourteen
steps each taller than her knee to the observation deck to
stand and look around. And then there was the groaning.

Soon she would know that the groan was that of strings,
aching as they stretched out for the wingflaps way out there
almost touching, it seemed, the treetops, while the sunglider
came down easily like a maple seed from the wide and blue
and absolutely motionless April sky. But right now all she
knew was that the sound both terrified and thrilled her. For
though she didn't know what it was, she was quite sure what
it *wasn't*: it wasn't a farm machine or any bird or one of her
stepfather's friends driving up from the city. And as far as
Vesica could think before she saw it, that covered all the
possibilities in the world.

But even had she known what sungliders were, and

known what wonders lay in lands farther off than any she had heard of, the tan diaphanous wings and silver struts and whirring upturned windmill of the craft would still have delighted her. As things were, she watched it come down with all the joy and trepidation she had felt when she was many years younger and first came here to Gravetye Farm. It was beautiful, she thought. It was strange and, for someone, it might be terribly fun. But it would never be—it was just not meant to be—for her.

The man in the sunglider was so big you could hardly believe such a delicate thing had ever held him and still gotten up in the sky. Vesica watched him climb down, one huge foot after the other, hands bigger than her thorn-pierced gardening gloves holding the lines above the little box where you sat when you rode it, with old clothes hanging from him, blowing in the breeze under the black rotor, like oil-stained blankets around a bear. A bear was what he looked like, Vesica thought. Or a giant, a creature from a story. (Most of her ideas of the world she had gotten from stories, and mostly childish ones; for fairy tales were all there were besides lawbooks in her stepfather's library.) But she also thought—a minute later, when the man looked around with his full-moon face pale and sweaty and the hair hanging damp over his brow—that he was kinder and sadder than anyone she knew. She found him more interesting, after that, than even the sunglider, and she had to learn everything about him. And *quickly*, before her stepfather came out.

The man lumbered to and fro (so much like a big old bear!) carrying things from the sunglider to a patch of young alfalfa near the pebbled road where he had landed. His hair was brownish, but lighter and redder than brown, like very old bronze polished with tongue oil and set out in the sun. The sun was so bright it made his movements seem slower, as though he were weighted down by having to drag his own dark noonday shadow. Something inside the sunglider was still buzzing, but it was barely an echo of the sound that, in later years, would be Vesica's sharpest memory. She approached them both covertly, man and machine, keeping behind the vines that twined up head-high blackened poles and covered the wires between them. The last pole in each row was set at a three-point angle, making a triangular space at ground level for Vesica to spy through. She tired of this quickly. The man wasn't doing anything interesting or secret, and after all she was fourteen years old. She stood up.

She stepped forward.

She put her hand out.

"Hello," she told him boldly. The man looked around, startled perhaps, but focusing gradually, his mind snagged on some inner hook she longed to know about. "Who are you? My name is Vesica."

The man returned a big, uncertain smile. She knew he was uncertain, possibly taken aback. Maybe also he was shy, despite his largeness—someone she must be gentle with. A timid bear.

"Hello there," he said finally. He inspected one of his hands and raised it to take her gardening glove. "I'm Groby. From Titchens. A field engineer. I'm here to fix some windmills. . . ."

He let his voice trail off as if expecting her to answer right away with "Oh, yes!" or "So you've made it!"—but Vesica withheld this satisfaction (though yes: she knew all about the windmills) pending further intercourse and perhaps some explanation of the sunglider. As she had known he was going to be, the man was the first to give up his claim to silence.

"I'm supposed to see someone—" He fished for a name in his memory, rolling his eyes to the left not the right, which meant something, but Vesica thought how much darker brown they were than her own which were pale as amber. The man, Groby, said, "Narthex. Commissioner Narthex."

"My stepfather," she informed him, willing to be helpful now that she had proven her ability to make him talk. "I expect he'll be around soon. He's *never* very far . . . when he's here."

Groby smiled. It occurred to Vesica that she might make of him, however briefly, an ally. Coming a step closer—so that, if he wanted to, he could have reached out and touched her feathersoft straw-colored hair—she confided, "He doesn't really live here, he lives in the city. He only keeps the farm because he has to Maintain his Constituency."

She thought saying this was all right; she wasn't quite

sure what the last part meant (it was something she had gotten from the foreman) but it always drew wide eyes and knowing smiles from everyone she repeated it to. Anyway, she still hadn't told him about the windmills. To her chagrin, Groby's face got even wider and he gave her not a knowing smile but another kind, the kind you give a child. He said, "Is that so"—as if it really didn't matter whether it was or not.

But Vesica had no time to feel betrayed by her new ally, for she heard the crunch of pebbles under well-cobbled heels and knew her stepfather was approaching. She hurried to close ranks.

The lean (or perhaps merely thin-boned) man came at them indirectly, by the road that clung to the contour of the vineyard instead of straight through the vines like Vesica. As he passed the gazebo they got a good look at him down an alfalfa-tufted aisle: tall and immaculate in his spidersilk suit, progressing at a slow march every step of which proclaimed, *This is my land. I own it.*

"Is that him?" said Groby quietly.

In a distant way Vesica was impressed by how readily the newcomer had taken up the role of conspirator. This may have been why, without any intention to do so, she touched his big-muscled forearm with a freckled slender hand and said, just as quietly:

"I hate him."

"Do you like to climb trees?" she asked Groby later. It was after the two men had finished talking Business, and Meggie from the kitchen had fetched them out a cool summery lunch.

"Very much," he said—not, I used to, or When I was a boy, which was something Vesica admired about him. He said, "Do you?"

"There's an old alder," she told him loudly (for his boots were a dozen feet over her head) "that's so dreadfully huge my stepfather hired a man to cut it down last year because it ruins the view from his observation deck. Only he couldn't do it. The wood was too hard or something. I'm the *only* one who's ever been to the top of it."

Groby hung like a large smoked ham from a sling that ran down from the scaffolding of his third windmill of the day. There were twenty-something more to do and it was already late afternoon: Vesica could see the mudmules lugging bales in from the amaranth fields. She calculated that three every afternoon and three every morning make six a day, into twenty-something makes Sunday at the earliest before he would leave. Groby said, "How can you be sure?"

"Of course I'm sure." Her bare athletic legs dangled from the crotch of two diagonal I-beams twenty feet from the ground. "My stepfather never lets anyone onto the property but the servants and laborers and people he pays to come here, like you and the pig-doctor."

"But before your stepfather bought the farm," Groby said. His voice was just loud enough to drift down to her, and he spoke without ceasing to turn the ratchet that tightened a belt-wheel whose rotation drove the generator in its gray box far below. "That tree's been here two hundred years, I bet. How do you know someone didn't climb it before any of you were born?"

Vesica considered this. She decided that she approved of Groby's refusal to patronize her. Most people would simply have made themselves agreeable, on account of her stepfather the Commissioner. This kind of argument—as opposed to the blunt rebuttals she often got from Narthex—was rare recreation.

"It was *smaller* then," she said decisively.

"Watch out," he said. "I'm done here. I'm coming down."

Her stepfather, of course, had wanted to dislike Groby as soon as they met, and had stood there searching with those zinc-colored eyes for a reason to do so. Vesica knew the look. (Her stepfather's eyes were slightly ellipsoid, so that when he stared intently at something they bulged translucently from their sockets. This gave him a look of hawkish acuity, while in fact it caused the focal point of his vision to fall somewhat behind the retina, rendering him badly myopic.) The problem, he told Groby, was the alignment of the blades.

"The fool that built them," he said, indicating with a sheaf of contractual agreements the gray towers that stood like overgrown fenceposts on the hills, "managed to point them *north*, whereas the prevailing wind is *west-southwest*."

It was his lecturing tone. Vesica strolled away, back to

the gazebo, to sit alone quietly and deny him half his audience. Then she realized this was being disloyal to Groby, her ally, and wandered back to stand in the middleground busying herself in the rigging of the sunglider.

"Actually," said Groby, with that long characteristic pause which Vesica knew must irritate her stepfather, "the wind has probably changed since the time these were built, what— sixty? eighty years ago?"

He turned around so that he could look past the blue-green slopes of the vineyard to where yellow meadows rolled out toward the mountains. You could barely see the forest, the dark forbidden forest where Vesica was not allowed to go, where the meadows ended and the land wrinkled up like a rug. Groby pointed a sausage-sized finger.

"See? The trees are young through there. A hundred years ago, fifty even, there was nothing to break the wind blowing down from the mountains. The climate's gotten a lot milder since then. You couldn't have grown grapes here, before. Those grapes, now—they're mighty fine-looking. Did you put those in yourself?"

Oh, how did he know to say that? Narthex stood even straighter, gazed out over the spare geometries of the vineyard. "To appreciate the design," he said, "you have to climb up to the deck on top of the gazebo." He set off, less stiffly than before, leading Groby in this direction. "It took a good bit of time to get right. And money, of course. So many dreadful trees to knock out of the way. And over there, you see, an entire *hill* needed to be bulldozed, so that one could have a view of the mountains."

"Is that right?" said Groby. He trailed after Narthex in great shambling strides. A bag of something heavy (tools, Vesica supposed) drooped from his hand as though forgotten in his eagerness to enjoy the Low Commissioner's earthmoving.

How smart of him! thought Vesica. To start right out on Narthex's friendly side, when most people tried so hard to get there and never made it. She didn't follow the two men up the fourteen steps of the ladder, and that was the last chance she would have to talk to Groby until Business was done and lunch was eaten and he settled down to work on the twenty-something windmills of her stepfather's farm.

*   *   *

Dinner at Gravetye Farm promised to be a contest between two unusually well matched adversaries. Groby possessed that very rare ability to maintain a comfortable silence, while Narthex had a maddening capacity to endure an uncomfortable one. Vesica had no weapon but a finely developed sense of when her stepfather was up to something, and tonight, she could tell, was one of those times.

Narthex's dining room was remarkable for managing to feel cramped despite its open ceiling crisscrossed by huge rafters and the tall curtainless windows along both of its walls, giving a view on one side of the distant blue mountains and on the other of the Blistered Moor, with the moon riding low over its wasted expanse. They gathered here, the three of them, to dine on several courses of perfectly cooked vegetables and a quail from the game park above the stream. In consonance with the room itself, the food managed somehow to be unappealing, causing Vesica to feel after the salad of watercress and dill that she had eaten quite enough. Groby alone seemed to bring to the table much appetite. Narthex seldom ate anyway, in public at least. Vesica entertained certain colorful fantasies about this, but they were not under discussion this evening.

For a course and a half it appeared that *nothing* was going to be under discussion. Groby fed himself placidly and Vesica fought an urge to squirm, wondering how long her stepfather could take it. He took it up to the marinated bog-trout. Staring down at those stripped and bloodless fillets seemed to remind him of something.

"I was speaking last week," he said, dabbing at something invisible between his narrow mouth and pointed chin, "to Lady Widdershins. Do you know who I mean, Vesica? From the Hardy Plant Society."

Vesica did—she remembered the huge powdered bosom in which the woman liked to suffocate small dogs and children—but she refused to make the concession of acknowledging this. Narthex did not mind.

"She mentioned, Lady Widdershins did, some sort of expedition or exploration or what was it called?—being launched here in the north somewhere. Traipsing off into the *forest*, if you can imagine such a thing. I seem to recall its being supposed to depart rather soon."

Groby raised his head politely, though it was clear his heart lay closer to trout than table-talk.

"Next week," he said.

The Low Commissioner adjusted an eyebrow.

"Where are they going?" said Vesica, and immediately felt sorry for it; for letting curiosity draw her into collaboration with her stepfather. Groby smiled: glad (she fondly supposed) to have reason to talk to her instead of Narthex.

"I don't know much about it," he said, "except that it's called the First Biotic Crusade, and it's being funded by some gardening club down in Riverrun. I gather that basically it's a bunch of herbalists, or maybe historians, looking for an ancient ruin. A lost ivory tower or something. Anyway, whatever they're looking for is way up north, on the other side of the mountains."

Vesica squinted slightly, trying to picture this. Heretofore it had not ocurred to her that there *was* another side of the mountains. She had vaguely assumed that the whole of life—certainly the whole of Society—was located down south, where her stepfather spent all his time and made all his money. She said, "But why are they doing it? Is there money hidden up there?—Or some horrible secret?" Such was her experience at Gravetye Farm that these seemed the two most likely objects of a large-scale undertaking.

Groby looked at Narthex, as though wondering whether to go on. The Low Commissioner's face had assumed what Vesica thought of as his Confessional look. It was utterly blank, a mask of incomprehension, the eyes hanging open until their lower lids seemed to rest on the cheekbones, and it generally had the effect of goading a speaker into spilling the entire contents of his memory in a doomed attempt to elicit some kind of response. In Groby's case the effect was different. The big man returned Narthex's gaze for a moment, then smiled and pleasantly said, "I guess so"—exactly as though Narthex had asked him something to which this was the answer.

He went on: "As I understand it, the Crusaders are trying to find out why plants are acting so strangely nowadays. I guess they're hoping to find some clues at this old place in the mountains."

Narthex nodded from his end of the table, his small mouth hissing slowly, "Ye-e-ss."

Right away Vesica knew that none of what Groby had said was news to her stepfather, that she was watching some private game, the purpose of which was to make Groby tell Narthex things he already knew. It was a maxim of the Low Commissioner's: Never ask a question unless you already know the answer. Until now, Vesica had not really understood what this meant.

"Master Groby," said Narthex thoughtfully, "you are remarkably well informed concerning matters of, one must think, largely academic interest. Might I inquire as to how you happen to . . . ?"

Groby smiled with bearlike shyness—the sort of deliberate diffidence that is possible when you're big enough not to be shy if you don't want to be. "Actually," he said, "I've been hired—after I'm finished here—to travel with the Crusade as its field engineer. Maintaining its equipment and so forth. I understand they've got some sort of big transport vehicle or something."

The bog-trout was disposed of and quail brought in. Vesica thought of a dozen questions for Groby, but held off asking them in compliance with her stepfather's rule not to speak in front of the servants. In the end Narthex preempted her. "You have not, then," he said with narrowed eyes, "actually seen the equipment? Or met any of the Crusaders?"

Vesica thought this must, for her stepfather, be coming awfully close to tipping his hand. She wondered why he cared at all, why this peculiar Crusade was important to him. Not knowing this, she couldn't steer her ally safely away from revealing anything important.

"As a matter of . fact," said Groby, "I did meet one member of the Crusade. It was a flower-arranger. It was funny, I thought. I mean, when you think of little flowers, and there they're going off to deal with those gigantic oaks . . ."

"A flower arranger," said Narthex, touching a fork lightly, tines down, to his quail.

"Yes. He told me that the Territorial Governor—I've forgotten his name—plans to lead the Crusade himself."

Narthex smiled. "Well," he said, his voice now surprisingly hearty, "I do wish the Governor every success. One can only sympathize with the poor man. Things have grown all but impossible for the citizens of this territory."

Vesica, recognizing his Oratorical Style, supposed that her stepfather had found out what he wanted to know, or at least part of it. Something, certainly, had made him cheerful. He kept on in this new expansive vein.

"You may be aware, Master Groby, that I have sponsored several pieces of legislation in the Low Commission pertaining to the ecological crisis. For example, it was I who argued for the establishment, during the last session, of a Guild of Refugees, to secure employment for those unfortunate citizens whom the forest has displaced."

Groby returned his attention to the remaining contents of his plate. Offhandedly he said, "I think I read about that. Quite a few of them are working around here, aren't they? On some of the larger farms?"

"We've got a lot of them at Gravetye," said Vesica.

Narthex regarded both guest and stepdaughter down the length of a protuberant nose. "It was not anticipated," he said dryly, "that the military activities in the West would have created such a drain of manpower from the agricultural sector. It was fortunate, certainly, that the Guild happened to be available to fill the void. But that was purely fortuitous. The art of statecraft does not have much in common with that of fortunetelling."

"A lot of them were farmers," said Vesica. "They had their own land, before the forest drove them off of it. Now they're working on somebody else's property like ordinary field hands."

"As I say," Narthex broke in firmly, "I wish the Governor every success with his Crusade. Anything that serves to resolve this baffling calamity will be much to the benefit of everyone."

Vesica slid an eye around toward Groby, and was pleased to see that he didn't believe this at all. She could tell by the way, in place of a reply, he got down to the business of mopping up gravy with a corn biscuit, as though that's what the dinner were all about.

Narthex settled back into the shadows at the end of the table and motioned for the removal of the dishes. "Do you know, Master Groby, I believe you might enjoy dining in the foreman's cottage for the remainder of your visit. It's so much . . . *warmer* down there."

He shot a spidersilk cuff. "Remind me, won't you, Vesica?"

Out on the hill where the last of the twenty-something windmills made its stand against gusts rising from the amaranth fields, a bank of anemones—descended from who-knew-what forgotten garden—had made a bright colony on the south-facing slope. They were of mixed colors, though for some reason the plants producing midnight-blue flowers had shown themselves more resilient over the decades or centuries and had come to dominate the hillside. Vesica found their color much too melancholy. Accordingly, for the past few seasons she had appointed herself an agent of natural selection, annually thinning the midnight-blues while encouraging the production of the tangerine-colored blossoms she preferred. They made a nice contrast with her blouse: an old loose-fitting thing of lemon ramie she had found in a farmhouse drawer, which only this year had begun to look something other than shapeless on her, now that her breasts stood out the way they finally did.

Her arms were folded neatly beneath them (for the morning breeze still carried a hint of winter, despite April and the sun) and her weight was on one long denim-covered leg as she examined the distribution of colors on the hill and wondered if anything more needed to be done. Groby was at work fifty feet away, probing at the viscera of the generator with an oak twig, but Vesica did not have time for *him*.

Something had changed in their alliance. New terms. A redefinition of roles. Vesica wasn't quite sure she understood it, but that was all right so long as Groby didn't either.

The blades of the windmill turned slowly. There were only two blades on this one, while every other windmill on the farm had three. Groby had said something about this (the one being older than the rest, or newer, or one design better than the other) but Vesica didn't care. She liked this one, the two-bladed one, better than the three-, and wasn't really worried whether the farm had electricity or not. Groby said five or six of the windmills would be enough for Gravetye, anyway, now that they were adjusted, and the rest were producing a surplus that Narthex could sell, but all of these numbers seemed very tiresome to Vesica, as if that were the only language men could think in—how many acres have you got, how many windmills, how many servants, how many votes, and how much money could I make if I sell so many at such a price, and how old are you, how many months a year are you alone here, for how many years now—and Vesica was sick of hearing it.

She would be glad when Groby left and her stepfather got tired of Maintaining his Constituency and she was by herself again.

At the top of the hill the big man shifted his weight, bent over the gray box poking at something with soft bear paws. He paused in his work and Vesica could see him looking sideways at her, not in the old way of just accepting her presence but *thinking* about it, thinking something about her, and she resented it. Didn't he understand how it was supposed to work? Couldn't they just be in the same place together, the way they had at first? Vesica had liked that, had liked the feeling of it. But it had changed now.

It was Narthex who had done it.

Since that night at dinner, Groby could no longer be with her without something going on in his head. Vesica could tell because he wasn't subtle about anything, like a big bear isn't subtle. She could tell he was wondering things, maybe even worrying about her: how she had come to live here, what her life was like, whether she had any friends or just the servants when her stepfather was gone, and how Narthex behaved when they were alone. Or maybe none of these things.

Maybe he just felt sorry for her.

Bending forward agilely, Vesica seized a crimson anemone and yanked it from its stem. It wasn't right, she thought. *Groby* was the one who should be felt sorry for. *He* was the one alone in the world, homeless, unmarried, trudging from one place to another. . . .

She wondered if it had begun to rain when she saw wet spots forming on the torn flower. Only a moment later and with genuine surprise—as though her body, too, had betrayed her—did she realize she had started to cry. She turned from the windmill and passed stiffly among the flowers, holding herself by the elbow and tweedling the red blossom until its stem was soft. Breathing deeply, she made a show of occupation at the task of thinning out until she was quite sure her eyes showed no trace of this unbecoming feebleness.

Then she turned to face the windmill. She advanced in long deliberate strides, resolved to confront Groby, to talk to him more blithely than ever, to *prove* to him . . .

But Groby was gone. He had finished the last of the twenty-something windmills and gathered his tools and left. She saw him walking, slowly, as though sorry to have really gotten it done, beside the gray towers leading back to the pebbled road where the sunglider was swaying gently in the warm southwesterly breeze. The morning sun clung to everything like a tight transparent skin.

Vesica was nowhere to be seen when Groby loaded the last of his luggage and provisions onto the sunglider and rolled it around to point westward, into the wind. Narthex had come to officiate at the departure.

"You've gotten everything?" he said, as people do on such occasions. The translucent eyes swung this way and that, perhaps expecting his stepdaughter to appear among the grapevines.

"Thank you," said Groby, "for having Meggie pack those foodcrates. I'm sure the Crusaders will appreciate your generosity."

Narthex remained unsmiling, but by the jerky movement of his head conveyed a rudimentary sort of pleasure. "Do give," he said, "his lordship the Governor my very highest regards. It has been a long time since I had the honor of an invitation to his estate. A remarkable place, really—but you'll be learning all about that soon enough, won't you? Are you invited to the Embarkation Ball?"

Groby's puzzled glance must have informed Narthex that he had pressed his good fortune a bit too hard, rambled on a few words too many, for quickly, as a man adjusts the set of his hat to the angle of the sun, he left off being Chatty and became instead Coolly Informative. He took Groby by the sleeve as the big man positioned the diaphanous wings of the sunglider for takeoff. With his other hand he pointed northward, past the game park, out over the Blistered Moor.

"You can follow," he suggested, "the streambed. It narrows, of course, and dries up a bit, but you should be able to see it from up there. That will take you to Deeping Lube, which isn't much of a town, I must say, though the Governor's home stands out rather conspicuously above it. You shouldn't have any trouble finding *that*—if you're looking for it, of course. If you need a place to stay, try the Hoar's Bed Inn. The woman that runs the place is an unsympathetic sort, but they say she keeps it clean."

"Thank you," said Groby.

He paused for a moment after adjusting his position in the dangling cab of the sunglider, and cast a final glance over the blue-green vines and towered hills and pebbled roadways of Gravetye Farm. Nothing in particular held his gaze, and he said with a nod to Narthex:

"Goodbye, now."

Narthex may not have heard him. The black rotor flung down a wave of cool compacted air, the strings groaned at their eye-bolts, and the sunglider rose slowly, reluctantly, into the empty sky.

From her quaking, cramped, and nearly airless berth in the carton labeled DRAGONPEARS, Vesica could only imagine what kind of landscape lay beneath them. She had ceased to wonder where they were going, or what Groby would do when he discovered her, or even what her stepfather would do when he found her gone. It was enough to hang there in the pregnant present, her whole life bundled up in one thrilling secret, feeling for once after fourteen years that she was absolutely alive.

Five

DEEPING LUBE, from above, looked as if it had been assembled from the pieces of a pop-up fairy tale, taken apart again, and after a lapse of time and memory put back together by someone who had never heard a fairy tale before. Master Field Engineer Groby, during his days at the Secret College, had heard a number of tales about the days when Deeping Lube was dug from the compacted glacial dirt. It was built (the tales said) as part of a governmental project to provide cheap temporary housing for workers in an industry that was expected to last for centuries. The industry no longer existed; it had predeceased the bureaucrats who planned it, and the government that employed them shortly followed; still, here was Deeping Lube. It continued to provide cheap and temporary housing—not for workers anymore, since there was no work to be had here, but for farmers seeking new lands the forest had not yet reached, for refugees seeking a haven from the Guild, for employment agents seeking cheap labor, for bankers and barristers and charity workers seeking to divert that splenetic gush of money that always attends a crisis, and for pilgrims of a dozen denominations crisscrossing in all directions seeking Truth, or Nature, or the End of the World. If these things were to be found anywhere, then Deeping Lube was a reasonable place to look for them. For it was a famous place, an important place, and this was a famous year: the year the forest went mad.

Groby banked the sunglider east, then west, drifting out over the horizonless waste of the Blistered Moor and back toward the run of sparkling water that looked so out of place here. Still he saw nothing of the landing strip. He tried to match the crabbing much-extended alleyways below with the tickweave of streets on his yellow chart. The landing strip should be *there*: in that paddock where the odd-looking building . . .

As the great astrologers are said to be able to glance at the sky and perceive immediately that a new comet has entered the heavens, an old star exploded, the sun become perturbed—not because they can *see* it, but because its presence changes the pattern—so Groby felt distinctly that there was something misplaced, something discordant, among the pop-up pieces of Deeping Lube. He was accustomed to looking for such lapses from a pattern; it was how he earned his living.

Frowning, he massaged the control stick with his hand—an easy, intimate movement—causing the sunglider to reconfigure its two hundred wings. Looking more like a butterfly now than a bird, the craft spun gently earthward, drifting down toward the long-shadowed paddock, toward what Groby might or might not have glimpsed there.

The odd-looking building was not a building at all. It was a monstrous machine; or more exactly, an assortment of machines, stacked up on cleated treads the size of railroad ties. It was, in other words, a vehicle, and unless Groby was badly off his mark it was none other than the Expeditionary Transport Vehicle, the object of his present employment. He surveyed it with misgiving. Forward, it bared blades as large and vicious as a sawmill's. Its midregions swelled to encompass an engine block. Moving rearward, it slimmed into what, on purely functional grounds, Groby guessed must be a passenger compartment, though this was windowless. And crowning it all like a ceremonial cap was the turret of a power-cannon, one of those venerable engines of death that were outlawed by the civic leaders of Riverrun a few years ago, when the seat of government moved to the suburbs;

they had been removed from the city walls, polished up and auctioned off, and these days you never knew where you would find them. Groby throttled down the small purring engine of the sunglider and made a reluctant landing.

The paddock was wrapped in a fence of beaten wood, most of whose sections had been stolen to feed the hundred cookfires scenting the air. The only reason any wood remained at all was an outer fence of thornwire, coiled like a spiny serpent around the field. A hundred yards away, small figures Groby took to be sentries were engaged in inaudible bickering. He supposed they were arguing over who should come to challenge him, and began fishing through the pockets of his coveralls for identification. He found none. Well, a couple of wrenches: would they do?

He stepped onto soil as dark as machine-oil and wondered about a place to spend the night. Narthex had recommended an inn—what was it called?—but he distrusted this, suspecting that maybe, like so much else the Commissioner had said, this might have been some sly ironic joke. Groby's mind was not attuned to irony. The concept of two levels of meaning—two realities present together, and one somehow more deeply true than the other—seemed to him odd and unsettling. Thus it fit well with his overall impression of Narthex. He thought of Vesica, the man's sad and lovely stepdaughter, and felt a fleeting kinship with her and with all the orphaned souls in the world. It was an unseasonal feeling, out of place in springtime, and Groby reckoned it was the product of hunger and sunset and a landscape that was particularly gloomy, with the soil so black and the ruins of the old industrial project rising at the northern end of town as tall and dark as a factory where night was being made.

Two figures approached. One was a young man draped in a cloak the gray-green shade of rosemary. The other wore a tunic with an officer's epaulet. The latter bowed, very slightly.

"Master Groby?"

Groby slid the wrenches back in his pocket.

"This boy," the officer began, and then the eighteen-or-so-year-old stepped past him.

"I'm here to take care of your luggage," the youth explained. His voice managed to be imperative and obsequious at once.

Groby said, "Well, I haven't got much. And I suppose it's all got to be loaded onto this, um—"

"I've come from the inn," the young man persisted, his voice taking on a bit of a whine. "They're expecting you for dinner. It's all been taken *care* of."

The mention of food was pivotal. Groby's stomach distended by a cubic inch, and autonomically, as though triggered by some enzymatic response, his head gave a nod of agreement. "At least," he said, raising a large cautionary finger, "let me show you where the luggage compartment is."

The youth followed him to the rear of the sunglider and watched as he unhooked the cargo hatch. Groby wondered how this young fellow, who looked to be constructed chiefly of skin and cartilage, was going to manage the heavy boxes. But he supposed if the boy was employed by the inn then he must be competent in such matters. The officer remained a distance behind them, as though to disavow any involvement in their affairs.

"You might need a hand-lamp," Groby said, producing one from a crowded pocket of his coveralls. For a moment, by its narrow beam, he studied the youth's face, which was the color of well-used cooking oil, with just enough hair at the mouth and chin to badly need a razor. As he turned away, glancing into the cargo hold, Groby noticed a rather large carton labeled DRAGONPEARS. Then he ambled toward the gate, guided there by the officer who, over that distance, remained half a step behind him.

The sign said:

🍾 Hoar's Bed Inn 🥖

''CHEAP EATS''

It hung not outside, in the disheveled little alley abutting on an age-old gasworks, but in the common room, staring down at the inn's equivalently ageless and disheveled patrons.

"I'm not," the proprietress declared, "about to have *that* torn down. If there was such a thing as law and order in this town, I'd hang it out front and maybe I'd get some decent customers in here."

"If there was such a thing as food in your kitchen," said one of the customers—a short man with a large mouth that was very dark inside, as though all sorts of unkind sentiments were brooding there—"then maybe you wouldn't have to advertise."

The proprietress gave this some thought. "Good point," she decided. "I think I'll fire that boy of mine and hire someone that can cook." Facing the kitchen, whose steamy confines were visible through a door permanently ajar behind her, she cried, "Thrull! Come here, lad! Where are you?"

Several seconds passed, and the proprietress turned back to the dark-mouthed patron. Spreading her arms in a gesture expressive of a ripened sense of existential despair, she said, "You see? He's not even around long enough for me to fire him. But: there you have it. It's the times. Another round of tea?"

Her name was Mrs Blister. Her hair was stiff, the color of bananas. Her face had lost its rosiness and begun to sag a bit, but her muscles kept their tone, and the hands that, out of a need to do something, kneaded a sponge, might as easily have been employed to discipline mudmules.

"It says here, Sheldrake," said a second patron, a study in opposites with the first, "it says here that, let me see—'In the past few seasons, many of our most popular cultivars have metamorphosed into strange, thorny varieties that are difficult to uproot and nearly impossible to kill by other means. Long the bane of landscape planners . . .' "

"What's that, your lordship?" Mrs Blister asked, squinting at the print—very expensive-looking print—on the reverse side of the pamphlet the man was reading from.

" 'Long the bane of landscape planners,' " he repeated, lengthening further his already very long spine, as though his words might carry better from a greater height, " 'ailanthus are larger and tougher than ever, and their leaves . . .' "

Sheldrake, the short man, muttered over the bar: "It's something those garden clubbers from the city are handing out. For six gold pieces and a peek at your teenage son, they'll send you twelve issues over the next eleven years. The manor's crawling with them."

" '. . . their leaves have *turned*,' " the tall man emphasized. "This should be of interest to you, Sheldrake. '. . .
have turned an objectionable shade of purple.' Isn't that your
favorite color? 'The once-barren Blistered Moor is now blan-
keted with a furlike mantle of gorse, so dense as to impede
. . .' " He read on silently. "Isn't *that* interesting. Have our
purchasing agents had difficulty getting around lately? Out to
the xantheé plantations and so forth?"

"Indeed they have, my lord. You sold all the carriages."

"Ah." The tall man saddened for a moment. "It was the
money, wasn't it? Well. We shan't have that to worry us
anymore, shall we?"

"We never had it to begin with," Sheldrake acknowledged.

The tall man gave no sign of hearing. Actually his ears
were quite acute, despite his being no longer exactly young,
except when it came to Sheldrake. Somehow he could never
catch just what the fellow had said.

"I'll tell you one thing," said Mrs Blister. "*I* wouldn't want
to be governor of this territory, no matter what the job
paid."

The tall man looked at her and brightened, as though
she had said something quite different. "Yes, by all means,"
he said. "Another round."

"Certainly, your lordship."

His lordship stood up and stretched. He laid the pamphlet on the bar and shook his head at it, as though to say,
He wouldn't want to be governor of this territory, either.
Unfortunately, he was: Governor of Deeping Lube and All
the Northern Territories—wasteland, most of them, and otherwise unreclaimable forest—a hereditary post he could not
have gotten rid of had he tried to, and sometimes he did feel
like trying. He glanced uneasily aside and downward at the
much shorter Sheldrake, afraid the little man might be speaking again. (Could it be, he wondered, the difference in their
height?)

Well, at least he looked the part. Besides tall, the Governor was impressively lanky and supple-limbed, which caused
him to appear relaxed no matter how tense he truly was, and
however erect he held himself his body gave off a comfortable air of slouching. His face, the color and texture of old
calf's leather, was reassuringly wrinkled around swimming-

pool-blue eyes that were set off (he thought) rather dashingly by an unbleached cotton safari jacket. He had been wearing this, or a series of jackets just like it, since the good news came this winter: the news of his being selected to lead the First Biotic Crusade—a position that provided not only an aura of concern for the common weal, but also full rights of publication and a weighty honorarium.

He had never fancied himself a crusader, upper-case or low. He thought of himself in grander and more nebulous terms, along the lines of Inheritor of Tradition. The particular tradition he had inherited, a goulash of genes and dreams and family debts, had left him with a title (the Eighth Earl Tattersall), a sprawling ancestral manor, and an income insufficient to maintain either of them in proper style. This puzzled him; he did not understand contemporary politics; he found it strange, for example, that the fellow Narthex, whose title was only Low Commissioner, had a very nice house and lots of money and . . .

Tattersall—which is how he called himself, how all seven forebears had called themselves—permitted himself a sigh. He had had his dealings with Narthex, and he had lost (so to speak) nine of the ten things in life he held dear. Thereafter he had resolved never to speak or even think about the man, lest the Commissioner nip back to filch the one he had forgotten.

"Thank you, dear lady," Tattersall told Mrs Blister, accepting the algae-colored beverage she pressed upon him over the bar. "Why, what a remarkable color!"

"It's made from yellow dock and dandelions," she explained. "Excellent for the blood. Drink up, now."

Tattersall successfully concealed his dismay.

"Here, my lord," muttered Sheldrake, producing something from his waistcoat. As the folds parted, the Governor caught a glimpse of bright checkered fabric underneath. "This will lighten it up a bit."

"What, a light?" said Tattersall, as Sheldrake allowed something to gurgle into his drink. "I haven't brought my pipe, thank you. Haven't I asked you not to wear that horrid shirt?"

"It wards off devils."

"It *does*," agreed his lordship. "*Quite* like the Devil."

The door creaked noisily open behind them, and a remarkable-looking figure shambled through. He was so tall he had to stoop to enter, and so broad-shouldered (broad-everythinged, really) it was difficult to encompass him in one glance. Tattersall, following the eyes of Mrs Blister, turned to look at him, and the very large man, for his part, turned this way and that, taking in the inn. The common room shrank around him: its faded drapes, ancient cedar paneling and small round tables, mostly empty, each with its yellow flower in a battered baby-cup, shriveled to insignificance before the imposing stranger. As the man lumbered over toward the bar, the Governor noticed something in one of his big pulpy hands, a small bottle . . .

"Excuse me," the man said. His voice was slow and his manner apologetic, as though he hadn't meant to be so terribly large but now there was nothing he could do about it. He continued: "Your door—I've got some oil here that might—well, perhaps I shouldn't presume. . . ." He stared at them worriedly. "This *is* the Hoar's Bed Inn?"

Mrs Blister, consulting the sign above the bar as though to be certain, said, "I've *told* my boy to grease that thing for oh, I don't know how long now. Are you here to eat? How did you find the place, anyway? You're not a barrister, are you? We don't serve barristers."

Groby relaxed a bit under this interrogation. "Actually I'm here with the Crusade. That is, I've been hired on as its engineer, and the young man told me—"

"What young man?" said Mrs Blister. "What crusade? Look, we don't serve crazy people either. I've got a heatgun under here."

"You serve his lordship," Sheldrake pointed out.

Tattersall rose (he had been on his feet all along, but with that air of slouching) and held out a hand to take the newcomer's.

"Do come in," he urged Groby, though Groby could hardly come much farther without upsetting the barstools. "Welcome, Master Engineer. I am Tattersall, the Crusade Leader, you know, and this is Sheldrake, my Chief Accountant."

Groby shook hands with them, stooping to reach Shel-

drake's. "I was told," he said, "that dinner . . . I mean . . .
Are the other Crusaders here?"

Tattersall coughed diplomatically. "Yes, well. They were
supposed to be here, but there were so many of them—and so
many of them ladies—that we thought, well." (A glance at
Mrs Blister.) "They might be more comfortable at the manor.
That is, my home."

"The place that looks like a glue factory," Sheldrake
explained.

"Yes, it is more satisfactory. That way, you see, they
have the run of the place, getting ready for their ball tonight."

"I heard about that," said Groby, frowning to remember
where.

"And Sheldrake and I," Tattersall went on, "are staying
down here. More comfortable all around, I would say. May I
buy you some food?"

The Governor gave them all his broadest smile, as well
he might have. For the first time since reaching the age of
majority, he wasn't worried about money.

"The Crusade," he said, "is going to be a very grand
thing."

The world outside the carton labeled DRAGONPEARS was like
the sounds that wake you up in the morning: bright confusing noises, urgent as trilling birds, everything alive out there
but you still wrapped in in the warm soft darkness of sleep.
Only, the darkness inside the box was chilly and hard and
Vesica was having trouble getting enough air, which she
thought might damage her brain if it kept up much longer, so
as soon as Groby's footsteps had lumbered away—and after
counting her heartbeats to a hundred, just to be sure—she
pressed upward against the lid until it opened, only an inch,
but enough to let the new air rush into her lungs and frighten
her, for it was that—the smell of this alien place—that made
her really know she was far, far from home.

She changed position to get an eye to the opening. The
day was almost over: a copper sun hung over the narrow
stretch of water she could just make out by the way it caught
the orange and white of the western sky. Close at hand was
another source of light, a smaller one, which Vesica saw as
she craned her neck and nudged the lid a little higher was a

hand-lamp. Someone had propped it on the rubbly ground, or forgotten it there. It shone on nothing of interest, and all Vesica could see from where she lay twisted in the box was the dirt and the river and a small group of figures by a fence. She figured it was safe to come out.

As soon as her feet found the soil—so much harder here than at home (no, than at her stepfather's home)—she saw something that frightened her more than anything about running away had yet managed to do. Beside the sunglider, twice as tall and a thousand times as massive, was an awful-looking thing she had no name for, but which captured fairly well her idea of *ominous*. Before Vesica could break it down into parts to think about separately, she heard a voice very nearby, and squatted down quickly beside the landing gear wishing the other side of sunset were a little closer.

Near the hand-lamp, a young man wearing a cloak the color of rosemary was waving his arms in dramatic overstatement at a cluster of people by the fence. He interpreted these gestures in a petulant, nasal chant: "Come *on*, come *on*! I've got to get *back* or the old witch will *fire* me."

Whether or not he managed to convey this message to the people across the field, the bunch of them started over, ambling like one of the work gangs at Gravetye Farm. The young man picked up the hand-lamp and swung it around, so close to where Vesica crouched that only the tightening grip of fear kept her motionless long enough for the beam to miss her. Clearly the cargo hold was out of the question. If these were thieves, that was the first place they'd go. She glanced hopefully over her shoulder, but thornwire gleamed around the paddock, red in the dying sun.

Choosing a moment when the eyes of the universe seemed to be pointed elsewhere, Vesica sprinted the distance from the sunglider to the huge vehicle beside it. Finger-sized teeth jutted from its flank, and she used these to clamber up until she reached a darker-than-black opening she could pull herself into. She landed on a steel deck, breathing oil and rust and her own chilling sweat. She had ripped one denim leg and felt blood sticking at the cloth there, but it didn't hurt enough to think about right now, and there were voices just outside.

"So," said one, a cocky boy's, "what goes in?"

The nasal voice said, *"Everything.* Put everything in, and be *careful."*

A round of complaints followed this, calling attention to the number and weight of the boxes. And what about this flying thing?

"That is Evil," the nasal-voiced young man said coolly, somewhat haughtily, Vesica thought. "It is an engine of destruction, just like the transport. We'll take care of that tonight, and the transport—"

From the belly of the black mechanical beast a rumbling noise arose, and Vesica missed what the youth said next. Outside, from the direction of the sunglider, she heard a carton strike the ground and crack open, hollowly like a great nutshell, and she guessed that it was the one labeled DRAGONPEARS.

Night came on quickly, with no moon. A haze the color of cobwebs lay across the sky. Collectively, out of winter's slow-dying habit, the citizens and visitors and squatters of Deeping Lube tossed another plank or another broken chairleg or another fencepost onto the fire. There were no proper logs here, where trees had not grown for centuries. This had once kept people away from Deeping Lube; now it drew them here in tremendous numbers. By its very barrenness, the place had become a kind of haven. What irony there was in this went mostly unremarked. Only those looking down at Deeping Lube from above seemed to appreciate it. Certainly the Territorial Governor did not.

Smoke curled up from tents and huts and market-stalls, taking with it a bit of the fragrance of ancient chemicals that mingled with the smells of cooking and nightsoil, rising until it reached the pocket of unmoving air that trapped the haze, and spreading out there, adding new streaks and highlights to the gray roof. In the alleyway abutting on the age-old gasworks, a door was flung open and, for a moment, lamplight made a warm golden carpet on the dusty street. Three shadows fell: stubby, lank, and bearlike; they remained there, leaning one way or the other, only for a moment, but so strange and convoluted was the twisting of that alley that the sound of their parting did not reach the street for some while afterward.

"Come now, Master Engineer, do join us."

"Well, I really need to get up early in the—"

"We'll have some music, and dance with the ladies! Gad, I hope the talking's done by now. There were to be speeches."

"You were to make one yourself, your lordship."

"I what? Perhaps there's some of that orange stuff left in the cellar. What *was* that stuff, Sheldrake?"

"Ant poison, as I remember."

"A grand potion, yes. But what was it? You never know . . ."

"Goodnight, Governor, it was a pleasure—"

"Are you certain you won't join us, just for a drink or two? Talk to him, Sheldrake."

"Better die here than in the forest, Master Groby."

"He's right! It will be much better in the forest! Well, tomorrow, then!"

The door slipped shut on newly oiled hinges, and the two remaining figures—the stubby and the lank—stepped cautiously down the alleyway. You never knew.

They passed through the quarter of Deeping Lube known locally as the Tanks: unlived-in, perhaps unlivable, though even here the sluggish breeze brought sounds of flights and scurryings. Cylindrical buildings hunched low on the ground, holes chewed through them by the worm of Time, though a few were intact, and others collapsed into themselves like ruined soufflés. Their shadows were kept from being smooth by the pits and trenches scored into the earth by the leakage of their contents. But that was forgotten now.

The soil of Deeping Lube was chiefly a nacreous black that the sun would make more colorful, lightning sometimes cause to smolder like peat, going on for weeks, burning belowground, the fumes rising in yellow clouds from sewers and drainpipes and even faucets, though for drinking purposes the townspeople went down to the stream they called Running Water, a term outsiders laughed at. The two men left the Tanks and entered the square that had been an open market before last year's riots. A pack of dogs sauntered by. Ahead, around the gallows, whose platform with the trapdoor provided the most elevated forum in town for the business of rabble-rousing, a gathering of gray-green-clad youths was underway. Two dozen young faces were concealed by hats and shadows and underdeveloped beards. A larger crowd of onlookers stood back a few paces, and in a powered wagon close by, taking notes, sat the half-dozen members of the Press Pool (spies, mostly, for competing interests in the great world beyond the Northern Territories, or perhaps not even that). In these remote postings they banded together for companionship.

"Good evening, Governor," a fat journalist said.

"Hello there. Small crowd tonight, is it?"

"There's something doing," the journalist said placidly, "at the landing field. Lorian's gone down to have a look at it."

"Well, just let me know if you need anything."

From the gallows a flickering hologhost, depicting a youth with a remarkably radiant brow, admonished the faithful on certain obscure tenets of their faith, or perhaps it was only a reading of lengthy bylaws. Tattersall was none too clear about the exact *raison d'être* of the Force, whether religious or political or, for all he knew, necromantic. They did turn up in surprising places.

"Urrrps izz self around us," the staticky image hissed, floating in and out of focus. "As those who came before us. The malevolent forces of so-called Science. Merchants of Bad Faith. Investors in Lost Causes. Advocates of Unnatural Diets. Gwipp fwwm mumm."

Sheldrake's dark mouth seemed to quiver as he and the Governor left the journalists to their story. Tattersall could not remember ever having noticed the inside of anyone's mouth before he met Sheldrake. Sometimes it was all he could think about.

"We must," he whispered, "keep on the good side of the Press."

They kept on. They entered what scant residential district there was in Deeping Lube: rectangular boxes, gray with age, set in little rows that defied the contours of the terrain. Another spring runoff from the manor had brought small bits of plastic and other debris scrabbling down the hillside, and instead of skirting these poor homes the stuff collected in their gardens and on their tiny stoops. No wonder, thought Tattersall, most people nowadays settled along the uphill edge of town, where the view from their huts of corrugated metal was better than the manor's; though they paid for it in the extra walk to Running Water. Everyone seemed to be indoors.

Turning a corner, the Governor came in view of his ancestral home, and (as had probably been the case with every one of his ancestors, though they had all kept a stiff upper lip about it) the sight immeasurably depressed him.

"Gad," he said, stopping in the middle of the road. "Doesn't the air smell awful tonight?"

"It's our guests," Sheldrake told him. "The old men are wearing perfume. And some of the ladies were burning incense."

"Ah."

The manor consisted of several interconnected structures in various stages of coming apart, as half a millennium's looters had made off with pipes and plates and sometimes whole sections of the place. Bless them, thought Tattersall. The portion that remained was vast and awful enough: a mass of tanks and valves and aqueducts, silos and smokestacks, catwalks and power-cells and a hundred other things that had outlasted their own names, which collectively Tattersall thought of as his Maze. He had read of another governor, lonely servant of some long-fallen empire, who built a maze for the amusement of his dinner guests; and he thought, By heaven, I've got one too!

It was his only consolation. The other governor (the dead one) had splendid gardens; neither Tattersall nor his progenitors had gotten so much as a single beet to root in the familial sod. The other one had thrown parties, with music; but even money, which Tattersall had never had much of, could not entice musicians to leave their cushy warrens in the south for this remote wind-shriven colony. And without music one could not have the things that went with it: the dance, the revelry, the amour . . .

"Well, come on," he told Sheldrake. "They'll be expecting me."

"They'll be expecting you sober, too, but it's too late for that."

Now and then Tattersall made out a bit of what Sheldrake was saying, but in the interest of friendship—which was his only *other* consolation—he declined to let the man know.

"It is a bit late," he agreed.

They strolled up the hill toward the manor.

In the Gallows Square, the crowd continued to thin. The fat journalist, turning to one of his colleagues, said, "Well, I don't suppose anything's likely to happen this late, do you?"

A younger man, busy copying expenses from a notebook labeled LIFE OF ST BOTO into another marked THE REVOLUTIONARY PHILANTHROPIST, looked up to see the last gray-green-clad youth slip off into the shadows. No one was left in the square but some mendicant priests and tourists, whose faces in the blue light of the hologhost seemed respectively dazed by hunger and the vapors in the air. He said, "I wonder where *they're* off to."

The fat man shrugged. "Blowing up the hospital? They've overlooked that so far."

"We could send someone around."

The fat man shook his head. "If we're caught there," he said, patiently giving his younger colleague the benefit of a long career that had lately turned unlucky, "we can be hanged as accessories. Not, of course, that old Tattersall . . . But it's a bad habit to get into. We'll just duck in at the post office to see if any manifestos have been pinned up, and then we're off to the ball."

Someone wondered what about Lorian.

"Ha!" said the fat man. "I told her not to bother. Next time maybe she'll listen."

He kicked the starting-pedal and tugged energetically at the wheel. The powered wagon coughed a bit and issued fumes that smelled badly, though no worse than the general atmosphere, and then it exploded. The wagon was hurled sideways, skidding across the square and landing on a knot of startled bystanders. A few of the mendicant priests and tourists were killed; the rest were carted off to the already-crowded hospital. The journalists, by some whim of the appropriate deity, were all right, though the fat one, on whom the others landed, was squeezed unconscious and

missed the ball. At the post office, a new manifesto was discovered. TO THE RETURN OF THE GREAT DRYAD, it said. It was signed
The Pure Force.

Six

THE EMBARKATION BALL
was well underway when its host, the Territorial Governor,
arrived smelling of gin with his unseemly little accountant at
heel. Advanced though the hour was, there was yet no music
or dancing, and the evening's featured speakers still sat rig-
idly on the dais. Behind them were arrayed the Crusaders,
excellent women and fussy little men selected from the ranks
of the Hardy Plant Society, apparently on the basis of se-
niority. Over their heads, draped in such a way that its final
letters were occulted, a banner proclaimed

When the Master is ready, the student appears.

—the Society's motto. No one was sure what it meant, but
the banner was magnificent. Indeed, the entire Upper Fractionating Chamber (as a plate above the doorway identified
this portion of the Maze) was magnificently done-up, hung
with silver drapes and banners and aglow with the landing
lights someone had thoughtfully brought up from the air-
field. These were hung pointing downward, for not even the
most inventive and energetic members of the Society had
thought of a way to decorate the ceiling. It was too high,
covered with rust and cobwebs, and there was something
alive up there: the brave soul who went up to investigate

wasn't sure exactly what, but there was a whole *colony* of them. This reminded Lady Widdershins, the Society's estimable Chairperson, of an experience in her own attic—whereupon it came to remind *all* the members of *something*—and further attempts to rehabilitate the upper reaches of the Governor's home were forgotten in the ensuing round of clever remarks. Still, the work that had gotten done was breathtaking. Even the Governor seemed to like it; but then, the Governor's was a pure and uncluttered soul, one could tell, and everything one did seemed to please him. His arrival was greeted with a heartfelt round of applause.

"And *here*," announced the Chairperson, spying his lordship slouching at the back of the Chamber, "is the nobleman who will *conduct* the Crusade through the *forest*. And *who*, ladies and gentlemen, has invited us into his *wonderful* home for the duration of our *stay*."

Lady Widdershins's luminous and voluminous form dominated the podium.

"*Won't* you," she asked the Governor, "come make a few Remarks to the members of the Society, as well as the Crusaders Themselves, and"—she added discreetly, though at the same stentorian volume—"their lovely Friends."

Tattersall smiled, tried to look as though he were standing upright (which he was, though gravity and direct lighting worked against him), and made his way through the several hundred people who surely couldn't, he thought, all be sleeping here. He joined Lady Widdershins—whom he had known all his life and with whom, on an occasion when they were both old enough to have known better, or even older, he had enjoyed a brief conjunction—at the podium, where she clasped her hands beneath an overabundant bosom.

"Tatty!" she greeted him, a safe distance from the microphone.

"Widdy!"

They cautiously embraced: the great lady careful of her pompadour and the vivid red flowers adorning her gown; his lordship, as ever, awed by the sheer volume of the woman.

"Let me *introduce* you," she said, assuming again her public persona, "to our other featured Speaker. This is Professor Tylyester, the Dean of the Secret College, and the leading Expert in the Field."

The professor was nodding impatiently, either out of modesty or because this introduction was superfluous.

"Good heavens," Tattersall cried, extending both hands, "they didn't tell me *you* were mixed up in all this. And a Dean now . . ."

"Hello, old man." Professor Tylyester smiled. "Yes—the Crusade has been something of a personal passion of mine."

He patted a bulky package under his arm, as though this might explain something. It occurred to Tattersall to wonder if his old acquaintanceship with Tylyester might have had the teeniest influence on his selection as Crusade Leader. It didn't do to forget one's friends, did it?

"*Well*," Lady Widdershins diplomatically broke in, "since we all *know* each other . . ."

"Yes," said the Governor. "Quite."

He turned to face the assembled guests. His blue eyes were bright and cloudless, none the worse for Sheldrake's flask, and his silver-blond hair caught the blaze of the landing lights and reflected it most favorably. Even his hard-worn safari jacket managed to look rumpled, which had its charm, as opposed to wrinkled, which did not. He cleared his throat.

"Hello, hello. Well. Isn't it wonderful, the way you have all come out here? Abandoning the well-known attractions of city life. Well. I trust you are all behaving yourselves."

He paused to acknowledge their good-natured laughter, judged his performance thus far to be a success.

"Well," he said, plunging onward. "It is certainly a grand and noble undertaking that has brought us all together. For we are here to honor the members of the First Biotic Crusade. These intrepid souls, whom you see behind me, have chosen to leave the comfort of their homes and their positions in society, to join us here in the defense of our very way of life. Yes—I think it is not going too far to say that. For are we not, here in the straited North, Civilization's front line of resistance? Yes: the battlefront, if you will, against that rapacious invader which has displaced uncounted thousands of our citizens, and leaves hundreds more homeless every day? I speak, my friends, of the forest. The dense and impenetrable forest, whose phalanx advances hard upon us even as we are gathered here tonight."

He paused, perspiring lightly, wondering which side of his family the grandiloquence had come from. At the entrance of the chamber there was a bit of agitation, as if someone were trying to crash the ball.

"Yes," he said. "And these bold Crusaders, who will embark with me in the morning—at eleven o'clock, I believe—we should all have gotten out of bed by then. Ha ha! These Crusaders will launch the very first counterattack against our vast and implacable foe. A counterattack . . ."

The Governor frowned as the agitation in the doorway spilled into the room. There was a young woman, not attired for a ball unless Tattersall was hopelessly out of touch with fashion, and several uniformed men who appeared to be chasing her. So *this*, he thought dryly, is how those fellows occupy themselves. He strove to continue:

"Well. A counterattack, I say, which will thrust deep behind the lines of the aggressor, probing for his weaknesses, stealing his secrets . . . Look here, you men down there, why are you chasing that woman? The dance floor has just been waxed, you know."

All motion in the Chamber came to a halt. The members of the audience who had been following his remarks turned to stare at the intruders, and those who had been sleeping opened their eyes and spotted Tattersall for the very first time. One of these, supposing that the Governor had just been introduced, started clapping.

The next person to come unfrozen was the young woman, who resumed her march across the floor. She came close enough for Tattersall to make out her cropped brown hair and flashing eyes before a couple of soldiers caught her from behind.

"Let *go* of me," she said firmly, and the soldiers, who had spent several years being taught to obey such commands, dropped their hold on her arms. "Governor Tattersall," she shouted. "You've got to do something. Someone's trying to sabotage the Crusade!"

"My lord," a voice purred behind him. It was that captain whose name Tattersall could never recall. "The woman must be some kind of fanatic. She should be taken into custody right away, before—"

Tattersall elbowed the man aside. He stepped down

from the platform (*leapt down* was what he was trying for, but his movements were too easeful for that) and into the mass of celebrants. Sheldrake, materializing in front of him, went charging through the crowd, bullying into existence an aisle down which the Governor strolled.

"Look here," he addressed the woman, "what is your name? What has happened?"

"Lorian," she said breathlessly. "I'm here with the *Daily Wake*, covering the Crusade. I was just down in the landing field, and a bunch of kids from the Pure Force are down there tearing up everything they can get their hands on. I thought you'd want to know."

"Sheldrake," Tattersall commanded, "bring my car!"

"You sold it, my lord."

"Ah." The Governor brushed aside a wave of sadness. "Bring something, then. I'll meet you out front."

As the short man bustled off, Tattersall took the opportunity to study the journalist, Lorian, with greater attention. Her green eyes looked especially large, he decided, because of how short she had cropped her dark brown hair. And her face *wasn't* pretty, there was no way around that, yet it had a certain . . .

"Are we going, or not?" she unexpectedly said. "I don't want to stand around here and miss a terrific story."

The Governor was startled, but not disagreeably so. He made a short bow. "Would you be so good," he said, "as to direct me to the scene of the disturbance?"

"Just hurry up," the woman said. She made off for the ballroom door, leaving the Governor to hurry along behind her.

"Oh!" Lady Widdershins exclaimed from the dais. "Isn't this exciting? Perhaps it's time for the *music* to begin!"

Tattersall hesitated; it pained him to miss the best part of the ball. Well, he thought, we shan't be gone *too* long.

The sallow-faced youth, having seen to the dismantlement of Groby's sunglider, assembled his followers for parting instructions over canteens of herbal tea. The other members of the Pure Force—mostly people his own age, though a few were old enough to have found something better to do—passed the tea around and regarded him with a sort of amiable vacuity, which suggested to the youth that the valerian and forget-all were already taking effect. He spoke quickly, from memory, before they nodded off altogether.

"The great forces of Nature are moving toward the final confrontation with Science, their ancient enemy. We at Deeping Lube are on the front lines of that old and terrible war. The outcome of the struggle may depend on us. What we've got to do—what Nature demands that we do—is to prevent this blasphemous Crusade from launching its attack on Nature's stronghold, the Carbon Bank Forest . . . by whatever means are required."

He droned on, scarcely paying attention to his own words. It was make-believe talk, Pure Force talk. The same slogans put together in different ways, like the pieces of a machine. And although it made him feel silly, it was very important that he talk this way, because most of the people in the landing field really believed it. He couldn't just come out and say, Let's go kill some scientists, or Let's blow up some machines. It had to be "weapons against Nature," or "seekers of the Five Forbidden Things." For many years he hadn't understood this; hadn't known hatred wasn't always enough; hadn't understood (except in the distant way one knows of such things) the Pure Force, or the struggle to crush the so-called great tradition, or the bright New Day that—for five hundred years or so—had been about to dawn. But then he had met Low Commissioner Narthex, there in the work camp, and . . . well, he had learned a lot since then.

"Okay," he said at last, to the few of his followers still conscious. "I leave now, and prepare for the decisive confrontation in the morning."

Then he turned his back on the landing field, musing privately that if Mrs Blister was still awake, the decisive confrontation might come a little sooner.

He did not notice the lithe shadow that fell behind him, for the reason that people do not customarily notice fairies: he was busy, and he did not expect it to be there. The night was moonless, and the field, with its landing lights removed, was very dark.

The youth strode quickly to Gallows Square, where he dismantled the hologhost machine. Set to replay the same drab lecture interminably, it had sometime during the evening gotten jammed, perhaps on account of the explosion. The youth hurried on to the Tanks. To his surprise the door of the inn opened silently. It closed again behind him, but not before something even darker and slyer than himself had slipped through the opening.

In the absolute blackness of the common room, Vesica listened while the youth's footsteps padded up a staircase—pretty quietly she thought, especially for a boy; but there must be something the matter with their muscles, they always make a certain amount of noise. She made no noise at all as she moved foot-by-foot across the uneven flooring. In the stairwell she paused, straining for a sense of where Groby might be.

"Ha! Caught you, you little bastard!"

Vesica recoiled from the pale face of a woman no taller than her shoulders. The woman wore a nightdress and a stocking cap that made her look even shorter than she was, and angrier, and she grabbed Vesica by the arm and pulled her downward, bringing the girl's face closer to her own.

"I'm not—"

The woman had discovered that. "You're not Thrull," she charged.

"Shh!" Vesica looked around, hoping the young man hadn't heard them. Probably not; there was something the matter with their ears too. She whispered: "Groby. I've got to find Groby. Is he staying here? It's really important."

The woman's eyes were wide in the darkness, but calm, merely evaluating. She said, "Who are you, honey?"

Manual labor is said to be good for sleeping. This turned out not to be true for Groby, or true in an unusual fashion. For while his body would gladly fall into long unstirring slumber, his mental faculties remained more or less awake, sometimes all the way to morning. It was a special kind of waking, though, full of mental torrents and doldrums, rising tides of consciousness that as slowly sank, and sometimes storms of light, as though tremendous energies were being dissipated along his synapses. He wondered where the energies came from, where they were going, where they hid in the daytime while he moved from job to job across the outlands of Civilization. Meanwhile the evening moved on.

The intrusion of light into his room therefore neither wakened him nor failed to; he kept still, presuming that the light came from within, and also the noise, but when fingers began tugging at his vest his large brown eyes popped open, fully alert and self-collected, to see what in the world was going on.

The expression in them frightened Vesica.

Vesica, the sight of Vesica, enormously disoriented Groby. He wondered if he weren't asleep and dreaming after all.

"Groby!" the girl whispered, coming closer. "They've ripped up your sunglider! They've stuffed it into that black thing, that machine . . ."

He rose up on the bed, saw Mrs Blister in the doorway, a lamp in one hand and someone's arm in the other. A boy's arm, someone he had seen before. He blinked.

". . . gray robes or something," said Vesica, whose voice he had lost track of for a moment. "Twenty or thirty or . . . I don't know what they're doing now; they've gone to sleep or something, but I followed *him* here."

Mrs Blister tightened her grip on the boy.

"Come on," said Vesica. "I'll show you."

But Groby would not be hurried. He moved at all times in his own deliberate pace, not because he was lazy or slow, but because the widely separated parts of his being required particular attention to hold together. His great body was quaking with adrenaline, but his mind had not gotten in sync with it, and there were questions it was thinking of that ought, probably, to be asked.

"Vesica," he said, to start with one of them, "what are you doing here?"

"Come *on*," she told him.

The two of them were halfway down the convoluted alley when Mrs Blister collapsed in a nightgowned wad in the middle of her common room. The youth removed from his palm a splinter of the sign he had struck her with, leaving it cracked and bloodstained behind the bar.

The landing field smelled of rotting hemp, though nothing grew there. Something had trickled down from the transport to react with the phlegmy humors of the soil, giving off a gas whose pale-lavender phosphorescence could be seen against the black hull, though only just. It woke none of the young people around it, whose slumber was reinforced by the tea they had drunk a short while before. Without question, they were meant to be here in the morning.

"I wonder what happened to the soldiers," Groby murmured, as Vesica led him through the maze of half-visible bodies.

"*He* probably killed them."

Groby reached the transport and, just behind the engine block, found a door. In her earlier panic, Vesica hadn't noticed this. She rubbed her battered leg. Behind them, at the edge of the landing field, a nasal voice began shouting:

"Wake up! Wake up, everybody! Enemies are among you!"

It was *him*.

The tea had been effective but not absolutely so; the bodies on the ground stirred as though sloughing off leaden nightmares.

"Wake up!" the sallow youth wailed. He came running across the field, kicking the nearest bodies. Twenty feet away, he drew something small from his cloak. To Groby he snarled: "And *you*—stay right there."

The faint light drifting down from the manor glanced dully off the burnished barrel of a heatgun. Groby, his massive body half into the transport, assumed a state of arrested motion that gravity, or something, must surely soon undo. Sleepily the young members of the Force climbed to their feet. They stood in the tangled night looking at Groby and the sallow boy and the pale luminescence around the transport, and might have thought very reasonably that none of it was real. Their leader cried, "These people are the agents of the Crusade! They're trying to ruin our plans!"

A voice from the darkness said, "What plans?"—groggily innocent, a girl's voice, no older than Vesica. The boy turned irritably to find her.

Vesica leapt. She struck the boy behind the elbow—not where she was aiming, but good enough. The heatgun clattered on the ground. From its muzzle a translucent rod of amber darted to the hull of the transport, made a crackling sound, and vanished. The boy lashed out, catching Vesica on the cheekbone. The night reddened. She staggered back.

"Seize them!" he cried. "Before they destroy us!"

Vesica wanted to fight him, to knock him down and kick him and punish him for what he had done to Groby's sunglider. But she knew it was hopeless; he was taller and stronger and (she was certain) more ruthless. While he was busy stirring up his troops she made a run for the transport, joining Groby by the door. He pulled her up, his bulky form still suspended from the running board.

"Get that big one!" cried the youth. "He can't fight all of us."

Without much conviction the members of the Force set upon Groby, eight or ten of them, trying to pull him down. He tossed them aside in great untroubled sidestrokes. The ringleader scrabbled over the ground, searching for his fallen weapon.

"Little bitch," he muttered. "I'm going to enjoy what happens to *you.*"

In the next instant his bloodless features were lit from above as though by a thousand candles. Points of yellow-white light flared and skidded across the sky like an invasion of dancing comets. They were accompanied by a series of small explosions. The youths fell away from Groby and stood dumbly beside the transport.

Across the field a voice exclaimed, "That's it! Bless you, good woman! Another salvo, if you please!"

There were more lights, more sonic claps. An inflorescence of fireworks blossomed over the landing field as a hundred glowing colors rained down.

"Forward, Sheldrake! Into the thick of them!"

At last Vesica spotted the source of it all: a wagon pulled by two panic-stricken horses, carrying a trio so mismatched it appeared some terribly comic mistake had been made. A short, dark-faced man held the reins, handling them like a jump-rope. Behind him a tall man stood calmly upright as though exempt from the laws of inertia. The third passenger, whom Vesica barely recognized as a woman, clung to the pitching cab, launching fireworks into the sky.

"Faster now, Sheldrake, and we'll stampede them!"

Vesica laughed, delighted by the absurdity of it all. The

wagon was just like those used at Gravetye for hauling
manure. It pitched and clattered over the landing field, scattered the crowd of youths like so many pigeons and plunged
onward toward the transport. Just when a collision appeared
imminent, the draft-horses rebelled, bolted to one side and
snapped their yoke from its mounting. The short man, still
clutching the reins, was dragged behind them. The wagon
tipped sideways, spilling the tall man then the woman and
finally a load of unfragrant cargo—the first two landing
beside the transport and the last sloshing onto it, drenching
the sallow youth who knelt dumbly in its shadow.

"Well done, Sheldrake!" With no more effort than it
costs a cat, the Governor had landed on his feet. He glanced
around. "Sheldrake . . . ?"

There was an indistinct reply some distance off, where
the horses had slowed to a canter.

"Ah." The tall man offered the woman, Lorian, a hand
up.

A few feet away, the youth stood wiping his face and
spluttering. "Come on!" he cried to his followers. "We've got
them all here now! All our enemies! Let's finish it!"

The excitement must finally have wakened them. The
Pure Force tightened its circle around the Governor.

"Stand back, young dastards!" Tattersall commanded.

For no accountable reason, they obeyed him. He turned
to escort the short-haired woman to the transport. Groby
reached down to help her aboard.

"Why, Master Engineer!" exclaimed the Governor. "Well
met, as they say."

"Hey, Groby," whispered Vesica, over his massive shoulder. "Who *are* all these people?"

Before the big man could answer either of them, a
thunderous vibration rose from the bowels of the craft, quaking the steel deckplates. The woman Lorian had discovered
what appeared to be a steering console, and was tugging
randomly at its knobs and levers. Her face was lit crazily by
an array of yellow lights.

"Hold on, everybody," she said. "I'm going to get this
thing moving."

"Um, I don't—" began Groby.

"Stop!"

The sallow youth stood outside the doorway, waving the little heatgun. He had caught Governor Tattersall in the act of climbing aboard. He shouted above the rumble of the engine: "You're going to have a short trip."

"Oh, good heavens," Tattersall sighed. "It's one thing after another. Here, give me that."

He reached out for the weapon, as though expecting the youth to meekly comply. And for all Vesica knew he might have—except that the transport chose that moment to engage its treads. It lurched six feet forward and halted, then moved as many feet back. The people in the field were nearly run over, and those inside fared worse. They swung their arms wildly, seeking handholds on pipes and ladders and bulkheads, and generally found it. Only Tattersall, perched uncertainly on the running board, seemed in danger of falling out and being crushed by the cleated treads. The craft moved forward in a series of shuddering lunges; the Governor wobbled off-balance.

"Oh my," he said, as though contending with a social dilemma.

"Here!" said Groby.

With a counterhold on the horn handle, the big man leaned forward to snare the Governor's safari jacket. He gave a casual, backhand yank; his lordship was hurled into the steering cab. The sallow-faced youth came behind him, clinging as tightly as a shadow.

"Oh, no you don't," he sneered—

—then Lorian rammed a lever over to FORWARD, and the transport made a final, decisive lurch. The passengers—all but Groby—slammed the bulkhead. The big man, already atilt, teetered for a number of seconds (enough for his practical mind to calculate the extent of his problem, and a few of its most likely outcomes) and then he began slowly but irreversibly to fall. It was rather—as Tattersall would remark upon retelling the story—like watching the collapse of the territorial banking system. The horn lowed mournfully for a long moment; then its handle snapped off in Groby's hand.

Just inside the cab, the sallow youth cringed between that great toppling body and the floor.

"No!" he shrieked.

Groby toppled into him and continued falling, for the

youth's insignificant body-mass was not adequate even to brake his descent. The two of them struck the deck together, the sounds of their separate impacts merging into something like the rupturing of a bladderball: first the solid impact of the ball being kicked (in this case, Groby's head hitting the deck and bouncing off it), then the sudden outward whoosh of air (as the boy's lungs were compressed and emptied).

The reduction gears of the transport reengaged. The vehicle moved ponderously ahead. Its treads tore at the earth. A pained warble rose up: perhaps the earth protesting, or an exclamation of dismay from the members of the Pure Force as their enemy rumbled away from them.

"Your lordship!" cried a panic-stricken voice from just outside the door.

"Sheldrake!" said the Governor. "Stop fooling around and come in here!"

Through the opening, the short man could be seen galloping along on a crazed draft-horse. He held his stubby arms out; Tattersall extended his long ones. For a moment they connected. Sheldrake made a leap.

"Whoops!" cried Tattersall. He was dragged halfway out the door. The woman Lorian grabbed his belt. After a moment of uncertainty all three of them came tumbling onto the deck. It was getting very crowded there. Over their heads a sign above the door flashed in red letters: STAND CLEAR.

"*Now* it tells us," said Lorian.

"Groby?" said Vesica, prodding his shoulder. "Are you all right?"

"Get him *off* me," whimpered the youth trapped by the big man's body. "I'm *suffocating*."

"Good," said Sheldrake.

From the front of the craft came a munching sound as the transport's blades tore through the fence around the landing field. Wisps of thornwire flew by.

"I say," said Tattersall, "who's driving this thing?"

And the transport shuddered
into the fastness
of the Moor.

Seven

THE BLISTERED MOOR drank the early yellow sun and gave nothing back but a steam of evaporation that clung to the ground like gauze. It was flat, featureless, and, in the manner of dried bones, immaculate: shunned for two dozen generations by all but the most determined explorers, the most desperate fugitives, the purest saints. Standing before it in the stillness of dawn, one could imagine them passing here—barefoot, wide-eyed with revelation or dread, stumbling from one waterhole to the next to stare down at the bearded face floating there yellowed by chemical salts, finally finding a dry and desolate peace somewhere, leaving the Moor again lifeless.

But none of it was real. Not on this spring-bright morning. There were no saints or fugitives here; at least, none that would have known themselves that way. There were no salt-poisoned waterholes. And the Moor, after five hundred years, was not lifeless anymore.

The black transport had growled northward through the night for thirty miles or so, and then of its own mechanical volition veered northwest, spewed fumes that smelled like burning vinyl, and forded Running Water, which narrowed to a fast-moving creek. Having gotten it started, its passengers found that they were powerless to stop the thing. Only

Groby might have made a decent match for it, but no one managed to wake Groby during two hours of trying, and no one managed to free the sallow-faced youth trapped beneath him. The youth, for one, finally gave it up and fainted, exhausted from sobbing and straining his diaphragm against that unmoving bulk. No one was very sorry when he did so. Sheldrake allowed that if he suffocated it would save a lot of paperwork back at Deeping Lube, if they ever got there, and anyway the prison had been converted to temporary barracks. (Weren't the Press sleeping there? The skittles lanes were top-notch.) An hour before sunrise, the transport fell into a sulk and slowed its treads, turning its imponderable attention to the scything blades and the power-cannon, which did a good bit of damage to the already ravaged countryside. At length even this stopped, and the machinery fell silent. The cobweb-colored haze blew away to reveal the moon a half-day short of full, setting as the sun prepared to rise. A tide of collective weariness engulfed the passengers. Vesica found a shelfful of velvet cots in the sleeping compartment. They all lay down.

It was very quiet, much quieter than Deeping Lube, where something was always going wrong, even quieter than Gravetye Farm, where all night there were sounds of animals. Birds, if nothing else. As the moon touched the featureless horizon, Groby sat upright, freeing the youth, and loudly said:

"My god, what was that?"

"Well," said Tattersall, rising again and dusting off his safari jacket, "I suppose we can sleep when we get back home. What a lovely morning!"

There was food enough for breakfast. Sheldrake complained but cooked it. Lorian, the reporter, provoked him to this by supposing aloud that he could not. He made a soupy gruel from the pressed flakes of some nondescript grain, perhaps barley? Undoubtedly it had been meant for some higher culinary purpose. The only thing they found to cook it in was a large silver punchbowl, ten-gallon capacity. He made a lot.

Tattersall was delighted: with the fine weather, and with the fact that Sheldrake was doing something useful. Who would ever have thought that an accountant . . . Well. You never knew.

The Crusade, he thought, was off to a splendid start.

Groby, refreshed by his hours of unintended sleep, made himself handy. He severed crucial connecting-wires to ensure that the transport would not abandon them. He verified that the young prisoner, though unconscious, was still breathing, and lashed him to a carton of tableware with steering cables from the sunglider. Then he pulled a heatknife from the depths of his coveralls and lit a fire for Sheldrake, who till then had been counting on the sun to warm the punchbowl. The only fuel they could find was a case of commemorative invitations to the Embarkation Ball. Watching these blacken and crackle, Tattersall permitted himself a lone, definitive sigh. At last Groby lowered himself beneath the transport with his knapsack of tools. It was striking to watch him burrow there: the transport made him look normal-sized, and he, the transport.

Vesica thought, insensibly perhaps, of an old fairy story. In an enchanted forest a boy and a girl, each traveling alone, run afoul of an evil scientist. They are lured into the scientist's laboratory, where after cruel and painful experiments they are left horribly disfigured, their once beautiful faces now inhuman and strange. Brought together by chance, the boy and girl manage to escape the scientist's clutches, and despite their deformities they fall in love. So innocent, so poignant is their love that a beneficent Spirit of the Woods appears before them, blessing them and making them perfectly ordinary again: just a boy and a girl once more.

Vesica suspected that beyond a certain age, the notion of finding happiness by becoming perfectly ordinary would seem a drab one. But the winter she had read the tale in one of her stepfather's books—alone at Gravetye Farm, forbidden to play with laborers' children and a hundred miles from any others—being ordinary had been the thing she most passionately longed for. And it had not yet, despite her being old enough to have thought more carefully about it, lost all of its appeal.

"Call me whum bruh wum mumbuh," Groby's voice reverberated from beneath the transport.

"We will," promised Vesica. She sat on the chalky dirt

and drew her denim-clad legs up before her, bare arms covered with goose-bumps in the April chill, pressing her knees together and watching Lorian.

Of all the things remarkable about that morning on the Blistered Moor (—the first morning she had ever spent away from home!—) Vesica found the short-haired journalist most noteworthy. The interest lay, probably, in how she could both identify and not identify with her, as another woman. The not-identify part came from the way Lorian chose to conceal all evidence of her gender. She had shorn her hair to an inch and a half, left her face bare of cosmetics, donned drab ill-fitting clothes that might have been a man's, and traveled all the way from Riverrun, which Vesica imagined must be the most wonderful place in the world, to Deeping Lube, which was crowded and ugly and smelled bad. There to sleep in a jail and be rattled by male companions. To Vesica, who was vaguely ashamed that she herself was not more feminine, Lorian was both a revelation and a puzzlement.

"What are you doing?" the girl asked.

Lorian was scrabbling through a well-worn leather satchel. "Just looking," she said, "for something I stole."

Vesica blinked. "You *stole?*"

"Right." —Nodding, not looking up.

Vesica—in whose mind the idea of stealing was linked with such concepts as chicken coops, sleeping in hedgerows, howling dogs, and the middle of the night—took half a step away from this peculiar new acquaintance, then eagerly a full step nearer.

"What did you get?" she wondered, not too eagerly she hoped.

Lorian pulled out a piece of paper. Very old, its edges the color of baked custard, the paper depended brittlely for a moment from two callused fingers, then casually was let slip like a leaf to bank sideward toward Vesica. As the girl snatched it from the air, she decided something that seemed (maybe, at least) more important than anything it could have contained. That Lorian was excited. That her air of journalistic dispassion was just that: an air.

"Not bad," said Lorian, coolly, as though dismissing all this. "Her prediction was pretty much on target. Look."

And at this, Vesica did get around to glancing at this old and faded hand-drawn diagram.

Sapper Grid Schemes

$F_2 \rightarrow$

$\leftarrow F_1 \rightarrow$

'Broken hex'
root spread

*Secondary spread after
progenitor die-back*

Vesica said, "Just like who predicted? What is it?"

"Amy Hayata," said Lorian.

And although this meant nothing, absolutely nothing, Vesica said, "Ohhh." And she said, "So, is that who drew it?"

"I got it out of an early monograph—well, an early version of her only monograph. Look."

Lorian was as close as Vesica could imagine her to seeming enthused. About what, there was no knowing; Vesica did not know what a monograph was, and was still puzzling over the deep resonance she had felt upon hearing the words *Amy Hayata*.

"When they assigned me to cover the Hardy Plant Society," Lorian explained, "I thought it was all over. You know, old ladies planting blue-eyed grass in the cracks along the Curtain Wall. Then this Crusade business started, and I thought it might be fun to do an exposé—"

"What's that?"

"Oh, you know, where you write about how somebody's sleeping with his partner's wife. Or in this case husband. Or something. So I started hanging around the Secret College, talking to the professors there, and finally I got to meet this old guy, the Dean, who's called Tylyester, who everywhere he goes he carries this book he's writing about Amy Hayata.

At first he didn't want to talk. But then when I kept at it awhile he said basically Here, you might want to put something in the paper about the Quest for Lost Knowledge, otherwise those fools will probably think they're on a picnic. And he gave me these old diagrams to study. And, I mean—here it is. Just like she predicted."

Retrieving the page from Vesica, she laid it (more caringly this time) with some others on the ground. Vesica crawled over to them on hands and knees, careful not to get dirt in the gash on her thigh. Her straw-colored hair hung down almost touching the musty pages. Where there were not drawings and neat handwriting there was some kind of lettering, midway in neatness between handwriting and the fine print in Narthex's books. On one sheet, centered above a chart, was this legend, possibly a title:

CORRELATION BETWEEN OBSERVED MUTAGENIC ACTIVITY AND SUBJECTIVE EXPERIENCE OF "DEPTH" DURING PROGRAM.

"I don't get it," said Vesica, enfolding many things in this sentiment.

Lorian, impatient, strode out onto the Moor.

"*These,*" she said, gesturing broadly. For good measure she scuffed the dirt with a hiking boot, dislodging something which came sailing through the air toward Vesica. It landed a few feet away, and Vesica saw that it was a tiny plant, the color and size of an asparagus shoot, but woodier, with dusty green embryonic leaves unfolding from the growth bud. The girl picked it up, nudged it with a slender dirty fingertip. Soft, round-lobed, a leaf uncurled looking very familiar, like something that grew on Gravetye Farm. And the Moor, now that she looked around, was dotted with them.

And it hadn't ought to be. It ought (she believed, and so she always heard) to be completely barren.

Attracted by all this—the plant, the talk, the mess of papers—Governor Tattersall climbed out of the folding chair he had set before the cookfire, the better to supervise Sheldrake, and greeted Vesica with, "Ah!" as though remembering something very pleasant.

"There are *plants* growing on the Blistered Moor," she

informed him, holding forth the evidence. Thinking, since he was Governor of the place he probably ought to know. And added in afterthought: "Your lordship."

"Call me Tattersall, my dear." The Governor smiled. "Why, of course there are. It says so in this pamphlet—let's see, I've got it somewhere." He patted the pockets of his safari jacket. "Gorse, I believe it mentioned . . ."

"No," said Lorian. She bent down and clawed at the Moor with blunt, graceless fingers. "Hand me that heatknife, will you?"

No fuss about honorifics for her. With a look of calm absorption that Vesica found remarkable (for she herself was so easily distracted), Lorian played the hissing beam of Groby's heatknife around one of the asparagus-sized shoots. Sparks and dirt spattered widely, but Lorian kept at it until she had blasted the sapling free. It was no more than five inches tall, but its roots, emerging in clumps from the battered soil, were wildly disproportionate. First a foot of them came out, then two, and by the time Lorian stood up with the tiny plant in her hand, its roots trailed all the way to the ground.

"It's an oak," she declared. "White oak, or a close relative. And it got here by sending out these underground creepers. Exactly like she predicted."

"It doesn't look like an oak to me," said Vesica. "And how did she know . . . what was her name?" (She wanted Lorian to say it again.)

"Amy Hayata. Right here, in these papers I took. I don't know *how* she knew, but you can just look at this . . . see how the roots spread out, and then the plant dies back from lack of water or something— Look, *I* don't understand it. But it's all right there, is what I'm saying."

Vesica and the Governor looked doubtfully at the stack of custard-colored sheets.

"That's why," said Lorian, "I applied to travel with the Crusade. I mean, not the diagrams. To find out more about this woman, this Amy Hayata. That was before they told us journalists weren't invited."

"Well," said Tattersall. "But all that's changed now, hasn't it?"

"It has?"

Groby's voice emerged from the bowels of the transport, appearing to say "Ah oonk oog aht up ahblum."

"What problem?" called back Vesica.

All the noise must have wakened the prisoner, who began whining loudly in the luggage compartment. Tattersall rambled off to see how breakfast was coming along.

"What does he mean," whispered Vesica, "all that's changed?"

"Who knows," said Lorian. Her green eyes were dark, inscrutable; she trailed the clump of roots behind her like a weapon not needed at the moment, but ready. "They say some pretty odd things about old Tattersall, back in the city. They say"—she bent her head confidingly—"he's just being kept in as Governor until New Arrangements can be worked out. Someone on the Low Commission is supposed to be in line for his job."

"Who's 'they'?" said Vesica.

"Of course you never know," said Lorian, straightening. "These aristocratic types—sometimes they've got Highly Placed Connections."

Tattersall was peering under the transport with his thumbs tucked comfortably in his canvas belt.

"How do you fare, Master Engineer?" he called down. "Is our craft ready for the great adventure?"

"Breakfast," announced Sheldrake, "is served."

In the luggage compartment the prisoner kept up his penetrating whine until he was satisfied that the others were going to ignore him. Then he set about shoving the carton of tableware to which he was tied across the deck toward another carton, a smaller one, lying unopened near the door. None of his limbs was free to operate the catch of this when he reached it, so he worked at it with his mouth—all in all, his most adaptable organ. The lid popped open on greased springs in due course. The young man leaned forward as best he could and peered inside.

"Yes!" he whispered.

Between mouthfuls, Groby gave his briefing. The five of them sat in a semicircle around the fire, which had died now to a few glowing clumps of paper.

"You see, there's something the matter with the programming."

"You could tell that," said Lorian sharply, "from down there?"

Groby shrugged. "It's where they put the computer. The point is, we can't make it go where we tell it to. Somebody's hard-wired a template of the forest into its memory map, and now all it knows how to do is chug along until it gets to where it's going."

"Can't you," said Lorian, "override that somehow? Or just break it? There must be some way to manage."

"I'm not really sure I'd want to try that."

Vesica watched Groby with admiration: the way he gestured with his spoon, pausing now and then to scoop up more of Sheldrake's porridge; the way his earth-brown eyes had grown quiet and intelligent; the way he spoke out of the absolute authority of his craft.

"The program that's ultimately in control—it's called the governor, by the way—"

Tattersall brightened.

"Anyway, it's the thing that runs everything else, the sawmill and the power-cannon and so forth. It has a certain amount of autonomy. And I'm afraid if we try to override it . . ."

"Yes, of course," said Tattersall, the very idea of overriding a governor being unthinkable to him, "I quite understand. Well, no matter."

"No matter?" said Lorian.

Groby told Sheldrake, "This really tastes good. What's in it?"

"The fruit of his lordship's fields," Sheldrake muttered. "Ox droppings."

Tattersall frowned at the contents of his breakfast bowl. (Actually this was a small ceramic flowerpot, embossed with the emblem of the Hardy Plant Society.) Everyone *else*, he thought, seemed to hear Sheldrake clearly enough. Could it be some form of ventriloquism? "I'm glad you enjoy it," he said uncertainly.

"So where," Lorian asked Groby, "is the machine programmed to go?"

"Didn't I mention that? Here—I had it print an abstract.

Well, it's sort of a map, actually." Groby mined the pockets of his coveralls until his oil-stained fingers extracted a piece of parchment, sheared at top and bottom as though by iron teeth. He spread it on the ground.

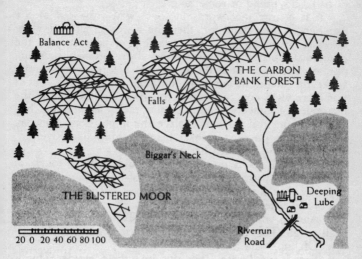

"That's us," he said, "just east of the place called Biggar's Neck. From the direction we've taken so far, it looks like we're headed up there to Balance Act."

"Why of course," said the Governor. "Hadn't anyone told you?"

Lorian's eyes flashed a brighter green, like sunstruck leaves, as they crossed and recrossed the little map, while Groby's eyes only blinked. Vesica wondered if the journalist's brain really worked that much faster than the engineer's, or whether it was just running around like someone lost in the woods, looking for the path that Groby had long discovered.

"That's where she lived," Lorian said at last, and Vesica knew, if no one else did, who *she* was. "On the other side of the mountains."

Sheldrake grimaced at the chart, as though disturbed by the enormity of creation. "It looks like an awful place," he said. "And they picked just the right person to find it."

Tattersall eyed his aide. "Why, thank you," he ventured.

"The other side of the mountains," said Vesica softly.

"That's right," said Lorian. "All by herself. Although this professor seems to think she might have once been married or had a boyfriend or something."

If it is true that words in some way grow out of the experiences they stand for, then the words *the other side of the mountains* provoked in Vesica a feeling of contact with the primordial experience that had spawned that ordinary-sounding phrase. She had felt a flicker of this before, when Groby spoke the identical words in Narthex's dining room. But it was more vivid now, as though this morning, away from the rectitudes of Gravetye Farm, *the other side of the mountains* had become more real for her, a place she might hope someday to visit, and not just a make-believe world like Riverrun, which could never touch her own.

"I wish I could go there," she said, with a touch of melodramatic wistfulness. The sound of her own words startled her, for her inner experience had been so vivid she forgot the outer reality of the Moor.

"And so you shall, my dear," said Tattersall happily. "So shall we all. That is the destination of the Crusade, is it not?"

"Oh, no," said Sheldrake.

"Sure," said Lorian, "but this isn't the Crusade. This is just an accident. Anyway, we're not the Crusaders."

"*I* am," said Tattersall. "The Crusade Leader, in fact."

"Well, but I'm not. And how about Vesica? She's just—"

"You wanted to go along," Vesica reminded her.

"With the Crusade! Not on some camping trip to the Blistered Moor."

Groby said, "Crusade or not, we're all going to end up in Balance Act if we stay on the transport. And it's a long walk back to Deeping Lube."

Tattersall coughed politely into his sleeve, as though he had heard enough of this. "I hadn't really," he said, sounding miffed, "intended to open the matter to discussion. I am, as you know, the duly chosen Leader of the Crusade. This is the duly chosen Transport Vehicle, this is the duly chosen Field Engineer, and this is the duly chosen Date of Embarkation. And as far as *I* am concerned"—he puffed himself up as much as possible in the sagging chair—"*this* is the Crusade.

Why, we've even acquired our first prisoner. I understand that Crusades normally take great numbers of those. If the others weren't around for our departure . . . well, I hope they enjoyed the ball."

"So that's it," said Sheldrake with an alkaline smile. "He's bitter about missing the music."

Tattersall sniffed contemptuously. "I didn't want to travel with that bunch of ninnies anyway."

Sheldrake gave the others a knowing nod. "He's afraid the whole thing will be called off and his honorarium revoked."

"That's right," said Tattersall, "my honor *has* been provoked." Then the gubernatorial mind darted off in a new direction, and he shot a worried look at Vesica. "Unless, my dear, you have to be getting home? Back to school, or something?"

"Oh, no, your lordship." Straightening her shoulders she explained, "I've run away."

To the Governor, this seemed to say it all. "I sometimes wish," he sighed, "*I* had run away. Well. That's settled, then. What should we do first?"

Sheldrake got up from the fire and peered about sternly, as though assuming command of the nonexistent territorial bookkeeping staff. In his firmest voice he said:

"Take inventory."

The young prisoner was asleep in the luggage compartment when Vesica entered with a tray (actually a face-down mirror) of food. She stomped to awaken him.

"Mm," he mumbled complainingly. Catching sight of the food, he sat up and tugged at the bonds around his wrists. "I thought I was going to *starve.*"

"The Governor says," Vesica informed him, "we have to treat all prisoners with dignity."

"The Governor," spat the youth. Quickly he covered his disdain in a show of miserableness. "But how can I eat," he moaned, "with these wires on?"

"You should have thought of that before you tore up the sunglider. Here, open your mouth."

She held up a lump of coagulated porridge, prepared to shove it in and get her fingers out of the way. The prisoner scowled.

"I'd rather starve than eat your table scraps," he said.

"I'm sorry," she said truthfully. "But it's all we've got. Listen, what's your name? So I'll know what to call you."

"Don't call me anything!" he lashed out. "You're all evil, and everything you've made is evil! Look at this machine— killing everything it touches, everything that's sacred: the earth, the forest—everything! Just as you've done for hundreds of years. And now your Crusade is trying to stop Nature from taking its long-awaited revenge. Was it wrong to hate this horrid thing? Was it wrong to want to destroy it?"

This outburst, which might have been effective in another setting, found the wrong audience in Vesica. "*We* didn't make this machine," she said simply. "We haven't been *alive* for hundreds of years. If you don't want to eat, I won't bother you."

She turned away.

"Wait!" he cried. "Thrull. My name is Thrull. Please give me some food, I'm so hungry—they made us go for days without eating, back in Deeping Lube. They told us if we didn't do what they said, they'd let us starve to death. Please don't go."

Vesica was simultaneously touched and repulsed by the young man's wretchedness. In an outburst of honesty she said, "What an awful name."

"I know," Thrull said miserably. "They gave it to me in the orphanage."

She narrowed her eyes. Well, *some* of it might be true. She laid the face-down mirror before him. "Here," she said. "You can handle this yourself."

Outside, the others awaited her report.

"His name is Thrull," she told them.

Four hundred and sixty miles southwest of Deeping Lube, in a walk-up flat of large, well-furnished but hardly ostentatious rooms overlooking the Tomb of Artists in the ancient city of Riverrun, a small electronic device blinked and sighed and reluctantly awoke. After a spell of puzzling over the signal that had disturbed its long slumber, it aimed a hot needle of light at a slip of paper, burning a brief message there. Then it transmitted a one-bit acknowledgment and went back to sleep. The message it had transcribed consisted only of two numbers, one of six and the other of seven digits, and the small machine in its dreamy carelessness had gotten one of these wrong. Still, it had been worth waking for.

The air was beginning to stir again.

"A hundred forty-seven flowerpots.

"Wings of sunglider, two hundred, sizes and shapes assorted.

"Brocaded table linen: three cloths, forty-nine napkins.

"Silver punchbowl, ten-gallon capacity."

"We know about that, Sheldrake. Can't we just leave off the, shall we say, frivolous items?"

"If you say so, my lord. But we'll miss you in Balance Act."

"It's hard to tell," Groby pointed out, "what we might need. Let's have him read the whole list."

"Oh. Well. If *you* say so, Master Engineer. Continue, Sheldrake."

"Navigation device, hand-held. Battery missing.

"Heatsaw.

"Winch.

"Incense, eight dozen packs, assorted.

"Champagne, one hundred forty-seven bottles."

"Wow."

"That's nothing, honey. You should have seen them sock it away at this reception I covered at Lady Widdershaw, no, Widder—"

"Please maintain silence during the reading of the inventory. Thank you. Landing wheels and struts.

"Toolbag.

"Sewing kit.

"Papers, assorted, in travel case."

"Hey, that's my stuff. You've got no business—"

"Property of the Crusade now, miss. Forward all complaints to the Governor's Office, Deeping Lube. Seven bags reprocessed nightsoil.

"One gallon marmalade.

"Six teapots. Two with lids cracked.

"Large drum of scones."

"What?"

"Sheldrake, how many bottles of champagne did you say?"

"One hundred forty-seven, your lordship."

"What an odd number. Change that to one hundred forty-five. And what do we have in the way of glasses?"

"I was just getting to that, my lord. Here, you'll have to initial the inventory."

"Oh, quite. Well. Break it out, won't you? We'll have a toast to launch the Crusade. And then we must hurry on. After all,
the forest is advancing
quite rapidly."

Eight

THE MOON swung around
on its gravitational tether. It had just reached that stage of its
repetitious journey at which it stood, vis-à-vis the Sun, in
that apposition called by learned astrologers, A Match. (The
image here, of course, being that of two opponents facing
each other across some contested court or stadium—in this
case, the Earth.) At this point it appeared as a Full Moon to
watchers below, of whom there were a large number, though
less than in centuries past, and none at all on that side of the
planet where the Sun showed its glaring presence, and where,
at that hour, despite the festivities around it, the Expeditionary Transport Vehicle sat looking black and sullen, its armored flanks growing warmer as their molecules were soaked
by the rain of particles flung out wantonly by the Moon's
much older and larger rival.

The Moon itself was less imprudent. It gave back a trifle
less than it got: reflected most of it, certainly, in the form of
moonlight, but hoarded just a bit here and there in transac-
tions among its constituents. In doing so it established a
pattern, a precedent. The Moon was known (to the same
learned astrologers) as the Mother of Habits, and the habit
of skimming a little off the top was not last among these,

though it received less publicity than, say, changeability, or having periods.

Poets and astrologers have long supposed that the Moon exerts an influence on humanity. They have had trouble, though, deciding exactly how this influence is effected. Botanists have never, to the best of anyone's knowledge, been invited to join the discussion. Had they been, they would ages ago have answered this age-old question, though perhaps not to anyone's satisfaction. They would have pointed to the Cleome Dilemma.

The cleome (syn. "spider flower") is a vigorous flowering annual which no member of the Hardy Plant Society wants in her garden. Its foliage is coarse, its seedlings prolific and ineradicable, its fragrance like that of bedstraw, and above all, its flowers a vulgar mauve-going-on-magenta that clashes angrily with everything nice. The cleome does have, however, one lovely white form (var. 'Helen Campbell') which is more delicate of flower, more refined of foliage, and in every way more suitable for the mid-to-back region of the mixed border. This desirable plant would abound in the gardens of the Hardy Plant Society, were it not for the Cleome Dilemma.

Which is, that as soon as 'Helen Campbell' is exposed to the presence or the proximity or even (some members would swear) the *mention* of the in-every-way common 'Violet Queen,' well: 'Helen' is no more, your adored bed of late-flowering yellows and whites is corrupted by 'Queen,' and you may as well cancel your plans to dine at the Silent Partners' Club because you will be spending the next few days destroying a flower that (you will protest) you did not pay for, nor plant.

You will be right. You have run against the Cleome Dilemma. Though genetically distinct, 'Helen Campbell' in the presence of 'Violet Queen' simply loses its identity, as two pendulum clocks ticking side by side lose their independence of timing, fall into synchronicity and become, in effect, the same clock. The reason for this, though technical, is summarized by the Cleome Corollary, which Amy Hayata did not formulate but gave its tongue-in-cheek name to. This states, to wit:

    1. 1   If something happens in a certain way, similar
           phenomena will tend to follow the same pat-

tern, to an extent determined by the strength
of their respective event-fields.

It is helpful (according to the bodyguard of commentary
by which the Corollary is attended) that the two things
being a certain way together should be related somehow:
e.g., two flowers, two women, two clocks. However, this is
not necessary, as the Moon, in exerting its influence over
humanity, gives testimony.

(It is wrong, strictly speaking, to say that the Moon
gives testimony to anything. As a cosmic body precessing
through the æther, the Moon cannot testify. It cannot talk.
To speak of the Moon as though it were behaving like a
mortal—to say, for example, that it finds the attentions of
astrologers gratifying, or is spiteful of the accolades heaped
upon the Sun—is to anthropomorphize, and several centuries' worth of serious thinkers have assured us this is wrong.)

The Moon swung farther on its gravitational chain. At
eleven past two in the morning on the remote melon-slice of
the planet directly opposite the sulking transport, it entered
into a relationship with Venus known to astrologers as A
Nudge. The image here is of a cozy aspect, as seen by an
observer shivering through another early-spring day in the
perpetually dank Observatory of the Secret College, where
most astrologers made their livings in that era. The Moon
Nudging Venus is not an aspect worth fussing over—oh,
sometimes it is associated with an uptick on the Fish
Exchange—but six minutes later, at seventeen past two, it
was followed by another cosmic event, equally uninteresting
in itself, but with Astrology as with so much else, things
must be considered together. At that moment, the Moon
jostled Mars in that square-dance known to astrologers as An
Elbow. The image here should be apparent.

Now, the Moon Nudging Venus, At Elbows with Mars
and Matched against the Sun, all at once: that really gave
astrologers something to think about. They had spent the
last departmental meeting at the Secret College debating
what this rare confluence might portend. A coalition cautiously formed around Stunning Metamorphosis. A minority,
however, rallied behind Old Accounts Settled, and a stalwart
few, mostly sympathizers of the Pure Force, declined to rule

out the End of Civilization. Few of these gave up their apartments in the city.

It is wrong, however, to say that the Moon took note of this. Being a cosmic body bound by cosmic law, it merely swung along as it had swung for a very long time now, neither watching the goings-on below nor ignoring them, plying the same orbit it always plied, its inevitable orbit, though moving a barely cognizable bit more slowly than it had moved in earlier eons. Not that the Moon was tired. Do not think that. It was just slowing down in compliance with some law that said it had to.

At twenty-one past two, there occurred a final cosmic happenstance that the astrologers had not taken into account. A very small comet, swimming energetically through the æther, trespassed into the Moon's inevitable orbit, smacking cleanly into that part of the Moon often (and wrongly) called its Eye.

Now, whatever ripe potencies all that Nudging and Elbowing may have laid bare, this infinitessimal swimmer plunged breathlessly into and, as it were, made fruitful. Several epochal events took place at once.

—Lady Widdershins's poodle, in a pique over being left at home while her ladyship attended the Embarkation Ball, burrowed through a decaying sewer main, setting off a subterranean hemorrhage that would go undiscovered for forty days and drastically alter the prospect from the Upper Garden.

—Low Commissioner Narthex stepped into the convoluted alleyway outside the Hoar's Bed Inn after an arduous morning of searching for his missing stepdaughter. A woman's hoarse shout seemed to drift through the door behind him. His search had turned up neither Vesica nor Master Engineer Groby nor Governor Tattersall nor even Thrull, his miserable shill, only a bunch of hung-over gardeners and some drug-weary youths. For the benefit of the Press he paid a call at the local hospital, staying just long enough to have his picture taken with some mendicant priests and tourists recovering from a bombing incident. Then he boarded an airskiff and left for his apartment in the city.

—One hundred and eighteen miles north-northwest of Deeping Lube, a small node of a vast network of interlocking roots, belonging to the lately arisen species Quercus robinia, began production of a pheromone whose odor, though detectable only in large quantities or by highly specialized receptors, resembled that of an old windowsill herb, long out of cultivation. At the risk of anthropomorphizing, we can liken this substance to a biochemical cry of alarm. The pheromone rose slowly through the soil and drifted on the southwesterly breeze. The subtle actions required to produce it, and the equally subtle responses to which it gave rise, fanned out slowly through the network of roots similar in design to a coupled-array antenna, creating a tiny ripple in the pond of unified energies that bound the roots, the Earth they sprang from, the Moon, its cosmic partners, and the sensing equipment in the Observatory of the Secret College. One of the astrologers there, a graduate student, somehow sensed this very slight, spreading ripple. He mistook it for something registered by his equipment, and jotted a note for Professor Tylyester.

—On the Blistered Moor, Sheldrake and Lorian clinked bud-vases.

　　　—In Balance Act, an owl cooed.
　　　—And the Moon blinked its Eye
　　　　　in the æther.

Nine

IN THE BLACK TRANSPORT time moved by, but irresolutely, lurching forward by fits and whims, heedless of the succession of hours outside the armored plating, as though after so many centuries the vehicle held in its inviolable lungs the air of an age gone by, the anger or aloofness, or maybe it was just tired of keeping track of things. It shambled ahead disconsolately, while on the Blistered Moor afternoon ebbed and the moon arrived to preside over a starlit evening. Inside, on velvet cots, the Crusaders slept, lulled by the monodic groan of old machinery. Even Groby, at loose ends because the transport had no need of him, lay down after a while and drifted into a doze; but his slumbering awareness would not abandon, quite, its fascination with the lowing throb beneath the deckplates.

Past midnight Vesica awoke, feeling a change. She rose from her cot and crept uncertainly, bracing herself against the bulkheads as the transport rocked like a railcar, from the passenger compartment forward through the steering cab, into the small passageway where the whir and grind of sawblades reverberated through the plates of the wall. From there, a ladder rose to a blackened hatch.

Owing to its military origins, the transport had no windows. It was lit inside by a series of dull crimson bulbs, the color of headaches, placed here and there where there was nothing especially to see. To look outside, you had to climb to the cupola that housed the power-cannon. Along its vaulted bulkhead, narrow viewports had been cut to give the gunner a glimpse, at least, of his target before he made a violet-tinted blaze of it. The violet came from the wavelength of energy used by the gun. Over the centuries this particular weapon had developed a sort of electric tic, so that every few hours, for several minutes at a time, power would leak from its deadly batteries and a pastel beam would pour from its muzzle like a spotlight. The beam was so pale that it could be seen only at night, and only if you were looking at just the right time. Past midnight, for the first time, Vesica was. She pressed her face to the viewport to see the beam brush over the branches and leafbuds of a nearby tree. It lingered there an instant; then the transport rumbled on, but not before Vesica threw off the blanket of drowsiness and opened her eyes wide in the crimson darkness of the cupola.

She thought: a tree. Here on the Blistered Moor, a *tree*.

She sat down in the gunner's seat. Well-worn, covered in something not much different from leather, it moved on squeaky gimbals and released a mixture of half-identifiable smells, as herb leaves do when you crush them. Vesica found herself at eye-level with a small chart someone had taped—how many ages ago?—between two rows of switches on the ordnance console.

WILD TURKEY POOL

Jesús	Wake
TJ	Blue devils
Finn	Heels
Doc	Hoos

She studied this for a minute or two, worrying that it might have some superstitious or magical significance—an idea she got partly from its terse, cryptic contents and partly from the shiver she felt when she read it. (*Blue devils! Hoos!*)

Yet despite its oddness and antiquity, the paper gave a comfortable, almost homey feeling to the gunner's seat, softening the edges of the armor plates, making the switches and lights less threatening. Maybe it was something innocent, to pass the time; a mix-and-match game.

"Wild Turkey Pool," she said aloud, contemplating the sound of it. Was it the name of a place? The place the transport had been heading for when it . . . When it what? What had happened, so long ago, so abruptly that its gunner had left this piece of paper to be read by fourteen-year-old eyes in an unanticipated age?

She returned to the viewport. The seepage of energy had stopped now. There were only blurred shadows creeping past her in the pale, illusive moonlight.

"WELL," said a voice behind her. Not really that loud; it only seemed loud because it startled her. The voice said, "What are you doing here?"

It was Sheldrake. *Little Sheldrake*, she thought irreverently. (He was no shorter than she was, but for a man as old as Groby that was pretty short.) She resented questions of this type, yet was too polite or too timid to refuse an answer.

"Um, nothing much," she said, turning back to the viewport. She could see Sheldrake's head—round and large for his body—reflected there. She kept Wild Turkey Pool to herself.

"Ha," the little man said, as though he doubted this. He climbed the rest of the way into the cupola. There was barely room for the two of them.

"I saw a tree outside," said Vesica. "I mean, a real tree—not one of those little shoots."

To which the short man vehemently replied: "The Devil's Oak."

Vesica hadn't yet made up her mind about Sheldrake, and remarks like this were the main reason for it. She couldn't tell if the man was being unpleasant, or if he simply *was* unpleasant, or if the whole thing was just part of his personality and he was therefore, in his own way, being friendly. Seeing that it was past midnight, the beginning of her second day ever away from Gravetye Farm, and she had nothing better to do, she decided to explore the question further.

"What," she asked him carefully, "is a devil's oak?"

"Ha! You may well ask."

He gave her a wink and a slow comradely nod, as though her simple and obvious question had introduced some dark complicity between them. Unruffled, she just looked back at him. Girlhood on Gravetye Farm had given her a certain tolerance for troublesome behavior.

"I *am* asking," she said firmly.

He frowned, which Vesica found modestly gratifying. "I don't know if I should tell you . . ."

"Then don't," she said, pressing her nebulous advantage.

"It's not a story you tell to children, if you know what I mean."

Vesica shook her head. "No, I don't. We were just talking about a *tree*, weren't we? I said, I saw a tree, and you said, the devil's oak, and I said—"

"Ha!" said Sheldrake: it appeared, his all-purpose syllable. "Not just *any* tree. But you wouldn't know, would you? You haven't heard the story."

Vesica sighed. She had thought she was winning the psychological skirmish; now it appeared that Sheldrake was prepared to wear her down. "All right," she said, conceding as little as necessary. "What kind of story is it?"

"A *horrible* story," said Sheldrake.

He had her on the run now. "I'm not sure," she said, but yes she was, "I *want* to hear a horrible story."

He drew closer, his dark eyes gleaming. "It was when I was a young man," he told her, just above a whisper, intimating by his very tone that Nameless Listeners might be eavesdropping on their crimson-lit discourse, "that it happened. Before all this got started."

"All this?"

"Deeping Lube. Refugees. The forest taking over. There were farms up here in the North, then. Farms just as pretty as your stepfather's."

"You know my stepfather?" said Vesica in surprise.

He waved the question away. "Anyhow, there were farms up here, and orchards, and I was working at Biggar's Neck as a tree pollard, and what woods there were were just some stands of trees nobody had thought to clear, or that shaded cattle—nothing you could call really a forest."

"Wait a minute." Vesica was determined to keep *some*

control of the situation. "How long ago was this? What's a tree pollard?"

He smiled gloatingly. "That's *another* story. Fifteen years, I'd say. The war in the East hadn't started yet, and times were fairly quiet. A little trouble in the hills, but there were mercenaries to take care of that. Anyway, while I was at Biggar's Neck—"

"That's on the map," said Vesica.

"Of course it's on the map. It was the biggest—oh, not just the biggest—the grandest, the most fertile, the most *everything* farm in the territory. It's gone now. It's all woods, I guess. But back then . . . I was working around the north border, been there a couple of months already. I worked very slowly, you see, very carefully. I knew the craft better than anybody—that's how I got the job. Anyhow, one of the gamekeepers at the farm was off on a trip to the mountains, hunting moose."

"Moose? What's that?"

"Ha!" said Sheldrake. "You'll find *that* out soon enough. Well, this fellow, the gamekeeper, had been gone a few days, and people were getting worried. So I said I'd go look for him. I knew the territory better than most people, and I was ready for a change anyhow."

Vesica squinted doubtfully, though it was probably wasted in the dark.

"It took me about a day to reach the mountains."

"On foot?"

"Of course on foot. How else—oh, never mind. You'll see that soon enough too. But then, as soon as I got under the orchids, I lost the fellow's trail."

"The what?"

"His trail. I had been on it, I was pretty sure, from the time I left Biggar's Neck, but as soon as it hit the forest—"

"No. Under the . . . did you say orchids?"

"Orchids, right. That's how you tell when you've left the—you know, just woods and trees and all that, and gotten into the forest itself. Orchids. In the treetops, millions of them. Every color. It's really . . . but you'll see *that* soon enough. Where was I?"

Vesica shook her head, still trying to imagine millions of orchids. "You, um—lost his trail?"

"Right. And I thought I'd just go on up the path anyway, and maybe I'd run on to it again. Gamekeepers aren't especially imaginative. So I followed it a ways, through the forest, and then even the path got lost."

"You mean *you* got lost."

"I mean, the path went into the woods and vanished. Just like the gamekeeper. I figured without a path and without any sign of the fellow's trail, there was nothing really I could do, so I headed back. Only I didn't get far before night fell, and let me tell you, night in the forest is *dark*. So I made a little camp, and by the time my fire was lit, it had gotten pretty gloomy. There were things crackling out there in the woods where I couldn't see them, and the trees must have been packed with owls, the way it sounded."

"I've never heard an owl."

"I don't suppose you have." He paused to perform an owl imitation which may or may not have been accurate (as Vesica was in no position to judge) but which was certainly spooky. It seemed to linger in the darkness of the cupola. "I tried to sleep but I couldn't. And do you know, after a few hours had passed—just after midnight, I'd say it was, the same time as now—I thought I heard somebody call my name."

Vesica, cuddling down in the gunner's seat, knew she was being taken in, but was taken in regardless. A tingle rose up her spine.

"It wasn't like any voice you've ever heard. It was . . . well, at the time I believed, though I can't tell you why now, it was the *forest itself* that was calling me. So I got up and started moving.

"Now, don't get this wrong. It's not that I was being brave. As a matter of fact, I was so afraid, just lying there in my blanket, I got up and started walking out of sheer terror. I didn't know which way I was going, and I couldn't have told one way from another anyway, there in the dark, but I just knew I had to go somewhere to get away from that voice.

"As soon as I started moving, though, I heard something else. Something even more terrible."

Sheldrake paused, and Vesica realized she was breathing hard, which was not surprising, and realized also that while

Sheldrake had been speaking, for the past minute or so, she had lost herself entirely in his story—not in the words, but in the story itself: in actually *being* there. She could describe, if he asked her, the precise sensations he had felt that awful night—the cool air against his skin, the smells of sweat and leaf mold, the dapple of moonlight, even (and this proved it all, somehow) the calling of owls. She had no time to reflect on how remarkable this was, that the story should contain in some way the experience it was describing, for Sheldrake was talking again.

"I was leaning, see, against this rowan tree, which they've got a lot of in the forest—but only in the deepest darkest parts, they don't seem to grow anywhere else. That's where this terrible new sound came up from. And I'm saying came *up* because that's what it did, from about the level of my knees, and no more than a couple of strides in front of me.

"*Wo*, was I scared. Like I said, this sound was even more awful than the first one. Because it wasn't something just vague and scary like maybe a ghost. It was a *human* sound, but all twisted like trees get when they've got vines growing around them. And it was *so close*—I could have knelt down and touched whatever poor soul was making it. No, really I couldn't, because something had got hold of me that wasn't even fear anymore. I don't know—nausea, maybe, like you get when you look at a corpse. So for a few minutes, I guess, or maybe longer, all I could do was stand there against the tree and try not to vomit.

"Well. What snapped me out of it was that the sound finally started to be like . . . I don't know, something you could halfway recognize. And when I listened a little closer, I figured out that it was *words*, that some poor soul was lying there *talking* to me. See, this is how I learned that you only tend to find what you're looking for, what you expect to be there. And I God knows hadn't been expecting . . . But anyway, there I was. So—

"*He's killed me*, it was saying, this voice was, in this feeble moan you wouldn't have been able to hear at all if the woods hadn't gotten as quiet as the grave. *The devil tricked me here, and now he's killed me.*

"I managed to get my nerve up and took just a little step forward, and then another little step, and then I knelt down at the fellow's side. Of course it was the gamekeeper. His face I could see pretty clearly by a little patch of moonlight. I won't even try to tell you what it looked like.

"He's killed me, the poor man kept saying, over and over, but when I asked him who he was talking about, what had happened, he acted like he didn't hear. I tried to see what was the matter with him—you know, felt his head and chest and legs and so forth, but nothing seemed to be broken.

"The devil tricked me here, and now he's killed me. He must have said that a hundred more times. I figured there was nothing I could really do for him, nothing until the sun came up, so I settled down beside him to wait out the night. The hours went by and went by—it felt like a month must have gone by there—and after a while the moaning got quieter and finally it fell silent. By the time it got light enough to see, I knew the gamekeeper was dead."

He took a breath—not Sheldrake in the forest; Sheldrake in the cupola of the transport. Vesica blinked. He raised a hand, as though warning her not to disturb the silence. (The cleats ground the soil beneath them, and the saw-blades rasped angrily ahead.)

"Around the gamekeeper's mouth was a smear that might have been made by blackberries. It also might have been made by deadly nightshade, which looks pretty similar if you've never seen it. Well, I figured that solved part of the mystery—the part about what killed him—but there was still the part about who it was, if the man wasn't totally insane, that had, like he said, tricked him into eating it.

"But all I wanted was to get out of there. I went off into the woods looking for fallen limbs. It was pretty far from Biggar's Neck, and if I was going to get him back it would have to be on some kind of litter. Not twenty feet away I stumbled onto the carcass of a young moose—a buck, though it was hardly old enough to have more than little nubs for antlers. It was shot clean through by the gamekeeper's rifle. At least, I *thought* it was the gamekeeper that had done it. I looked for a while after that, though, but the man's gun wasn't anywhere around.

"Well," said Sheldrake, rocking on his haunches, "that got me to thinking. The man had said, you know, 'The devil tricked me' and so forth. And I had taken that to be just a manner of speaking, the way you or I might call someone the devil who's done us some dirty business. But finding the buck like that, and the gun vanished, I began to wonder what the fellow really *had* meant. I thought of all those stories about a spirit protecting the woods—do they tell those stories down south, too? Yes, so, I started to think that maybe the fellow had meant, actually, the Devil. You know, angry over killing the young moose and whatnot. Anyhow, I picked up a couple of branches and found my way back to the dead man, *and this is the awful part.*"

Vesica knew she should tell him to stop, but at the same time she knew this was the point of the story. Sheldrake took a breath.

"So. I made a litter and got the dead man on it and dragged him off toward Biggar's Neck. Out of the forest and down onto the prairie. I kept going till nearly dark, and by that time I could see the hills ahead where Biggar's Neck was, nice rolling hills covered with barley. I was pretty tired by then so I put the litter down. I left the gamekeeper there, on a little rise, and walked the rest of the way myself. Next morning a few of us came back up in a wagon, to get the body.

"And what do you think. When we got back, there was the dead man, just where I had left him. But something was strange: There was this big bulge, right here, over his stomach, that I hadn't noticed before—like something was stuffed up underneath his shirt."

Sheldrake demonstrated by puffing up the front of his own shirt, as though Vesica could possibly have trouble visualizing it.

"Of course, we didn't want to disturb the dead or anything like that. But the bulge was so . . . pronounced. So, after a minute or so of looking at it and talking about it, we went ahead and loosened the fellow's shirt and undid a couple of buttons—and what do you think popped out?"

Vesica shrank into the gunner's chair, as though whatever it was might pop out of Sheldrake's shirt right now.

"It was the stem of a tree! An oak tree—just a tiny thing—but it was *growing out of the dead man's stomach.* Can you imagine that?"

She could not do otherwise. She felt the blood draining from her head.

"We didn't know what to *do*. We tried to pull the thing out of him—there was clotted blood all over the stem, can you imagine? But it wouldn't come out, and we couldn't break it off. So we thought, well, we'd have to carry the gamekeeper with the tree still in him back to the farm and let her ladyship, the woman that owned the place, figure out what to do. *But*—let me tell you, when we tried to pick him up and put him in the wagon, we couldn't get him off the ground. The damned little tree had put its roots right down through the poor man's body! Right through his spine, and they had spread out so much in the ground we couldn't pull them out. We had to take pruning shears and cut them, where they came out of his body, and I'm telling you, when we were done we threw the body on the wagon and got *out* of there."

For the first time in their one-day-old acquaintance, Vesica could empathize with what Sheldrake was telling her.

"So this," the short man said, rocking back reflectively, "is how I finally figured it. The gamekeeper had eaten something that he probably thought was a blackberry. Maybe somebody had tricked him into doing that, and maybe they hadn't. However it happened, the thing he ate turned out not to be a blackberry; it turned out to be the seed of an oak, which sprouted right away and killed him. And it kept on growing, and bored right through his guts while I was carrying him on the litter. It put its roots down in the ground, and those roots are still there, still growing and spreading. And they're sending up these crazy shoots that grow overnight, so tough you can't pull them up, and they're taking over the whole territory, and nothing can kill them. Because all these other trees"—he waved his arms around—"all these oaks you see around here, they all started with that tree that grew out of a dead man's stomach. And that's why it's called the Devil's Oak. And that's how this whole thing got started."

Sheldrake leaned back with an air of self-satisfaction. *There*, he seemed to say. How's *that* for a horrible story?

Vesica reclaimed enough of her self-possession to think of a couple of things wrong with it. "But oaks don't grow from berry-seeds," she said, which was the foremost problem. "They have acorns. And how could somebody trick you into eating an acorn? How could you even *eat* an acorn? Except in a pie or something. And if you did, and it sprouted, it couldn't grow *that* fast. Besides, if the Devil wanted to kill somebody, he wouldn't go to all the trouble of planting a *tree* in his stomach—he'd just zap him dead by touching him or something. Wouldn't he?" (She wasn't entirely certain of this last point, but it stood to reason.)

To all of which, Sheldrake could only shrug. And seemed perfectly content to do so.

"If I had made the story up," he assured her, "I wouldn't have kept that part in. But that's the way it was."

By way of punctuating this, he placed a foot on the ladder leading down from the cupola. "You should get some sleep," he told her. And then he went down as he had come up, in silence, his large round head disappearing last.

Vesica looked at the little chart on the console. WILD TURKEY POOL, it said. Sheldrake's story had made the words on the little page no less mysterious. If anything, a dozen different and darker threads of interpretation now suggested themselves. Frustrated, she pressed her eye to the viewport, expecting to find daylight slanting through large malevolent oaks outside the glass. But the moon still shone, and the
transport still lumbered inexorably
toward the forest
in the dark.

Ten

*

BIGGAR'S NECK was a dis-
torted reflection of Gravetye Farm. Or more likely, from the
way Sheldrake had described it, a distorted reflection of
itself. Sloping up from the river, which was draped with
willows and carpeted from bank to bank by coarse, purple-
leafed lilies not yet in bloom, land that not so long ago had
been a meadow was overrun and ruined—but ruined intriguingly: a place as odd and intricate as the Maze at Deeping
Lube.

There had been a few specimen trees, dawn redwoods,
freestanding on the slope. Now they were monsters, two
hundred feet tall, their fernlike leaves turned large and toothy,
their upper branches locked against the sky. Still, enough
sunlight made its way to the ground to feed a crop of what
looked (to Vesica, drawing upon the only image that presented itself) like savage delphiniums. The stalks of these,
rising twelve feet above hairlike ground-cushions, were covered with blooms so large and fertile one expected, in place
of bumblebees, to find buzzards flitting between them, drawn
by their drooling nectar. Their color-range gave disturbing
new dimension to the seedsman's catchall category, *mixed*.
And their fragrance, along with the oily droppings of the
transport, made the Crusaders decline (at the risk of offend-

ing Sheldrake) this morning's variation on the theme of lumpy porridge. Only Groby had much appetite.

"I don't know," he said, tucking in his brocaded napkin. "I guess it goes with the job. Weird odors have always made me hungry."

A breeze blew over the hill, stirring the flower bracts and shaking loose palm-sized petals. The transport gave a sympathetic belch from one of its dozen exhaust ports.

That was where they stopped, in that mad meadow. It had not been Groby's doing. The transport seemed to recognize Biggar's Neck, to choose it as a resting point. From the console in the steering cab a sky-blue panel spelled out

TIME TO GO: 02 HRS 43 MIN

and had been counting down, evidently, for some while before Lord Tattersall awoke, frowned at the silence, and said out loud:

"My goodness. We appear to have stopped."

"Very observant," said Sheldrake—already, despite his late night storytelling, at work on breakfast.

The green wall outside the passenger door was so thick as to block an assault on Biggar's Neck from that direction. Accordingly Tattersall led the Crusaders—they were all awake now, and quietly excited—down the narrow passageway to the rear of the vehicle, where Thrull, their disagreeable prisoner, slouched before a hatch in the cargo hold. He was no longer lashed to the carton of tableware. The dictates of compassion, as well as a frequent need for the contents of the box, had led Tattersall to order him placed on a long retaining-wire that gave him room to rove about, as far forward as the sanitary facilities behind the passenger compartment, on condition that he be well-behaved.

"Like a good dog," Sheldrake interpreted.

And he *had* been, from what they could tell; but that was probably due as much as anything to a lack of any alternative— and maybe to the fact that (as even Thrull must realize) his fate was now tied, in more than a literal sense, to the fortunes of the Crusade.

They found him crumpled this morning in a bodily configuration that suggested not only an absence of bones (which had been noted before) but an actual dissolution of the cartilage. Lord Tattersall took pause. He stared down at the youth, who for his part did his best to look downtrodden. Vesica felt like kicking him; she would have bet he spent all night rehearsing this posture. Yet Tattersall—a more innocent soul, in some ways, than she was—let go a sigh.

"I just don't have the heart for this," he told Sheldrake.

"Don't have the brain, more likely," Sheldrake replied.

"It *is* a strain, to see another human in such a state." Tattersall stepped forward, coming to stand upon the greasy spot Thrull's head had left on the deckplates. "Tell me, young man, have you taken the opportunity to contemplate the gravity of your offenses against the law?"

"Oh, brother," whispered Lorian to Vesica. "He must have gotten this off the editorial page of the *Wake*. I *told* them people actually read that stuff."

On the floor, the youth fawned and cringed extravagantly. "Oh, your lordship! I'm so sorry I let them talk me into it. It was those Pure Force agitators from the city—they want to keep everything stirred up so they can recruit new members. I realize now you're *not* the tyrannical fool they said you are."

"They said that?" Tattersall bristled.

"There's some honesty in everyone," conceded Sheldrake.

"Yes, your lordship. And a lot else. I wish I had never met them. Oh, I wish I could go back home."

"There, there," said the Governor sternly. "You'll have to tough it out, like the rest of us. Here, Sheldrake—cut this poor wretch loose."

Sheldrake grudgingly complied, making every effort to crush Thrull's wrists in the process. Lorian shook her head.

"But see here," said Tattersall, not wishing to appear unduly lenient. "The first sign of trouble, and back in chains you go."

The hatch slid open as Thrull was whimpering his thanks to Tattersall and casting dark glances at Lorian. Then the Crusaders stepped down onto the grounds of Biggar's Neck.

In the transport's meandering wake, the tangle of vegetation had been razed to a two-inch stubble. What had become of the missing stems and leaves and flowers was mysterious, the transport seemed to have swallowed and digested them. The shorn earth was like a hallway, walled by leaves and flowers and roofed, here and there, by misshapen trees. The air was heavy with spring dampness. It was all disconcertingly quiet.

"So," said Lorian—an urbanite, unable to stand silence for very long. "What do we do now?"

The others looked to Tattersall, naturally enough, for some sign of response or at least attention to this, but the Governor strolled off down the verdant aisle, nosing here and there among the flower stalks like a schoolmaster snuffling out truancies. Thirty steps away, he bent to sniff a saucer-sized poppy.

"Is he safe, do you think?" Lorian bit her lip, looking worriedly around her. "I mean . . . going off by himself?" She fingered her satchel as though it might hold some discreet but lethal weapon—which, for all anyone knew, it might.

"Sure," said Vesica—and *feeling* sure, for some reason. "He's okay. It doesn't seem dangerous here. Is it, Sheldrake?"

"Ha!" The short man feigned a shudder. "You don't see *me* marching after him."

"Good," said Lorian. "Then you can march after me. I want to collect some plant samples, and see if I can match them with these diagrams."

Sheldrake turned to stare at her, his black eyes meeting green ones as stubborn and unblinking as themselves. One could sense, thought Vesica, a certain rapport here: a balanced antagonism. Sheldrake dourly nodded.

"If we're going," said Groby, slowly of course, "to be here awhile, I'd like to have a look underneath the transport. Check the engine and so on. Could anyone help me? With the tools and the light?"

Vesica opened her mouth to volunteer, but another voice spoke ahead of her.

"I will!" said Thrull.

Groby alone, perhaps, did not instinctively distrust this offer. He only nodded, indicating the place he had dropped his toolsack. Lorian handed Sheldrake a pair of florist's shears. The Crusaders divided. Vesica was left alone in the flower-tufted aisle. The meadow felt not just quiet, she thought, but *hushed,* as though like the transport it had purposely come to a pause. And where could Lord Tattersall have gotten to? Someone should have kept him company; and the truth was, Vesica wanted to be kept company herself.

She ventured up the transport's wake a hundred yards or so, glancing frequently back as the other Crusaders grew smaller behind her, until she came to a place where the meadow looked more or less assailable. The swollen delphiniums grew sparser as the trail wound up the slope, and between them grew clumps of what *might* have been red clover. It was too big for clover, with six or seven leaflets instead of the usual three, but it *looked* like clover, and this was somehow reassuring. Vesica put a tentative foot on top of it.

An arresting, tangy-sweet aroma filled the air, as though the earth were telling her she had taken the proper turn.

"What could it be?" she wondered aloud.

"I can almost remember," said Tattersall. "But not quite."

She looked up, in less surprise than one would have thought, as though she had expected the Governor to be there. He was only a few steps away, though inconspicuous, for his safari suit was so less brilliant than the surrounding flora. Not in response to Vesica, but following some inaudible prompting of his own, he bent over a cluster of leaves, rubbed one vigorously between his fingers, and sniffed the air. He nodded slowly, smiling, as one encourages a child or animal to approach.

"Well," he said, "I suppose it will come when it's ready to."

"What will, your lordship?" asked Vesica.

Tattersall looked up in surprise, as though just now taking note of her. He smiled. "Call me Tattersall, my dear, or I shan't call you Vesica. Will you walk with me to the manor?"

He stepped past her without waiting to receive an answer or give an explanation. She had little choice, really, but to follow. The red clover, or whatever it was, was up to her thighs.

"To the manor?" she said, hurrying in his footsteps. The Governor covered a good piece of real estate with each indolent-seeming stride.

"Unless," he said, "there was somewhere else you wanted to go."

"Oh, no. I mean . . . but what manor? Where are we going?"

They were climbing the hill. Already they were high enough to look down at the transport, its flanks half-buried in leaves. Still it was hard to get a good look at the countryside; you could see just so far in any direction before something big and malformed (yet like the flowers, half-recognizable) rose to block your view. Tattersall seemed only vaguely aware of the girl behind him, and this chiefly suited her, for looking over people's shoulders was a familiar position; nonetheless it was annoying to have her questions ignored. She drew alongside.

"The *manor*," she put to him, like a challenge.

He looked down at her. His eyes were different from what they had been: still bright, still swimming-pool blue, but for the first time in her acquaintance, melancholy. In a tone that matched them he said, "Ah. So you've been there."

"I haven't been there," she firmly corrected him. The Governor, she saw, was a man who needed to be *spoken* to. "Have you?"

"I spent much of my time here, until a few years ago. Well, maybe more than a few. It was the most beautiful place in the territory."

"Sheldrake told me that."

"He did? Ah, of course: I *met* Sheldrake here. He was something else at the time, not an accountant—let me see . . ."

"A tree pollard?"

"Yes! Quite! You're a very knowledgeable young lady."

Vesica was going to ask him what a tree pollard was, but he rattled on with his remembrances, which all things considered she was more interested in. They started walking again.

"It was when Widdy was still living here. She was younger then, of course. Though not exactly *young* . . . Well, perhaps that's best forgotten. Perhaps everything is best forgotten, after all this time."

"Oh, no," said Vesica, not perfectly sure what they were talking about. "Don't say that."

He smiled wistfully. "Oh, you're right, I know. One

should cherish one's memories, shouldn't one? When one has lost so nearly everything else, at least the memories remain. The old stories. What's this?"

They had reached a place where the hill topped out and flattened. At their feet the clover gave way to something softer, lower, more nearly emerald-green. It was like a carpet of the lushest and thickest pile—so perfectly smooth that Vesica wanted to roll on it. To her absolute astonishment, Tattersall did just that: turned a broken cartwheel, came to a precarious halt with his riding-boots in the air and his silver-blond hair dangling almost to the ground, and then collapsed in an untidy pile, his body wracked with what Vesica, in alarm, mistook for sobs, then recognized as the silliest form of giggles. She stared at him as he rocked back and forth on the ground, staining his safari jacket beyond any realistic hope of coming clean again, until the shock of it wore off and the hilarity overcame her. This did not take too long. Then she joined the Governor on the ground, rolling log-style across what really *was* a carpet-soft surface.

"What is it?" she said. "On the ground, I mean."

"Why, it's tennis grass. Don't you know, the stuff that covers . . . well, perhaps you don't. I've never seen it quite so thick before. But isn't it splendid?"

"Yes, but—what's it doing here?"

"The croquet field," Tattersall explained, and exploded in giggles again. "The . . . croquet . . . he he! We used to play . . . oh my, ha! We used to play croquet here. After luncheon."

"Who?" said Vesica. And the expression that came over Tattersall's face made her think the question had been an earth-shattering one.

"Dittany-of-Crete!" he exclaimed.

"*Who?*"

"That smell! It's dittany-of-Crete!" He was positively sweating in his excitement. "A . . . an herb—I'll never forget it. They used to grow it here. In little baskets. It trailed . . . You know the way a smell can bring back old feelings, old—"

Vesica frowned. "You mean back there on the hill?" she asked him sharply. "That smell, when you stepped on the clover?"

"Oh, no, not clover. Dittany-of-Crete. A windowsill herb. It was once thought to have some form of magical—or was it healing?—powers."

Vesica narrowed her lips, withholding comment; yet she knew that while the fragrant clusters on the hill might not really be clover, they weren't any windowsill herb, either. And smells can't jump from one plant to another. Can they?

Tattersall rose to his feet. He looked . . . well, undignified might not be putting it too unkindly. Everything about him was asunder—everything but the eyes, which had regained their impetuous fervor.

"Well," he said, sweeping his personality into one neat pile again. "Let's go up to the house, shall we?"

The glass-walled manor was crescent-shaped, an architectural marvel. It lay against the hillside away from the transport, staring with clematis-lidded eyes southeast over what once must have been a remarkably lovely view and which was still, in a different way, quite stirring. The land rolled languidly away, each blue-green hill rising not quite so high as the last, like waves losing their power as they neared the beach. And the Blistered Moor, thought Vesica, *was* something like a beach, all gritty and one-colored, though not as lifeless as you thought before you got there. And this land was like an ocean, a vast, turbulent, life-spawning ocean, lapping onto the Moor.

But the house: from the back, which was how she and Tattersall approached it, it did not seem much more than an oblong, slate-roofed cottage. You could look right over the top of it and see something the color of wheat growing high and wild on the opposite hill in what had been, evidently, open farmland. The walls were wrapped in wisteria, and the roof was squatted on by monstrous house-leeks. But when you walked around the side, on flagstones nested inches deep in the tennis grass, you began to get an idea of the size and splendor of the place. The hill fell away dramatically. First two stories, then three, then a sunken terrace with a lily pool revealed themselves. The lily pool was full of the same coarse-leaved plants that filled the stream. And the air, even this early in spring, smelled of lavender, which should not have survived the northern winter. But the *house*:

"Look at it," said Tattersall, shaking his head. "It used to be magnificent."

"It *is*," insisted Vesica, "it is magnificent. Look at the old stonework. You can't get people to do that anymore, my stepfather says, no matter how much you pay them. Look how big the windows are! And up there, the top floor—look, it's all glass! It's all . . . and that balcony . . . wouldn't you love to walk out there in the morning, in the sunshine, and smell the air and listen to the birds and—"

"It was marvelous," Tattersall agreed. "Well. Shall we look inside?"

They elbowed their way through the early blue clematis—whose blooms spanned an uncharacteristic distance of seven inches and whose stems leapt three stories up the stone facade—and entered a hall that rose rafterless to a skylight forty feet in the air. The light that filtered down was tinted aqua-green by algae on the glass, and this, plus the humidity, gave the place an underwater feeling. Vesica sniffed. That smell—dittany-of-Crete, or whatever it really was—was stronger here. And the air was unseasonably warm.

"It's the sun," explained Tattersall. "This place traps the sunlight, somehow. It's been warm like this—for all I know—forever."

They processed up a winding stairway, into rooms that were broad and sunny and endless. Where you expected to reach a wall, the room just turned a corner and there was more of it, boundless brightly carpeted space, the inner walls hung with bold color-field tapestries and the outer ones open to the sun and the air. Yet for all its beauty, and for all that its interior had remained, by most standards, perfectly livable, the place had an eerie and inhospitable air, and Vesica never wondered why its owners had moved away. They must have felt, as she did, unwelcome here. Unwanted. Hostility pressed in against the bright ageless walls.

They separated, each taking his or her own heading through the abandoned corridors, and Vesica soon found herself standing at the edge of what would, on a simpler scale, have been a bathtub. In this sad and magnificent place it was a swimming pool, set in a grotto beneath a ledge of plants that had not only survived their abandonment but thrived, multiplied, gone native. They sprawled over the ledge, tickling with rose-colored blooms at the edge of the water, which was clear and blue and—to an experimental toe—as warm as the sunshine. The pungent smell of herbs was more intense here. It was all so wild, so natural, that Vesica wanted to take off her clothes and plunge in. And she thought, Well, why not? If she heard Tattersall coming she could warn him away, and besides, she did need a bath.

Cautious at first, she unbuttoned her jeans. She slid them down her tan slender legs, seeing for the first time the bruise that covered most of the thigh where she had gashed it, and stood beside the pool in her underpants. The warm scented air was much more comfortable than denim had been, and she felt herself, without trying to, relaxing. She took off the blouse of lemon ramie, regarded its torn and shapeless form for a moment, then laid it on a mound of flowers. And in an instant, surmounting her misplaced modesty, she removed the last shard of cotton and stood naked and elated in the sunshine. Gratefully she slid into the pool.

Water felt so *good*. Had she ever realized it before? She moved her limbs slowly back and forth, feeling the silken intimacy as the water wrapped itself around them. She dipped her head in, closed her eyes and opened them, staring at herself, at her naked, water-refracted body, then came up with a small splash, blinking, and found herself eye-to-eye with a tiny motionless squirrel.

At first she thought: *Oh*, in startlement, and covered her breasts. But, a squirrel!

"Tch, tch," she told it, squirrel-sounds, squeezing air between her teeth. The squirrel wiggled its nose.

She said, "You're not afraid of me."

The squirrel was obviously not.

"Do you live here?" she asked. "Where's your mommy?"

The squirrel seemed happy to go on watching her, enthralled by her alien scent, perhaps, or hoping for some handout. Well, she didn't have anything to give it, and if it had the run of *this* place it didn't need charity anyway. She settled back, drifting tummy-up across the water, allowing the squirrel and the sun and the whole hidden cosmos, if it could see this far, to behold the secrets of her long smooth body.

The truth was, Vesica hadn't quite made up her mind

about all that. Her body. And all that. It felt at times (though this was not one of them) as though it belonged to someone else. It was not *her*, not an expression of her real self, the way the squirrel's real self was expressed in that fur, those black eyes, that tiny wiggling nose. She remembered a time when she hadn't been aware of having a body at all—unless it got sick, or she bruised it. Then there was a while, more recently, when it had just been *her*, and in no way remarkable. But now: now it was different. It was something to wonder about, to be suspicious of; whose oddities of behavior and desire were apart from, even opposed to her own. Not *me* anymore, she thought. Whatever *me* is.

"Well," she said to the little animal, "are you a boy or a girl? Or does that matter to squirrels?"

Oh yes. It did matter, to this squirrel at least, and Vesica felt it. She felt something else, too, very peculiar—though as soon as she tried to get a grip on it, the feeling was gone. So many feelings are like that. This one was about the squirrel, something odd about this particular squirrel, as against the hundred and fifty or so other squirrels Vesica had known in her girlhood at Gravetye Farm. She blinked repeatedly, the way you do when you have water in your eyes. Between blinks she thought she had it—then the water cleared and it was gone again—but for a moment there . . .

The squirrel turned and scampered away, vanishing into its bright ageless home.

In the wake of the transport Lorian knelt and tugged at something that seemed to have sprouted from the ground that very hour. It seemed so, because it stood a hand-width higher than the surrounding stubble, and its tender purple-green leaves bore no scars from the transport's passage. As she touched it, the tiny stem appeared to wilt; it drooped and curled at the tip, like a vine searching for a limb to twine on. Lorian expected it to break, but it proved surprisingly resilient. Studying the crown of its roots, just visible above the soil, Lorian thought it must have grown from an underground stem or rhizome, like the oaks on the Blistered Moor. She wondered how far away its parent was. But the rhizome branched repeatedly for as long as she could follow it, and the branches lost themselves in the general unruliness of the meadow. Well. It had just been idle curiosity. Shrugging it off, Lorian stood—

—or tried to stand, but something held her—

The tiny shoot. It was five or six inches longer, now, than when she had first noticed it, which was only a couple of minutes ago, for god's sake, and it was wrapped around her wrist like a bracelet, a very tight constricting bracelet, and Lorian said:

"Damn you, don't grab hold of *me*."

"Hadn't dreamed of it," muttered Sheldrake, who stood by obliviously, browsing the stack of custard-colored papers. He said, "What does 'inter-specific transposition' mean?"

The tendril seemed to tighten. All right, Lorian knew that was impossible, it was only her imagination, but it *was* pretty strange; and there was a burning sensation on her skin and she wasn't imagining *that*.

In the cool morning air of the hillside, she began perspiring.

Lord Tattersall strolled down a hallway he remembered almost perfectly, with the omission of where it led to, when he noticed near his feet a small cotton-furred squirrel. For several years his only involvement with wildlife had been the more-or-less-annual efforts to rid the upper stories of his home of irksome pigeons, and the winecellars of rats. He came to the squirrel, therefore, with a presumption that their relationship would be adversarial. Moreover he had the distinct impression that the squirrel was waiting for something. Some sign.

"Pardon me," he told it, "for intruding upon you. I shan't be here long. Just as soon as I find Vesica . . ."

The squirrel made a chittering sound, which to Tattersall's unschooled ear sounded disturbingly like laughter.

Well!

It's strange, thought Groby, breathing deeply the dark oily air between the rows of cleated treads, that they would have built this thing without an airfax transmitter. Here underneath the steering console was an indentation where a transmitter might have fit, but it was empty. Loose wires dangled down. Groby twiddled one of these between his fingers, noted for future reflection that its copper lead was bright, barely tarnished, as though it was only recently disconnected.

But his train of thought had scarcely left the station when Lorian started to shout. Though her words were muffled, their timbre of pain and alarm cut through the mantle of greenery.

"Here," Groby told Thrull, who skulked in the shadow of the motorblock. "Hold this wrench. I'm going to see what's the matter."

His voice was rounded out and amplified by the metallic cavern. Thrull nodded neutrally and took the wrench while Groby scrabbled toward the yellow-green daylight. By the time he emerged into the fragrant air his heart was throbbing like an engine, as much from foreboding as from the exertion of the crawl.

Lorian stood a short way off, Sheldrake beside her. Papers were strewn on the ground. Groby reached them just as the journalist was sloughing off an arm-length vine she seemed to have gotten caught in. The vine was thin but wiry, and had something sticky on its climbing-pads, for in places it clung to her skin.

"Like a stinging nettle or something," she said. "Wow! It really burns."

"Could I see that?" said Groby, taking the vine in his work-gloves.

Yellow stains remained on the gloves where the tiny plant touched them. Some kind of acid, Groby thought. Maybe the vine was a parasite, and this was how it penetrated the bark of its hosts. The bark, or the—

Sheldrake looked at Lorian and away from her in alternate rapid glances, as though the extent of his concern, if any, was a matter he wished to keep in the dark. "Has anyone," he said, "seen the Governor?"

Neither of the others responded; Lorian was busy rubbing her arm and Groby was staring at the length of vine.

"I guess I'd better go find him," Sheldrake decided, "before we miss our ride. You can look after her, can't you?"

"I don't," Lorian tersely informed him, "need looking after." Her wrist showed signs of wanting to swell. "Damn! What *is* that thing?"

* * *

Dittany-of-Crete had been used as a windowsill herb for centuries, and was thought to have tonic or alchemical qualities, but was not seen much anymore. Its leaves were like small pillows covered with downy white fuzz, and its flowers were rose-colored, appearing at the ends of trailing branches. Among the things people once said of it was that if you placed it in a sunny window, its smell would lure angels out of the *akasha*, causing them to take on bodily form and possibly befriend you. But this (as a professor of the Secret College remarked to a graduate student in astrology) was just the sort of story one expects an herbalist to tell. For if no one has ever seen an angel, or knows quite what the *akasha* is supposed to be, and no one grows dittany-of-Crete anymore . . . well, why not? Who can say it isn't so?

It was complexly aromatic and its seeds were very small.

Vesica lifted the lemon ramie blouse from the mound of trailing flowers and brushed it off, for it had picked up tiny black dirt-specks. She felt cool and clean and silky, and the caress of the blouse as it slid down over her breasts was queerly exciting. Before she left the bathing pool she tucked one of the sweet rose-colored blossoms in her hair. It clashed happily with the yellow blouse, and brought out the copper-tan of her freckles.

"Tch, tch," she said, glancing around for the squirrel, but he was gone now. She found Tattersall lounging in a deck chair on the sunken terrace, almost hidden by a fan of wand-flower that thrust itself exuberantly through the cracks.

"I had thought," he said, staring over the aquamarine hills, "it would be sad here. But it's just . . . different. Like a place you once lived that's owned by someone else. One could even say it was nicer this way."

She knew what he meant. "Like a wild garden."

"Good heavens, Vesica," the Governor exclaimed, staring as though he had never seen her before, "what a beautiful young lady you are! You look a bit like someone, someone I . . . Well. You never know."

They crossed the terrace and waded into the tennis grass.

Back in the meadow they were received with some excitement. Sheldrake bustled toward them, waving his stubby arms. The checkered shirt bobbed up and down like a signal-flag.

"Your lordship!" he said, stage-whispering, as though fearful of being overheard. "It's the forest! It attacked what's-her-name, the woman—"

"Lorian?" said Vesica. "What's happened?"

Muttering, Sheldrake threw a pregnant glance across his shoulder. Vesica followed it: Groby in the middle-ground, the transport in the back-, and between them Lorian (favoring one arm? or does it only look that way to the presupposing observer?) gathering papers from the ground. The meadow teemed with unruly life on every side, but there was nothing new about that. Sheldrake shuddered.

"I don't see anything wrong," said Vesica (except the black speckles that clung to her blouse, which she swatted at). She walked on.

"I don't wonder," called Sheldrake after her, "that *you* don't see it. You have to know what you're looking for. You have to know your enemy, if you're going to outsmart him."

Tattersall shook his head. He thought perhaps he had missed some explanation, but what it had been he no longer cared to know.

"What nonsense!" he said. In several stately strides he overtook Vesica, and the two of them strolled together down the stubbly green.

"By all that stinks in the cellar," muttered Sheldrake behind them. He performed with quaking hands a series of quick and cryptic gestures: down at the earth, up at the sky, back and forth before his forehead. (Who knew? It might have been some sacrament of tree pollardry.) At the end of this he declared: "Well, I guess we're in for it."

Down at the transport Lord Tattersall was saying, "Where's that young man? The prisoner?"

"I think we've got a problem," Groby said, concluding, though no one knew it, half an hour's silent rumination.

And Lorian rubbed her forehead, not feeling so good any longer.

Tendrils of the purple-leafed vine found their way over the treads of the transport and through the intake ducts just forward of the motorblock. From there the vine grew very quickly. The limiting factor in its growth was not, as might have been presumed, its rate of cell division. The vine had solved that problem a few hundred years ago, when it borrowed some genes from a slime-mold. Now its entire upper length was a single elongated cell, with certain sites specialized to perform chores which, together, amounted to playing for time, while a more conventional multicell structure was, so to speak, retrofitted. The limiting factor now became the speed at which the vine could manufacture cellulose, which was needed to extend and fortify its outer wall. This problem was solved in short order, as such things go, after two hundred years of trial and error. The new trick was borrowed not from fellow flora but from a small component of a hot water pump, around which the ancestral plant happened to have twined. Thin plates of silicon, the vine discovered— "discovered" in a purely descriptive sense, for who can know the inner state of a plant?—were assembled to form a tough and pliable shell vaguely akin to the unnatural substance, Plexiglas. But by now the line between the natural world and the other one, whatever it was, had blurred considerably. For reasons the vine had no inkling of—probably—the glacial mantle underlying the Carbon Bank Forest was silicon-rich. Thus a store of raw material could be accreted over months and molded into segmented wall-plates a few molecules thick, to be moved quickly forward by capillary pressure and snapped into place whenever the occasion for rapid expansion should present itself. All of which enabled this vine to grow with unprecedented alacrity. It was really quite remarkable.

Or again, it was not. Something cannot be "remarkable," can it, unless there is someone around to remark? And the vine had evolved in a world that, for all its myriad species, was uninhabited, in the customary sense. The vine lived and grew in a kind of vacuum, an absence of observation. The essence of the vine—the thing-in-itself—must remain a mystery.

We cannot know, for example, what drove it to creep on acid-secreting climbing-pads down the transport's intake ducts until it entered the old black motorblock. We can only note that it discovered there (again, in a purely descriptive sense) the old rubber coating of the power lines leading rearward to the great reduction gears. Rubber, like the woman's skin—like, indeed, the old unhappy slime-mold—was especially susceptible to the vine's corrosive secreta. It was chemically disassembled, as the woman's epidermis would have been had she not yanked the vine off. There was a faint sound of sizzling, and then the vine broke through: through the insulation, to the power cables themselves; and there the vine got (speaking very, very loosely here) quite a surprise.

Electricity surged. It crossed the narrow gap between the power line and the rusty body of the motorblock. It raced along the highly conductive metal, until it reached one of the several places where the motorblock was bolted to the frame. There it veered and took a shortcut through the navigation computer. This device, no larger than a deck of fortune cards, offered only momentary resistance; then its components fused into a blob as shiny and flat as a molten tea tray, complete with charred scones. As the flood of energy passed on, a small runlet spilled over into the bank of servo-motors that directed the sawblades. It overrode the safety switch and revved the blades to a dangerous torque, meanwhile pointing them down toward the earth which was, in some unfathomable manner, the cause of all this. When at last the current reached the portion of the machinery called the governor, the tread-wheels gave a series of convulsive jerks, tilting the vehicle forward at an angle of ten degrees or so, which was enough to bury the sawblades in the dirt. They made a rapid excavation, flinging, as they were designed to, everything they touched back into the processing chamber, thereby filling it with soil which it vainly tried to ignite. It ignited the servo-motors instead. They vanished in a gush of oily yellow flame, the spectacle of which could only be imagined, since the Crusaders—the only prospective witnesses around—were on the other side of a great body of metal and engaged in a discussion of where their recently freed prisoner might be.

Some inconsiderable fraction of the energies released in those seconds was dissipated in the form of electromagnetic radiation. The radiation shot outward in all directions, giving rise to an age-old and almost irresistible analogy with ripples spreading in a deep clear pond. After a few millionths of a second, the ripples encountered a device that was specifically designed to receive them. It was an airfax machine, which, had it been left in its rightful place beneath the steering console, would have first been discovered by Groby, and now destroyed. But it had not; it had been removed by the prying screwdriver of a young member of the Pure Force, placed inside a carton in the luggage compartment, taken out, activated, and hidden beneath a mound of gray-green laundry. It had most recently been moved some fifty feet and set down in the mad meadow, out of harm's way, between savage delphiniums, where it transmitted a repetitious series of first six digits, then seven, then the whole thing over again.

Now it paused, sensing the incoming radiation. It spent several thousand cycles analyzing what it mistook for a reply. At the end of this, reaching no firm conclusions, it became excited. Tiny red lights blinked on. It began a new transmission, relaying not the usual six- and seven-digit numbers but a stream of raw data which it hoped, in its naïve electric way, might be of interest. These data were dutifully transcribed in a walk-up flat overlooking the Tomb of Artists, by a sleepy machine which as usual got several of them wrong. As with many news reports, however, the fictitious parts were more interesting.

The glowing red lights caught Thrull's attention. He picked up the machine, shaking it to see if anything was broken inside, but heard only the usual faint crackle. Then he heard something else, not from the airfax machine but from down in the meadow. A hollow *thoomp*: deep and loud, but muffled. Thrull's heart raced and he started to turn, to flee, but wait a minute—it wasn't *him* that had done it, whatever it was, and anyway there, right in front of him, between the delphiniums, looking up, was a small stupid furry gray squirrel.

"Tchee tchee," said the animal. (Squirrel-talk.)

"Get shot," said Thrull, who hated animals, though he had known few of them.

The squirrel appeared to wrinkle its small nose; no doubt this was a characteristic gesture merely, but it angered Thrull. He took a menacing step forward, raising the airfax machine in his hand.

"Tchee," said the squirrel, holding its ground among the flowers.

Thrull, irritated mostly by the distraction, when what he wanted now was to go back down to the meadow and see what that noise was, whether (as he hoped) something terrible had happened, took another step forward, nearly treading on the squirrel now, and when the tiny
creature still didn't move, he brought the airfax machine
in his hand slamming down
and killed it.

Eleven

CIRCLES formed around news-
vendors in the ageless city of Riverrun, hub of that loose
agglutination of states and estates and wastelands of which
the Northern Territories were arguably the least important
part, when the morning edition of the *Daily Wake* appeared,
as usual, at three in the afternoon. On the cover the hawkish
eyes of Low Commissioner Narthex seemed to bulge from
the finger-smudged newsprint into the soggy air. The rest of
the Commissioner's face, as grainily depicted, bore a troubled look, and his posture suggested apprehensiveness. He
stood stiffly by the bed of a middle-aged woman in a garish
sundress whose bandaged forehead was largely concealed by
the silk flowers drooping from her hat. It did not require
great imagination to suppose that the Commissioner, whose
long-fingered hand rested on the woman's shoulder, had
been surprised in the act of strangling her. The caption read:
COMMISSIONER COMFORTS CLERGY BATTERED BY YESTERDAY'S
BOMB.

"It doesn't *look* much like a priest," the fat journalist
conceded to a younger colleague at the bar of the Silent
Partners' Club. "But that's what they told me at the hospital.
You wouldn't believe how bad the food was."

"Uhm," said the younger colleague. He put the newspaper
aside and opened an account book. "Do you think this lunch

qualifies as a business expense? I'm not a member here, you know."

"Claim it," the fat man advised. "Knock the ball into *their* court. Isn't that Professor Tylyester?"

They stared down the murky bar at the cowled figure disappearing into the Deep Game Room.

"Here, Evergrey," the younger colleague said. "You can have this paper back. How about another round?"

The aged bartender accepted the hard-thumbed copy of the *Daily Wake* and moved shakily down the rail, delivering it to the next patron on the reading list. As were all other things in the Club, the news here was disbursed according to a strict hierarchy of which Evergrey was the chief custodian. He delivered the paper into the hands of a uniformed man whose face and insignia were rendered indistinct by poor lighting. (Evergrey was also the custodian of lightbulbs.) Ignoring the photograph, the officer spread the paper before him and rapidly scanned the lead story.

CRUSADE OFF SAFELY, he read, AFTER BRUSH WITH "PURE FORCE."

The story was only two days old, which made it—by the standards of the *Wake*, and even more so of the Silent Partners' Club—unusually current. It proceeded:

The First Biotic Crusade embarked from the frontier town of Deeping Lube late yesterday evening, marking the first scientific effort to halt the expansion of the Carbon Bank Forest, which has displaced thousands of farmers and villagers throughout the North. The departure was not a smooth one, however, as a violent raid by youthful militants resulted in the loss of many of the Crusade's supplies, and forced a last-minute change in the expedition's roster.

"They very nearly knocked the whole thing off track," said Commissioner Narthex, who represents the Northern Territories on the Low Commission, in an exclusive interview this morning. "But the Embarkation Ball ploy caught them napping."

Information was received on the eve of the Crusade's start, the Commissioner explained, of plans by the so-called Pure Force to disrupt the scheduled embarkation. In order to mask the Crusade's departure, a lavish "Embarkation Ball" was staged at the residence of the Territorial Governor, featuring a number of supposed "Crusaders" —actually members of the Hardy Plant Society who volunteered to pose as members of the expedition while the real Crusaders slipped unobtrusively aboard the Expeditionary Transport Vehicle at an undisclosed staging area near the town.

The key to the success of this diversion, according to Commissioner Narthex, was the last-minute substitution of the Eighth Earl Tattersall, described as "a mid-level administrator held over from the old aristocracy," for the Commissioner himself as the Leader of the Crusade. While admitting that he "regretted very much" not being able to command the expedition on its historic journey, the Commissioner stated that, in his view, "My presence in Deeping Lube that night would have jeopardized the entire mission. In any case," he continued, "I have no doubt that Lord Tattersall will perform quite admirably, given his lack of training or experience in ecological matters."

Commissioner Narthex sponsored, during the last session of the Low Commission, a number of initiatives aimed at reducing the burden of refugees on the city, including a "borrowed worker" program to relieve labor shortages in the armaments industry. "We now have," he claimed, in a rare mood of boasting, "the most comprehensive resettlement program in the history of Civilization."

As to the ultimate success of the Crusade, the Commissioner was less sanguine. "It has taken five hundred years," he pointed out, "for the forest to expand to its present boundaries. It may take more than a few weeks or months to figure out how to beat it back. Meanwhile we can only hope to minimize the destabilization of our society. No one has anything to gain from that—no one, that is," he added, his voice taking on an undertone of bitterness, "but those filthy little anarchists."

A spokesperson for the Pure Force, the organization reportedly responsible for the disturbance at Deeping Lube, denied that his group had any involvement.

"We *do* oppose," acknowledged this young man, who agreed to be interviewed on condition that

he not be identified, "the pursuit of Science, which
we think is *exactly* the wrong way to solve this
problem. But we also oppose the use of violence
to prevent it. Basically we believe that a certain
amount of folly, in the name of Science or Politics or whatever, is part of the human condition. All you can do is try to combat it with the
Truth."

The Truth, the young man continued, can only
be known through direct personal experience.
"You either know it or you don't," he explained.
"There's no sense going out into the woods trying
to find it."

Asked to clarify the position of the Pure Force
on the First Biotic Crusade, this source replied,
"You have to understand that Science is what *created* this situation. To think that you can solve
everything by throwing *more* Science at it is really
taking this fight-fire-with-fire thing too far. If the
scientists had just left the forest alone, back in the
days of the Madness, everything would be all
right now. But they couldn't stop fiddling around,
and now they've got Nature all screwed up, and
that's why the Pure Force was founded in the first
place."

The Force lays claim, according to this spokesperson, to a 500-year history of "peaceful but
strenuous opposition" to the expansion of scientific knowledge. He added, "These accusations
of violence and terrorism have been thrown at us
all along. And it's totally ridiculous. You might
as well accuse those little blue-haired ladies in the
Hardy Plant Society of planting land mines in
with the petunias."

"Have you *ever*," Lady Widdershins demanded, tossing
her copy of the *Wake* as hard as she dared into the antique
plastic in-basket atop her armoire, "read anything to *beat* it?
Do you know, I believe I will cancel my subscription."

This sentiment was taken up by the large number of
guests around the second-floor sitting room at Marshmain,
her ladyship's in-town home. She persisted in thinking of it

as her in-town home, though it had been fourteen years since she abandoned her happy rural seat at Biggar's Neck. Not that she had abandoned hope of someday returning there. This very hope, or a faint glimmering of it, had lent an eensy bit of added enthusiasm to her zeal in promoting the Crusade. *Her* zeal, she wished to emphasize. Not the Low Commissioner's.

The crowd in the second-floor sitting room was unusually large today: large even for a Thursday, when Lady Widdershins was At Home; large even for a Thursday in *spring*, when she was At Home in her grandest manner. The chamber was packed with the entire membership of the Hardy Plant Society (or at least that portion of the membership still able to read). It was packed besides with caterers, musicians, and servants spilling large amounts of wine, with the membership's standing corps of marriageable daughters, and with its equally numerous corps of impassioned Friends. They had gathered here—this glittering, though these days just a *bit* tarnished trayful of Riverrun's social gems—To Hear (as their invitation had informed them)

> The Very Distinguished
> Professor Tylyester
> Dean of the Secret College
> Discuss the
> First Biotic Crusade

—a topic which, in light of the foregoing events, had acquired a timeliness undreamt of even by the Chairperson herself (nothing if not a dreamer) at the time the invitations were printed on pennyroyal-scented parchment. But this timely attraction—like all other attractions, if you only wait them out—had taken on the nature of a wry ironic memory, for the Dean had not yet delivered himself, and was now three hours overdue. The guests, left with no one but themselves and one another's escorts to entertain them, had done as they usually did on such occasions: they had all gotten badly drunk. Lady Widdershins, who did not drink, or more exactly did not drink any *longer* (having wised up after an Indiscretion with still-echoing complications), gave up trying to divert them and sank into her vermiculated writing-chair to read the *Wake*. With what result, we have already witnessed.

Her eloquent ire was interrupted by a commotion below, as a new guest emerging from a powered car was deposited on her doorstep. She heard her retainers scuttling about and bootsteps traversing the grand, though poorly ventilated, Marshmain hall. It *must*, she thought, be the Professor. Rising, she ran her hands down the floral pattern embroidered on her dress—on no account but that of impatience, for her ladyship must know after all these years that her corporeal wealth was equitably distributed. She pressed through the tottering crowd, determined to be the first to greet the long-anticipated *arriviste*—and got there just in time.

Just in time to be taken as violently aback as though she had been slapped in the face.

Before her stood Low Commissioner Narthex. (In her own sitting room! The cad.)

Blessedly her ladyship was given a few moments in which to edit her reaction. This gift came from her poodle, Paracelsus, which sank its teeth into the Commissioner's gray spidersilk trousers.

"Nice little puppy," Narthex oozed, meantime doing his best to choke the animal to death. "My, what a pretty little dog!"

Glancing up from this mortal contest, he managed a thin treacly smile at Lady Widdershins.

"My darling Widdy!" he gamely croaked.

"Don't *ever*," she began, then paused to be absolutely certain she was speaking loudly enough to be heard above the merrymaking, "*ever* call me that again. Only one person has ever called me that, and he is incorrigible, and *that* is neither here nor there between *us*."

She fanned herself. Paracelsus let go of the Commissioner to trot over and bite the lutar player. This resulted in a chord of scandalous atonality. The rest of the ensemble, perceiving the go-ahead for improvisation, let fly with a polychromatic fusillade.

"How *dare* you," Lady Widdershins continued, her voice ringing through the music like a gong, "how dare you *come* here after that horrid story in the *paper*?"

Narthex's translucent eyes momentarily clouded. He took

a step sideways, as though trying to rise from his own social ashes, and said, "Why, my dear lady, that is precisely why I *have* come."

Her ladyship could only blink at this audacity.

"Yes," Narthex hurried on, continuing to tiptoe sideways until he had half encircled her. "I have come, you see . . . to express my outrage! Yes! To express my outrage at the scandalous abuse of the public trust which that newspaper has committed. What paper was it, Widdy?"

"The *Wake*, of course, and don't—"

"The *Wake*, yes! And do you know, I have also come to tell you, that is . . . Ah! To tell you that I have arranged to have all copies of that edition removed from the shelves! Torn down from the newsstands! Yes—rather than allow this outrage to go on. Which story was it, by the way—"

Lady Widdershins offered Narthex the expansive prospect of her back, searching (thus far, vainly) for a Hardy Planter able-bodied enough to end, by whatever means were required, this unwelcome encounter. That newspaper story *did*, she was pressed to concede, have its nasty little point about blue-haired ladies. And the servants, poor old things, were little better. . . .

An inhuman howl interrupted her. Lady Widdershins turned just in time to see the poodle Paracelsus fly in a low arc across the drawing room, land with a woozy whimper in the lap of the harpist, and vomit. The foot by which the animal was launched entered the room a moment later. It was clad in a no-nonsense black shoe, the laces of which were brushed by the tattered hem of an academician's robe, which in turn swayed imperiously from the shoulders of an academician's broad and hairy body.

"Damned animal," the academician's mouth intoned. "Ought to be stuffed—use it as a pincushion."

Lady Widdershins nearly swooned in an effusion of relief. "Why, *Professor*," she gushed, "what a charmingly original idea!"

"Somebody's carriage was blocking your driveway," the Professor went on to complain. "I'm having it towed."

Low Commissioner Narthex, seeing himself not only ignored but possibly deprived of his means of transportation, made an efficient if essentially graceless exit as, on cue from

Lady Widdershins, the ensemble (less the harpist) began mewling that season's unforgivably glib sensation, "Saraband of Lost Time."

"Sorry I'm . . ." Tylyester muttered, his low-pitched voice breaking intermittently through the barrier of music, ". . . just coming over when . . . most unfortunate . . . drop in at the . . . retrieve my papers . . ."

The papers he had retrieved bulged under his arm. Unable to determine quite what her honored guest was trying to say, Lady Widdershins contented herself with deciphering the title on the topmost tattered sheet. She read:

NOTES TOWARD A CRITIQUE OF HAYATA'S COMMENTARY
ON THE "ORGANIZING PRINCIPLE" OF GENETIC TRANSPOSITION,
WITH EMPHASIS ON THE HISTORICAL AND BIOGRAPHICAL CONTEXT
AND HER EFFORT TO END THE CRISIS OF INDETERMINISM

Her ladyship took a deep breath. Now *that*, she thought, is the sort of thing that makes you wonder if the Pure Force, too, doesn't have its nasty little point.

"You must be *so* upset," she soothingly suggested, "about the Crusade. After we had all worked so long . . ."

"Upset?" The Professor hoisted the brow from a heavy-lidded eye. "Is something wrong with it?"

"Why . . . that is," said her ladyship, her social instincts faltering, "that trouble the other night . . . leaving without the Crusaders . . ."

"Ah." The Professor's black mane shook as he nodded his head. "See what you mean. Bit of a disappointment. But the *vehicle*, you see—big frightful thing, can't break it if you try—ought to do well enough without them. Programmed it myself. Anyway Tattersall's still on board, isn't he?"

Lady Widdershins frowned. One didn't quite know what to say to this. The Professor went on:

"Shouldn't matter anyway. Except to Tattersall, of course. Any idea who he's got with him, by the by? No? But the transport, you see, is going to Balance Act whether there's anyone to drive it or not. And when it gets there, it'll send back its coordinates, and we can use those to fly on up there. I always intended," he added confidingly, "to do the *real* research myself."

Lady Widdershins, on behalf of the Society, felt a tiny bit taken advantage of. She said coolly: "Do you take tea?"

"Ale, if you've got it," rumbled the Professor, turning up his voice now to an amplitude suitable for note-taking. "Don't trust the water, anymore. The Plumber's Guild will be the ruination of this city. Who was that thin fellow just leaving when I got here? Had the look of a thief about him, I thought. Everyone got their pocketbooks?"

On her way to the dumbwaiter, Lady Widdershins permitted herself a glance out a lace-curtained second-story window, followed by a slight, and slightly worried, smile.

Down in the courtyard, Low Commissioner Narthex waded through a damp yellow profusion of marsh marigolds to the place where his carriage had been reparked. Angry, embarrassed, and still perplexed by the matter of his missing stepdaughter, he gave the driver incorrect instructions and found himself soon caught up in afternoon traffic on the Aleatory Strand. Something in the atmosphere—damp and stagnant from the nearness of Faerie Sump—was familiar to him. After looking at passers-by for a time and resenting their stares in his direction, he realized where he was.

"I'll get out here," he said, and launched himself to the crumbled pavement.

The Silent Partners' Club was situated in a cul-de-sac beside a luthier's shop. It bore no sign, save for the wheels-within-wheels motif said to be derived from the fortune card THE RANDOM WALK, which someone had etched in its façade. As such things will, this grafitto had endured a generation or so while the name of the establishment, once bold above the double doors, had become weathered and unreadable.

No matter.

Narthex paused in the cloakroom to slow his breathing and coordinate his limbs. He made his way through the Club at a confident saunter, waving off halfhearted approaches from the journalists at the bar, until he arrived at the dark corner where the faceless captain sat staring into a bowl of tepid stew. The stew looked less like a meal than a set piece; reason enough (though none was needed, in this incurious chamber) to explain his lingering so long. He gave no greeting to Narthex, but spoke quietly through lips that remained nearly motionless.

"I've found an aircraft for you. It's just a lorry, but it should do for what you want it for."

"Good enough." The Commissioner delved into an inner pocket of his now dog-bitten spidersilk suit, extracting a long and tightly scrolled piece of paper. The captain unraveled this far enough to discover an indefinitely repeating list of the same two numbers, one of six digits and the other of seven. He stared upward, calculating.

"Are you sure about this?" he said. "It's pretty far north."

Narthex nodded impatiently; he did not intend to discuss it here, in an even marginally public place, and at any rate there were more immediate problems to resolve.

"You know," said the fat journalist a few stools down, "I believe that *was* old Tylyester. I wonder why he left in such a hurry. Something to do with the Crusade, do you think? They say he's the brains behind it."

"If he's such a hotshot," said the younger colleague, mildly slurring his words, "why's he eating in a place like this?"

"Oh, he's not eating," the fat journalist said. "Not in the Deep Game Room. They don't *eat* there."

"What do they do?"

The fat journalist did not know. He had never penetrated that shadowy sanctum. "I understand," he said, hoping to sound mysterious, "they throw dice."

The younger colleague appeared to doze.

An hour later, as the great orange disk hurled itself behind the western battlements, a hundred shadows moved out from the Armaments District, forming circles around newsvendors in the ageless city.

Twelve

IN THE LUSH GHOSTLY manor at Biggar's Neck, Vesica discovered a dresserful of baby clothes. She held them up, puzzling over them; this seemed an odd place for children, even only imagined ones. But the clothes (pink snap-up shirts, tiny socks, soft blankets) were adorable.

In the meadow Groby paced around the burnt-out wreck of the transport. Everything was ruined but a backup generator, saved by a corroded crossover switch. It now dispensed intermittent doses of energy to the power-cannon, which sprayed lavender light across the misshapen redwoods on the hill. Groby, watching this, took more interest in the trees than in the transport, for they seemed far better equipped for this disaster. When one was struck, its bark popped open like a pastry shell, laying bare a sticky underlayer of resins and sap-ferrying phloem. These liquids (Groby surmised, from closely observing the process) vaporized explosively, forming a cloud of waste gases and steam that suffocated the flames, saving the tree from all but superficial harm.

As an engineer and as a practical philosopher (if indeed there is any notable difference between the two), Groby could only admire this. He patted the stricken transport on the flank.

Sheldrake, delighting in the manor's supply of shining cookware, foraged among the weeds around the terrace for something to make a salad of. He found violets, wild onions, wood sorrel, and dandelions, the last of which were doubly useful, as their roots, roasted and ground, could stand in for the xanthée his lordship must by now, Sheldrake supposed, sorely crave. While he harvested he thought about his old life as a tree pollard: nights spent camping on this same sprawling landhold, mornings gathering firewood in the chilly northern sun. He had no regrets, he decided. Nor was his life much worse now, fundamentally. Only a little more confusing. But that will happen.

The sallow youth, Thrull, glancing around him, placed the airfax transmitter down in a clump of something like clover. With a stick then he lifted the mutilated body of a squirrel, slung it over his shoulder, and slipped by way of a back door into the manor. This admitted him, by luck, to a broad immaculate kitchen, where afternoon light poured through the glassy walls.

"Look," he told Lord Tattersall and Lorian, whom he found there. "I've brought dinner!"

Lorian—not at the sight, though Thrull took credit anyway—collapsed onto the floor.

"Oh my!" exclaimed the Governor. He was quick to her side, lifting her head and brushing the hair from her paler-than-usual face. She seemed all right, only weakened. The pink spots where the vine had touched her wrist were forming blisters.

The Crusade, thought Tattersall, staring down at her, barely two days old, was already unraveling.

"We have got," he mused aloud, "to make some Difficult Decisions."

His tone suggested that he wished the making of them, whatever they were, would fall to someone other than himself; also a fear that this was not to be the case. Lorian sighed, coming around.

Thrull, anxious to be helpful now that the transmitter was safe and he was confident of being rescued, bent down beside them.

"You want to put her on a sofa or something?"

"A sofa?" Tattersall looked up, bemused. "I didn't think

Widdy *owned* any sofas—but of course we can check. Love seats, though: that's what she went in for."

Thrull had lost interest anyway. He moved silently, out of habit, down the row of cabinets, thinking how great it would be to have *broken into* a place like this. Finding the door unlocked had taken a lot of the fun out of it.

Lorian's eyes flicked. "What's . . ."

"Just rest," Tattersall advised her. "It doesn't appear we will be going anywhere very soon."

Though even of this he was not very sure. *Anything*, he felt, and feared, might happen.

Lorian's condition grew more puzzling, though not necessarily worse. She dozed through much of the afternoon, while around her a silent debate as to the future of the Crusade was conducted in sighs and tapping fingers and things not said while gazing southeastward, the direction of Deeping Lube, through the drapeless algae-green windows. A ceaseless undercurrent stirred the air, drawn by convection as the sun heated and northerly breezes cooled alternate sections of the single twisting room, the inhabitable Klein bottle that was the manor. The sensation of things held in abeyance, a pause between great conflicts, was as plain as the smell that Tattersall swore was dittany-of-Crete, though none of the plants that spilled from ledges and crept across the floor even faintly resembled it.

When Lorian awoke at five thirty-five, the sun had touched the brow of the western mountains, Sheldrake paced moodily near the love seat where she lay, half-propped, while Thrull stared up through a skylight as though expectant. Groby and Vesica and Tattersall were there as well, though like a supporting cast, doing nothing of note: perched on the arms of overstuffed furniture. In fact they all seemed to be waiting for her—for *her*—which startled her into alertness. The Governor looked kindly down.

"Feeling better?"

"Oh . . ." (sitting up, she said). "I remember this *dream*."

Sheldrake looked at, then away from her. He seemed to have expected this. (How very odd, thought Lorian. Or perhaps she had misread his brief expression.)

"I could hear," she said slowly, "this really deep voice.

Humming. Inside me, like. Or all around. And there was light, and wires, and things on the carpet. Toys. A gun and a tree and a rocketship. But not a real tree. You know, man-made, like a model or a demonstration thing."

The sun swelled up like an orange balloon outside the window. The clouds, whose undersides it stained acrylic colors, stretched high above the earth; remote; indifferent. At the edge of visibility—where they always lived, at the edge—great birds reduced by distance to fledglings patrolled the sky. Vesica, feeling an evening chill, slid down her chair-arm into the impersonal embrace of feather cushions. Fabrics brushed around her: the silk of upholstery, the pastel cotton of a sweater found in a bedroom closet which perfectly fit her, for which she had given up the ramie blouse that was dirty now, anyway, and still dusted with stubborn black specks.

"So what happened," she said, "in the dream?"

Lorian squinted. "I think I had to pick which toy I wanted to play with. And I guess just throw away the others. Or maybe, I don't know, they would just—you know, disappear, poof—if I didn't choose them."

Sheldrake's dark mouth opened and closed, as in silent incantation.

Thrull said, "Other people's dreams have always bored me."

"But the one that I picked," said Lorian, earnestly now, as though a matter of personal conviction were involved, "would come to life. Or maybe . . . no, gosh—I'm sorry. I can't quite remember."

Lord Tattersall sighed. "I never remember *my* dreams. Though perhaps that's just as well."

"So go on," said Vesica—accustomed to beginnings, middles, and ever-after ends. "What happened?"

"Not much, I don't think. I picked up—or anyway I ended up holding in my hand the little toy tree."

Audibly now, Sheldrake groaned.

"But it didn't come to life." Lorian looked around, as though surprised by a sudden access of clarity. "It . . . healed me."

"Of what?" said Vesica.

The journalist's green eyes seemed to glisten, to shine.

Color rose into her cheeks, as though she were blushing. But not the same color, quite, as a blush. She opened her mouth, closed it again, swallowed.

"Of the fever!" Sheldrake snapped. He thumped across the carpet. Lorian, befuddled now, stared up at him.

"Yes," she weakly murmured.

Sheldrake touched her forehead. He challenged the others: "Feel her! She's burning up!"

Vesica thought, You don't even have to. You can see it all the way from here. Lorian's whole demeanor seemed—right now, as they stared at her—to change from something ordinary, simple exhaustion, to something strangely but definitely wrong. Her eyes passed from glistening to glazed. The flush of her cheeks matched the sun's dying color.

"I don't . . ." she murmured, and then fell quickly and heavily into the kind of sleep that Vesica thought might happen if someone cast a spell on you. Deep, troubled, giving no true rest, yet also dreamless, denied that lone consolation.

"Wow," the girl barely whispered.

Sheldrake knelt by the unconscious woman's side. The others—even Thrull, for the sky was too dark to hope for anything now—gathered behind him. Tattersall stammered:

"Is she . . . Will she . . . ?"

Sweat ran down her temples. Sheldrake lifted and seemed to consider in turn each of her sagging limbs: as a tree pollard, one could imagine, carefully but dispassionately examines a failing tree before setting his saw to it. He cleared his throat, unencouragingly.

"This reminds me of something," Vesica said, two thirds to herself, the rest to Groby on the padded chair-arm beside her. The big man placed a bear-paw on her shoulder. She confided, up to him, "A fairy tale."

He nodded, as though this were not out of place at all; in fact perfectly understandable.

Lord Tattersall turned to face the Crusaders, his swimming-pool-blue eyes floating helplessly. "Well," he said. "This does complicate our decision, doesn't it? One might say, immeasurably."

"What decision, your lordship?" said Vesica.

"About the Crusade, he means," explained Sheldrake, as from her love seat Lorian softly moaned.

Absently Tattersall nodded, staring down at her.

"But," Sheldrake added, "that's what *he* thinks."

"It is?" said Vesica.

"Who?" said Tattersall, having lost the thread of it. "About what?"

Sheldrake ran a surprisingly gentle hand across Lorian's brow. "About," he said patiently, "the *Crusade*."

"Ah!" said the Governor, remembering now. "*About* the Crusade: I was just thinking, you see . . . we really must, somehow, decide . . . but now that *this* has happened . . ."

"It's all pretty simple," said Sheldrake, "if you ask me."

"It is?" said the Governor, worried once again that he had missed something.

Solemnly Sheldrake nodded. His stern gaze passed among them. "There's only *one* thing," he intoned, as though this should have been obvious to everyone, "we can do."

And Groby—who might, in fact, have been paying close attention to all this, but whose tone suggested he was somewhere on a thought-path of his own—said softly down at Vesica:

"What fairy tale was it?"

From the ageless, nightblack, almost magical city an airlorry rose, desultorily. Its fluted wings shuddered as its engine, improperly maintained, struggled to hold it aloft. The faceless captain at its helm spoke a curt farewell into the mouthphone, toggled ON the navigational computer, and peered by the light of orange diodes at the torn-off scroll of paper down which the same two numbers marched in unwavering columns. South of the mountains at least, he thought, and hoped there wouldn't be trouble. Or paperwork.

The Low Commissioner, as usual, had bargained him down, this time with a vague promise of a transfer to the seacoast—"*if*," as it had been carefully half-explained to him, "there is a girl among the, shall we say, pilgrims."

A girl? It brought numerous things to mind, among them blackmail opportunities, and shed an illusionary light—like moonlight—upon the Commissioner: a light in which, the captain reflected, Narthex looked really very much at home.

*   *   *

"Well, but there's all this forest business," the Governor pointed out. "Isn't it supposed to be dangerous in there? That is to say, isn't that how this whole Crusade thing got started? And without the transport . . ."

"We're better off," said Sheldrake. He lifted from a pan of cool water a faded burgundy polo shirt, wrung it lightly, and laid it on Lorian's brow. Without rising quite to consciousness, she nonetheless gratefully sighed.

"That shirt looks familiar," said Tattersall: a ploy, since he wasn't altogether sure what Sheldrake was talking about.

"The places rowan grows," the short man went on, no more loudly, "*that* thing would never have taken us."

"Rowing, you say?" Tattersall squinted as he tried to imagine this. "Surely you don't propose to travel by *raft* . . ." but trailed off, because it was perfectly plausible, after all, that Sheldrake might propose exactly that. Or anything.

"That's in the story too," whispered Vesica.

Groby, her only audience, sat hugely amid the coils and coils entangled in the pattern of a rug. The moon, a day past full, shone down on them through a skylight that domed the upstairs sitting room they had chosen for at least the early evening. Its chief attraction was a fireplace, by whose light and the moon's Groby was busy at some project involving an ironing board, two dismantled bicycles and a stack of pancake-sized silicon plates, part of the wreckage of his sunglider. As Vesica watched he picked up a plate, pressed it between the wheel-spokes, jiggled it, took it out again, fitted it somewhere else and let it stay. That was engineering, she supposed.

"But are you *certain*," Lord Tattersall implored, "that this tree or bush or whatever it is that you're talking about will even *be* there? Not to mention that it will be in bloom. How can we know—"

"Beats me," Sheldrake admitted, "how you can know anything."

"Well, there you are."

Sheldrake looked up from his ministrations over the love seat, his dark mouth moving up and down as though chewing over several tasty replies, when Groby set the ex-bicycle wheel among the coils of the carpet and said, smilingly, "A raft or a rowan tree?"

Vesica said promptly, "A rowan"—for having gotten to be friends with Groby, she was accustomed to waiting out these great long pauses. "But I know another story with a raft in it. And a boy, and a river."

"The Speaker," said Thrull, whom for a while now she had successfully forgotten, "says that all stories are the Story." He said this sneeringly, as though it were an obvious truth, a platitude, that ought to be known by any schoolgirl.

Vesica, never a schoolgirl, said, "Why don't you be quiet? Nobody was talking to you." Out of unthinking curiosity she added, "What speaker?"

"He's talking about some loud-mouthed kid," said Sheldrake. "The current hero of the Pure Force."

"The Speaker," sniffed Thrull, "is a great prophet. He came all the way from Seastaithe, and he says that Civilization is doomed because Nature is going to avenge itself."

"And if Nature can't swing it alone," said Sheldrake, "you'll help out by tossing a few bombs around, eh? Actually," he added for Vesica's information, "they've been predicting the end of the world for years now."

She nodded, finding—like most young people—the notion of the end of the world quite plausible.

"You'll see," said Thrull. He glanced once more, hopefully, through the skylight. "When we get back, you'll see what's going to happen."

"If we get back," said Sheldrake. "Not too many people do, from where we're going."

"Oh my," said Tattersall. He sat uneasily beside Lorian, who lay motionless except for the shallow rise and fall of her chest. "Would you tell us," he asked Sheldrake, "why we're going there, again? To Balance Act, that is?"

"Because," said Sheldrake, as though making a slight concession, "it's the only way *she* is going to get better. It's the forest that's made her sick, and only the forest can make her well again."

"And what," said Tattersall, "has this tree got to do with it?"

Groby smiled. A bear-paw came up to signal Vesica.

"Why don't you tell your story?" he suggested.

The Crusaders looked at her. Vesica blushed. She felt funny, to have been made the center of attention: flattered, in a way, but at the same time inadequate, because she was relatively certain that compared to all the others, who knew about things—even Thrull, who knew about this Speaker—she didn't know much about anything, except stories she had read, and in consequence had almost nothing to say.

"Yes, do tell it," Tattersall seconded, more supportively. "We could do with a little diversion, heaven knows. I hope it's a cheerful one."

"The Story of the Young Pucca."

"Pooka?" said Tattersall.

"You know," said Vesica, "a hobgoblin or something. This is the story of a young one, not the old one that has a lot of other names."

"Ah."

"A pucca, see, can change itself into anything it wants to. That's because it's part fairy and part human. The human part sometimes comes out, and then the pucca can walk around and talk and be like everybody else—for a while. But generally the fairy part is in charge, because fairies are smarter than we are, or more powerful or something. And the pucca wanders around playing tricks and stealing things and spying on you.

"Now, the Young Pucca had been a pucca all his life. I mean, his human part had never come out and he had always been just, like, this thing and that thing, and lived in the woods with all the other fairies for a million years. Then one day a human, a girl, walked into the woods where he lived, and the Young Pucca fell in love with the girl as soon as he looked at her."

Thrull groaned. Vesica took a sharp-edged kind of pleasure in knowing that she was annoying him.

"The problem was, the Young Pucca didn't know how to tell the girl he loved her, or even let her know he was there, because all he knew how to be was like a horse or a tree or a hummingbird or whatever, not a human, and he knew if he was any of those things the girl would just look at him and not know. So what he did was, he waited for the girl in the woods, and when he saw her coming he turned himself into a rowan tree—just this *huge* tree full of rose-red flowers, the most beautiful rowan tree in the world. And he knew the girl would see him and smell the flowers and come over to pick one. And she did.

"And when she did, the Young Pucca said to her—because even though he didn't know how to *look* like a human, he could talk like one—he said, 'Hello there, girl.'

"The girl was frightened. But she stayed there anyway, because the voice had been so beautiful, and she said, 'Who's that?' And the Young Pucca said, 'I'm the Spirit of the Woods, and you're the most beautiful girl I've ever seen.'

"Well, the girl, as soon as she heard his voice, she was in love with him. That's how puccas are, too—they can charm you with their voices. But the pucca wasn't trying just to charm the girl. He was really in love with her, and as soon as she heard his voice she was in love with him, too. And she said, 'Come out where I can see you.' But the Young Pucca said, 'I want to but I don't know how. You'll have to help me.' She said, 'How can I do that?' and the Young Pucca didn't know. But he made her promise to come back to the woods the next day, at the same time, and maybe they would think of something.

"The girl came back the next day and every day after that. And each time she'd come, the Young Pucca would try to turn himself into a human. But it didn't work. He turned into a rosebush, and a looney-bird, and a piece of beautiful music, and even a reflection of the moon in a pool of water. But he didn't know how to turn himself into a human, and the girl fell into despair, because she loved him but all she had ever seen of him was his voice. Or heard, I mean. But at least they could talk.

"Then one day the girl got an idea. She thought maybe if she made the Young Pucca some clothes—a shirt and some pants—then he could give himself a body to fit them. You know, instead of the clothes fitting the body, the body . . . So. Anyway, she stayed up all night sewing, and in the morning she fell asleep and slept right through the time she was supposed to go into the forest.

"The Young Pucca was so worried and sad when the girl didn't show up, afraid that she had given up and stopped loving him, that he decided to go into the village and find her. Now, this is another thing about puccas: they can't leave the forest, because their fairy part can't live where there's civilization. So as soon as the Young Pucca came out of the woods, when he was just at the edge of the village, his fairy half fled out of him, and left him with nothing but his human half, which fell down weak and sick beside the road. And some men who were coming into the village saw the Young Pucca lying there with no clothes on—they thought he was just an ordinary boy and some robbers must have taken his clothes away—and they lifted him up and carried him into town and laid him in a bed, but nobody could figure out how to make him well. And the Young Pucca was in a coma, like, or dying, and he couldn't talk.

"Then the girl woke up, and when she ran outside to go to the woods, she heard people talking about the young boy that nobody knew, and how he was lying in this bed dying, and she guessed what had happened. So she took the clothes she had made and ran to the house where they had taken him, and she said, 'Here, put these clothes on him.' They didn't do it right away, of course, because they thought the girl was crazy or something. But after a while they went ahead and tried it, and the boy—who was really the Young Pucca—sat up and he was suddenly well.

"When the girl saw him, she knew he was the handsomest boy in the whole world, and she was twice as much in love with him as before. But he said, 'I can't stay here. I've got to go back to the deep woods where the rowan tree grows, because I can't live with just my human half.' And the girl begged him to stay and marry her, but she knew he couldn't. So she said, 'Then I'll go into the woods with you, and become a fairy.'

"And she did, and they lived there for a million years together.

"And that's the Story of the Young Pucca."

Breathless, Vesica sat back to await her audience's response. The audience sat thoughtful for a few moments; then Lord Tattersall (whom she should have expected to be an expert on fairy stories, had she thought about it) said:

"But that seems rather too easy, doesn't it? I mean to say, all that trouble about turning the boy into a human, but the girl is able to turn into a fairy . . . just like that."

Vesica frowned. To tell the truth, the ending had always bothered her a little.

"But that's the story," she said.

"Well, but," said Tattersall, "maybe the person who told it, originally, didn't really know how it came out. Perhaps the happy young couple were, let us say, lost sight of, after they vanished into the woods. Perhaps the tale doesn't end there at all."

Vesica nodded doubtfully. It had never occurred to her that a story could be anything but what it was; that it could be criticized like something you had made up yourself, or caused to turn out differently.

"And besides," the Governor went on, growing enthusiastic in his critique, "it doesn't shed a great deal of light on our own situation, does it? We're not coming out of the forest, we're going into it. And we don't have any puccas along. At least, I hope not." (He glanced worriedly at Sheldrake; though he did that often anyway.)

"But, it's just a *story*," said Vesica.

"Ah. So it is," said Tattersall, as though he had forgotten this himself.

"It's a *stupid* story," said Thrull. "And it's a lie, like all the rest of them."

On the love seat, Lorian weakly moaned, as though trapped in a story of her own.

The Moon arrived at the meridian. Were time reckoned this way—by the Moon, and not by its larger, slower, less temperate rival—the time at Biggar's Neck would now be midnight precisely. As things stood, it was in fact twenty-three past twelve. The Sun was almost, but not quite, exactly opposite the longitude described by the seven-digit number that marched down the scroll of paper in the cramped and rusty-smelling cabin of the airlorry. The Moon on the other hand was at that longitude precisely. It was a coincidence— the Moon and the airlorry arriving at the same time—that certain types of people would have appreciated, and others not. The faceless captain, an earthy sort of man, was among the would-nots. Which was a pity, since at that hour at Biggar's Neck he was the only one awake to have appreciated it at all, unless there were observers of whose existence we do not know. There is so much we do not know, really; including the reasons why some people are interested in celestial correspondences while others are mainly concerned with avoiding trouble, and paperwork, and with the reward that might be waiting in the city when they return, if, of course, there is a girl among the, shall we say, pilgrims.

The airlorry banked in low across the meadow, its hot rumbling exhaust stirring the moonlit delphiniums; but the captain was not the sort of person to appreciate that, either.

At the forepeak of the airlorry was a jumble of old, intriguing, and mostly misunderstood electrical machines. These little engines reacted, each in its own way, to the nearness of the great metallic body of the transport. Some could barely contain themselves; they registered their reactions on dials and video screens, which the captain ignored. Others, made for different purposes, were unable to comment; they knew the transport only by the induction it caused in their circuitry, like a great magnetic sag.

Meanwhile the transport, the object of this attention, reacted in its own dumb way to the sudden shimmering advent of the airlorry.

It was mostly dead now. Its power-cannon no longer spewed fire across the hill. What energy it retained had been laid in hastily, before Groby dismantled the backup generator that was its source. This energy was shunted into a great bank of capacitors, big as a bathtub, at the base of the matte-black barrel. Had Groby known of this, he might probably have drained it off in one last lavender shot. He had not known, however, because he hadn't looked, and he hadn't looked because he hadn't expected it to be there. His impression of the long-dead designers of the transport (too numerous, too ponderous, too single-minded) had not inclined him to expect this kind of surprise.

The surprise, though, when it arrived, was not for Groby. Groby was asleep in the ghostly manor. As were all the Crusaders, at that hour.

The control mechanisms in the gunner's console, where WILD TURKEY POOL had been taped until a few hours ago, when Vesica removed it, did not require much energy to operate, and their needs were more than supplied by the dribs and drabs of electricity that seeped from the bathtub of capacitors. The power-cannon had all the life it needed, and then some, to detect the approach of the airlorry, to track it along the streambed and through the meadow at the base of the hill, and to rouse the slumbering serpent of energy to STAND-BY from STORE. A red light blinked on the panel where Vesica's hand had rested, and a pair of servo-motors began to creak their oil-encrusted gears. The matte-black barrel swung southeastward, the direction of the nightblack, ageless, almost magical city—from which the airlorry came throbbing up the transport's wake.

Then the serpent of energy uncoiled, and the power-cannon shuddered in a final ejaculation.

The airlorry became a spectacular low-hanging sun, running down the spectrum from blue to mauve to scarlet to orange and at last to smoky yellow, as it sank beneath the delphiniums. A frightful show: but with the faceless captain dead, there were only squirrels, and the Moon, to watch it.

Vesica sat up in the darkness of a baby's lavender-papered bedroom. Something—a sound just fading—echoed in her ears. It might have been laughter, or someone shouting. Vesica strained her attention, but the manor was quiet.

: almost quiet: there were watery sounds of air sliding through the endless chambers, and somewhere the shivery warble of a bird.

Something turned over in her mind. A dream, imperfectly remembered. With a bird in it: or no. It might have been a person.

It was Vesica. She had worn feathered earrings, and the earrings, no, the feathers, had grown like a bird's to cover her. The wings that formed at her shoulder blades took her soaring into the sky, until she could look down and see the alder tree at Gravetye Farm she had once climbed all the way to the top of. The tree was in trouble and was calling to her for help, but when she swooped closer she saw that it wasn't the tree that was calling at all, but a boy stuck in its upper branches, held there by two great limbs that embraced him with a relentless passion that made Vesica tremble. The boy's eyes were wide and imploring, the color of the sky, and his imprisoned arms reached out to touch her, but at the last minute Vesica became frightened and swerved away, spinning downward through the branches of the alder, which changed to become a thorntree and then an oak, an ancient oak, and she spun through it lower and lower until her muscles contracted with a jerk and she sat up in the darkness of the abandoned manor, feeling her heart pound and her breath come hot and fast from her naked chest under the bedclothes.

The waning Moon gazed through twined branches that covered the windows. Across the lavender wallpaper danced make-believe rabbits and squirrels.

It took her several moments to understand that she was all alone, that there were no animals or puccas or wide-eyed boys there in the silent chamber, that she should try to sleep again. She did try, finally, but was still half awake, her skin glistening with perspiration, when the Moon set and the Sun appeared above the bulging delphiniums. Vesica felt very odd, dislocated, as though she were rapidly and without much intending to, growing up.

Thirteen

❧

THE SUN WAS blowing up.
Its fiery essence spewed out into a vast and hungry void.
Eventually this would kill it. It would roll at its stately pace
down the nearly linear curve by which learned astrologers
described its destiny. Toward the end, the curve would slope
downward sharply. The aging Sun would become inconti-
nent. Its thermonuclear heart would begin to fail. It would
grow faint and dull and, finally, dark. This was called Evolution: a long slide into silence.

When Vesica awoke in the glass-walled manor, however, the Sun was still alive. Alive and unruly. Scornful, like
a monarch, of the expectations of lesser souls.

Thought to be round, the Sun was markedly oblate. Its
supply of light, which seemed so steady, so assured, was in
fact the product of violent and unpredictable explosions,
some of which, volcanic, welled up from its gut to vomit
their new-minted elements into the emptiness. Perpetually
disturbed, the Sun wobbled on its axis and altered its shape.
It vented deadly emissions. It disrupted the operation of
cells, faded expensive fabrics, garbled airfax transmissions,
and freckled fourteen-year-old skin.

But to all of this, even its own dying, the Sun was
indifferent.

Majestic, awful, radiant, it stared everywhere like an evil eye.

Learned astrologers knew the Sun as the Father of Chaos. By whose sole dispensation, conditionally given, Order was sometimes (but briefly, precariously) possible.

People worshiped it, and they were right to.

"What are you doing?" demanded Tattersall, rapping on a countertop.

Sheldrake failed to answer. What he appeared to be doing was braiding a fistful of limp, semidessicated leaves around a twig. The rest of the Crusade—minus Lorian, who was awake but had not yet summoned the strength to come down from the sitting room—regarded him over a breakfast counter. Sheldrake inspected his work, apparently for tightness, then turned to play it over the stove. The leaves emitted smoke in an acrid, yellowish plume. Tattersall, as Crusade Leader, leaned forward to sample this, then turned away, his lordly nose upwrinkled. He said:

"Well, whatever it is, I hope you're done with it soon. We're leaving here, you know." He glanced down the counter. "That is to say . . . aren't we?"

Groby looked up from his bucket of barley stew. "That's right, your lordship. The battery's charging right now."

"Ah." Tattersall nodded as though this answered somebody's question, no doubt, but not his.

"Then," Groby went on, riding a slow but dependable train of thought, "I'll hook it up to the cart, and somebody can wake Lorian, and somebody else can help me load the supplies on—"

"I'll do that," said Vesica, her words fitting easily into his comma.

"—and then we'll be set to go."

Sheldrake crossed the kitchen to stand, Vesica thought, provokingly close to Tattersall's stool. Declining to actually sit on this (which would have made him too tall to eat) the Governor was using the stool as a kind of pivot, leaning heavily against it while he turned now this way and now that: eastward to gaze across the plush croquet lawn, north-ward into the manor—but no Lorian yet—westward along the row of open cabinets, their contents plundered and ready for Groby's cart, and now southward, at the sunny expanse of tile where Sheldrake had commenced a hip-hopping dance. The ludicrous character of his movements was matched by this singsong doggerel:

> "Oakwood, rue, and betony,
> Keep the fiends away from me.
> Boldo leaves and ague root,
> Kick the Devil's brown patoot."

Vesica, watching this, was torn. For though this was perfectly ridiculous, the sort of thing you entertain small children with, at the same time it was delightful. A grown man making a fool of himself. The sunlight seemed to dance along with Sheldrake, sparkling in his small rodentine eyes. Compromising, Vesica allowed herself a quiet chuckle.

Sheldrake spun around.

"Don't laugh!" he admonished. "You'll encourage them!"

"Encourage who?" said Tattersall. "What in heaven's name are you doing?"

Sheldrake resumed his purgative dance.

> "Black cohosh and sandalwood,
> All your tricks are foiled for good.
> Smudge-stick foul and smudge-stick black,
> Keep the Devil—"

"Good *heavens*," Lord Tattersall exclaimed.

Sheldrake gave him a look of nasty satisfaction, but the Governor had forgotten him.

In the kitchen doorway stood a gaunt, diminished-looking Lorian. She wore a bathrobe, monogrammed with an immense purple T, the sleeves of which were rolled to the elbows, laying bare the welts on her forearms.

"Are we," she said, in a voice little better than a croak, "going somewhere?"

Tattersall crossed the room in a motion so fluid and so perfectly reflexive as to be almost invisible. He took the short-haired woman by an arm, then by both arms, sliding his own around her shoulders.

"I'm fine," she said, making a noble effort to shake him

off. Tattersall guided her firmly to his breakfast stool. Sliding onto it, she scowled—a more convincing gesture, this—at Sheldrake, who had halted in midhop. "*He's* the one," she said, "that *I'd* be worried about."

Vesica thought how hard it would be not to admire her. Sheldrake, with a wounded look, took up his ritual again.

> "Elm and asafœtida,
> Begone or you'll regret it-a . . ."

"Yes," said Groby—typically, two sentences too late—"as soon as all our provisions are loaded, we're going into the forest. By foot. It'll be slower that way, but there's some kind of tree that Sheldrake thinks will make you better."

Lorian looked at him, then at Sheldrake again. In her expression mingled cynicism, weariness, and hope. Sheldrake solemnly nodded.

"Well, you won't get far!" burst out Thrull. The sallow youth leapt down from his stool as though he had taken quite enough of this. (And taken also, Vesica noted, quite enough of barley stew.) "They'll get you before you're even into the woods!"

He left the kitchen in a state that seemed to Vesica too tame, too controlled, for genuine rage. He's up to something, she thought. "I guess," she said, getting up also, "I'll start loading up the cart."

"Remember to save room," said Sheldrake, "for *her*."

"I remember," said Vesica, going out—and leaving Lorian to wonder whether they were serious or not, and if so, room for her in what?

Thrull crossed the terrace and ducked—furtively, Vesica was sure—into the small jungle of gooseberries that encroached upon the flagstones. She tried to follow him, but several things, a conspiracy of circumstances, interrupted her.

In the first place, there was her reflection in the lily pool. She caught just a glimpse of this as she cut the corner, hoping to gain a few steps, and that briefest of glimpses brought her to a halt. But when she looked again—leaning out as far as she dared over the dark still water—the thing she thought she had seen wasn't there, and she felt extremely childish. What, after all, would the *moon* have been doing, reflected there at nine o'clock in the morning? Because even if the moon was out, which it wasn't because it was just past full, and . . . but even then, you wouldn't have been able to see it, because of the sun.

Which brought her to the second place.

Which wasn't the sun. But in looking up at it, to reassure herself, Vesica saw a great bird, a broad-winged predator, circling slowly, with no air of menace but rather as a sentry strolls the parapet, expecting no evil but prepared for it, and Vesica wondered if this wasn't one of the birds she had seen yesterday afternoon through the algae-green window of the manor, reduced by distance to a fledgling, patrolling the sky. But had no time to wonder what the bird was doing *here* before the third circumstance arose.

Thrull shouted, "It's gone!"

His voice came out muffled by gooseberries. Again: "It's gone! It isn't here!"

"What's gone?" she shouted back crossly.

Thrull's eyes were wide and panicky when he emerged scraped red by branches to stand before her on the flag-stones. A stalk of wand-flower, wagging in the breeze, swung over and hit him in the face. He slapped it angrily, cutting his hand on its papery edge. He wailed:

"Somebody *took* it!"

Vesica turned up the corner of a lip, as pleased to see him so discomfited as she was annoyed by his immaturity. "Well, whatever it is," she said, "you probably had no business having it in the first place."

He glared at her and stomped at the flagstones, which brought her to the fourth place, but by now she was no longer counting.

"Look at this," she said, bending down to pick up a tiny, gray-leafed sapling that Thrull's stomping had uprooted. She rolled its stem between her fingers. It smelled peculiar. She said, "It's just like the ones on the Blistered Moor."

"So what?" Thrull was without hope now, too unhappy even to ignore her.

"So . . . it just is, that's all. Look, here's another one."

The terrace, actually, was dotted with them, popping up through all the cracks, even cracks much too small to have admitted an acorn. Which was odd because she hadn't noticed any saplings yesterday, when she and Tattersall had come and gone again and then come back: three trips, and she hadn't noticed. But what did *that* mean? Only that she hadn't been looking, probably; but then she saw another thing odd. The saplings, the little not-quite-oaks, which she was stubbing gently with her toes as she walked between them, weren't really *everywhere* on the terrace, no, but only, like, along *here*, making a line toward the doorway. And they moved in this same line in the other direction, over toward the deckchair where Tattersall had slumped, where there was a whole big clump of them, and then the line turned and moved off into the tennis grass, so by now the whole thing had gotten pretty mysterious.

"Where are they going?" Vesica wondered out loud, when the more obvious question would have been How did they get there? Which made her wonder—later, when there would be plenty of time to think about it—if maybe she hadn't caught on to it right away, and only had to think out all the steps.

But all the steps were easy. Following the line of not-quite-oak trees. Because they were the same steps she had taken yesterday. Twice. From the manor and back, with Tattersall, after finding the pool, and taking her clothes off, and meeting the squirrel, and picking up her lemon ramie blouse which was covered with tiny black specks. Which she had changed out of after she tried, the whole way back to the transport and then to the manor again, to brush the specks off. Without success. And along this same line, across the tennis grass and through the clover and down to the flower-mad meadow again, there were all these tiny trees.

"NO!" shrieked Thrull, behind her, up on the hill, as though a monster had gotten hold of him.

"NO! PLEASE, IT CAN'T BE!"

But it was, or must have been, though Vesica couldn't see it, because she was engaged in a fifth circumstance—Thrull's shriek making the sixth—and barely heard him.

"The trees," she murmured—

—beside the mown-down wake of the transport, were taller, thicker, more ominous than they had been only yesterday. Misshapen redwoods, she had thought, but now it was clear they were really something different, something more twisted and scaly and frightening to behold.

"Oh, we're doomed," sobbed Thrull. "That was our last chance, and now it's gone, and I can't even find the airfax machine."

He came down the hill so limply that, though his feet stayed beneath him, he seemed to tumble. He stopped at Vesica's side, forgetting for the moment that he despised her, recognizing only that she was another person, a comrade, with whom his terrible fate was to be shared whether he liked it or not, and just then in the flower-mad meadow, beneath the wreck of the airlorry, its oily electric stench still in his nose, the new experience of in-this-together was a strong and surprising one.

"Be quiet," she said. "I'm trying to see."

"See what?" he said.

She pointed:

: but that was impossible

: at the hundred colors as bright as jewels that glowed at the top of the tallest trees.

"It looks," said Thrull, wiping his nose, "like orchids."

Which was either the seventh circumstance or maybe the eighth, depending on whether you count the extraordinary strangeness of Thrull's having any idea what an orchid looked like. Though yes, that's exactly what Vesica had been thinking. Two hundred feet overhead, gleaming in the still-sparse canopy, a thousand orchids refracted the sunlight and fluttered in the restless air.

"This must be it, then," she whispered.

It, it came out. And before Thrull could ask what, she said:

"The forest. We must have come to it already."

Or, the thought imposed itself, *it must have come to us*.

"But, um . . ." said Thrull, and of course there were objections, but not even that heartless youth could bring himself to raise them.

"Let's go back," she said, "and tell the others."

Taking, after a moment's hesitation, the young man's arm, she led him along the line of saplings, following once again her own footsteps,

while overhead the hundred-colored orchids glistened

like glass,
and still higher the advance guard of eagles patrolled the sky,
and higher than anything in the world the Sun stared
down
majestic, awful and radiant
like an evil eye
at the forest,
              the last great forest
                  in the world.

Springs

In the garden of God are regions of darkness,
waste heaths and wan waters, gulfs of mystery,
where the beleaguered soul may wander aghast.
— RANDOLPH STOW

Sorbus aucuparia
Rowan tree

Conspicuous blood-red fruits of dubious value.
Its pale wood is the material of choice
for magic wands.

Fourteen

AN APRIL WAS going on, according to habit. What winter had kept warm was waking. What it had frozen thawed. And what it had killed (for winter had been, as winters are, destructive) rose again . . . just possibly. We will leave that to learned astrologers.

But April was going on. Breeding lilacs, stirring dull roots, and all that. Mixing memory and desire. Growing branches out of the stony rubbish of an ageless, dreamlike, but all-too-real city. And so feeding a little life to Lady Widdershins, who this April began her fifteenth year as Chairperson of the Hardy Plant Society. And who, also according to habit, organized teams of volunteers to set out annuals in the crater beds, burnt-out vehicles and empty ammunition casks that lay along the Aleatory Strand, from the Observatory down to Faerie Sump. For one must take what solace one can from the arrival of yet another April. From the unbroken life-renewing habit of spring. And from the companionship of so many of one's well-meaning and good-hearted though God knows generally wrongheaded fellow men. And a few of one's fellow women too; though these mostly had the sense to stay indoors till the rains stopped. (But how one missed, even now, after fourteen springs, the magnificent solitude, the purer pleasures of one's lovely, often thought-of but sadly long-abandoned manor!)

From the upstairs sitting room of Marshmain, her grand but, all things considered, less than satisfactory in-town home, Lady Widdershins watched as Faerie Sump climbed its mudslick banks to lap along the Strand, flood out basements and alleyways through the old brick warrens, and submerge, by midmonth, her ladyship's Lower Garden. Which, as far as she was concerned, was all to the good, because when the waters receded they would leave behind a fine and nutritive silt that would work wonders for her peonies, two months hence, and in general turn everything that was now brown the most sparkling emerald green, and besides, no one had any business living in that rat's nest across the Sump anyway, which attracted the wrong element and spoiled her ladyship's view.

But if all this—these habit-bred banalities—embodied the April of the Chairperson, then it must have been another April entirely that was in progress for the Dean of the Secret College. Professor Tylyester did not especially care for green, on the whole preferring brown, or at any rate the comforting shade of alabaster cast on old paper by a warm-white electric bulb. He preferred his plants in monographs, with crisp laser-etched cross-sections of critical parts, sex organs and the like, neatly labeled in india ink. Moreover, as a founding member of the Silent Partners' Club, the Professor frequented at least fortnightly the old brick warrens around the Sump, where the Club paid taxes on a small rat's nest of rooms. And most importantly (though the full meaning of this was none too clear, even to Tylyester), this April, his April, was *not* the same as all the others.

After all, the First Biotic Crusade was afield. Against the potent attack of the forest, Society had at last marshaled a vigorous defense. And he, Tylyester, had conceived it. Had drawn on all the knowledge accreted during a long scholarly lifetime. Had trained the Crusade like a sword—or better, like a questing ink-quill, thrusting it blindly, plunging it down into that well of knowledge that must, Tylyester *knew* must be waiting there—and aimed it (the Crusade not the inkwell) at the legendary research station at Balance Act, a site that had defeated generations of determined, career-minded archaeologists. Which was why, in the end, the Dean had not chosen an archaeologist to lead the expedition. But had instead, after plumbing his memory—all the most cobwebbed corners—selected his old friend Tatty. Whose mental lights may not have been the brightest (heaven knew), but who, more than anyone the Dean had ever known, was possessed, even obsessed, by Obligation. To friends, to duty, to family honor: to anything and anyone, it seemed to Tylyester, that one could plant in his head. But especially to the Preservation of Things As They Are, which is how Tylyester had put it to him. While promising a liberal honorarium. And now, in this April unlike other Aprils, the Crusade was afield.

Pleased with himself, yet unaccountably apprehensive, Tylyester canceled his lectures for the remainder of the term and secluded himself behind the doors of his black-porticoed townhouse to ready the final, the definitive draft of his compendious and nearly complete NOTES TOWARD A CRITIQUE OF HAYATA'S COMMENTARY ON THE "ORGANIZING PRINCIPLE" OF GENETIC TRANSPOSITION, WITH EMPHASIS ON THE HISTORICAL AND BIOGRAPHICAL CONTEXT AND HER EFFORT TO END THE CRISIS OF INDETERMINISM. Which task he pursued with a warm (though, as he liked to think, objective, purely objective) passion, suffering only the fortnightly interruption of dinner in the Deep Game Room at the Club.

While the Dean was thus secluded, his faculty of learned astrologers staged a cookout on the catwalk of the Observatory, celebrating the New Age which they were agreed, after their last department meeting, was about to arrive. They announced this, in a carefully phrased invitation, as a Mysterium Coniuntivus, which they were fairly certain would ensure that only like-minded individuals would attend, and were thus surprised when several members of the Psychology Department showed up. Fortunately these bespectacled gentlemen brought an interesting green beverage, and the party turned out quite lively. Those astrologers who, a few days before, had interpreted the rare celestial confluence as portending a Stunning Metamorphosis had good reason (for a few hours at least) to feel vindicated; while the End of the World crowd were privately thankful they had kept their apartments in the city.

Only a sniffling graduate student, hired for the night to tend bar, happened to glance at a bank of sensitive though seldom used equipment in the darkest part of the Observatory, where xanthée mugs were stored, and noticed the odd goings-on being registered in the lower atmosphere. Across an arc that corresponded roughly with the northern mountains, an unusual pattern of electrical activity was in progress. An evanescent dance, like heat lightning, though it was the wrong time of year for that. The shimmery display seemed to originate at ground-level, dissipating outward into the æther, as though a very rapid discharge of stored-up energy were taking place.

It was like nothing the graduate student had ever seen before. Indeed, it ran against the major currents of astrological thought. That it had been detected at all was surprising, for the Observatory's equipment was not attuned to the vibratory characteristics of earthly phenomena. The graduate student paused to blow his nose and wonder whether he ought to bring this . . . anomaly . . . to someone's attention.

He repocketed his handkerchief. He decided instead to bring out more xanthée mugs, replacing those that at a very rapid rate were being dropped from the catwalk into the crowd of young people assembled in the street below. The Pure Force, he supposed. The learned professors exclaimed, shook hands, and passed money back and forth whenever one of the errant mugs struck someone's head. The sums exchanged were larger if a mug struck but failed to shatter. One of the psychologists appeared to be keeping score. All in all, the graduate student thought, a typical bit of academic fieldwork.

All too typical, the Pure Force might have thought. The ancient enemies of Science (few of them more than twenty years old) gathered in the street that bisected the Secret College for the rite they called Evening Knowledge. Tonight it would be conducted by the Speaker himself: not his hologhost, nor his circle of disciples, nor his several impersonators—the last of whom were often employed by one or another politician to whip up the Force in favor of some cause, in hopes that this would rally popular opinion against it. Which it generally did; not that popular opinion had much occasion to express itself. The last general ballot had been several years ago, before the Ecological Emergency was declared, though one still heard of elections in the outlying districts.

Larger and younger and livelier crowds had been turning out for Evening Knowledge this April, this very different April—logically enough, since the weather was improving, and the full moon made the dark city streets less intimidating; though there might have been some other factor at work, some immanence that certain members of the Pure Force might have sensed. And not they alone: also gardeners out late turning the soil; and farmers from the North, displaced now, from long habit watching the sky; and poets roaming the streets looking for parties; and plumbers letting their hands hang down in aqueducts running cold with the spring melt. Any one of these might have felt some new flow of energy, something almost but not quite physical, a subtle current entering and leaving the world's spine.

"Sit down," said the Speaker, and they obeyed him, even those too far away to hear.

"Try to feel it," he told them. And they tried, even those who didn't know what he was talking about.

"Let the Presence come near."

One would have known him—if one had been there at Deeping Lube the night the Crusade left, and also here at Evening Knowledge—by the intense radiance of his brow. Otherwise he was an inconspicuous young man, a boy for practical purposes, slimmer and shorter than his hologhost, though his shoulders were disproportionately wide.

"It is beginning," he said, and all his followers listened silently, which was necessary because his voice was very quiet—

"The Noosphere is aroused."

—and yet it carried. Amplified, as it were, by the five-hundred-year tradition out of which it spoke. Half a millennium of steadfast, earnest, unwavering, and periodically violent opposition to all forms of scientific inquiry, and most particularly to those disciplines (less numerous than the partygoers in the Observatory liked to think) which threatened actually to succeed in learning anything. For it was Knowledge, and not its poor cupbearer Science, against which the Pure Force had long ago taken up arms. And contrary to the general consensus, the Force held the view that after a long and bitter contest, it was winning. Winning, indeed, overwhelmingly.

The Speaker said: "Open your lower chakras." And those few of his followers sufficiently schooled to comply—especially the teenage boys—felt a lively welling-up of awareness.

In each phase of its long struggle, the Force had chosen the weapons most appropriate and most readily at hand. Though yes: in five hundred years it had known its share of disappointments.

Old sciences had been obliterated, only to be replaced by newer (but weaker, always weaker) ones.

And the Secret College: so named for historical reasons only. Though the Force still vandalized its buildings and agitated among its students, the days were past when secrecy was a condition of the College's very survival; when its professors were forced to study alone; when its library was dispersed among a thousand cellars in the understory of the city.

And yet—how much Knowledge was lost! How many classrooms and laboratories and far-off research stations destroyed! How many books and disks and monographs turned to ashes! And of those remaining, how few were understood, and by what ineffectual pedants!

If the professors, partying in their poisoned tower, liked to think of the Force as a pack of young know-nothings, acting out some collective rite of adolescence . . . then let them think it. Let the thought comfort them in their perplexity.

Or, as the Speaker said, in a final version of April:

Let Truth remain forever behind her veil.

Let Science lose itself in a labyrinth of hypotheses.

Let the First Biotic Crusade vanish in the forest.

Let the Mother of Habits diminish in the sky.

Let the Father of Chaos roar from his seat in the heavens.

Let the Blank Card lie unturned
upon the table.

Fifteen

❧

NOT TO PROCEED DIRECT-
ly, following Groby's map with the help of a compass sal-
vaged from the transport, Lord Tattersall directed that the
Crusade should follow the streambed that meandered vaguely
west-northwest before turning decisively north, making for
the Falls, transecting the mountains, and seeking its source
near the legendary settlement of Balance Act. Perhaps he felt
in an odd way (though not so odd as to be unfamiliar to any
of us) comforted by the nearness of water. Probably he
distrusted anything mechanical, with good reason by now.
Privately he may have held to the notion that if Sheldrake's
worst forebodings proved out, they could build a raft—this
raft idea having somehow taken hold in him—and drift, if it
came to *that*, downcurrent to Deeping Lube. But whatever his
reasoning, which he did not announce, the Governor set
forth from Biggar's Neck with provisions and an incapaci-
tated Crusader loaded onto a bike-wheeled top-heavy-looking
cart that his Master Field Engineer had constructed, and
began moving at the rate of between seven and twelve miles
a day through the Carbon Bank Forest.

Vesica walked next to the cart, where she could talk to
Lorian and to Groby, whose constant attention was needed
to keep its small sun-powered engine humming like some-

thing going on in a beehive. Of them, Lorian was the more responsive, as Groby spent much of his time tinkering, or otherwise engaged in large thought.

"I wish they'd let me walk," she complained. "Look, my arm's all better now, the red marks are fading, and really, I feel good enough to . . ." She dozed off almost invariably in the middle of sentences like this. Nonetheless Vesica took the case forward, twenty feet or so, to Lord Tattersall.

"I think Lorian's getting better," she said, with a side glance at Sheldrake. (This mannerism of the Governor's was hard, really, not to copy.) The ex-tree pollard, now as one imagined in his element, stalked the woods ahead of the rest of the Crusade, choosing a path as near the stream as it pleased him to go, in accord with some unspecified instinct for the terrain rather than, as Tattersall repeatedly requested, a view to where the cart would fit.

"Ha!" he cried, out of sight in a choke of brambles. "She's not getting *well*, though, is she? The symptoms are just getting harder to see, is all."

He stuck his head out. Round and overlarge like a baby's, Vesica thought, as she always thought, without attention anymore. The Crusaders had been together long enough that their association was a matter of habit. Sheldrake said darkly:

"It's not on her skin anymore. *It's gotten inside of her.*"

"Pish-tosh," said Tattersall. "Look out where you're going, now. You'll have us all tangled up if you aren't more careful."

By this time Groby with the cart and Lorian had caught up, and they were off again, Thrull remaining an indeterminate distance behind the body of the expedition—far enough to be safe from routine chores like shoring up the luggage, though never out of hearing of the dinner bell.

It struck Vesica as they really got into the forest, past the disorganized places where it was like at Biggar's Neck, with trees just popping up between the weeds and flowers—it struck her then that you could only be *in* a forest, not *at* it like a place on a map, or *on* it like a farm. You went into it like you were this little animal, this ground-creature, crawling along, and the forest just swallowed you. And then you were part of it, just another part of this great huge forest itself.

Because the forest wasn't just trees, once you got inside it. Though the trees were there, of course. They swelled up out of the ground as wide as silos, unbelievably tall, like pillars holding up the sky. But also they grew down, their roots embracing deep in the darkness, hugging the world together like the yarns of a fat brown blanket. And between the one and the other—the root tips where small things burrowed in the dirt, and the treetops where orchids fluttered and eagles made their nests between the clouds—all the million million things that lived and died were part of the forest, just by being inside it, and the forest was somehow, too, part of them. It *was* them, really. Not just trees. So when Sheldrake said, about Lorian, *it's gotten inside of her*, maybe that's what he was talking about. Vesica didn't know.

But she wanted to.

But one thing, at least, she did.

She knew that the Carbon Bank Forest was beautiful.

From outside—from the cupola of the transport, say, listening to Sheldrake, or from the gazebo at Gravetye Farm, seeing the forest like a purple quilt lumped up at the feet of the mountains—she would never have expected it. Back then, the forest had been a great and horrid mystery. The Enemy of Civilization. And of course it was an enemy still; and Vesica was a Crusader. But now the great mystery had splintered into a hundred smaller ones—like the eagles, flying surveillance in the sky—that were more unsettling, yet also more appealing, than the purple quilt had been. They had that beguiling strangeness, like the mood you're in after a fairy tale, that leaves you thinking, dreaming, wondering, long past the happy-ever-after. And *that's* how the forest was beautiful. That strangeness.

The treetops bright with orchids.

Water-sounds, like distant music; and the reedy percussion of moving branches.

Air that smelled of fermenting leaves and rain.

And sunlight. Scarcely penetrating the cloud-thatched roof. And where it did, spilling like a cataract down wooden walls, or splashing on boughs that extended, like eaves, to intercept it.

And then, of course, the Crusaders. For they were part of it too. Six small organisms, short-lived and trifling when seen against the forest as a whole, they added minutely to its bank of carbon, its store of organic molecules, its reservoir of genes.

They did not see themselves that way. Their discrete awarenesses were full of other ideas: historic quests, five-hundred-year-old struggles, the Preservation of Things As They Are. And smaller things, too: headaches, hunger, callused feet, and curative herbs; the color one would paint one's bedroom; the fear of one's stepfather; the trouble with a makeshift cart. No, these six beings did not see themselves as a pack of animals, did not see their Crusade as an extension of the tribal foraging behavior that had been part of the survival strategy of their species for a million years. The fact that they *were* conscious beings, they thought, made them unique, and uniquely important.

Into the great slow rhythms of the forest these six creatures entered like a snatch of some bright and noisy melody— the sort of thing that enters your mind when you're not quite sleeping, gets caught and lingers there, reminding you of music once loved but now old and gone and, you had thought, forgotten. Such melodies are said to be infectious. They live inside you, vigorous and possibly inimical invaders. Eventually you realize you are not asleep any longer; you are hearing endless choruses of a song no one has played for quite some time now. You shift beneath your fat brown blanket, trying to remember where you heard it last. Some part of you recalls the lyrics, wants to sing along; the rest of you wants to go back to sleep. But the song has infected you.

You grow restless, eventually. You stir.

In the deeper woods, a week beyond Biggar's Neck, oak became predominant, replacing the birch and hickory and ash of the broken prairie. The trees here were older members, it seemed, of the same hard-to-identify species that sprang from the cracks at Biggar's Neck and shattered the hardpan of the Moor. Here they grew so large and so close together that in places Groby had to disassemble the cart and carry it piece by piece, Lorian leaning on his arm, between them. You would not have thought the earth could have supported so many. It buckled between them like a cloth over bulging muscles. There were no rowan trees, yet. Only oaks, and vines, and fragrant ground-cover; on random hillocks, last stands of dark-needled spruce; and bent beside the stream, a clutch of thorntrees. No paths wound between them anymore, and there seemed little chance of blazing one. Sheldrake made a few passes with a heatsaw, but the oak bark showed the same defensive talents that Groby had admired back in the meadow. Sheldrake gave up when Lord Tattersall remarked that the heatsaw was really, supposing they should need one, their only weapon.

Would they need one, really, though? It seemed to Vesica that since they entered the forest, she had felt nothing like a sense of danger. And they didn't need a weapon, surely, to eat. On the contrary, Sheldrake, by dint of daily foraging for herbs and roots and berries, was turning them all into vegetarians.

"We didn't have time," said the little man, reminiscing while he worked, "to go trotting back to the main house every time we got hungry."

Vesica smiled: the tree pollard coming out. And Sheldrake pleased with it.

Prairie turnip, she learned, could be recognized by its early cobalt-blue blossoms, dug up, and its tubers pounded into a starchy flour that tasted nutty and was allegedly nutritious.

Sego lilies, another staple, were something like potatoes; but so also were girasols and bush morning-glory roots, and really, the three had nothing in common. Vesica guessed that *potato* was what your mind came up with when it couldn't find another comparison—the way it reaches for *chicken* when you're trying to describe the taste of frog's legs.

They ate soups of fritillary, bearberry and yarrow. They stocked, as seasonings, spiderwort (tart and salty) and native ginger (pungent and sweet). And as a breakfast gruel of choice, Sheldrake's allegiance transferred easily from barley to wafer-parsnip, whose grainy roots he baked, ground, and boiled to a watery mush that, to Vesica's surprise, was nearly delicious.

After two weeks in the woods she found she did not miss eating meat, did not miss home, regular bathing, laundered bedclothes, or the comforting rhythms of farmlife. There were campfires in the evening now; stunning scenery; Sheldrake's tales of monsters and magic springs hidden in the woods; Groby's benign lumbering presence; Lorian to help in small ways, as her strength ebbed and flooded like an unpredictable humor; Tattersall to worry about; Thrull to despise; new food; new ideas; even—packed off from the manor— new clothes! (These were flamboyant, loud-colored things, too large at the bust and hips but exhilarating to go about in. She had packed off some of the baby clothes, too, finding it too sad to leave them, but kept those to herself.)

Nor did the others, mostly, seem to mind the privations of the journey. It was what a Crusade was all about, wasn't it? Tattersall said it was. Only Thrull objected to the dirt and their new diet—though not enough to bathe in the icy stream, or go squirrel-hunting.

"They move too fast up here," he complained. "The other one just *stood* there."

So Sheldrake kept them filled with his concoctions and they all lost a couple of pounds and Vesica, for one, felt wonderful.

Then things changed.

Things changed. A condition of life, they say.

In the space between the long twilight of morning and the slow-moving shadows of afternoon, something happened to the world around them. The sounds of animals receded through the underbrush, remaining audible, but distant. A new sharpness in the landscape forced them farther from the stream, onto ground that was rubbled from the last passage of the glaciers. And:

"There's something the matter with the engine," said Groby, in a voice empty of inflection.

He looked up from his inspection of the sun-powered cart, and the other Crusaders looked back at him. It was impossible to tell if he was worried. Come to think of it, it was hard to tell if Groby *ever* worried. Or if life and all its imponderables were just, to him, like problems in engineering, which you thought about when you had time, and tinkered at, but always put aside for dinner, and left off completely when it got too dark to work.

"Well . . ." said Tattersall, letting the syllable drift out into the silence. "I suppose we could camp here, then, couldn't we? While we're still a short walk from the stream . . ."

". . . it might take a while," Groby was saying, though whether in reference to the stream or the engine or the Crusade in general was uncertain. He stood beside the cart with two wrenches crossed between his fingers, like the hierophant of some grotesque or comic ritual.

Vesica helped Lorian to her feet.

"I had another dream," the short-haired woman said sleepily.

"Ha," said Sheldrake—seeming to imply that this confirmed his most dreadful suspicions.

"There were green . . . I don't know: *twisty* things. Snakes maybe, or something. But they were down in the ground, though. I'm not making this up."

Sheldrake hadn't said she was, but just the same shook his overlarge head. Lorian allowed Vesica to lead her to a corner of the fate-chosen camp, where they were partly hidden by an upthrusting granite spur. Vesica dipped into her knapsack for something to serve as a cushion. Her hand brushed a baby blanket, whose cotton nap she caressed with an odd sense of deprivation, of long-forgotten despair. "So, go on," she said.

"Hm?" said Lorian, straightening into a posture of alertness. She looked around. "What were we talking about?"

And right away without knowing why, Vesica said:

"Amy Hayata."

Lorian sighed. "Poor Amy," she said. "Why were we talking about her?"

Vesica shrugged. At some point she was going to cross the fuzzy frontier and be out-and-out lying. "I just wanted to know."

Lorian looked at her then. *Looked* at her: city woman to country girl. And Vesica got the message. That this wanting-to-know business was really asking for trouble.

"Well, sure," said the journalist, after a moment or so. "Although I haven't got the story straight, myself. Or not all of it. But what did you want to know?"

Vesica shrugged. Unknown territory, here. But Lorian, now awake, was a willing talker. There was experience waiting to be had. (And if this implied innocence lost, Vesica did not think of that.) She said, "I don't know. Um, what was she doing up there? Or up here. And whatever happened to her?"

"What happened," said Lorian carefully—journalistic habit showing—"no one really, I think, knows. But there was a visitor, a mail-carrier or something, who visited the research station two, or no, three years I think, after the date of the last draft of her paper. And when he got back he said that the place was in ruins. Not just empty. But like something terrible had happened—an attack or something. Professor Tylyester thinks that means that Amy must have been . . ."

"Dead?"

Lorian gave her the look again. "Well, but. Not *just*. Don't they teach you history in the North?"

To explain that no one had taught her anything—deliberately, at least—would have been too complicated. Vesica simply shook her head.

"Well"—Lorian shrugged—"things were pretty horrible back then. Especially for scientists."

"They deserved it," said Thrull, who had settled not quite near them but near enough. He did not look up, however, from what appeared to be an examination of his toenails.

Lorian took a breath, started over: "But what she was doing. That's understood a little more clearly. —Does anyone hear music? Like whistling? Or maybe a flute?"

"Birds do that," suggested Thrull, with feeble irony.

"Thanks for letting us know," Vesica told him. She looked at Lorian. "No—I don't."

The woman sighed. "The fever coming back, I guess. But what Amy was doing had basically to do with what's the matter with the forest now. You know, what makes it act like it's out of control and so forth."

"I understand that," said Vesica, partly out of self-consciousness, because Thrull's presence at her back made her anxious not to seem childish.

"Do you?" said Lorian, sounding weary. "I'm not sure I do anymore. It was something to do with order versus chaos, or rather randomness, that she disagreed with most of her colleagues about, except for a few people who were mostly dead."

Well, in that case, Vesica didn't understand either. She kept silent.

"So, Amy came up here when she was still a young woman—I'd say late twenties or thereabouts—so that she could do her research with just a few other biologists for company, and no one telling her what to do, and no one throwing bombs through her window"—a glance at Thrull—"and started working on this paper that she kept rewriting for the rest of her life."

Back on familiar ground now, Vesica said, "How long was that?"

"What?"

"The rest of her life."

"Oh. I don't . . . no one knows. Ten years or so? Probably less. The basic idea seems to have just, like, *come* to her, so the first draft went pretty fast. It was the details, the data, that took time. Getting her evidence together. Because she knew she was right, from the very beginning, but the problem was how to convince her colleagues. It had to all be written out very clearly and circulated around, and in Amy's case there was the problem of telling a lot of people that they were wrong and she was right, when they all had probably better things to think about anyway."

"Like what?"

Lorian frowned. "Like, the world was coming to an end, they thought, because of everything people had done to it. The only forest on the continent was dying back, and the farms were turning into dustbowls—"

"Dying back?" said Vesica. "The only forest was . . . did you say dying?"

Thrull leaned over in their direction. "See?" he said pointedly. "*That's* why science ought to be done away with. Everything was under *control* before they started screwing it up."

Vesica looked around for something to throw at him, but Lorian said, "Oddly enough, that's exactly what Amy thought. I mean, that things were under control. Which is what put her at odds with her colleagues, who thought, you know, everything was coming apart. *They* were arguing basically over whether the solution was to try to get things under control again as quickly as possible, no matter what it took, or whether—and this I think was the majority view—that's how things had gotten crazy in the first place, by too much meddling, and now the only hope was to sit back and leave them alone. Whereas, what Amy said, in her paper, was . . . I forget the exact words, but . . . things are very *much* under control. Everything is meaningful and orderly. No matter what it seems like. It's not just a bunch of random events, like statistics in the newspaper or something. But what we have to understand, she said, is what the Organizing Principle is, and why it's behaving this way—because there must be a reason. And then we have to influence the . . . growth fields, as she said . . . to, like, calm things back down."

Vesica considered this. "That makes sense, I guess. Why did everybody think she was wrong?"

Lorian frowned. "I must not be explaining it right. The part of it that got everyone all worked up was the part about the Organizing Principle, which she said must exist if things were, like she thought, meaningful. Because what Amy meant by *meaning* wasn't like, two things on opposite sides of some equation. It was more to do with . . . the idea that equations can exist in the first place. Or that we can imagine that they do. Does that make sense? See, Amy thought that the very *idea* of the forest, just being there, was much more remarkable and interesting than whether it was dying or not. And if we could get some understanding of that, of what the forest really was—what it really *meant*, in the sense that she was talking about—then we would understand this much more mysterious thing, this Organizing . . ."

"Yes." Vesica nodded. She had, for a lingering moment, a strong sense of things becoming clear. And she added: "I agree with her."

—As though Amy were still around to be agreed with. And as though it made any difference, to Amy or anybody else, what a fourteen-year-old girl thought.

Then—as Lorian looked oddly at her, and Thrull twisted his mouth around, thinking of something mean and sarcastic to say—the moment of clarity ended, and Vesica was left feeling young and ignorant and very, very small beneath the orchid-hung ceiling of the forest. She sighed, in tune with the warble of a bird.

The bird warbled more urgently. Vesica looked around

to see the tiny creature, a puffball of blue and white, perched on a bayberry twig at eye level. Well, maybe an inch higher. It clutched its twig exhaustedly, or perhaps Vesica was projecting onto it her own weariness.

"Poor thing," she said. "How'd you get so high? Where's your mommy?"

"What?" said Lorian, screwing her neck around.

"Shh. It's just a little bird."

The young bluebird ceased warbling, as though she had disheartened it. Then it began again, forlorn now, and No, thought Vesica, it is *not* my imagination. "Are you lost?" she said.

"Dwoit dwoit," the bird told her. "Dweee-leell-ll."

It occurred to her that there was food in her knapsack, little fruits Sheldrake had harvested from sagebrush buttercup. She pulled one out and tossed it to the bird.

The gesture must have frightened it. It shot from its perch, flapping its wings in an uncoordinated manner, as if—like the laborers' sons at Gravetye Farm—it was growing so quickly it was not used to its own limbs. Vesica smiled as the little creature rose higher and higher, flitting in and out among the foliage. It diminished to a speck against the distant sky, then less than that: a mote, a memory. Vesica wondered how such a tiny thing had found the courage to fly so high—and wished that she could follow.

As she sat that way, staring upward, it seemed to her that a small piece of blue sky broke free and began floating down. If it was other than a piece of sky, this slight thing dancing on currents of air, there was no way to tell while it was thirty feet above her, or ten, or even five. Not until it landed, unbelievably, in her outstretched palm did Vesica realize—to her great delight—it was a flower.

Its petals, four inches across, were the purest azure. Across them like clouds floated speckles of gray and white. There were a few leaves, deployed behind the petals like wings, and a snub-necked stem. Vesica drew her breath in and held it, as though such a delicate thing might be crumpled by her breathing. But beautiful things can be surprisingly resilient.

"I can't believe it," she said. "It's *perfect*. Look, Groby—"

She crossed the campsite to show him. Lorian weakly

followed, and the Crusaders drew around her, examining the delicate trophy.

Sheldrake said, "There's something the matter with it. It's got a smell."

"It smells rather nice, I think," said Tattersall, in the flower's defense.

"But orchids aren't *supposed* to have a smell."

"It's sacrilege," declared Thrull. "You shouldn't keep it. You should return it to the forest right away."

Vesica pulled the orchid away from him.

Lorian, leaning against the broken cart, shook her head. "You know, it's funny—in her paper Amy talks about how in any system, like in a forest, every little part plays a necessary role. But what I don't get is . . ."

Groby nodded. "Like a machine."

As though to demonstrate this, he tapped on the small electric motor of the cart. It sputtered a bit, but when Groby held its throttle calmly down, it settled to humming like a happy beehive again.

"What I mean is," said Lorian, with a nervous eye on the suddenly functional cart, "these flowers—what necessary role do *they* play?"

Vesica stood by, sniffing the beautiful bloom. "Well," she suggested, "they look nice."

This so disgusted Thrull that he spat vehemently on the spot. "Nature," he declared, "doesn't do things because they *look* nice."

But Vesica, staring down at the pale blue petals, hoped fervently he was wrong.

Something crept on narrow feet through clumps of wake-robin not blooming yet, but astir, buds raised to the pale moonlight, between the two oaks like towers guarding the fate-chosen camp. There were three hours left until morning, and the great nave of the forest was dark and dimensionless. The feet moved cautiously among the sleeping adventurers, one foot falling softly inches from where the last buried itself in damp loam. Near Vesica they paused. For half a minute they shifted a body's weight between them, deciding, then retraced themselves, made their way around again. Behind a fern-covered embankment they found Groby, mouth open to the stars.

A wattle of wires and silicate disks lay on the ground beside him. Nesting there, with several wires attached, was a molded plastic handgrip to which small waveguides and a chipped enamel tag had been affixed: FOR SERVICE CALL— Narrow hands lifted it, wattle of wires and all, like a bird's nest, careful not to crack its delicate contents. The feet moved noiselessly away. Groby shuddered, thinking—in his nightly state of half-dreaming turbulence—he had felt the presence of a snake.

Dawn came ever earlier and ever warmer. Vesica awoke, perspiring lightly beneath an embroidered tablecloth. She opened her eyes in the twilight, saw the North Star suspended motionless between two trees, and moved her hand to touch the tablecloth, her clothes lying beside it, the sack behind her head: a ritual performed unthinkingly, renewing her attachments to the world. The night's last dream (a great adventure, and she its heroine) slowly faded, its chiaroscuro blending with the murky light of the new day.

She dressed languidly, with no witness but the forest, in jeans and a billowy silk shirt. At the center of the camp she found the fire cold and no one else awake. Without a clear reason for doing so, she kept walking past the fire, beyond the perimeter of the camp, into the dim and trackless forest. A sense of imminence unsettled her. For more prudent souls this would have been reason enough to stay close by the others, build the fire up, rouse the camp—but not for Vesica. The heroic dream, the adventure, had not quite slipped from her awareness, though little was left but the mood of it. The dream-events themselves (which must have been marvelous) had faded to an indistinct backdrop, giving context to her thoughts, investing her actions with the weight of the inevitable.

A hundred yards from the camp, the stream lay as though in wait for her. She paused on its bank. To her right it ran deep and narrow, back toward the manor, the blown-up transport, Deeping Lube, everything they had left behind. To the left, very near the place where Vesica stood, it took a detour, jagging around a crop of boulders and rippling through shallows where its bed was filled with fingernail-sized rocks. The large trees stood back, fifty feet from the streambed, allowing the North Star to sparkle in the water and the woody underlayer to grow particularly rife—aged thorntrees crowding the banks and scraping Vesica's wrists as she brushed among them. She began walking again without knowing quite where, but without losing that sense of inevitability.

Her foot slid down an algae-slick incline and entered the water, which was cold but easily fordable. Some inner logic told her that because she could, she ought to, and in a mood of complaisance she splashed across the stream. The North Star blinked at the corner of her eye, signaling approval.

It was a kind of passage. Vesica stood on unexplored ground, the other bank of the streambed, with the forest crowding thick and black ahead of her and the morning still a promise from the East. Her skin tingled in the warm wet air.

Well? she wondered, directing the question—if any-where—at the North Star, which seemed somehow to have conducted her here. *What happens now?*

(The North Star hung very still. The universe pivoted around it. Whatever secrets it may have known—and astrologers tell us that the North Star has learned quite a few during its long unbroken vigil—it spilled none of them to Vesica.)

Well, maybe that's it, she thought. Just stay here and keep quiet.

She remained very still for a couple of minutes, just stood and listened to the silence of the woods. It was not an ordinary silence, a mere absence of noise, but rather a fullness, a Presence—as though many sounds had come together and somehow canceled one another out, in the same mysterious way that many colors can combine to make pure white. Vesica fancied, as she stood there, that her ears must have changed somehow, become attuned to vibrations more delicate than gross movements of air. A few days ago she would not have heard this fullness of sound, this Silence. Now she felt it humming all around her, passing through her, and felt her inner self resonating like a sympathetic string.

And her eyes: had they changed, too? The patterns of the forest were too dense, too overwhelming for the normal kind of vision. The gradations of light and color from leaf to stem to flower, one layer laid upon another in painterly exuberance, were too subtle for mere acuity to resolve. Yet she saw now that a profound unity underlay it all—a unity her straining eyes could almost but not quite bring into focus, as though it were carried on a wavelength apart from ordinary light.

If her eyes had changed, and her ears, then by extension so must her other organs of perception. And if this were so, what did it mean? Was it like finding a telescope, being able suddenly to see things that had been there all along, but hidden? Or was it something even stranger—a new world opening up that had *not* been there before?

These thoughts seemed to occupy her only a few instants. But when she looked up she found that morning had fully arrived. The North Star had faded into the blue of the morning sky.

She turned back to the camp, refreshed and clear-headed as though at last completely awakened. The world around her was bright, many-hued, writhing with life. Halfway back across the streambed, with water rippling coldly around her ankles, her eye—her ordinary eye—was caught by a glint of something silver below her, where her crossing had disturbed the pebbled bed. She bent down and poked at it. The smooth-worn pebbles separated, and more of the silver appeared. Pressing her fingers into the muddy bottom, she pried at it from beneath, shivering from contact with the cold dirt and water and possibly from the chilly intuition that rose up her spine like the thought of ghosts or spiders, and then it came free

—sparkling into the sunshine, almost weightless in her hand

—a tiny double flute with nine fingerholes and engraved below the mouthpiece,

the legend GOODFELLOW.

Sixteen

BEYOND THE GRAVELED
ford the forest was a different place—not in the kind or
distribution of its species, or from any change in climate or
topology. It was different because the Crusaders knew the
graveled ford *was* a ford, and not just a shallow bed of
fingernail-sized stones. And knowing this, they knew the
curving path that crossed it was a road: a road that began on
the other side of the ford and pointed west-northwest more
or less toward Balance Act, but certainly toward somewhere,
for paths and fords do not make sense without destinations—
two at least—to connect them, any more than holes in a flute
make sense without fingers to cover them, long-dead fingers,
the fingers of a ghost that had crossed the stream at this ford
and who still, in Vesica's imagination, stalked the woods
before them, blazing a trail which the Crusaders could only
follow.

And they *could* follow it, which was maybe the strangest
thing. Though its paving was crumbled and long overgrown
and they would simply have stepped across it an hour earlier,
now that they knew it was there they could follow it quite
easily.

But for Vesica, everything was wrong: the road, and the
manner of their choosing it. A great misunderstanding. It was

because of the flute, she knew, that they had left the streambed, turned away from cool beguiling North to trudge through briars and nettles toward a hazy orange-red West, fighting the terrain instead of following it. True, they were headed in the direction of Balance Act, and yes, there had been the flute. But the flute hadn't been on the *road*—it had been in the stream, the stream that flowed gently between the mountains, the stream they had now abandoned as an unknown pair of hands had abandoned their shining instrument.

And died for it, her mind said, but Vesica hushed it.

It wasn't a real road, anyway. It once had been; the forest parted where it crept; trees grew beside it in two thick rows like the locust drive at Gravetye Farm, only old and wild, twined together at the top. But the road itself was as overgrown as a hedgerow. What kept it passable were pockets of disintegrated stone and oil-black patches where nothing grew, like the soil of Deeping Lube—and who wanted to follow *that*?

Thrull declared, "This is an evil place. Built by evil people."

And Vesica found herself, for once, in agreement. She remembered what Lorian had said: The world was coming to an end, because of everything people had done to it. And this road, she thought, must be part of the Everything.

Disconsolate, she fell in beside Lord Tattersall. "I'd like to walk with you," she said, "if that's all right."

As did most things she said, this cheered him. "By all means, do," he said kindly. "We can chat about the pleasant things we shall do when the Crusade is over, and we all go home again."

"After they've paid him," Sheldrake translated, "the rest of his money."

Tattersall indulgently smiled.

"Well, *I* want to walk in front," said Thrull. "I want to get this whole thing over with and not waste any more time."

"Go ahead," said Sheldrake, yielding the position of point-man with, under the circumstances, reasonable grace. "*Anybody* can follow a road."

Groby said, "You know, I don't think I've seen my heatsaw lately."

*   *   *

The double flute was a great treasure. Vesica guarded it with her other valued things: the robin's-egg-blue orchid, the scrap of paper that said WILD TURKEY POOL, the baby clothes from the manor.

Her stepfather, the Low Commissioner, had built his career on the philosophy—which he declared frequently in public, particularly on his visits to Deeping Lube—that the accumulation of wealth (as practiced, for example, by un-named members of the old aristocracy) was something to be despised. It was better, this philosophy maintained, to drag old valuables out of their attics and into the public domain, where they could be made good use of. If no social purpose could be served with them, well, then they must be value-less, and could be discarded—often, in Vesica's experience, discarded onto the walls and mantels of Gravetye Farm. It was a philosophy of wide appeal. It had never appealed to Vesica, though, and this had long disturbed her.

Now she understood that it was merely a question of temperament; that she herself was more in the mold of Tattersall, with his Maze of enigmatic relics. She shared with him an impulse to embrace the past, to cling to it, whether it was comprehensible or not. She valued old things irrespec-tive of any use that might be made of them. The odd fact was, uselessness in many things was an advantage. This flute, for example. That it was delicately made, that it was ancient, that it emblemized a great mystery—these were attributes far overshadowing the fact that she did not know how to play it, nor did any of her comrades. Maybe someday she would learn. Or maybe she would meet someone who already knew, whose lips could touch and fingers dance along the flute, releasing its long-imprisoned music.

As for the orchid—which unlike her other treasures could not be simply packed away and guarded—she placed it in a dubious medium of leaves and rags. Queerly enough, it seemed to thrive there. It produced, a day after the Crusade turned onto the roadway, a second flower bud. Two days later this opened and a strange new blossom emerged: dark and mottled brown like moth-wings, smaller than its sibling. Promptly, as though the plant's attention were diverted, the original blue flower began to fade.

Oh, yes, and that smell—the complex odor that an orchid might or might not be supposed to have—Vesica finally recognized. It was the same smell, the *identical* smell, Vesica was certain, that Tattersall had said belonged to dittany-of-Crete. Which obviously it didn't, or how could it be coming now from an orchid? Yet Tattersall had said so, and Vesica felt an almost daughterly compulsion to believe him.

Angels, Vesica had heard, found the smell of dittany-of-Crete alluring. She wondered if demons liked it too. They often seemed to go after the same things, though their motives were different.

But this was a disturbing line of thought, and she steered away from it. She took her place beside Tattersall, and the Crusade moved westward on the crumbled road through the mountains.

Thrull's eyes, the eyes that now led the expedition, were focused on knots of smartweed and thistle, neither of which he recognized or cared about, just ahead of his feet. He seldom raised his eyes to the horizon, because he did not expect the horizon to be there, and did not care about *that* either. Besides, there was so much to think about.

Thrull was scarcely the most credulous member of the Pure Force. He had, in fact, served as an informant and provocateur within its ranks—in effect a traitor—for some years now. And yet, traitorous or no, he was a member. He had spent crucial years of his boyhood reciting the movement's slogans. He did not believe them. Yet he believed nothing else in particular. He might mock Vesica for her childishness, or scorn Tattersall's devotion to a dry-rotted code of behavior, or hold in contempt Lorian's adoration of a dead botanist—but he could not, and did not try to, construct a belief-system of his own. The only one he possessed was the one he had borrowed (and not returned, though he saw no value in it) from the Pure Force.

Now, with nothing better to do and no other source of solace, he contemplated the teachings of the Force as he traipsed through the mountainous reaches of the Carbon Bank Forest, the very temple of an aroused and angry Nature. And the more deeply he considered it, the more it seemed to him that this Crusade *was* wrong, not simply, as it had seemed before, inconvenient. And that something really terrible *might* come of it.

When, therefore, something monstrous loomed before him on the roadway in the sharp-edged light of afternoon, Thrull was astonished yet not altogether surprised. Which may explain his failure to scream or faint or even take a second look, just to be sure—or indeed to react in any thoughtful way at all—until his wits returned and he found himself hurtling through waist-high thistle, gasping and wide-eyed and unable to stop before colliding head-on with Groby. The big man grunted and rubbed his stomach. Thrull sprawled on a patch of paving stone at his feet.

"There was . . ." he panted. "I saw . . ."

Lorian, from her seat in the cart, looked at the fallen youth in satisfaction. Sheldrake overtook them.

". . . something," Thrull sputtered, "huge . . ."

"Speak up," Sheldrake told him. "We can't understand you. Not that we really want to."

"It had horns," Thrull managed to explain. "It was huge. Brown—awful—right there in front of me. *Evil.* It was evil."

He was beginning to collect himself now. He sat upright, his spine rigid with the memory. "It wanted to kill me," he said.

"Ah, what's this?" said Tattersall. He and Vesica ambled along—in no great hurry, for they were enjoying each other's conversation. Spying Thrull on the ground the Governor said, "Did you *strike* this young man, Sheldrake? I must say it's taken long enough. What did he do?"

Vesica laughed; Sheldrake waved a denial. "He claims he saw something up the road. It had horns, you say?"

"Horns. It was . . ."

Sheldrake nodded. "A moose. The boy saw a moose and it scared the stuffings out of him."

"It wasn't," Thrull said almost meekly, for the memory still cowed him, "a moose. It was . . ."

"A moose!" said Vesica.

"I told you," Sheldrake reminded her, "you'd see one. You'll have to be on the lookout, though. They can be pretty shy."

Thrull was still protesting, denying all this, but the

others had gotten firmly into the habit of ignoring him. They resumed the journey indifferently, leaving him to catch up, except for Vesica, who stayed a moment behind.

"Was it really that scary?" she said. For all she knew it might have been. She couldn't remember a moose from any of her stepfather's books.

Thrull sat fuming. Worse than frightened, he had now been humiliated. He yanked the satchel from his back and pawed through it impatiently.

"You'll see," he rasped. "All of you. You'll see your moose, all right."

He waited until Vesica had turned and gone before plunging a hand more deeply into his pack.

Vesica slipped away that night an hour after dinner, which was as long as she could wait. The Crusaders were telling stories—stories she had heard weeks ago—around the fire. From her pocket protruded the tendrils of the orchid, tendrils that now resembled more than anything the vine that Lorian had gotten tangled in at Biggar's Neck. Vesica had grown leery of the thing. Maybe Thrull had been right: maybe there really had been something wrong about taking it and carrying it around, as though it belonged to her. Maybe she *should* return it to the forest right away. But if she was going to give it back, she meant to do so in a civil manner—a way that Tattersall would have approved.

A faint dusting of daylight remained on leaves and fronds and needles, though this deep in the woods it was hardly bright enough to notice. Vesica noticed it only because her senses were enlivened: by the silence of the woods, by the thrill of having a secret plan, maybe by a dozen factors she had no inkling of. Whatever the causes, she knew once more that sense of heightened awareness she had felt on fording the stream. She stepped easily between half-seen trunks, each foot falling naturally in a spot that seemed ordained for it, heels coming down gently in the loam, rebounding from massive roots, effortlessly missing sharp rocks and brambles. The trackless forest, she realized, was a truer path than any that had been imposed upon it. The easeful, rhythmic quality of walking, something she had not felt for days, made her briefly forget her resolve not to wander far from the fire. But this "briefly"—when she looked up and wondered how far she had come—was like the "few instants" she had lingered by the streambed. The stain of sunlight had washed away, and the stars hung low in their millionfold brightness.

She had reached an open space where the second-quarter moon shone through trees held apart by great rocks. From somewhere she heard a trickle of water, a sound that both soothed and energized her, making her hope they might have returned by their blundering roadway to the stream. But no—the sound was coming from above her, higher in the rocks. She climbed without thinking more about it, because it was so obviously the right thing to do.

The invisible path led her to a gap between bulging blue-black stones. She peered into it, wondering distantly what she was doing here, and then a glimmering caught her eye. She inched her way through the opening and came out at the edge of a stone-lipped bowl, twenty feet across and barely ovoid, filled to her toes with clear, dark, and nearly motionless water. What motion there was—a trembling, as though of nervousness—was the subtle network of interwoven ripples spreading out and echoing off the stone and joining again in intricate combinations, caused by a tiny cataract that spilled down the cliff-face on the opposite side. The moon rested on the edge of the cliff; its shivering image floated on the water.

"Wild Turkey Pool," Vesica said.

It fit. It named the place.

She drew the orchid from her pocket with fingers that were tingling as though magic rippled just below the skin. She knew nothing about magic, though she had read a hundred stories in her stepfather's library, but she imagined this was what it felt like. The tang of dittany-of-Crete expanded in the air. In the short time since dinner, when she had tucked it in her jeans, the moth-wing flower had begun wilting, and a third, larger bud swelled some distance along the stem. Solemnly Vesica set the plant and its fabric cup down on the cool blue stone.

She stepped away. She had done what she came for, found a home for the orchid, and it was time to go. But the legs she stepped away on grew weak. Around her, the immense Silence changed in some way, became even fuller as though ready to burst with noise, or else—just as likely—became even deeper and more perfectly quiet.

Vesica, out of respect or fear for that Silence, clenched her teeth together, for otherwise she would surely have cried out, it was growing unbearable, it was, Something was . . .

AND THEN

And then the forest fell silent. Not: Silent. Just quiet. Nothing had happened and the orchid was sitting where she had left it by the pool.

Vesica was terribly disappointed, though she expected nothing and *wanted* nothing, just to go back to the camp. So she turned again, and at the corner of her vision something huge and brown and terrible swelled up to grab her with hands that would drain away her life.

She shrieked

—and there was nothing. The orchid lay undisturbed in the moonlight. There had never been anything, and Vesica forced herself to think this over and over regardless of how little she believed it. Her heart pounded and her breath came in short spurts. Yet her excitement was that of joy as much as terror, for this was an adventure all right: every adventure contained some terrible trial, a test its protagonist must pass before she could be truly a heroine. She closed her eyes and squeezed her mind shut, forced out all memory of the monstrous thing that wanted to destroy her, turned away from Wild Turkey Pool and then calmly, magisterially, turned back again. She stood with her eyes closed.

"I'm sorry," she said very slowly and clearly. "I'm sorry for everything that people did, back when you were dying. I don't know what-all happened, but I'm sorry anyway. And I brought this flower. I know it was your flower to start with, but I'm giving it back to you."

It was silly, the way it sounded, talking aloud to the empty forest, but it was all she could think of to do. She opened her eyes.

In front of her, as close as the orchid had been, stood a ghost-white naked boy.

She gasped.

The boy gasped too.

He must have been even more frightened than she was. His eyes stared back at her from the same height as her own.

Well, maybe an inch higher. From this she guessed that he must be her own age. Yet something about him, his manner, the way he held his slender body, made him seem impossibly young, as though he had stepped into the world that very hour. Perhaps also there was something about his eyes . . . She couldn't make out their color in the dark, but she could tell his hair was just lighter than oak leaves in autumn, and his body was not really white except in contrast with the stones around him; in fact it was similar in color and in certain other arresting respects to Vesica's own. Her eyes were wandering down it—she had never seen anything like it before, nor ever wanted to—when a sense of the boy's alarm brought her eyes snapping back to meet his. They were filled with a jumble of new feelings, and as Vesica stared into them the feelings passed from him to her and she knew there could be no more than a few moments left before one of them turned and fled. And because she desperately did not want that to happen, because the outcome of the adventure depended on it, she held her hands out, palms open, and tried hard to think of something she could possibly say, only to find that she had forgotten how to talk.

The boy opened his mouth at the same time, closed it again, swallowed, and then he was gone.

"No, wait!" she cried, finding her tongue when it no longer mattered.

She started to run after him, but for some reason she was not sure, exactly, which way he had gone. There were only Wild Turkey Pool and the moon shivering in the water. The orchid, with its new just-opening bud, was gone.

Yet in all her bewilderment and sorrow, there was one thing Vesica was sure of.

She had recognized him.

It had been the boy from the dream: the one imprisoned by the limbs of the alder tree:

the one who was calling her
to save him.

Seventeen

"**N**EW CLOTHES?" said Lorian. "What for?"

Vesica had been caught sewing baby blankets together in the hazy light` before dawn. She had been at it since before she could be sure what she was doing, what color the pieces of cloth were, after lying awake hearing her heart pound through the night, and the quality of her stitchwork showed it. What had woken Lorian she had no idea. She herself had maintained an expert silence, a silence she learned, so to speak, at the knee of its master. This was one of the problems, she supposed, with having a journalist around.

Lorian's sharp green eyes shone at her through the twilight, as though Vesica's sewing tools might be the accoutrements of some delicious scandal.

Vesica said, "Oh, you know. I'm tired of wearing these things that don't fit right, and everything being dirty all the time." She held a patchwork pants-leg against her own.

"About half an inch too long," Lorian judged.

Vesica nodded, hoping that was right.

"Well," said Lorian, rearranging her blanket, "I couldn't sleep either. I kept hearing noises out in the forest. I know it's nothing—"

"Noises?" said Vesica, too eagerly. But Lorian didn't notice.

"The usual things. Owls hooting. Little things hopping around. The moon seemed awfully bright last night. Do you suppose that affects them?"

Vesica supposed it did. The sun edged up a bit, and with it her work went more smoothly. She wanted to get it done this morning, wanted it finished before they got too far away from Wild Turkey Pool.

In time they heard a stirring on the other side of the camp. Someone moving, pushing blankets aside. The day would be a warm one.

Lorian said, "I'm going to talk to Tattersall." She struggled to her feet, brushing bits of leaves from her hiking pants, and stood there weakly, as though the merest brush of air would knock her down again.

"Are you all right?" said Vesica.

Lorian nodded; then, more honestly, shrugged. "I'm going to ask him if we can't stay here and rest—at least for the morning. I just don't think I can go on without a little sleep."

"Oh, good," said Vesica. "Tell him I couldn't sleep either."

"Yeah, that ought to do it. He'd stay all summer if that's what *you* wanted."

She stepped carefully away, leaving Vesica to wonder if this last remark was bitter or jealous or just, in journalistic fashion, the facts as Lorian saw them—and wondering, besides, if it was true. She did not spend much time on this; she had little to spend. She chose another piece of baby cloth from her knapsack (a tiny coverall this time; her supply was fast diminishing) and decided it could go to make a sleeve. Blinking at her own heartlessness, she grabbed it hard in both hands and tore its seam out. A sense of haste informed her movements as she rethreaded the needle with robin's-egg blue. Her eyes, which had stayed open and alert by moonlight, felt heavy, swollen, glazed with pointless tears in the glare of the sun.

The month of May was nine hours old: who was keeping track of that? It was the first really warm morning. Spring, which here in the North had entered haltingly, one blossom, one leaf at a time, now rushed ahead in an inflorescent flood.

Tattersall was happy to declare a holiday. The time felt right somehow. He joined Groby and Sheldrake on their morning forage; herbs and salad greens were abundant along the road, in the greater sunlight, and of late they had eaten rather sparingly. A feast was in order, then. Sheldrake spoke wistfully of moose steak—but Groby's heatsaw had not turned up, and there was no other effective weapon.

When they were gone, Lorian lay down for a nap. Vesica pretended to but, after giving Lorian time to nod off, forced her eyelids apart and took up the final bit of sewing. There were only the hems to go; and the decision about a drawcord, or buttons. She squinted, tried to get some sense of how her work might look to a disinterested eye, if such an eye existed. She could only think: shabby. But it was her best, her honest best, and maybe that would count for something. She thought it might, from her memory of the story.

But what story was she remembering? It had all gotten tied up in her mind, the old tales sewn up together like fragments of unconnected dreams, contrasting happily there in dream-space but a gaudy mismatch in real life. But wasn't real life also the great adventure? Oh, forget it, Vesica was too tired to decide. She had to think about buttons—a drawcord or buttons. She closed her eyes to concentrate. And then she would take the finished shirt and pants to Wild Turkey Pool, and lay them down beside the orchid. She had thought the orchid was gone, but no: there it was. Its scent drifted over the makeshift clothes, filling the pores of the fabric, displacing the smell of the manor at Biggar's Neck— not the manor all overgrown with vines and flowers, but an earlier one, dry and warm, noisy with guests, a gigantic place, the whole world it seemed to Vesica. But that was another story, as Sheldrake would say; and what story was it? What story was she remembering now?

Only a dream, Vesica. Only a happy, long-forgotten dream.

Nature drew a blanket of serenity over the earth. A warm breeze moved through its branches, carrying from some-where north of the road the music of a waterfall. The sun rose languidly, the first sunrise of May, and primroses turned from pink to white and bared their fragrant sepals beneath it. In the campsite by the crumbled road, the breakfast fire burned low.

Vesica passed into motionless slumber. The tension flowed from her spine like water from an unquiet river, merging in whatever silent ocean lies waiting far downstream. Her arms and legs uncurled like petals; her dreams flowed out like an exotic fragrance on the æther. And the things that are drawn to such rare scents—the things that come to sate themselves or bury their secret spores—gathered quietly over the campsite and extended dark proboscides to feed.

But a movement from the forest alarmed them. They scattered on the immaterial breeze. Something great and slow and powerful had returned from a long absence, and the world that lay untouched by the sunlight grew bright with its approach.

The Presence entered the campsite. It came from no direction—rather, from the realm in which all directions exist together it entered the one where they stand, like compass points, apart. It stood there, tasting air and smelling dirt and hearing the sound of water for the first time in, oh, a very long while now. Or a very short time, by the standards of the forest.

It was a trifle bemused.

Stepping carefully between the two sleeping Crusaders, it examined their inconsequent consciousnesses as one examines the handiwork of a child. If such a Presence could be said to feel, in any comprehensible sense, then what it felt was a serene and encompassing acceptance of all it saw—an acceptance almost identical with indifference, but leavened with sympathy and affection. Certain things had changed, it observed, since the last time it was summoned here. Other things had not. But the Presence had expected no surprises. With some fondness it studied the remains of a humble meal, the fading embers, the knapsacks on the ground. A small metal-and-plastic object, tucked in a cloak the color of rosemary, caused it a moment of consternation. This was the sort of thing the Presence had seen entirely enough of. For a moment it entertained a whim to intervene and dispose of it—but then it found what it had come for.

The patchwork clothes were fitted together with pitiable

unevenness, as though by unpracticed hands. Their colors clashed alarmingly, in combinations the Presence could not have conceived if it tried to, nor ever conceived of trying. On top of that, the shirt and pants, from a sartorial standpoint, were poorly cut and badly sewn. The hips were too baggy; the shoulders too narrow; the crotch too tight. They were made for the wrong kind of body.

The effulgent Presence was touched.

From somewhere close at hand, in that dimensionless and unfathomable Silence, there came such a stirring or agitation as one would not have expected to find there. The Presence turned within itself to attend. A mysterious sort of dialog then seemed to occur—a dialog without words or gestures and possibly without participants. The boundary between the world of the campsite and that other world, whatever it was (perhaps the land where stories end happily ever after), grew strained, translucent. Two awarenesses clashed in the vibrant æther: one half-grown, the other ageless and immeasurable. When it was over, the forest rumbled with a single epoch-making sentiment, unremarkable except for being without precedent in either world.

The illimitable Presence said:

All right, then. Go.

And with no passage of time and no trace of anything at all having occurred, there were only the warm spring breeze and the music of the waterfall and the May Day sun swelling in the sky.

And a hundred and twenty pounds were added to the mass of the world.

Vesica awoke at the return of the foraging party. In a lightning-flash of awareness she understood that she had fallen asleep, that it was now late morning, that she had missed her chance to slip away to Wild Turkey Pool without giving an explanation, and that the shirt and pants were gone.

Gone.

It must have been Thrull. Thrull must have taken them. It was like him, and he was the only one the clothes could possibly have fit. (They would actually be too short for him, but he wouldn't know that until he tried.)

She stormed into the center of the camp, demanding, "Where is he? Where's he gone?"

But the others only looked at her quizzically, Tattersall with alarm, as though she were sleepwalking. Well, they wouldn't know anyway. She went to the place where Thrull had slept last night—but of course he had vanished, and taken his knapsack with him.

She said, "I'm going to find him. I'll be back."

And she marched straight ahead, in the direction she happened to be facing, into the woods.

She did not have a plan. She did not know where she was going. Anyone who happened to meet her that way— supposing that someone might have materialized then before her—would have gathered very quickly that she had been awake all night and now was wandering angry and confused and at substantial risk of becoming lost. (Tattersall had gathered this already, and was directing Sheldrake to follow her. On second thought he and Groby went, too, because whatever might be going on, it was interesting.)

The direction she walked in did not take her to Wild Turkey Pool. Instead the woods grew thick and tangled, falling gradually to a moist lowland of sycamore and ash and another species she didn't recognize. The air grew musty, but agreeably so—like the smell of a half-remembered or maybe imaginary attic, of sweaty undressed children trying on costumes from an old treasure-trunk, posing in them before a dusty mirror. Some part of Vesica's mind must not have been awake yet; or the membrane of reality must have ruptured, letting dreams leak through.

In this low place was a clearing where a dead oak rose like a maypole. Its branches were rotted and gone, the trunk supported by vines that fretted it like rigging lines. From its base sprang an opportunistic thicket of saplings, glowing now in carmine bloom. The sight of this—the bald trunk, amidst so much blossom and verdure—gave halt to Vesica's blind march. She drew up beside it, rubbing her temples and blinking the blear from her eyes.

A thrashing came from ahead of her—a stomping of clumsy feet somewhere inside the clump of saplings.

"Leave me *alone*," she demanded, as Thrull might have done, for thus does a hunter mock her prey.

The thrashing continued; a young tree shook, raining carmine petals.

"Is that you?" she said. Probably meaning Thrull, though she wasn't sure anymore. Losing sleep was a strange thing, a drug, in its effect on you. "What are you *doing* in there?"

She went to look. She stuck a hand out, parting the branches, and when she did the saplings shook more violently than before. A hole opened in the green wall. Vesica peered through. From the other side, a long face stared back.

It was not one of the Crusaders. It was—

Vesica cried, "A moose!"

—It was a moose. It was stuck in the tree, caught by the antlers. It stared at her imploringly, as though begging her to set it free, or at least to encourage it in some way.

"Wow," she said, feeling more drugged than ever. "Are you really a moose?"

Well, not a very old moose. Its antlers were only nubs; adolescent antlers. Maybe it had gotten them tangled in the bush because they were new and unfamiliar, like the wings of a baby bird, and it was experimenting with them.

"Poor thing," she told it. "Here, let me help."

The moose seemed agreeable. But a new sound came from behind it, and they both—moose and human—looked around in alarm. (At least they tried to; the moose was still entangled.)

Crack, went more branches—and between them stepped Thrull. He entered the clearing where Vesica stood, the green-and-carmine wall blocking his view of the trapped animal. He was carrying Groby's heatsaw. Its black plastic handle and metal waveguides looked large and dangerous in his hand.

The moose became agitated, thrashed its head back and forth in a frenzy to escape.

"There you are!" Thrull cried, as Vesica might have done, for thus does the prey mock his hunter. But he was not addressing the girl. He turned to her now, warning, "Stand back!" and waving the heatsaw.

She was frightened; she complied. Thrull pulled back the safety latch and pressed the button ON. From the tip of the heatsaw spouted a yellow stream. Sparks fell away from it, dust motes ignited by its outpouring of energy, dying as they touched the soggy ground. Thrull swung it around him like a saber, then leveled it at the hedge.

"No!" cried Vesica. "Don't hurt it! It's just a young one . . . and it's caught . . . no, stop!"

"Young?" said Thrull, making deadly infinity-signs with the blade. "You're crazy. It's as old as the forest. It's been tracking us for days now. I knew it as soon as I saw it on the trail."

"Knew it?" said Vesica. "Knew a moose?"

"A moose!" He laughed—a harsh, unnatural sound. "It's no moose. It's a *devil*. The Devil of the Forest. It's been sent to kill us."

Vesica made a lunge for him. She dodged the heatsaw, but ran into his elbow as he cuffed her away.

He raised the blade. The heatsaw flashed in the air, momentarily surpassing the sun's distant fury. Then it came down—slicing down through the leaves, through the interwoven branches, through the carmine petals, through—

The helpless beast gave a howl heart-rending in timbre, as though its soul were compressed in that instant of agony to a single sound, almost human in quality.

For a moment so brief that it seemed no time at all, Vesica saw or sensed or even less than that—imagined—something huge and brown, not the moose—something truly monstrous—rear itself up, tower over the saplings, glare down with eyes cold and wild and feral, not at Thrull in particular but at humanity in general. At Vesica.

And then it was gone. The branches were hissing smoke, and a wide gap had been slashed between them.

Thrull clicked off the heatsaw and stared numbly through the leaves. He seemed exhausted by what he had done—and puzzled by it, too, as though it were done not of his own choosing but, like the actions of a soldier, required of him. Vesica got to her feet. There were noises behind them. But all of her senses were focused on the hole made by the antlers through the leaves. There were no antlers there any longer. There was no moose, nor any devil.

"I didn't . . . " said Thrull. "It wasn't . . ."

There was only a boy, lying on the ground.

The body of a boy.

"I was *sure*," said Thrull, almost wailing now.

The boy was lying face-down in carmine petals. He was about Vesica's height, or an inch taller, his sun-gilded hair just darker than oak leaves in fall.

"What happened?" shouted Sheldrake, rushing up to them. "Hey—those look like rowan blossoms, there."

Vesica started to cry, to cry loudly and shamelessly as she had hardly ever cried, ever, even when her stepfather had been as cruel as he could possibly be.

"Um . . ." said Groby, as Sheldrake took the heatsaw and looked down into the space between the branches.

The boy was dressed in patchwork clothing, its pieces poorly assembled as though by unpracticed hands. But they fit him: the hips, the legs, the shoulders—the slender body lying there seemed to have been made for the clothes as much as the clothing was made to fit it.

Tattersall put an arm around Vesica, who could not, who refused to pull her eyes away; and Sheldrake, for the sake of doing it, threw Thrull to the ground like an outgrown plaything.

"Who," said Groby, his thoughts still widely proliferated, "is . . ."

He leaned down to examine the body. He took in his large careful fingers the pink sleeve that had once been a baby's coverall and tugged at it, easing the boy onto his back. The body flopped over like something that had never been alive. The face was just as Vesica remembered it from her dream: fair skin palely freckled, slightly upturned nose, lips flesh-pink and barely parted. The eyes, which in the dream had been wide and imploring, were closed now.

"Go on, your lordship," said Sheldrake. "Get her away from here."

"No!" said Vesica. "I want to see . . . I want to know . . ."

"This isn't right," said Groby—as though as usual he were following some wholly separate conversation. He took the boy's fragile, lifeless hand.

In Vesica's mind, an already-ruptured membrane now tore open all the way. Through the opening, memories poured in uncontrollable succession: the boy the moose the squirrel the bird the eagles the forest, the Devil of the Forest, the fairy tale, a boy and a girl, wandering in the woods, the pucca, the rose, the rowan, the orchid, the oak, the alder, the boy trapped in its branches, no this isn't right, not a real tree, manmade, a demonstration thing, stored in a trunk, the baby's clothes, the double-flute, the smell of dittany-of-Crete, the Silence, the Presence, the North Star, the Sun, the Moon, Wild Turkey Pool, the robin's-egg-blue orchid, the naked boy, making clothes to fit him, the boy again, somehow all of it:

She broke free of Tattersall's arms.

"Groby," she said, trembling with a life's worth of uncertainties and only one thing she was sure of. "Could I just—?"

Groby lifted the boy's hand and Vesica took it. Just took it, flesh still warm in hers. And on that the story turned, became what it is, what it could only be, being a story.

The boy's slender chest rose. Remained still a moment. Fell. The warm hand drew tight around her fingers. Then he opened his eyes. They reached out to Vesica's and entangled with her own,

> clear and deep as pools of water, flecks of white
> like clouds drifting across them,
> blue as the May morning sky.

Reprise

I was the shadow of the waxwing slain
by the false azure of the windowpane.
I was the smudge of ashen fluff—and I
lived on, flew on, in the reflected sky.
—JOHN SHADE

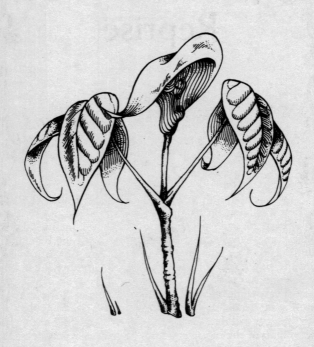

Trillium erectum
Wake robin

The distinctive flower-head shows itself in early summer. The root may be chewed as an aphrodisiac, though large doses can slow the heart.

Eighteen

AFTER THE LONG DREAM the boy was lying on his back in the warm bed of the forest. He opened his eyes a crack, listened to mountain larks and bluejays argue over whose eggs would rest on the branch of a witch's ash. The branch overhung the dragon path, which only the boy could follow. Not even his mother knew how, though she was the one who had found it, she who sat in its coiled heart while the boy lay dreaming beneath the ash tree. His mother would be expecting him now, waiting for him with her eyes closed as the sun slipped down beneath the lowest limb of the old white oak, the limb that reached down to the path like an arm about to scoop something up and hold it. The sun would touch her eyelids and that would mean it was time for the boy to be home. Then they would walk across the meadow, orange with afternoon and marigolds, past the orchard of thrice-coppiced oaks and through the tall gate that rolled up on tiny gears like the door of a picture-book castle. Together, back at the dome, they would repeat the agreeable sunset ritual of making dinner, to which the boy's contribution would consist of climbing the ladder to the pantry and fetching down pasta or flour or rice while telling outrageous lies about his adventures in the forest: tales of friendly giants and axbearing woodsmen and princesses disguised as simple farmgirls. The kitchen where his mother would stand opened on to a balcony where herbs grew in planter boxes some man had made before he left. . . . But that was a long time ago. Now, in May, the herbs would be pale-green and fragrant—sweet cicely and sage and dittany-of-Crete spilling onto the cedar planking, burrowing with tiny roots between the cracks.

But what man was it that built the boxes? The boy squinted and tried to think away the dream, which still confused him, but the harder he thought the more the dream came back to him, as though despite his efforts to concentrate he was falling asleep again. It must have been the man who lived here once, while the boy was very young, years and years ago.

My father, his mind told him, but no, his father was—

The boy's heart thumped as though someone had called him. He strained to hear his mother's voice, but there were only mountain larks. The image of his mother was blurred, as though some translucent barrier stood between them: as though she were part of the dream and not real, not waiting for him under the oak tree.

Dead, his mind thought. *My mother is dead.*

The boy sat up in panic. Sunlight warmed his legs through the patchwork pants.

My father is dead too.

The boy breathed rapidly, tugging the air in short gasps, sweat running into his eyes warm and salty as tears, big-knuckled hands white and trembling. He lifted one of those hands to his eyes; the crazy yellow sleeve that turned pink at the elbow came with it, trailing a thread of robin's-egg blue down his wrist. The hand stopped inches from his face, obeying the boy's command as though it belonged to him, but it did not, could not.

I know it's true. My father and mother are dead. I'm the only one alive, and I'm . . . I'm not really . . .

Small brown hairs covered the wrist and ran up the arm like an army of ants. The boy flexed long, unfamiliar fingers. They were clean and uncallused, as though they had never dug moats around the dome to sail whittled boats in, or climbed the stooping oak. (But they *had*. The boy argued stubbornly and silently as though expecting a reply from somewhere within.

None came.)

He shook his head. Sun-gilded brown hair fell to his eyebrows. He ran his fingers through it, found the left-hand part, the cowlick. The hands moved down to the forehead, to temples that felt more squared-off than they should, cheeks less rounded, a chin more tapered and firm.

Something had happened.

A very long time had passed while the boy lay dreaming. Years, maybe. And it had been terrible, that long restless dream—oh, but wonderful too, full of stars and silence, beautiful as a song. With all his heart the boy wished he could go back to that dream again. He wished that nothing had happened to wake him, that no one had come to end his easeful slumber. No one . . .

. . . had come.

In the space between one thought and the next, when the boy's mind was empty and sad, a memory rose to fill it. Or perhaps not a memory—not *his* memory—but part of the spell-woven dream. If so, it came from near the end, when the boy was already half awake, his dream-limbs stirring beneath the covers. Like all such memories it was bright, unbelievable, its image out of focus yet in certain aspects sharp, as though seen through a window streaked with water.

Water, yes: a window:

—The small animal that was the boy, or was seeing for the boy, or that the boy was dreaming about, sniffed the air. Unknown odors drifted through the corridors of its bright ageless home. Animal smells, but from an animal that had not lived here in the creature's lifetime. And musty fiber, from a plant not native to these uplands. The squirrel—it was a squirrel—followed the smells until it came to a flower-hung alcove, where polished rock was hollowed into a pool. There in the clear blue water—splashing, wetting the squirrel—was something long and golden and smooth, something the squirrel had never seen before, nor ever wanted to. The squirrel twitched, grew warm and uncomfortable. No, it was the boy who was uncomfortable, watching, or remembering—it was all so confusing—the long golden body rolling over and sliding through the water, blinking its large amber eyes, speaking in a voice like a boy's bell-like soprano, but different. Very different.

"Do you live here?"

The boy was trembling now, unsure what he had been for that very long time while he was dreaming, or what he was now, what kind of thing this was that sat beneath the witch's ash with the boy's mind living inside it. Whatever it was, it was quaking and hot with the image of wide amber eyes, smooth shoulders, small pink-nippled breasts, and the boy was ready to burst with a kind of desperation, a feeling that *I can't stand it* but not knowing why or what. His mind swelled with that single image; the glassy alcove vanished, and the hollowed-out pool, the trailing flowers, the water, even the squirrel, until there was nothing left but that tan, that naked, that long- and downy-limbed soft-as-warm-bread body, and the boy

Gasped.

And looked down at himself, his angular form thrusting out at wrong angles inside the patchwork clothes. And not understanding himself, or his new ill-fitting body, or anything that had happened, the boy began softly and almost silently to cry.

And crying, he whispered not a dead woman's name but—

"This is terrible."

Lorian stared at a chipped crystal bud-vase, once used to serve champagne and now the receptacle for a blood-brown infusion of flowers from the rowan tree—the same carmine blooms the boy had lain in. "Deceptive, too," she said, swirling the liquid in front of her. "It tastes awful but it smells sweet."

"I wonder," said Lord Tattersall, "if there's a moral in that."

Sheldrake commanded: "Just drink it."

"I'm drinking." She braved another swallow. "Though I don't know why. I feel fine now."

"There, you see?" said Sheldrake. He peered down into the battered and tarnished punchbowl that squatted on smoky coals before him.

They were down in the damp clearing, the place where

Vesica had wandered in her midmorning daze. The shadow of the dead oak fell across them, as though they were figures on a huge and ominous sundial. They had not left here since the astonishing advent of the boy, though they had not quite resolved to stay here, either; little by little their encampment transferred itself down to this musty-smelling hollow, while the Crusaders kept a languid vigil just outside the curtain of rowans. The boy remained within. Asleep, they thought. At least lying with his eyes closed. No one cared to disturb him; not out of fear (although Thrull clung to his Devil of the Forest idea) but from a need to reconsider *everything*—the Crusade, the forest, the month of May—in light of it all having hurled them against this wall of impossibility.

Vesica said, getting back to the bud-vase, "I'm not sure I understand. Why does she have to drink it, if she's feeling better anyway?"

Sheldrake put on a wounded look, as though she had insulted his cooking. "Rowan blossom tea," he said, enunciating with great care, "is extremely potent. It starts to work *even before you drink it.*"

"Oh, good heavens," said Tattersall. Sometimes he wished Sheldrake would stick to muttering, so he wouldn't have to understand. Thrull, in contrast, rolled his head around from where he had averted it as he lay in a sulk beyond the fire, and seemed to renew his interest. Groby squatted on massive haunches studying his map of the North. What he saw there was no more knowable than ever. Vesica persisted:

"But how could . . ."

"Shh!" Lorian waved them into silence. She squinted, straightening her spine, like an overbred and nearsighted quail hound trying to justify its expense. Elaborating the analogy, she gave a short sniff at the air and pronounced, in a melodramatic whisper:

"He's awake!"

Groby folded the map and repocketed it. "He's been awake for a while now," he said. "I think he's trying to figure out where he is. Or maybe whether he trusts us enough to come out."

Come out, he meant, from the carmine-garlanded bower. It struck Vesica as she thought about this that they were like characters from an illustrated fairy tale: a circle of loyal advisers, waiting beside the curtained bed of the King. Or no, the Prince—the enchanted Prince, languishing under an awful spell. A spell from which he would never be free, or at least not until . . . She searched her memory, sorted through the innumerable stories she had collected there. But like the cluster of rowan trees, whose leaves and flowers intermingled in the sun, all the stories ran together, their plots and characters getting jumbled—as though Thrull had been right: there was only one Story, and everything you thought was separate was really part of it. All the once-upon-a-times and the happy-ever-afters were not true beginnings and ends but only transitions, places where the plot spun around on itself like a staircase, spiraling to yet another story, and suddenly you were there in the middle of things again. So even the notions of *inside* and *out* didn't mean much anymore; and you couldn't even hear a story, the Story, without being part of it.

Maybe such thoughts were part of growing up—which she had decided she must be doing, though she didn't particularly want to.

". . . awake," Lord Tattersall was saying, "then I suppose we ought to go talk to him."

"About what?" said Lorian—the old sharpness back in her voice.

"Well, you know: who he is. Where he comes from. That sort of thing."

Thrull sneered, "It's not a *he*. And it doesn't come from anywhere. It's been *sent*, to destroy us."

The Governor gave the youth a glance that seemed to deplore his lack of charity. "Well, then. We should in that case talk about what *it* is, and where it was *sent* from." He stood up. "Would anyone care to—"

"Vesica."

The name, faintly spoken, seemed to hang in the air before the boy's face. And maybe it was that name, something in the sound of it, that made his face feel warm. Then, quickly—

"*Wait, I'm coming,*" said someone. Very nearby. A female voice, not his mother's, a girl's bell-like soprano. Footsteps thrashed through the leaves on the other side of the witch's ash, and the boy moved stealthily around the dead oak. He felt the tingle of the dragon path curling around his toes. He was remembering now.

"That's odd," said a man's voice—an older man than the one who built the planter boxes, but not as old as—

"Well!" The footsteps halted. "Perhaps he's just, ah, stepped out for a moment. You know."

The boy remembered the voices now, the tall man and the teenage girl they belonged to. He remembered a crude cookfire, shiny things spilling from knapsacks, the smoke and chatter of the camp. He remembered many more things quickly, sounds and smells and textures tumbling from the corners of his mind like the contents of a tightly packed cupboard. At the same time, as he remembered these things, he began to forget: to forget the long dream and all its horror and all its beauty.

"Just stepped *out* a moment," a new voice muttered, mimicking the last. "He thinks we're in the drawing room at Marshmain."

"What's that, more champagne? That would be nice, Sheldrake, thank you. But just now . . ."

The boy was safe on the dragon path. If he wanted to, he could slip unseen into the forest, as he had a thousand times before. That part was easy.

The hard part was, he didn't know who these people were, or whether they were a threat to him, or what they had to do with . . . with anything. His head was awash with so awfully many things—memories of a past longer and stranger than the boy could possibly have known. Yet some-how the memories had gotten there, cramming his brain in no particular order, running together like drops of water in an ever-shifting sea. Each memory that surfaced came snared in associations: the act of hiding behind the oak carried in tow a scene of old terror, a stranger chasing the boy around a maypole, or the maypole might have been a tree, the strang-er's heatsaw might have been a gun, the screaming might have been the girl's, or his mother's, the stranger might have been his father, they might have been playing a game, it all might have ended with a happy dinner together, or a bloody rape, a merciful rescue, a woozy afternoon having his wounds dressed by a tree pollard, going to sleep behind an ancient oak and waking alone and bewildered under a witch's ash.

In the glass-walled manor of memory, everything is an imperfect reflection of everything else.

Prompted by a thought he had since discarded, the boy brought a hand to rub his stomach, and something wrong or unexpected there put a brake to his spinning awareness. He lifted the crazy-quilt shirt and exposed someone's flat, pale belly—not his own, surely, though the warm flesh tingled at his finger's touch.

Across the stomach ran a thin white scar. Though healed, it was clearly never going to vanish. It was like a second navel, a flawed one: sign of a troubled birth.

The girl's voice said, "Well, I don't see why we're just standing around. I'm going to find him."

"Oh," said the tall man. "Well, then. Sheldrake, go along with her, won't you? Or Groby. Where has Groby gone? I don't want anything—"

"I don't *need* to be watched over," the girl's voice said. Not unkindly; only explaining something that should have been clear. (The boy understood this, understood everything about that voice, and nothing else about anything.) "I'll be back. But not until I find him."

The boy remembered then why he had hidden behind the tree; at the same time he forgot having hidden behind another tree, under other circumstances. He remembered the girl's face, and forgot other faces he had once known very well. He forgot and he remembered, remembered and forgot; the two must happen together now. As agile footsteps neared his hiding place, he vanished like a sprite into the forest.

The dragon path wove its way through the dark bottom of the woods. The boy moved along it cautiously, having trouble with his legs. They were too long and the knees too high and the joints not as smooth as they should be. Instead of bending with his weight and springing back, they exhibited two contrary and unpredictable tendencies: at times not bending at all, which made him tall and stilted like a fawn, or else collapsing altogether, which was frightening at first and finally bewildering, for balance was crucial to following the path's abrupt sinuosities.

The dragon path was not like any other. It wasn't a path at all, in the sense of connecting this place with that. It was simply a pattern of the forest, part of its fiber, as the patterns etched in bark are part of a tree. When the boy was very young he thought the path was plain to everyone, that its serpentine stretches were there for anyone to tread. By degrees he realized this was not so; that the pattern of the woods was like a code that only he could read, or an image in one of his mother's holographs: if you stand *here* you can see it, but from *there* it vanishes behind the leaves.

He drew up in puzzlement. Ahead of him, the bottomland narrowed to a gully, where the dragon path twisted around a stream. Dimly the boy remembered someplace cool and dark that way, a grotto, where he might be safe. But his feet, clutching the moldy soil with long bare toes, urged him sideways, out of the gully, up a hillside overgrown with mountain laurel.

He frowned.

A tug of intuition. The phrase—his mother's—floated into his mind. But though he remembered the words, he could not remember, anymore, the sound of his mother's voice saying it. He tried; he thought of the games they had played—on this very hillside, probably—and the way his mother had taught him how to elude her, how to avoid being caught.

Just be still, she told him. *Don't think. Wait for a tug of intuition.*

—Hiding-games. The boy racing ahead on the dragon path, ducking between the trees, while his mother moved quietly down the streambed, seeking him out. And though he had been very good at this—had made no noise and hidden very cleverly—his mother had nearly always found him. She couldn't feel the dragon path, as he could; yet she had always known where to pause, where to stoop, where to peer around a rock or up into the branches. *How,* he would ask her, *how did you know,* and she would try to tell him, but the explanation was roundabout and confusing.

It's the fields, he remembered. *Everything has a field around it—little boys, and trees, and squirrels—and the fields control the things inside them. Tiny things, smaller than you can see, that dance all around inside.*

Inside of me?

Inside of everything. Everything alive. And the fields help everything to be healthy, and to grow into taller trees and long-legged boys. Like you'll be one day.

Had there been a note of sadness in her voice, something on her face like a shadow? The boy couldn't remember. He remembered only staring at his mother as she spoke—the orchids of the dome bright and many-colored above her, and deep blue sky beyond that—trying to imagine a field surrounding her like a cartoon halo: bright and shimmery, moving as she moved, suspended like a magic veil around her head (though she said it wasn't like that, wasn't like anything you could think of). And as he thought about it now, on this distant May afternoon, he found that he could remember that image, that swirling halo, which was just something he had made up, but could no longer remember his mother's face, which had been something real.

It *had* been real, hadn't it?

And if it was, then where had all of it—her face, her voice, her memory—where had they gone? Where did memories disappear to?

Twenty yards in ahead of him, a twig snapped among the thorntrees by the stream. *Bear,* he thought: the kind of thinking that occurs without conscious effort; a recognition of signs. In the boy's mind the image formed of a large and wary animal, contemplating his presence as he contemplated its own. And waiting.

The tug of intuition came again. *Get out of the gully,* it told him. *Go home.*

Go . . . where?

Wild Turkey Pool stood black and deep before Vesica. She peered around it, feeling more than anything else a sense of irritation.

Why had he run away like that?—when anybody could see they were his friends and nobody was going to hurt him. After all that she, Vesica, had done. Going without sleep. The baby clothes. Didn't he realize . . .

There were to be no strange encounters here today. She neither saw the boy nor felt any niggling premonition of his presence. Was it all a bad mistake, then? Was the notion of the Enchanted Prince, and the great adventure, nothing but girlish fancy?

She lowered herself to the cool blue-black rock and looked down into the water. By daylight you could see how deep it was. Cold and black, it drank the sunlight and quivered like some icy, opalescent jelly. She gazed into its depths, hoping with half her mind that some message, some clue, might be descried there—but there was only her own face, imperfectly reflected.

Home.

But where—and what—was that?

Of all the things the boy had forgotten, or become confused about, he had forgotten this one most thoroughly. All he could remember of where he had once lived were discrete, unconnected fragments: orchids, wistful music in the air, the sharp smell of dittany-of-Crete. Smooth wood, milled from oaks, standing around him. And birds, some kind of birds—aloof, imperturbable, marking the dark hours with their cooing. And what else . . . chickens? Brood hens, were they, plumping-up on their nests?

But that was all of it. Only the pieces. The important things—the place itself, what life he had lived there, and with whom—were gone.

But here was the boy, returned by some whim or miracle from the long silent dream; and here was a bear snapping branches in the thorntrees just ahead of him, and an inner voice urging him out of the gully.

He surrendered, let his eager toes direct him. They dug into the pliant earth of the hillside, passing silently between mountain laurels and mounds of honeysuckle. Sun slanted between towering oaks. It must be late. The boy strained for some glint of recognition; but how could he expect that? After so much time had passed.

The hillside leveled off, and the boy found himself in a place where the small trees of the understory grew thickly beside a clearing. He had not lost the sense of a large and wary animal behind him, but now he was more troubled by what might lie ahead. Clenching his teeth, he stepped quickly and silently through a screen of bayberry and out into a meadow glowing orange with the haze of afternoon.

The sudden brightness astonished him. How long it had been since he had stood in open sunlight there was no way to tell, but from the effect it had on him—indrawn breath, squinted eyes, racing heartbeat—it must have been a very great while. He ran his feet through the daisies and prairie grass exulting in the sun. If the forest had been a sanctuary of silence, this meadow was a teeming marketplace of life. Bumblebees danced on clover. Earthworms excavated the sod. The season's first butterflies fluttered above the wild thyme they treasured, and robins darted with beaks stuffed full of thatching, alighting in the shaded bowers that would be their homes. And all these things the boy observed with a feeling of acknowledgment or approval. *Very well*, his heart seemed to say. *Go on with it*.

An odd sort of thought, but not the first that had occurred to him on this unprecedented day.

Crrkk, went more twigs behind him.

The boy crossed the meadow without looking. He had encountered bears before (at least the situation felt familiar) and the general principle involved was one of avoidance. Reaching the meadow's end, a hundred yards away, he allowed himself one glance across a shoulder. There was something there, all right, behind the bayberry. He couldn't tell what, but it didn't worry him. *Home* was where he was heading, and home—whatever else it may have been—was the place where you were safe.

In his preoccupation the boy had not noticed the peculiar character of the woods he had reentered. Here, instead of springing up randomly, the great columnar oaks stood in rows, like a giant's orchard. They were so old that their fattened trunks almost touched, and their upper branches were more dead than alive. Beyond them were cedars, aligned in an evergreen wall.

The boy moved ahead. Whoever had planted these trees (and it was impossible to think that *no* one had) had placed them much too close together, or never meant for them to reach their present size. The huge roots pressed upward, wrestling for the nutrients that seeped into the soil. The boy climbed over them like half-buried barrels. He drew near the cedar wall.

Something about that wall . . .

"AHA!" cried Lorian. She stepped from behind a tree.

The boy nearly collapsed.

"I KNEW you'd come here!"

The short-haired woman came forward with what may have been the most self-satisfied look ever to form on a human face. The boy stepped away but—other than natural startlement—felt no impulse to flee. It was somehow clear that she was harmless, despite her aggressive affect.

"I don't know how I knew," she said, looking around and speaking rapidly, "but I *knew*. Wow." She blinked. "That's really amazing, isn't it?"

The boy said nothing, but for the first time since awaking from the long dream he *knowingly* said nothing—which carried the implication that, if he wanted to, he could speak.

Lorian studied him, her eyes now showing concern. "Hey, I'm sorry if I scared you."

The boy shook his head. This woman—whom he was *sure* he had never seen before—seemed somehow, very strangely, familiar.

"What is this place, anyway?" she said. She looked around. As with the boy, the wall of cedars somehow called her attention. "I mean, I had this idea you would be here and all that . . . . But what, um—"

Snkk, went another twig. So close behind them, the boy seized Lorian's arm without thinking, ready to hurl her out of the bear's way. But it wasn't a bear.

It was Groby.

The boy recognized the giant who had knelt beside him, holding him with great soft hands, while he lay on the petal-strewn earth. Yet seeing Groby now, the grace of his lumbering movements, the boy seemed to know him in a way that transcended that brief memory. He held his ground.

If Groby noticed the two of them at all, he gave no sign. He was a dozen paces away, staring at a sheet of paper. His footfalls were bringing him obliquely toward the place where the boy and Lorian waited. They remained that way, united in patient wariness, until Groby paused, looked up at the boy, then Lorian, and smiled.

He said, "It looks like you're both feeling better."

And the boy shook his head—in disbelief, not denial. For Groby, in his slow unerring shamble, had *tracked* him here. Which meant, for most of the way, that he had tracked him along the dragon path, which only the boy could follow.

"What's your name?" the big man asked. "You can talk, can't you?"

The boy tightened his lips. Silence was his only refuge, and even that was imperiled.

"Do you know where we are?" said Groby. "Is this where you come from?"

The boy frowned. He had followed the impulse, the tug of intuition that urged him home. Yet he no longer knew what home he had, or whether to believe the memory of having one at all. His lip quivered. He began walking toward the wall of cedars, because that was, ultimately, where the tug of intuition led him—toward the row of old trees that grew so close together that their bristled, interpenetrating limbs blocked out the light.

He experienced in that moment—between one footfall and the next—a bit of linguistic sorcery: as if a witch had muttered, "Fire," and lo, a flame had leapt up before him, the boy discovered that the thing he had been calling, in the metaphoric language of thought, "a cedar wall" was nothing else but an actual wall of cedars—a wall, in that hundreds of thick timbers had been placed side by side and braced up and nailed together—a *wall of cedars* because from each of those timbers sprouted dusty-green needles like those that grow from living plants. The closer the boy got the more certain it was—and yet the more impossible—that the wall before him *was* a wall of naked, bark-stripped planks, and that at the same time it was alive, as though the cedars had never been sawed and planed.

As the boy stared at the miraculous planks, his eye was caught by a rectangular signboard, nailed high on the wall and all but smothered in needles. It was embellished in an old-fashioned way, with a garland of flowers around the lettering. And like the wall itself, the sign was somehow, miraculously, alive: its flowers were not carved wooden things but real—real flowers, really blooming. Beneath them, weathered but still readable after the long dream, the sign proclaimed:

Balance Act
Reporting Station 12

And from above the sign, its source still hidden behind the living wall, a mellow, smooth-as-polished-wood voice came drifting down:

"Wow, hey! Visitors! Hey! Let me figure out how
this gate works.
It's been a real
long time."

Nineteen

WITHIN THE WALLS of the ancient city of Riverrun, Professor Tylyester left his black-porticoed townhouse for his fortnightly dinner at the Silent Partners' Club. He carried under one arm a dictionary-sized sheaf of papers whose label, before its dissolution by palm-sweat, had read NOTES TOWARD A CRITIQUE OF HAYATA'S COMMENTARY ON THE "ORGANIZING PRINCIPLE" OF GENETIC TRANSPOSITION, WITH EMPHASIS ON THE HISTORICAL AND BIOGRAPHICAL CONTEXT AND HER EFFORT TO END THE CRISIS OF INDETERMINISM— the compendious and nearly complete work upon which his reputation, he hoped, would ultimately incline.

Night was overdue. A low-flying formation of clouds caught the conflagrations in the Military District—celebrating a calamitous victory over heathens and appliance-sellers in the South—and trapped their smoky effusions above the catafalques and office buildings that a more self-confident century had seen fit to erect along the western battlements. Somewhere among those hundred-foot granite ashcans and marble highboys stood the dome of the Observatory, like a half-deflated ball cast out with grander garbage. Tylyester gave a dutiful glance in its direction, failed to locate it, and entered a cab. The driver was barely awake, perhaps kept that way by the din of fireworks; he cranked over the ill-tempered engine without need of encouragement. Slipping it in gear he remarked:

"Feels slimy out, don't it? Must be summer."

The Dean did not dispute this, for his mind was set on graver problems. It was not, however, summer. It was Flora Day. Tylyester believed in accuracy at all costs: accuracy and woolen socks. They were equally hard to come by, as the Pure Force increased its influence over both the Press and the garment trade. But Tylyester intended to outlive the Pure Force, as firmly as he meant to predecease his stockings.

Halfway down the Aleatory Strand the cab ran afoul of a manifestation of the very movement he had been, in the forum of his mind, decrying. Two hundred young people, drugged or drunk or maybe just disaffected—the Dean was not certain how disaffected youths look, though there were said to be quite many of them—jammed the street around the overturned wagon of an incense vendor which had been pressed into service as a podium. The speaker tonight was one Tylyester had noticed before: tall and mostly thin, wide only at the shoulders, which made him unbalanced-looking. From his face radiated a certain presence or aura that had an undeniable effect on the crowd. None of the red-eyed demonstrators showed any inclination to wander off, and a few seemed actually to be listening to what he was saying.

Which was, at the moment, " 'Reality wraps itself around us.' By this he meant that we can change by our actions and our thoughts not only the direction of events but actually the contours of possibility, the stresses that play along the great interwoven fretwork of chance. For as Action arises from Intention, so do the forms of things grow from the seed of ideas . . ."

"Yo!" barked the driver. "Out of the way there!"—depressing his horn handle. The nearest youths shuffled aside like cattle and the cab crept through. From where Tylyester sat it was impossible to tell whether the vehicle was still on the roadway, but that was always a problem with the Aleatory Strand. They reached Faerie Sump half an hour behind schedule and there ran out of fuel. The Dean sat for some time absorbed in the chortling of quail, who were drawn to the Sump by a profusion of Jerusalem artichokes, until he noticed the cab had stopped. He cleared his throat, but the driver was asleep now—the martial festivities were over and the evening had fallen quiet.

The Dean disembarked, unsure whether the driver was narcoleptic or merely impertinent. He gathered up his bundle and realized as he stood ankle-deep in smartweed and mud that he had lost interest in the fortnightly dinner. They would miss him at the Club; they would speculate about his health; whether he would die, if he died, intestate; and that would be good for them. He smiled.

The Moon was three-quarters full, Cold-Shouldering Venus.

Tylyester was no more than a medium-size man, but he had—like the Speaker behind him—a certain presence. Largely this emanated from his face, which was dark-browed and broad. His build was indeterminate under the robe he wore, on loan from a banished colleague, now dead, as rumor had it; though a contrary rumor (—these things often come in pairs—) held that the colleague was alive, disfigured to a degree that human eyes could not bear to look upon, and living on a farm in the West. Tylyester sighed. He must try to keep the robe clean, just in case, though it would be difficult with all the mud around. He wondered if he was still on the Strand.

Had anyone been following his movements from, say, the Observatory of the Secret College, it might have seemed (supposing the hypothetical observer was equipped with an optical instrument of sufficient resolution) that the Dean was floating in the air, hovering before the backdrop of the swamp. This illusion was engendered by the long robe which concealed his trudging feet while his upper body remained motionless: arms wrapped thoughtfully around their brain-taxing bundle, head canted down, mane thickened by moonlight. He would have appeared, through that distant, slightly out-of-focus lens, to be deep in concentration, as befitted his honorable, if underfunded, station.

The fact of the matter was, Tylyester could not decide whether to turn his attention to the lusty caterwauling of quails, the oddly pungent aroma mixed with the customary stench of the Sump, the laughter and shattering glass of a party warming up across the water, the onlooking moon, or the rapid clop of footsteps approaching along the Strand—

the Strand itself, and not the muddy byway onto which the Professor had wandered. In the end he chose the footsteps, since the other four points of interest would likely be there later, and there was something about the footsteps he seemed to recognize.

In the long robe Tylyester was nearly invisible. In any case Low Commissioner Narthex would not have recognized him; their acquaintance was slight. The Commissioner was in a hurry, if one could judge from the heated character of his movements as he jerked his arachnoid frame along the street. Though the night was dark, a shadow flowed behind him. Some slight discord in their respective motions—the Commissioner's quantized, the shadow's continuous and smooth—suggested to Tylyester that they were separate entities, albeit part of the same phenomenon. This was borne out when Narthex said, quite audibly in the stillness of the Sump:

"Where is that damned footbridge?"

The shadow, never faltering in its liquid stride or flickering for an instant into visibility, murmured an interrogative.

"No, damn it, and that is precisely why I am going. But invitation or no, her ladyship shall not turn me away. You may be sure of that."

He stopped. His body and the shadow's seemed to merge, as though the two aspects of that single, detestable phenomenon (thought Tylyester, imposing like any observer his own bias on the material at hand) became for an instant united—jerky particle and flowing wave merging in perfect blackness, negative existence, the Blank Card whose face no one may see. But here Tylyester's thoughts, like his feet, were straying wildly.

". . . understand?" Commissioner Narthex was saying.

"How about my money?" the other figure replied—and Tylyester understood why he had thought it a shadow. It was a tall youth dressed in the characteristic garb of the Pure Force, his rosemary-green robe nearly as unnoticeable as the Dean's gray.

"Your money," said Narthex mockingly. "Yes, yes: here. Is that all that's important to you?"

"What about you?" the youth jibed, grabbing the tidy bundle. "What are *you* in this for? Fame and honor?"

The Commissioner's lips curled in an invisible sneer.

"The Triumph of the Noosphere," he said, his voice bone-dry with irony. "The fulfillment of the Speaker's prophesies. Nature's reconquest of the Earth."

"Ox balls," said the youth. He broke, unexpectedly, into a loud and carrying laugh.

"Now if you'll excuse me," murmured Narthex, "I have a party to attend."

Without further ado he spun about and tucked himself away into the night, with a degree of stealth hitherto associated with viruses.

"What could be the matter?" Lady Widdershins inquired of Paracelsus, her poodle. "I have such a peculiar *feeling* tonight."

Paracelsus wagged his tail, then remembered the pink bow attached to it. Dogs have come a long way since evolving from the wolf; but not, perhaps, *that* far. Sniffing, he stalked indignantly away, stopping just short of where cascading aubrietas, beaded with spray from the gardener's hose, threatened to get his paws wet.

Lady Widdershins's lawn party, held annually on Flora Day, had reached that intermediate stage when the guests were feeling talkative and most of them could still talk. They staggered happily about the Upper Garden, while above their heads strings of lights glowed citrine and vermilion, making bright muddy puddles in the stagnant reaches of the Sump, and over *them* hung a third-quarter waning moon. Alone with her poodle on the patio, Lady Widdershins fanned herself with a spray of waxwing feathers and directed her ear to the front of the house, where a cab had squished up the Marshmain drive and some members of the Hardy Plant Society were exclaiming over its passenger. Judging from the sexual inclinations of the exclaimers, her ladyship need not bestir herself. She sighed.

Here in Riverrun, the red numerals of Flora Day glared out from an awkward stretch of the garden calendar, a row of squares as empty as a hopscotch board. Early May was an in-between time, when spring bedders—so festive only a week or two before—were looking bedraggled, while roses and phlox and dephiniums were not yet out of the bud. Lady Widdershins made do with the double red 'Robin' strain of aubrietas, which spilled from tubs and baskets around the patio, and the hardy geranium 'Charles Kinbote', whose regal purple made a soothing contrast as it lapped onto the flagstones leading down to Faerie Sump, of which Marshmain commanded the best, the very best view.

It had been different at Biggar's Neck. There, on Flora Day, spring was at its most glorious. The air tumbling fresh and clear from the mountains seemed to whisper a ceaseless promise of wonderful things, happy days ahead, as it slipped between the primroses and forget-me-nots and snow-white scented violas. Here in the city, the air scarcely moved at all, and what promises it made were of another dull and muggy summer. As to anything slipping between the primroses, Lady Widdershins had learned in the last fourteen years not to inquire.

Yet it was better, she thought, to have a party, even a wrongly timed one—to celebrate Nature in her abundance, even if that abundance was unfairly doled out—than to have no party at all.

Onto the long sloping lawn beyond the Upper Garden, some of her guests had deployed themselves for a moonlit game of croquet. The sounds of mallets striking balls, balls striking balls, contestants howling, bottles being hurled across the Sump: Oh!—how it took her back to the long-lost glass-walled manor, and all she had left behind. You don't know, do you, when you give something up, how much, how terribly much you will miss it. Behind her the latest arrival had entered the grounds, surrounded by admirers.

On thinking it over more carefully, Lady Widdershins decided it *wasn't* the croquet match that had reminded her of Biggar's Neck. In fact, as she now recalled it, she had thought the sport fiendishly annoying, being played as it often was at great volume just when she was in the mood for a nap. No, some smell had done it, some very odd but familiar kind of smell; not entirely, she thought, a pleasant one.

"My dear lady," said a voice behind her. She turned, quickly donning her party face (delight, mild amusement, ladylike distraction) to greet one of the fussy little men of the Society—good-hearted things, most of them, though prone to fits of envy, and anyway useful at licking envelopes for the monthly mailings. This particular gentleman was leading on one arm, an arm that visibly trembled, a boy or very young man of striking radiance. He was not pretty, this youth, and even less handsome, but his narrow face was suffused with a kind of glow or effulgence such as girls his age sometimes get when they make the vast mistake of becoming pregnant. Only more so.

"May I present," said the aging escort, whose next words were partly lost in an uproar from the croquet field—evidently one of the players had gotten caught in the quicksand at the bottom of the lawn—and Lady Widdershins didn't quite catch the name of the newcomer. It might have been Owen.

". . . is the Speaker," the poor old fellow continued (as the boy seemed absolutely to ignore him, instead studying Lady Widdershins with a look of intelligent interest), "of the Pure Force! Isn't that *exciting?*"

"I should say," said Lady Widdershins, eyes narrowed. "So you're the one telling us we should stop trimming the weeds from the sidewalks and just Let Everything Go—let ourselves revert to cave dwellers."

"Tree dwellers, perhaps," the boy purred. His airy voice had a moving quality, like the northern breeze. "We shall have little choice in the matter by the end of summer. Nature shall have made our choice for us."

"Oh, what nonsense," Lady Widdershins declared. She fanned herself and thought she rather liked this boy, if only for his perfectly applied mascara.

"Have you noticed," he said, "how wild-looking your flowers are this year? How the stems have grown woody, even on the annuals? Has 'Charles Kinbote' ever been so . . . *robust?*"

"Now, now," said the elderly invert, trying with a series of mincing gestures to quiet his charge down. The boy only smiled at Lady Widdershins as though the two of them shared some wonderfully horrid secret that the rest of Society was salivating to know.

"That is perfectly ridiculous," she said haughtily. "And I shall be happy to convince you of that on any Thursday afternoon, when as you may know, I am At Home. Paracelsus! Stop that!"

She turned and strode gracefully, as in a solitary tango, across the patio, toward the spot where one imagined her troublesome pet to be. In this case the dog was, as it were, conjectural: adduced as a means of amputating the conversation at the knees. It would resume, she was certain, at a later date; she hoped it would; but not until she was ready. Tonight there were other things on her mind, and something was definitely the matter down at the foot of the lawn.

She had barely stepped onto the flagstone walk when a ruckus erupted at the front of the manor. It sounded as though a large declamation of poets was trying to crash the party: there were huzzahs, whistles blown, small bombs or firecrackers detonated in succession, and a couple of people screaming as if someone dear to them had thoughtlessly died. Meantime on the croquet lawn the playing stopped and someone shouted "Take your hands off me!" in a very nasty voice. Lady Widdershins hesitated a moment; then her mind was made up by the sound of crashing masonry. Her front porch was guarded by two *precious* hand-carved Pucks, and if anything had happened to them there would (mark her words) be Trouble.

As she turned back to the patio, a mob of ill-clad youths rounded the house and came charging like a wolfpack in her direction.

"Grab that old bag," the tallest of them directed. "She looks like she's worth something."

Much too organized, Lady Widdershins thought, for poets; which was some consolation.

"What *are*," she demanded, "you ghastly people doing?"

Two of the youths grabbed her by the flabby-looking forearms, to find them surprisingly well muscled. Not for nothing did she spend five hours a day digging in the dirt. She brought the youths' heads painfully together (an old Finishing School trick) and pushed them aside as one gently but firmly clears last year's growth from a perennial. This cleared the mob and her mind considerably. She now saw that there were only a dozen of them, and none of them looked well fed.

"Forget her," the tall one said. "Just trash the place."

The pack of young wolves dashed around her, and Lady Widdershins thought, Trash the place my potash.

"Sportsmen!" she cried to the croqueteers. "Here with your mallets at once!"

The ensuing mêlée was, though noisy, neither the strangest nor the most violent to have occurred at one of her lawn parties. In this—the fact that the party-crashers were new at it, and she was not—the hostess had a firm advantage. Her troops were generally older, and many of them had trouble hearing her bellowed commands, but this gave them a greater tendency to be treacherous, to administer with mallet and trowel and flower-stake wounds that mere youths would have shrunk from. It was not a rout, by any means. The patio, the garden, the luscious lawn were all badly injured, as were a number of partygoers' clothes. But they all had more clothes back home, heaven knows, and one had to allow for party damage in filling out one's wardrobe.

At some point in the battle it occurred to Lady Widdershins that Low Commissioner Narthex had achieved an entrée to the grounds, despite her strict instructions to the doormen to impede him. Well, but the doormen might have been knocked unconscious—and had better have been, if her Pucks had met with any harm—and anyway if one is staging a dogfight one has got to expect a few curs.

"My dear lady," the Low Commissioner accosted her, "I came as soon as I heard the disturbance. I believe I may have helped in dispatching three or four of the ruffians."

For some reason he was oozing mud from about midthigh downwards. Lady Widdershins noted with satisfaction the resemblance of this substance to the result of feeding Paracelsus too many chocolate bars.

"It is disgraceful," Narthex went on, bringing his unseemly person closer, "how the Home Guard is unable to maintain any semblance of civil order anymore. I should say, if anyone asked me, that things were worse than ever this year. As luck would have it, some members of the Volunteer Militia—which as you know was created by legislation I introduced in the last session . . ."

"No one," said Lady Widdershins, dabbing at her brow and trailing a sentence or two behind him, "would dream of *asking* you, Commissioner. And I refer not only to your opinion of the Home Guard. Well done, gentlemen!"

The troop of croqueteers trudged wearily onto the desecrated patio, where red petals of aubrieta 'Robin' had bled from their containers and lay drying under the decumbent bodies of the beaten youths. A platoon of fussy gardeners stood guard over the prisoners with a frightsome assortment of weapons procured from the Marshmain toolshed.

Behind them, as Narthex had begun to say, were a brooding contingent of militiamen—looking on the whole like unemployed farmers with scarlet armbands. What contribution these worthies had made to quelling the Flora Day Riot (as it would be dubbed tomorrow in the *Daily Wake*) was open to question. They had not gotten very dirty doing it. Their sole prisoner was a youth dressed, like the others, in a gray-green robe, but who somehow stood apart from the rest. As they led him—for he offered no struggle—toward the street, Lady Widdershins recognized the enigmatic boy she had invited back for one of her Thursdays.

"Why are they taking *him*?" she demanded of Narthex.

"Ah," he said. "The ringleader. The Speaker. We've had our eye on him for months. He's the one that gets them stirred up in the streets, and sends them off to do his dirty work."

She wanted to argue, for clearly this was an absurdity, a grotesque (she assumed, until she thought about it) misunderstanding. But in that moment the gang of militiamen trudged past her leading the boy, and the look he turned briefly in her direction was one of complete serenity, like THE DISSIDENT in a deck of fortune cards.

"Good night," he breathed softly, prompting a militiaman to thump him behind the head with a padded club, the kind that leaves no bruises.

"Good night," bowed Low Commissioner Narthex, beaming as though he had made a quiet move in some deep game. In a suspiciously casual tone he added, "By the way, my lady—I'd like to have a little chat with you, at your convenience. Nothing urgent, you know. It's about your goddaughter."

"My—" Lady Widdershins frowned; then frowned more severely as she began to understand.

Professor Tylyester arrived home to discover that he had forgotten his doorkey. He wasn't worried; it was the sort of thing he never expected to remember. He made his way to the rear of the black-porticoed townhouse, where there was an overgrown kitchen garden and a door left perpetually unlocked. Out of habit he bent to sniff the herb bed (a tangle of thriving species, the more varied because Tylyester never weeded it). The lower he bent, the more distinct became the smell that pierced his nostrils. It was a tart-but-sweet smell that had been in the air all evening, and he recognized it chiefly for what it was not: it was *not* anything that belonged here. When he could lean no further he stooped on rickety knees, and at that instant, in midstoop, it occurred to him.

It was dittany-of-Crete—that herb that had once been popular in planting boxes and windowsills. Oh, but surely no one grew *that* anymore. Besides, it was not hardy here; it would never have lived through the winter.

He traced, by noncommittal moonlight, the odor to a particular plant. It was a woody thing, though its leaves were small and it looked, on the whole, recently sprouted. He tugged at it, and immediately the stem appeared to wilt, as though he had uprooted it. Then it began to wrap itself around his finger: a bean plant, seen in time-lapse exposure as it curls around a pole. Of course it was no such thing; it was nothing Tylyester had ever seen before, and its clinging-pads stung where they touched him like a nettle. Very quickly the sting grew painful, and shortly unbearable. Tylyester cried out.

The strange plant grew nineteen inches that night, its stem became erect and turgid, and its leaflets widened into round-lobed, dusty green leaves reminiscent of *Quercus alba*, white oak.

But it was not white oak. The Biology Department of the Secret College, arriving in force at the predawn summons of its Dean, was unanimous on that. Nor was it a nettle, nor a vine, and least of all was it dittany-of-Crete—though in some ways it possessed the traits of each of these, and more besides. (One biologist was particularly struck by how its bark was remarkably resilient, soft yet leathery; in a word, skinlike.) No, this plant was something else, they said:
something remarkably
different.

Twenty

THE DEAD BOTANIST'S garden rose again from the black soil to stand like a floriferous mirage against the backdrop of the half-collapsing dome. Two thousand species—selected by the staff of the old Reporting Station for their fruitfulness, their rarity, their promise as subjects for research—had been brought in pairs and half-dozens and (in the case of favored flowers and herbs) hundreds into this four-acre earthbound ark. And when all the plants were aboard and the snow had battened them down, the ark had loosed its moorings and floated out across Time. It had drifted over the centuries; its passengers had bred and crossbred and mingled with wind- and bird-ferried migrants; and now it had beached itself on the soil of a different age.

The garden had changed in innumerable small ways. Mulberries still lined the chicken run, though their ranks had grown ragged. Strawberries had gained ground on what once had been a lawn. Dwarf apple trees were no longer dwarf. The grape-and-kiwi arbor, like a channel in need of dredging, was clogged and unnavigable. The row of windbreaking nut-pines formed a second, taller and less negotiable wall in the south.

Yet what was striking about these changes, these rearrangements of the grounds, was not that they had occurred but that *only* they had occurred. The five-hundred-year-old landscape was astonishingly intact. Only its edges, its lines of demarcation had been jumbled, but this was on the order of a shift in artistic fashion, a slide from crisp portraiture into robust if less orderly impressionism—through which the subject had sat patiently, wearing a smile that grew minutely sadder, wiser, more enigmatic.

The first person to behold this (as the gate groaned up like the door of a picture-book castle) was the boy with an unfamiliar body and fading memories of a long, impossible dream. He ducked through the opening when the gate was inches off the ground. When it was high enough for Groby to follow, the big man found himself on a walkway of flat stones among which pennyroyal crept, shaded by walnuts. Pendulous branches framed his view of the grounds. In the center of the frame, twenty feet away, stood the boy, his patchwork pants hidden by a patch of young raspberries among which self-sown bellflowers bloomed. He was motionless, but with the jittery stillness of a bird, ready to fly at the first shadow. His head jerked sideways: right, to the comfrey cage, the chestnuts, the decrepit shed; left, to the broken ranks of corn and squash, where bees called on violets among the rotten windfalls of a pear tree. His mouth opened in a silent shout, which he quickly swallowed, and his eyes—which Groby just glimpsed when the boy snapped his head around, as though hearing footsteps behind him— glistened like sky-blue crocuses after a shower.

Whatever the boy was hoping for, listening for, perhaps fearing to find, it was not the easygoing voice that floated down from a walnut tree beside the gate.

"Hey . . ." the voice drawled, finding an extra half-syllable somewhere in the *y*. "Be right down, soon as I get this gate—"

The voice was gobbled up by a loud metallic crunch.

"Oh, wow," it said, no more loudly. "Think I might've broken it."

There was a disorganized clunking, and Groby looked up to see the lower part of a man (boots, torn trousers, sagging leather toolbelt) descending a ladder whose planks were laid almost invisibly against the scaly bark. When an orange-bearded face came into view it bore a look of mild vexation, but at sight of Groby—who stood eye-to-eye with him, though the man was still two rungs up—this became a broad and unmistakably lazy grin.

"*Wow*." Its owner nodded, as though the effort of climbing down had paid off. "Good thing that gate opened high enough to let *you* in. Don't think it's going to close again, though. Little buddy gone somewhere?"

Little buddy? Oh: Groby turned to the boy, to where the boy had stood among the raspberries, but he had vanished. It seemed to be something he was good at.

"Bashful," suggested the man on the ladder. "Probably turn up for dinner. The others coming soon?"

"Hm?" said Groby, who was still wondering about the boy, wondering many things about the boy, and had not yet dragged his thoughts into the compound with this relaxed and wholly unastonished stranger.

"Hope they will be," the man went on—quite happy, it appeared, to carry both sides of the conversation. "Wife won't be ready for a while, anyway. *Wow*. Guests for dinner, and we don't even know if there's extra plates!"

Groby frowned. His great brain was foundering in a flood of stimuli.

"But hey," said the man. "Getting ahead of myself here. They call me the Owl."

"They do?" said Groby, his attention caught at last. He had never heard of such a thing.

The man—the Owl—stepped off the ladder, holding out a hand. His movements matched his voice: the loose-jointed frame seemed to be engineered to seek the most effortless path between two points. Groby took the hand, seeing its owner, in a sense, for the first time, as though a name had been needed under which to file him.

The Owl, yes: it was a right enough heading. He stood a head shorter than Groby, which did not make him exactly short. His hair was orange, as Groby had noted, and also tangled and thick. It flowed onto his shoulders and from there, becoming at no certain point a beard, onto his chest. It was pressed flat from being slept on. He had an air of very quiet exuberance: eyes narrow but bright, mouth flattened into a semipermanent inward-turning smile. His build was wiry, though this had to be surmised through several layers of unkempt (though impeccably laundered) clothing.

But all that aside, who *was* he?

"Couldn't have come at a better time, anyway," the Owl reflected, stroking his beard (meaning, Groby presumed, *You* couldn't, though it developed that he was talking about the gate). "Wolves aren't so hungry anymore, and it's early yet for deer. Of course there's rabbits. Care for a cup of tea?"

"How," said Groby, "did you, um . . ."

"Oh, right," said the wiry man, waving away the unasked question. "Been expecting you for a while now. Hey, wow," (stooping to snatch a clump of dandelion, which he tucked carefully into his number-two shirt) "shame you missed Flora Day!"

The compound was essentially elliptic, yielding to the idiosyncrasies of the terrain and bulging a bit at the end where the dome stood, or rather squatted. Egg-shaped, then, really. The two thousand species of plants were massed in clusters on either side, leaving the center open to haphazardly furrowed beds. These gave way nearer the dome to a small meadow or wild lawn, where segregated stands of grasses and wildflowers had crossed each other's borders to form one riotous knee-high impediment to pedestrians, through which the residents, traveling to and from the berry bushes along the chicken run, had beaten a network of footpaths. The gate was at the egg's narrow end. Outside of it, the Crusade arrayed itself as though to commence a siege, although the guardians of the living walls, who stood before them, gave no sign of resistance.

"My wife," said the wiry Owl, shuffling aside in the gate-opening to clear the field of vision.

"*His wife,*" the person in question said, in a tone of gentle mockery. "Gerta's really my name. *He* may have forgotten, it's been so long since he used it. Around here he calls me—"

"Hey, hey," said the Owl, winking a half-descended eyelid. "Guests, now."

Gerta smiled. Her smile was wide; her face was wide; her shoulders and bust and hips were wide; and yet she was not fat, nor did she give the impression of being slow or lethargic. Her wideness was an aspect of her being, it seemed, rather than just her body, and gave her a comfortable look, a restful and placid look, as though (thought Vesica) she had been very still for a very long time, ripening like a fig, say, and was planning to keep doing so for a considerable while longer. She sought Vesica's eyes. "Do you think your friend will be back soon?"

As though Vesica would know. As though he were even her friend at all, which he wasn't, or else why had he disappeared again? Without even waiting for her.

The Owl said, "Probably turn up when he's ready to." —Rather slyly, it seemed to Vesica, as though omitting the personal pronoun were an act of purposeful ambivalence. "But hey," he said, "come in. It's as cheap in the parlor as on the porch."

The gate had risen no higher, despite Groby's having put his shoulder to it. On the other hand it was no lower. The Owl was probably right: it would never close again. Already the thatching of cedar needles, ripped apart as the door panel rose, had begun to sew itself back together.

One by one, Lord Tattersall first (bending ceremoniously from the waist, remarkably supple), the First Biotic Crusade crawled like suppliants into the compound.

"I can't believe it," said Lorian. "This is it. Really *it*."

"This is what?" frowned Sheldrake.

Like a barrister adducing some crucial cornerstone of her case, she held out a sheet of custard-colored paper.

She said: *"This."*

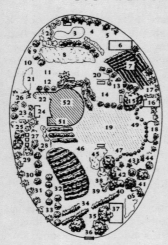

1	Dense forest	27	Beehives
2	"Bog garden"	28	Nectar flowers
3	Pond	29	Willows
4	Robinia	30	Alfalfa
5	Composting area	31	Nut pines
6	"Field" lab	32	Peaches
7	Grain crops	33	Pears
8	Perennial vegetables	34	Raspberries
9	Apples	35	Walnuts
10	Hardy bamboo	36	Gate
11	Grasses	37	Shed
12	Roses	38	Rhubarb
13	Bush cherries	39	Thyme walk
14	Camomile lawn	40	Lovage
15	Medicinal herbs	41	Chinese chestnut
16	Coop	42	Persimmon
17	Black locusts	43	Mulberries
18	Comfrey cage	44	Sumac
19	Wildflower meadow	45	Strawberries
20	Lavender	46	Clover walk
21	Daylilies	47	Blueberries
22	Grape and Kiwi Arbor	48	Chicken run
23	Red currants	49	Gooseberries
24	Methane grill	50	Girasol
25	Cherries	51	Kitchen deck
26	Fig	52	LIVING QTRS

"See what I mean?" said Lorian. "It's all here. Everything. It's like it's only been a couple of months since she . . . went away."

The Crusaders looked down at the diagram and up at the disheveled but still recognizable compound it depicted.

It was late afternoon. A wind whirred briskly from the southwest, but the row of nut pines soothed it to a gentle breeze, cool without threatening to be chilly, sharp with cedar. The shadows across the garden, complementing the orange tinge of the sky, were midnight blue. They shifted restlessly, altering the perspective of the compound with every shuffle. Somewhere ahead, near the dark slumping hill that was the dome, a set of windchimes played a random melody from the austere, rather monkish notes of the Parched Scale, so named by the saint or refugee who invented it on the Moor with paint cans.

"We like to think of ourselves," said Gerta, "as caretakers."

Lorian squinted suspiciously.

"Yeah," said the Owl. "Until the folks that really belong here—whoever they are—come back."

He said this with a wink, implying perhaps that this was purely a convention, that his residency was as good as title to the place. This did not settle well with Lorian. With an assumed air of casualness she said, "Where do you two come from?"

The Owl shrugged. His eyes were merry, sliding from left to right as though the answer to Lorian's question might be lying around somewhere but he had forgotten where he put it. He said:

"Oh, you know—here and there."

"We've wandered a great deal," explained Gerta.

"Been here a while, though." The Owl rubbed his brow, as though trying to remember how long. "But hey—never mind *us*. How about you all? I bet you're a whole lot more interesting than we are."

Lorian frowned, doubting this, but Lord Tattersall straightened himself by another inch and took a symbolic half-step forward, assuming a pose suitable for making a minor proclamation, as for example the christening of an irrigation trench. In his clearest voice he proclaimed:

"We are the First Biotic Crusade. We have come on behalf of the Secret College of Riverrun, seeking to solve the great mystery of why plants have gone mad, and to prevent the forest from conquering the world."

"Wow," said the Owl agreeably. It seemed a form of applause. He and Gerta exchanged brief, apparently innocent smiles. Gerta said, "We're sorry, but we haven't heard about that."

"The Crusade?" said the Governor. "I don't suppose you would have. It just began, you see—"

"No," said the Owl. "She means the other. The college. And the part about plants. Going mad, you say?"

Lorian drew nearer. "Where *do* you people come from?"

The Owl said, "Places *we've* been, plants aren't crazy at all. Always found them right cooperative, myself."

Gerta nodded, gesturing with soft white arms around the compound. "That's why we like it here."

"But the Secret College," persisted Lorian. "Surely you must—"

Tattersall clucked his tongue. "Sometimes I wish," he said, "we had none of us heard of the Secret College. *Well.* But here we are."

"That's right," said Thrull, who since the incident in the hawthorns had kept himself subdued, or at least inconspicuous. "Here we are. Little cancer cells in the body of the forest."

The Owl studied the sallow-faced youth like a naturalist before an interesting new specimen. "What's cancer?" he said, blithely smiling.

Thrull returned the smile with a silent smirk. "Oh, you'll see," he said. "Just wait."

Unexpectedly (and yet, Vesica thought, appropriately) the woman, Gerta, laughed—a rich, liquid sound—as though this suited her fine; she would be happy to wait in this cluttered wonderland forever; as though whatever happened it would always be springtime, the flowers always blooming, the north wind always benign.

"It's getting late," she said. "Will you be staying for dinner?"

"We shall be staying," said Tattersall, "until the Crusade has succeeded."

The dinner table was set for nine, which left one space untaken.

"Hey," said the Owl, "why doesn't everybody sit down?"

The polished, age-darkened wood of the table caught the twilight that drifted with the breeze through the missing panels of the wall. Here on the north-facing side, the frame of the dome was generally intact, only sagging a bit from centuries of snow and fallen leaves, but the panels of foam and Plexiglas had gone the way of all walls. Someone in the intervening years (the work was too old to be the Owl's) had replaced the blown-out panels with oak slats, themselves probably pirated from an outbuilding, and these in turn had begun, like outgrown scales, to shed. The flooring was dry, but suspiciously pliant. Groby moved over it carefully, easing himself into the nearest creaky armchair.

In the center of the table, a lone indigo iris stood in a handblown vase. Gerta lit candles around it, and the six Crusaders and two caretakers sat down together to dine.

The boy had not reappeared. He must be in the compound, it was generally thought; but this was saying very little, for the compound was a small jungle, intershot with paths that led intriguingly into the shadows, offering hundreds of places to hide.

Vesica stared uncertainly at her plate—without contest the best meal she had been offered in a month—wondering if it would be all right to eat without him. It wasn't *her* fault that he had run away, was it? She toyed with her tableware.

"Don't worry," the Owl said kindly. "He'll turn up."

She took a few spoonfuls of curried lentils, which were delicious, but her heart wasn't in it.

"Excuse me," she said, pushing her chair back.

The others either looked at her or not, as their individual senses of courtesy required. Groby made a show of engrossment in a particularly large and steamy dumpling, for which Vesica rewarded him with a squeeze on the shoulder as she left the room.

"Oh my," said Tattersall. "Perhaps I should . . ."

"I think she'll be all right," Gerta said gently. "She just needs to feel her way around, I think. Bread, anyone?"

"Now that bread," said the Owl, "we just baked this morning. Lucky thing."

Tattersall frowned, accepting a fragrant slice. He wasn't entirely certain whether these unexpected hosts were steering the conversation toward, or away from, some subject; and in either case, what the subject might have been. He was certain only that this genteel dinner in the ruins of the Reporting Station was not what the Crusade's planners had had in mind.

"Now see here," he said, determined to assert himself in some way or other. "You people are being most hospitable, and we are grateful for that. But we haven't come up here, you know, on a vacation."

"Came looking for a wild goose," put in Sheldrake.

Tattersall glanced doubtfully into his stewbowl. "What I mean to say is, there is important work to be done. We are here because we believe this place may hold some important items of information. Lost Knowledge, you know. The key to the ecological mystery."

The Owl blinked.

"See," said Lorian, her elbows skating onto the smooth expanse of the table, "a long time ago, there was this very special woman—this botanist—I mean, someone that studies plants—"

Gerta smiled.

". . . any old records," Tattersall was saying. "Books, journals, photographs, that kind of thing. One never knows what might prove useful."

"Even machines," suggested Groby.

"Newspapers," said Lorian.

"Drugs," said Thrull.

"See what I mean?" said Sheldrake, helping himself to more curry.

"Believe I do," the Owl mused. He faced his wife. "Sounds like they've come to look at Amy's stuff."

Motion halted around the table. The Owl, smiling diffidently, said in a tone of good-mannered pride:

"Don't you worry, now. We've been taking good care of things."

The dome was a complicated hollow like a beaver house, one chamber leading to another a few steps up or down, with tall spaces open to the air and twilight in between. As she passed from the southern side into the sagging north, Vesica came against a two-story tier of filing cabinets, sealing off the habitable portion of the dome from the rest. The upper cabinets were overgrown with vines which must have crept in through the skeletal roof, where the building was covered only by a sheet of early stars.

Vesica watched the constellations perform their invisibly slow pirouette: Ixxta, the poisoned princess, slender and bright; Popoco, the drunken pretender, twisting toward the Rock Star, which shone like a stagelight before his glistening eyes. The sky was lower here than at Gravetye Farm. For the first time since Vesica tucked herself into the carton labeled DRAGONPEARS, a wave of homesickness swelled and slowly receded in her breast. Yes, she did miss home; but just home—not living there with her stepfather. She started walking again. In the center of the dome she found a stair.

It was sunk in a shadowy indentation, almost invisible. A poor attempt had been made to seal it off with tar paper, but after a few steps the stair broke free and spiraled away into the rafters. It disappeared in the darkness of the upper levels of the dome. It was, of course, irresistible.

Enjoyable shivers rippled down Vesica's arms as her fingers traced out the path of the handrail, and guided by this she found the wedge-shaped planks with her toes. She climbed slowly, and slowly her eyes adjusted to the dark. This fell short of being absolute; there were horizontal bars of light through the wall of filing cabinets, and a diffuse glow that hung like dust in the air. She reached a second landing but the stair kept going, and Vesica did not even consider stopping short of whatever long-forgotten garret lay above her, snuggled against the night sky.

When her eyes cleared the floorboards of the uppermost story of the dome, she found herself staring into a small and not-at-all-spooky loft. There she discovered the source of the vague illumination: a glowing ball of pale, silver-white light, like a miniature moon; its face was pocked and shadowed like the moon's, though it bore a different expression, and Vesica understood right away what it was. At the age of six or seven she had kept a lightsaver in her bedroom. Hers had been shaped like a duck. This one was very dim, for so little sunlight penetrated the roof. But it served its purpose, or rather purposes: it gave Vesica enough light to see her way up the last steps, and it assuaged her mood of homesickness. She even found it possible, in a queer but satisfying way, to sit on the dusty floor and squint her eyes and half-believe this was her own room again; that she was safe, and where she belonged, and really home.

A voice behind her said, "Get out of here."

Vesica jumped. She opened her mouth to yell, but recognizing the voice (of course) she merely slid across the floorboards and turned to look by stored sunlight at the ghost-white face of the boy.

He was drawn up into a bundle on what once had been a mattress. His eyes were angry. He hugged his drawn-up legs against his chest, bare feet and ankles sticking out of the patchwork pants, and toes digging at a moldy bedspread.

"This is *my* room," he said forcefully. "Get out."

Vesica was prepared to do that—she planned to, in a moment—but first she said, "Look, I guess you think I'm not your friend or everybody is against you or something. But that's not true. We all want to help you. . . . No, that's not right, that really sounds stupid doesn't it? They always say that in stories. Let's see . . . "

She took a deep breath, preparing to start over, but realized that through his glistening eyes the boy was—against his will, perhaps—smiling.

"That's right," he said, his voice coming out deep and throaty. The Adam's apple bobbed in his narrow throat. "They do. Don't they?"

Vesica smiled back, gratified by what she thought must be a really tremendous effort to be nice, to let her know he hadn't meant for *her* to leave him alone, necessarily, but just, basically, *everything.* Circling back to an earlier thought—and so reminding herself of Groby—she said:

"This is your room? Really?"

He nodded. He drew his legs in tighter, nervously wiggling his toes.

"Wow," said Vesica. "What a great place."

He looked away from her.

"How long ago?" she said. "I mean, did your folks live here once or something? Like Gerta and the Owl?"

The boy stared at her helplessly. He wanted to answer her, she thought, but something made it impossible.

"Or I guess you haven't met them," she said quickly. "I don't— I mean, I'm not trying to pry or anything." She looked around. "It just seems like an interesting place to live. Better than where *I* come from."

He considered this and slowly nodded. She wished he would say something again, for his voice—even though it was unhappy—had been soft, and even somehow musical.

She told him: "My name is Vesica."

She started to put out a hand, but the boy, sensing the impending motion, pulled back. When she checked her hand he relaxed again, as though this silent, uncompleted interchange had defined their private system of etiquette, and now they could go on.

"I know," he said. "And I know you made my clothes. Thanks."

"You do?" Vesica stared at him, less certain yet more comfortable than before. She nodded. "You're welcome. So, anyway, what's your name?"

His Adam's apple bobbed. He said, "I . . . " as unthinkingly his long white fingers sought a sanctuary in his ruffled hair. His eyes lost themselves in brown lashes. "I . . . "

"You don't remember!" guessed Vesica. "Is that it?"

He gave a slight frown; boyish wrinkles fleetingly crossed his forehead, surrounded his mouth, then vanished. His skin was as clear and smooth as Vesica's own, though paler. Something in her—the little farmgirl, picking flowers on a hill—wanted to touch it, to smell it like warm earth, wondering what it was made of. The rest of her did not. Her two halves regarded each other with distrust.

"I could *give* you a name," she supposed. "Just, you know, so I'll have something to call you. Until you remember your own."

The boy shrugged. Then, deciding, he said, "Go ahead."

"Okay." She regarded him carefully, scientifically. Where do names come from, she wondered . . . and then it came to her. From stories. Like narcissus, the flower named after somebody looking in a mirror or something, and the beautiful red aubrieta called 'Robin', named after . . .

"I know," she said. "*Tamlin*. I'll call you Tamlin. Is that okay?"

The boy mouthed the word a couple of times, evidently finding it satisfactory.

"*Tamlin*," she said, holding out her hand, this time confidently.

He reached slowly to take it. His hand was larger than hers, his wrist pale, covered with tiny hairs like a light-brown ant caravan; hers was tan and freckled and dusted with golden down. Their fingers momentarily embraced.

"Tamlin," she said again,

                    and the boy, Tamlin, said,
                         "Vesica."

Twenty-one

THE PAST RECAPTURED
the attentions of the Crusade after a flurry of interest in the
present.

"We are here, after all," Lord Tattersall reminded them
on the camomile lawn next morning, "for the purposes of
scientific inquiry. And it seems to me we could start by
getting *that* mess" (turning to consider the impressive leaf-
mound that was the northern portion of the dome) "out of
the way."

"Exactly," said Lorian.

Tattersall beamed at this unusual show of support.

"It's where the greenhouse would have been," she explained. "You know—northern light."

"Ah," he said, a trifle disappointed. "Well. Then perhaps
you and Groby . . . and Thrull there . . ."

Groby nodded. If his training at the Secret College had
equipped him for any nobler task than sifting through centuries' worth of broken glass and leaf mold, he did not point
this out. Thrull behaved less gracefully. With a sound like a
dry expectoration, he turned his back on the proceedings.
Lorian, contrastingly eager, rolled up the sleeves of her lab
smock, an exotic item of clothing she had guarded in her
backpack until now. She said:

"Amy kept . . . I mean, what we want to look for especially is a bunch of disks"—forming a circle of thumbs and forefingers—"about this big. That's what the records were kept on. And a machine to play them."

Groby nodded, as though he had hoped for this.

"Now, Sheldrake," said the Governor, "you and I will interview those two caretakers. Who knows? They may have stumbled on to something. Something whose importance they cannot judge."

"And you can?" said the small man, miming incredulity.

"I don't *know* who can." His lordship shrugged. "If nothing else, we can transcribe the interview and include it with our report to Tylyester. Data," he added, with emphasis, "is the thing. Academicians are very big on that."

Vesica shifted her weight impatiently. "What can *I* do?"

The boy, Tamlin, stood a few feet away from her, contributing to her discomfort. He stared at the dome, the variegated lilacs, the first golden leaves of a *Robinia*—the world at large, but not Vesica.

The Governor smiled a not condescending yet still not properly serious smile. "You, young lady, are assigned to investigate the compound. Very thoroughly, mind you: no stone unturned and all that. And your young friend can help you."

"Tamlin," said Vesica. "His name's Tamlin."

"Mm?" Lord Tattersall cocked a deductive brow toward the shy, grave-faced boy. "Ah, I see. So it is."

On the sunny, south-facing kitchen deck the Owl watched his wife pull dead twigs from an herb just emerging from the soil of its box. Plant and planter looked equivalently aged. Yet here they were, alive for another spring.

"Expect it won't be long now," the Owl mused, more or less for the sound of it.

"Oh, I *hope* so," said Gerta: passionate though very calm. She stood back from the planter to judge her work. Not bad, her expression said. But not quite perfect. "Still, there's time yet . . . ?"

The Owl did not quite respond to this, though clearly it was intended as a question. "The boy," he said, "looks about fourteen, I'd say."

"Or fifteen," said Gerta. "They change so quickly."

"Hard to tell," agreed her husband.

Gerta inhaled the pungent fragrance her pruning had let loose. "I *do* love the spring," she sighed.

"Careful," said Lorian.

Needlessly. On the camomile lawn the figures of Groby, Thrull, and the Owl—diminished by altitude from Lorian's perch in the *Robinia*—stood beside an apparatus that looked like something designed to send the biggest blimp in the world aloft. Only in this case the object to be levitated was not a dirigible but the dome. From what remained of its northern end, a dozen steering cables ran through a network of blocks and cleats (assembled from defunct plumbing) through a vortex of pulleys tended by Lorian in the tree, and finally to a winching device that had once been a birdbath, a rain barrel and four laundry poles.

"I don't think this is going to work," she said.

Groby nodded, as it appeared, happily. "We'll see," he said.

The men took their places at the laundry poles and waited there, scuffing like horses, until in a moment they were joined by a slighter figure that seemed to materialize from the roses. Lorian strained her eyes, not recognizing for a few moments the boy they were calling Tamlin, though this was generally acknowledged not to be his name.

"Okay," said Groby.

The excavation team heaved. The steering cables made that groan which Vesica so vividly remembered. As the barrel rotated and the cables drew tight, the collapsed framework of the dome rose trembling from the heap of its own substance, gradually expanding to a semicylindrical shape like the fibrous lining of a diamond-ball.

"Whoa!" shouted Groby. His engineer's intuition throbbed somewhere behind his right ear-canal (its location, as yet, not having been precisely anatomized). The groan of cables fell silent. Groby thudded across the compound to Lorian's tree. With remarkable alacrity he lashed and spliced the cables in place until he was reasonably certain they would stay there; then he signaled the other members of the team to take a breather.

They had already wandered off: the Owl to have an extra bite of Gerta's mulberry muffins; Tamlin to wherever he disappeared to; Thrull to roll in silky paper another cheroot of the devilhemp he had found growing among the rhubarb. Just short of its glowing tip, a line of small black print read:

ACT II. SCENE 1. – A Wood near

The smoke rose in the warm scented air, drifted south across the compound, and irritated the bees hived in the shade of pussy willows.

Groby, alone in the clearing, regarded the winch and the cables and the resurrected dome with an existential gratification known most commonly, if not exclusively, to engineers: the pleasure of seeing chaos routed, usefulness summoned from objects lying at hand, inanimate things invested with responsibility. Behind him, the breeze made a forthright westerly assault on the windchimes, banging out crisp, almost martial chords and passing on to stir the big man's clay-brown hair.

On the sun-bleached planks of the kitchen deck, the Owl wolfed down muffins like a man congenitally incapable of either satisfying his appetite or gaining the slightest amount of weight. Gerta softly smiled.

"Do you think he'll be the one?" she murmured.

"Hey," said the Owl with his mouth full. "Might be. Might be, at that."

"Excuse me," said Lord Tattersall behind them.

He stood next to Sheldrake, the smaller man grinning evilly and holding in a stubby hand an accountant's pad and a pencil.

"I was wondering," Tattersall went on, "if we might have a little talk."

Gzzhh gzzhh gzzhh, goes the blood through Thrull's brain. He can feel the vessels above his ears dilate and contract with his pulsebeat, the sunlight crawling down through his oily hair and into his scalp and through his skull and oozing into the fluids of his head and leaking out again through his eyeballs. His eyes shine like the glaze on pottery. They blink in the blue northern light.

Gzzbb gzzbb gzzbb.

:feet thumping the dirt: zigzagging through the compound: watching the walls converge as the cedar-shelled egg constricts around him: getting tangled in raspberries: God, are they everywhere? Chickens cackling in the chicken run: windchimes banging like gongs behind him: escape, escape!

Gzzbb gzzbb gzzbb.

:the gate: pale green light visible under half-raised timbers beyond the cool tunnel of walnut trees. The gate.

Thrull tries not to look around, makes himself not look around, just keep moving this way like you're invisible toward the gate, walls sucking up around you, gongs banging, slip into the tunnel here and quick on your knees through the gate and: *Ahhhh.*

His blood cools down. The shadow of the wall spills over him, drapes him like dark fabric. He bounces on the loamy soil, rabbitlike hops down the hill, stumbles over his own feet, falls and lies there laughing.

:!!!

Thrull hasn't felt this good since the last bag of coins from the Low Commissioner. He pats his gray-green cloak to see if there's any devilhemp left. Then he remembers there's a whole bunch of it—a *thicket* of devilhemp, a *grove.* A summer's worth for sure. If it takes him that long to get out of here. A summer's worth: as much as he can smoke as fast as he can smoke it. Oh yes. Oh yes.

:sitting up

:*what was that?*

It comes again, Scrunch scrunch, footsteps is what it is. Right down the hill behind him, slow and one-at-a-time.

Luckily Thrull is invisible. He shivers with spasms of delight as the footsteps turn as if they're following a trail; of course there isn't any trail down here but the footsteps turn anyhow; now they're moving *that* way. Luckily Thrull has ears as sharp as a bat's. Luckily he is weightless. He gets up and weightlessly invisibly drifts behind the scrunching feet through the mountain laurel blooming pink along the hill.

Just when he wonders whose footsteps these are he's following, the mountain laurel thins and there in front of him is that weird little punk boy—Tamlin, they're calling him—of course that isn't really his name, Thrull knows *that*—right

there twenty feet away scrunching along slowly with his head
bent down—and what in god's name is he looking at? Thrull
has eyes like an eagle but he can't see anything on the
ground there, but the boy is barefoot and that must be it.
He's looking down so he doesn't step on anything. Scrunch
scrunch.

Now and then the boy stops and turns around as if he
doesn't know where he's going, or maybe he's running like
Thrull, hiding from something, and luckily Thrull is invisible
or the boy would surely notice him. Thrull holds his breath
until the air seeps through the fleshy walls of his lungs and
into the muscles and hisses between the ribs and drifts out
through the zillion holes of the gray-green robe, smelling
like protoplasm. Then he's about to faint but luckily he has a
memory like an elephant. He remembers how to let the
breath out and how to take another one. The boy starts
walking again, scrunch scrunch through the mountain laurel,
until he reaches a kind of open space where the sun comes
down all fuzzy and there are these orange flowers everywhere, a meadow sort of, but not like the meadow in the
compound where everything's jumbled together. In this one,
everything is separate, just sitting there in the sun, really
quiet.

:*god* this is good.

The boy goes on and Thrull holds back a little now,
because this place is awfully bright and the gray-green cloak
maybe isn't as invisible as the rest of him. Across the meadow
the boy stops and stares this way and that way as if he's lost
something but is pretty sure he left it around here somewhere, and sure enough in a minute or two he finds it. Of
course a minute or two is like all afternoon to Thrull, hunched
down far enough back in the undergrowth that the sun can't
see him or Tamlin either. Then the boy slips into the shadows and Thrull goes racing through the open before his eyes
can slide away from the place the boy has gone to, which is
just a little patch of black in all that orange.

:*damn it.*

The boy has disappeared. How does he do that? The
ground slopes down covered with big trees overhead and
small trees beneath them with blossoms the color of flesh.
The trees are far apart so that Thrull with eyes like an eagle

can see as far as he wants to, but the boy is gone. He might be hiding behind one of these flowery trees but why should he want to do that, since Thrull is invisible and silent, and if not, then he must have just, you know, *vanished.* Thrull waits for what he thinks is three or four hours, which makes it probably ten minutes, and still no Tamlin so what the hell, he reaches in the pocket of the gray-green robe and gets out another cheroot.

Something about devilhemp seems to always inspire the thought: This is the best I've ever had. But it *is,* really, it has to be. Thrull pulls in the smoke and lets it drift peaceably through his nostrils. The vessels over his ears dilate and contract again. Sunlight leaking through the trees causes the ground to melt and run gooey down the hill like a brown glacier.

Thrull discovers he has lost all connection with the arm holding the cheroot and snaps his head around in alarm just to make sure he hasn't caught his hand on fire or anything. The cheroot is still there, smoldering with only a millimeter or two of paper gone. He has taken a single puff. Just above the burning tip, a line of small black print says:

that shrewd and knavish sprite called Rob

My god, thinks Thrull. This is the best I've *ever* had.

As another lungful of smoke infiltrates his bloodstream, crawls up his spinal column and sabotages his synapses, Thrull has the crazed idea that something is looking down at him from the limbs of a nearby tree.

It's a bluebird, his overloaded cortex tells him. A god-damned bluebird, looking at me from a goddamned rowan tree.

But how does he know this? The rowan especially, which he's pretty sure he's never known about. He shudders at how great this devilhemp is—first it made him invisible and now it's making him omniscient.

"Get snapped," he tells the bluebird.

The scenery changes somewhat; Thrull blinks and fairy stagehands race out and start shoving things around, then hide again, so that when he opens his eyes all the trees have shifted a few inches this way and a few inches that, and the color of the rowan blossoms has changed a tiny bit, oh but Thrull with eyes of an eagle detects the change right away, you can bet on that—their flesh-pink tone is more flushed now, like cheeks that are embarrassed or angry. Thrull congratulates himself. He thinks maybe he will take another puff, but the cheroot in his hand has burned down to his fingertips and the black charred place on his skin doesn't hurt at all, owing no doubt to sabotage in his vital ganglia.

:oh yes oh yes. Thrull sproings up onto his feet like a rubber toy that was twisted out of shape. The fairies rush out and shove the trees around some more while he's getting his balance, so that by the time he's stabilized, everything is a few more inches this way and a few more inches that, and the ground has sloughed farther down toward the streambed and the rowan blossoms are the color of bloodshot eyes. *Really* bloodshot like Thrull's are.

Something tells Thrull: Don't go down this hill into that dark mysterious grotto. Which is as good as inviting him and sending a taxi to pick him up, and he smiles at how he's going to show them they can't tell *him* where not to go to.

Don't go *down* there I said, the bluebird tells him.

"Eat dirt," he tells the bluebird.

Ha!—the bluebird gives up and turns into a squirrel and races down from the rowan and bites Thrull somewhere around the ankle. Luckily the nerve-saboteurs have left no axons functioning, and won't the squirrel be sorry when Thrull goes down the hill and finds the five-hundred-year-old heatweapons and makes squirrel pancake of him.

:oh yes oh yes, it's unbelievable—he's not only omniscient but also clairvoyant. He sees himself entering the grotto just like he was already there. Maybe he *is* already there. There are these huge rocks all around, big dark-gray rocks that swell up as they drink the brown electric energy that pours into them along the serpentine pathway hidden in the earth, and the roots of the gigantic old tree wrap themselves around the rocks where they're ninety percent buried like icebergs, turning the energy from brown to green and pumping it into the leaves, which turn it blue and discharge it to the air. No, not the air; the æther or *akasha* which isn't it amazing, Thrull has never known was there before, not till now having been omniscient. He walks or foresees himself walking into the vibrating space between the rocks, and feels his feet burning like he's crossing hot coals, the first thing he's felt in some time now, so he looks down to see what's going on and his feet aren't there at all—somebody's feet are there but they can't be Thrull's because they're barefoot and the legs are skinny and naked with dark hair matted over goosebumps, and Thrull is terrified now and wishes he hadn't lit the last cheroot because this is getting almost too intense for him to handle.

When he looks up again a rowan tree is standing there, its blossoms red the color of blood. The tree is exactly as tall as Tamlin. It speaks to Thrull, telling him *I told you not to come here now get out.*

But Thrull says, "Cough up turds you pucca brat," and there in his hand is a five-hundred-year-old weapon of the type once favored by guerrillas. Oh yes, thinks Thrull, I know the future and the past and now I'm all-powerful too, and points the gun at the rowan tree, but now the tree turns into a great brown fur-covered monster with hooves and horns and evil angry eyes. Thrull shrinks at the very sight of this, becoming small like a rabbit or even smaller. The monster reaches down with gigantic claw-tipped hands, and Thrull knows that if the fingers even touch him they will drain the life right out of him.

I can't believe this is happening.

It happens. The ungodly fur-covered monster touches Thrull and his life ebbs away like *that.* Then he's floating in the *akasha* dead and disembodied, and the monster takes a breath and exhales with the fury of the North Wind, blowing the insubstantial remnants of Thrull out of the grotto, up the hillside blooming with mountain laurel, across the orange meadow and through the grove of thrice-coppiced oaks whose roots embrace in the darkness, under the half-raised gate and into the compound, where the North Wind stirs the wind-chimes and the spare, monkish tones of the Parched Scale wake Thrull up an hour before sunfall. He opens his eyes in the raspberry patch, where he must have tripped and passed out while trying to escape the shrinking egg.

The smell of boiling soapwort is in the air. Thrull sits up and dusts off his gray-green robe and thinks: That's the best I've *ever* had.

"Amy's things," said Lord Tattersall, touching at last upon the crucial point with all due delicacy, at the same time eyeing the Owl with sharpened swimming-pool-blue eyes determined to let no nuance of furtiveness slip by him. Sheldrake sat with pencil poised on the kitchen deck, where a familiar-smelling herb unfolded its flannel leaves in a planter. Gerta's full-throated hum floated from the kitchen. The Owl yawned.

"You mentioned," Tattersall reminded him, "*Amy's things,* last night at the dinner table. You said—"

"Wow," said the Owl. "Forgot to tell you." He turned to the kitchen door. "Soapwort ready yet?" he called in.

"A few more minutes," his wife replied.

Sheldrake scribbled vengefully.

"Now see here," said Tattersall. "I asked you—"

With slithery efficiency the Owl was on his feet, lank body poised as though for flight under its loose coverings. Sheldrake, not to be eluded, leapt up and expanded at the shoulders, blocking the door.

"And just where," began Tattersall.

"Hey, don't worry," said the Owl. "Going to show you."

"Show us . . ."

The Owl smiled benignly. "Amy's stuff."

Feeling, among other things, like a man foredoomed never to complete a sentence, Tattersall motioned Sheldrake to step aside. They entered the sunny kitchen of the dome, where Gerta stood before a large simmering stewpot. The Owl conducted them up a ladder to a small loft lined with shelves: a pantry. It burgeoned with the surplus of last year's garden, or the year's before that.

"Glad you came," the Owl said, "to help us with all this."

Sheldrake grunted—a prod—and the Owl indicated a hatch through which the blurred signature of sunlight could be seen on a further floor.

The next chamber was a sitting room. There was a rapid impression of mats and pillows, and then they were beyond it, onto a catwalk that circled the inner edge of the dome where its curving walls crossed the tangent of forty-five degrees and became its ceiling. Below the catwalk was an expanse of mostly nothing: a floor as wide as a ballroom, across which leaves had drifted in broad furrows, like burial mounds. The echoes of their footsteps were damped by dirt and rotten flooring. Overhead, the roof was reduced to a lacework of intersecting triangles, suspended at critical nodes by Groby's steering-cable. The effect was ambivalent: the dome here looked either half demolished or half built. In either case, the project was unfinished.

"Where are you taking us?" Tattersall thought to ask.

The Owl whistled in excitement. "Been waiting for *years* to see this place. Your friend Groby's really done something."

They had entered, then, the lately elevated section of the dome. Beneath them the catwalk swung like a jump rope. The Owl slid quickly along it, counterbalancing its sway, making for a ledge that jutted ahead of them. Accepting his hand, the two Crusaders clambered behind him onto the creaky promontory.

"Well!" said Tattersall, puffing from exertion. He looked around.

The ledge was cluttered, but it was hard to tell with what. Examination, conducted cautiously, gazing into the shadows, revealed it to be more extensive than it had looked from the catwalk. Not a ledge at all, really, but a whole new level of the dome.

"A lost cause," declared Sheldrake.

"The library," grinned the Owl.

Tattersall nodded. The title made some sense of the place—unlike "Upper Fractionating Chamber," which gave off only a stale air of mystery. Let's see. Those lichenous crates must have been storage cabinets of some sort. And those wall-sized sections, tumbling into one another, shelves. And this narrow gorge between them, an aisle.

"But I wonder," he said, in the manner of thinking aloud—gazing up at a webwork of wires that spanned the broken ceiling, among which dozens of cracked and empty flowerpots were snared like dessicated prey—"what could those be?"

The Owl said, "Looks like somebody was really into orchids."

"Ah." Did this mean anything? Tattersall prompted the Owl: "There was something you wanted to show us . . ."

"There was?" The poker-faced caretaker blinked.

The Governor tightened his lips in an extremity of irritation. "Well, *I'm* going to have a look around, in any case. Bring him along, Sheldrake."

To the north, east, and west, the aisles of the ruined library ran down to walls of tesselated Plexiglas, mostly broken now. On the south they ended in a balustrade above the empty chamber. The ceiling was open, admitting much light, but the geometric tension between its sixty-degree vertices and the library's nineties, on balance, made things worse. People had gotten lost here. Tattersall, about to join them, ventured inward, clucking his tongue. The shelves around him—where once a vast accumulation of human knowledge had been stored in a dozen media—were now a heap of rusted canisters, deteriorated film, acid-eaten paper, and melted mylar. What food for philosophy was here, were Tattersall a different sort of person! But Tattersall, only himself, surveyed the wreck of library with the same exalted wistfulness that befell him when he glimpsed the ruined industrial project that was his home. In his mind this feeling was inseparable from the experience of confronting the past; for what was history, anyway, but an effort to keep track of all that has been lost? And what was heroism but a holding action? Turning another corner, having forgotten his companions completely now, he drew a deep breath in readiness for a sigh.

. . . But held it. At the end of the aisle, Lorian sat cross-legged on a cherry writing desk, the broken balustrade at her back. In one hand she twirled a fountain pen, its pink plastic cylinder intact after five centuries, though its nib had rusted away. In the other, with equal hopelessness, she hefted a flattish object whose size and thickness suggested a picture-book, perhaps a notepad. Whatever it *had* been, it was now an enameloid lump of owl droppings. Lorian raised her head.

"It's gone," she said flatly. "I mean—this is all that's left. And it's nothing." She dropped the notepad. It fell with a lifeless thud on wood wiped clean by her own palms.

"Amy's desk," she said. "Amy's journal. And look here— Amy's pen. And there's nothing left of any of it."

Shifting, letting her legs fall like a dispirited girl's over the table edge, she stared up at Tattersall with eyes that pled for consolation. All he could think to offer was something trite and conventional, something along the lines of Don't worry now, things might not turn out so badly—when for all he knew they probably would. Precedence suggested it. Fortunately he did not have time to bring this up. From the room below came a sizable commotion, and Tattersall looked down to see Groby and Gerta winding their way between leaf mounds, hefting the great steaming stewpot on a broom.

"Hey, wow," the Owl exclaimed, leaning dangerously hard against the railing. "Just in time!"

"Throw it down, then," said Gerta.

The Owl turned to Lorian. Gently he said, "Go ahead, now. Let her have it. —*That*," he explained, as she looked back dumbly. He pointed at the clump of paper on the table. "Don't worry, now, she'll be careful with it. Just soapwort, you know."

As a child, barely comprehending, does the bidding of an adult, Lorian handed the notepad to the Owl.

"But don't throw it," she said, beginning to collect herself.

"Don't have to," he told her. "Stair's just over here."

The small congregation gathered over the stewpot while Gerta dipped a swatch of cotton cloth into the foamy, sweet-scented decoction; lightly wrung it; and swabbed it gently down the guano-glazed spine of the ancient paper.

The coagulated goop was slow dissolving, but under Gerta's persevering treatment it began slowly to give up its hold on what could barely be recognized as a stack of irregular, possibly hand-milled sheets.

"That's *right*," Lorian murmured. "She would have made it herself, because of the acid."

Gerta smiled, happy at her task. From the topmost page before her, plumbago-blue lettering swam slowly into view.

PROGRAM NOTES: January —

January to what? thought Lorian. (*To now*, of course, she realized.)

"Program notes," read Tattersall. "Something to do with music, is it?"

"Here," Gerta told Lorian. "You can open it now."

She extended the notebook like some trifling gift. With a markedly different air, Lorian accepted it. As patiently as she could manage she slipped her fingers under the topmost leaf, not quite visibly trembling.

The leaf turned.

"My goodness," said Tattersall.

"Is that all?" said Sheldrake. "Some kid's coloring book?"

Groby frowned, as though he doubted this, but said nothing.

Some kid? thought Lorian. In her most earnestly neutral, journalistic voice she told Tattersall: "If you don't mind, I'd like to hang on to this."

"Suit yourself." The Governor sounded a trifle disappointed. "Well. I suppose our next step is to go though the library more carefully. Piece by piece, as it were. There must be *something* left there—wouldn't you think?"

This plea for encouragement rang hollowly. Sheldrake mumbled something about dust or rust or must. Groby gazed at the paper in Lorian's hand. The two caretakers stood placidly, as though awaiting some further opportunity to oblige. And Lorian thought: Mommy?

Surprise Mommy. Surprise.

Twenty-two

PALE FIRE DANCED above the burners of the methane grill when Tamlin ducked beneath the gate of the research station. He paused to consider the smell of roasting food—warily, as though there must be something behind it.

From a branch of the walnut tree, a lithe form sprang onto his shoulders, knocked him to the ground, and rolled on top of him. By the time he got his frightened eyes in focus, he was firmly pinned.

"Vesica," he panted.

"No joke." She let his arms go but maintained her perch straddling his stomach.

"*Vesica*," he said, struggling against her. "Let me up. What is it? What's the matter?" He studied her face in the uncertain light. "You're mad at me, aren't you?"

"Why should I be mad? All you've done is hide from me the whole time since we've been here. Like I was your worst enemy or something."

Tamlin stopped struggling and closed his eyes. His face was as pale as starlight. After studying that face awhile and waiting for the eyes to open, which they didn't, Vesica relented and swung a leg off, setting him free. He continued to lie there.

"Tamlin," she said, "hey, I'm sorry. I don't *mean* to be mad at you. It's just . . . I wish you weren't afraid of me."

He blinked. His eyes were dry and empty. "I'm not," he said carefully, "afraid. Of you. It's more like, I'm just . . . confused, I guess."

Vesica frowned. "Something's happened, hasn't it? Something's happened to frighten you."

"*I'm not frightened.*" He set his jaw, and Vesica could tell she had stepped too far again. "I told you. I'm just . . . confused."

She touched his hand. He made a quick move as if to draw back, but stopped himself. In tiny steps, one by him and one by her, their hands turned around, palm to palm, and closed around each other. Tamlin sat up.

"I waited for you," Vesica said. "I looked for you all afternoon, and finally I figured you'd gone. I mean, out of the compound. Where'd you go?"

He shrugged.

"Come on, Tamlin. You can trust me."

He narrowed his eyes to stare into hers. With soft intensity he said, "I don't know. I—really—don't know."

"But . . ." She pointed. "Look. Your feet are muddy. You must have been down to the stream."

He shrugged again. "I guess. I don't remember."

Vesica thought about this. She believed he was telling the truth. It didn't make sense, was the only thing. "You mean," she said, spelling it out, "you really don't remember what you've been doing all day."

He let go of her hand and turned away. The bald fact of it seemed to embarrass him.

"Tomorrow," she said, "why don't we stay together? So I can keep track of what you're doing, in case you forget, and tell you about it later."

"Mm," he said, which Vesica thought might as well be No. He said, "You know how when you wake up, and you've forgotten the dream you were having but you can still sort of remember it? It's like that, kind of. Only it's all the time. And it's like, I feel like I'm forgetting more, too, all the time. So I've got to—I think sometimes if I can just be by myself and just think about it, then maybe I'll remember. . . ."

Vesica stared at him. She had never in her life tried so

hard to understand something, and so far she wasn't having much luck. Mostly thinking aloud she said, "It's almost like you . . . you're leading two separate lives or something. Or maybe even . . . two separate people. That happens in stories a lot."

He shook his head. Not in denial; sharing her puzzlement.

"But it's all right," said Vesica. "I'm still your friend."

He looked embarrassed again.

"Oh, you don't have to say anything," she said quickly. "I just wanted you to know . . . you know, that you're not all by yourself or anything."

He thought about this. He nodded.

Side by side, one hand apiece almost touching but not quite, they walked across the meadow to join the others for dinner.

The fire burned magically in its pit beside a fig tree, where no wood or coal or anything else combustible was to be seen. Its flames were blue and yellow, palely flickering. They gave the chief illumination to this breeze-sweetened evening, for the moon had not yet risen and the embowering vines and trees hid the pale glitter of stars. Only the Pole Star, finding an improbable route through the shattered panels of the dome, spied down on the proceedings. Closer by, the fig leaves, the archway dark with roses, the terrace stones padded with pennyroyal, all faded to black in the tenebrous night. The only things the firelight found to reflect from were the semicircle of faces and the eight-inch blooms, more startling now than by daylight, of clematis 'Richard Curtis'—a hybrid whose enigmatic ancestry was believed to include *C. textilis*, and whose abundant petals managed to be at once extravagant and restrained, their cheery cream-yellow petals edged lightly with melancholic amber that caught the firelight and shimmered like gilt.

"How does it work?" demanded Lorian.

She meant the fire. The Owl scratched his orange beard, blond in the darkness, and said, "Heard it burns swamp gas."

"Sure," said Lorian. "So where's the swamp?"

He shook his head. "Quite a puzzle," he said, sounding like someone who enjoys a puzzle very much.

"My, my," said Lord Tattersall, polishing off his seventh

vegetable fritter. "You people certainly seem to want for nothing."

"Oh, no," said Gerta. "Nothing at all."

"Wait a minute," said Lorian. "What do you mean, you *heard* it burns swamp gas?"

"Ha!" said Sheldrake. He rolled back from the fire rubbing his stomach and tilting his ale-nog.

"Yeah," said the Owl, "got about everything we need."

"Heard from *whom?*" persisted Lorian, but nobody seemed to hear her and perhaps by now she preferred it that way. Every few seconds she glanced around at Groby, who stared by inadequate light at the precious old notebook. She had loaned this to him reluctantly, because really, how could she not? She did not own the notebook any more than the Owl owned the Reporting Station, or Tattersall the past. Yet there were certain perquisites of custodianship.

"This is pretty interesting," the big man said, as though he felt the weight of her attention. "She says here . . ."

"Later," hissed Lorian. "Read it later." (Meaning that the words of Amy Hayata, written in her own hand, were too sacrosanct to be profaned by reading with food in one's mouth.)

Groby nodded. From the blackness under a fig tree, Thrull was heard to groan.

"Whatever has become of him?" wondered Tattersall. "I hope he isn't ill."

The Owl shook his head. "Sounds like something might've bit him."

Lorian said, "How can you tell that from . . . oh, never mind."

Vesica laughed softly from where she and Tamlin sat facing each other in a dark mossy corner of the terrace.

Quietly, catching their attention by her very gentleness, Gerta said, "My, what a wonderful evening. Shall we have some music?"

"Music?" said Lord Tattersall, in a tone of childish wonder.

"You've heard of that," Sheldrake reminded him. "It's what they do at parties down south so you don't have to listen to people talking."

"I *know* what music is, Sheldrake."

"You do? Fancy that."

Tattersall said, "Yes, by all means, Mistress Gerta—let us have it."

The Owl fluttered into the dome. He returned in a few minutes with an armful of odd-looking objects, few of which looked especially musical.

"One for everybody," he said merrily.

"But—that is to say," objected Tattersall, "none of us knows how to play."

Gerta touched his arm as though this were stupendously modest. She said, "Oh, Governor. Of course you do. Here, just try."

She handed him an elongated box of polished maple, over which a dozen strings had been stretched in non-Euclidean parallels. Tattersall accepted it doubtfully, his long arms extended as though he would be quite happy, should Gerta have second thoughts, to give it back.

"Don't worry, Governor," said the Owl. "Can't hurt *that* thing. Go ahead, give it a twang."

Tattersall complied to the extent of taking the box by its narrow end and giving its strings a hesitant stroke: dog lover attempting to pet cat.

From the box arose a chord of remarkable depth and clarity. It swelled for a few seconds as the strings built up a resonance with the wooden cavity of the box, then slowly faded, lingering for perhaps ten seconds as an enchanted sweetness in the air. Tattersall stared at his own fingers with astonishment.

"See there?" said the Owl. "*Anybody* can play."

"Evidently," said Sheldrake.

Tattersall tried another combination of strings with an equally mellifluous effect, then gleefully another and another. Whoever had chosen the ratio of frequencies the strings produced, and built the box to house them, must have done so with the intention that all possible permutations of notes-into-chords should blend as beautifully as possible.

"That sounds great," said Vesica.

The Crusade Leader beamed. Sheldrake grumbled, "Let *me* try one."

The thing the Owl gave him had no strings at all. It was a shiny tubular assemblage that looked like the daydream of a plumber. Sheldrake took it eagerly, turning it up and down and sideways, seeking a clue to its operation.

"Here," said Gerta, guiding him to a narrow port like a nozzle. "Just put your mouth there."

"Put my mouth here and what?" said Sheldrake worriedly.

. . . And from the contorted bowels of the contraption came a mellow, chimelike reiteration of his voice. The sounds that bubbled up from the reverberating depths of tubing were not words any longer, though they retained something of the pitch and cadence of speech; upon this raw input, however, the device elaborated as dramatically as the thousand canes of a bamboo stand elaborate on the breeze.

Sheldrake tried it again, perhaps unintentionally, with the sentence: "Well, kiss a fish." The result was so rewarding that Tattersall joined in with a lusty strum. For half a minute the two unlikely entertainers traded plucks and mutters, to the substantial delight of the onlookers, particularly those (like Vesica) to whom the musical arts had always been among the more arcane.

"Hey, come on now," said the Owl. "You all grab something."

Vesica reached into the pile and came up with a kind of junkyard gamelan. A dozen glassy objects of varying shape—bulbs and jars and beakers, things you expected to find on a mad scientist's workbench—had been installed with wires along a green-patinaed plant stand. Two honey-dipper mallets were fastened to its sides. Vesica took them up, and—as Groby bowed a coffin-sized koto—and Lorian bent over a keyboard that had once been a data entry device—and Tamlin strapped himself into a leather harness—and the Owl raised the product of crossing a clarinet with a vacuum cleaner—she gave the gamelan a tentative tap.

And music rose (it really did!) to fill the air.

Laughing, tapping at random on her watery-sounding chimes, Vesica turned to Tamlin and found him just sitting there, propped against a battered plastic box with a harness sagging around him, doing nothing at all.

"What's wrong?" she whispered. "Doesn't it work?"

The old leather harness had slipped around his shoulders, ensnaring him. "I don't know how to do it," he complained. "Look—there's nothing to play. There's just this box and this board and these strap things."

"Look here," Tattersall told the Owl, bringing the performance to a halt, "why don't you give this young man a real instrument?"

The Owl scratched his beard. "Only one there is," he said.

"Well, at least," suggested Vesica, "you could show him how to play it."

The Owl was abashed. "Don't know," he admitted. "Never heard it played before. Quite a knack, they tell me."

"Who tells you?" said Lorian, fingering her tiny clavier.

"Maybe something will come to you," the Owl told the boy.

Tamlin seemed satisfied, perhaps by the reassurance that he didn't *have* to play the plastic-and-leather contraption, if nobody else could either. Straightening in the harness he said, "Okay. I'll try."

Vesica turned to Gerta. "What do *you* play?"

Gerta smiled in surprise. "Why, I don't play anything, dear. I sing."

"Hey, all right," said the Owl. "Ready to go now?"

The Crusaders raised their instruments.

"We will perform the ballad," Gerta announced, "of Fair Janet and Young Tamber Lane."

On cue, the Owl began eking out a melody from his ominous-looking horn. Belying appearances, its timbre was sweet and clear, somewhat reedy, rich with overtones. It may have been the only instrument present whose range exceeded the lovely, if limited, scale the others were tuned to. The Owl made the most of this, indulging himself with grace notes and quarter-tone warbles as he spun out the wistful theme.

"Hey," he said when he was done, "you can play now if you want to."

One by one, hesitantly, the Crusaders joined in. Some of the notes they struck were rather surprising, even bizarre, but none was truly incompatible with the rest. They rounded the chorus, and the next time through, Greta lifted her voice beside them.

> Janet has kilted her pretty green skirt
> A little above her knee,

> And she has snooded her yellow hair
> A little above her bree,
> And she is to her father's house,
> As fast as she can flee.

The melody was soothing, as nearly hummed as sung, though accompanied by the ragtag band the lyrics sounded exotic and even slightly menacing; and maybe that was Gerta's intent.

> Out then spoke her father dear,
> And he spake meek and mild;
> "And ever alas, sweet Janet," he says,
> "I think thou goes with child."

> "If I go with child, old Dad,
> Myself must bear the blame;
> There's not a lord about your house
> Shall get my poor child's name.

> If my love were an earthly knight
> As he's an elfin gray,
> I would not give my own true love
> For any lord you say."

> Janet has kilted her pretty green skirt
> A little above her knee,
> And she has snooded her yellow hair
> A little above her bree,
> And she's away to Carbon Wood
> As fast as she can flee.

It sounded familiar to Vesica, though she couldn't imagine how, for she had little acquaintance with songs. She tapped out an occasional note on her gamelan, but inattentively. Gerta sang:

> She rode on out to Carbon Wood
> And stopped by the rose tree;
> But though she found his steed tied up
> Tam Lane she couldn't see.

So then she plucked the double rose,
The rose as red as wine,
And up there came young Tamber Lane,
And said, "Why plucks thou mine?

Why plucks thou my rose, fair girl,
Among the groves so green?"
She said, "Before I kill the babe
That we got us between,

Oh, tell me, tell me, dear Tam Lane,
What binds you to this rose tree?
Why do you hide in Carbon Wood
And will not marry me?"

"It chanced," he said, "upon a day,
Long years ago, they tell,
When we were back from hunting come
That from my horse I fell;
The Queen of Fairies she caught me
In yon green hill to dwell.

And pleasant is the fairy land,
But, eerie tale to tell,
At every end of seven years,
We pay a tiend to hell.

Tonight is Halloween, fair girl,
The morn is Hallow Day;
So win me, win me, if you will,
For well I want you may.

Just at the mirk and midnight hour
The fairy folk will ride,
And if you would your true love win
At stream-cross must you bide."

"How will I know thee, Tamber Lane,
Oh, how my true love know,
Among so many fairy knights
The like I never saw?"

"I will ride the milk-white steed,
And linger near the town;
Run quickly to the milk-white steed
And pull the rider down.

But in your arms they'll turn me, girl,
Into a snake and adder;
But hold me fast, and fear me not,
I am your poor child's father.

They'll turn me to a bear so grim
And then a lion wild;
But hold me fast, and fear me not,
As you shall love your child.

And last they'll turn me in your arms
Into the burning gleed;
Then throw me down into the stream
And throw me in with speed.

And then I'll be your own true love;
I'll turn a naked knight.
Then wrap me with your pretty green skirt,
And hide me out of sight."

Well gloomy, gloomy was the night,
And eerie was the ride;
And Jenny in her pretty green skirt
By stream-cross did she bide.

About the middle of the night
She heard the bridles sound,
And fast she ran to the milk-white steed
And pulled the rider down.

So well she minded what he said,
And Tamber Lane did win,
And hid him under her pretty green skirt
As blithe's a bird in spring.

Out then spake the Queen of Fairies,
Out of a bush of broom:

"She that has gotten Tamber Lane
Has gotten a stately groom.

But had I known, Tam Lane," she said,
"What now this night I see,
I would have plucked thy blue eyes out
And hid thee in a tree."

Though the lyric was done, the music drifted onward by
its own momentum. The band had outgrown its need of
Gerta to propel it; and soon it lost Vesica too. For when the
girl glanced aside at Tamlin, she realized two things at
once—things, both of them, she should have understood a
while ago.

"Young Tam Lane," she whispered—not in slow separated syllables but run together, the vowels blurred, as they
are when you tell a story. She recognized it now; for though
the song was strange, the story it told was an old and a
familiar one. Or perhaps as Thrull had said, all stories were
the same, and this was the Story again, only not told but
sung.

But that was the first, the lesser discovery. The greater
came when she looked at Tamlin, strapped in the ancient
harness. From the harp—no, from the air around the harp—
drifted a haunting, haunted song; a child of the one Gerta
had sung, but a child that bore only scanty resemblance to its
progenitor. He must have been playing it for some time now,
because its shimmering chords had filled all the spaces of
Gerta's melody.

One by one, as they noticed it, the other players lowered their instruments. Each time another stopped playing,
the sound of Tamlin's harp grew louder to compensate. Its
tones became fuller, more complex, until after a minute or
two there was no one playing but Tamlin, and nothing at all
missing from the rich and vibrant tapestry of the song.

As for the young musician himself, he was blind to their
attention. His eyes were closed, and his face had taken on a
roseate aura of serenity. It was an innocent face, unclouded,
dreamy; the shadow it had worn was gone now, washed
away by a light that glowed from within.

What he was doing, exactly, to provoke the old harp to

such peaks of expression was not at all clear. It looked as if he were sitting there on the plastic box in a trance. The Owl nodded—a gesture that encompassed the boy and the harp and the firelit scene around them.

"Got the knack, all right. Not many people do, they say."

Gerta said, "Not many at all."

They stood watching Tamlin, listening to Tamlin play, and Vesica wanted to go over and touch the boy, to contact more directly the radiant source from which that astonishing music flowed—and more than that, to make him stop playing it. For despite its beauty, there was something frightening about the way the song streamed forth from, as it seemed, Tamlin's very being. It was as if his innermost self were being *spent*, like fuel, to generate this loveliness. Vesica fidgeted, gaining resolution, and rose to her knees, when—like a power cord severed—the music ended with a small electric *plup*. Tamlin opened his eyes, stared blank-faced back at her.

"You're not . . ." he struggled to say.

"Nope," the Owl chuckled. "She's not."

"Not who?" said Lorian and Vesica together.

Tamlin, seeming not at all himself, rose from the battered plastic power-box and wrenched the harness from his neck. He stared at the harp in awful wonderment, as though it were something very different, something alive. His eyes were fixed and starry. His lips formed a string of quiet syllables, then stopped and started over again, like someone trying to remember the lyrics of a song. Of the few words Vesica heard, the most distinct were also the most implausible. In a windy breath that rose from deep within his throat the ghost-white boy sang softly:

"Ho ho ho."

Twenty-three

IS IT HOPELESS? read Lorian. She sat alone in the chamber below the library, her presence concealed by a leafy hummock. Stacks of hand-milled pages lay on either side of her. Footsteps and voices and the groan of moving furniture could be heard overhead as Lord Tattersall directed the exploration of the library.

Lorian was not hiding, precisely. The formulation she preferred was *conducting private research*. And there was nothing wrong with that, was there? She felt pretty sure there was not. She read on.

Or is it just spring? All these biographies I've been read-ing lately, and all they've done is remind me how little I've accomplished and how much there is to do.

The funny thing is, even though you know it's not going to be finished in your own lifetime, there's a real irrational comfort in knowing that it <u>will</u> be finished, that these mysteries <u>will</u> be understood someday. And you can't help feeling that you're going to be there when it happens—right there, yourself—to see how it all comes out.

Like McClintock said, I think in her 80's: "And I can't wait. Because I think it's going to be marvelous, simply marvelous." Like she was going to live, and work, and be there at Cold Springs beside her colleagues, right up to the

end of it. And <u>this</u> from a woman who'd been ostracized
for three decades, who'd been called a "mystic" in the days
when that was a term of worse than derision—a form of
dismissal, a way of sweeping the woman and her work and
her piercing—if often barely intelligible—arguments
under the rug.

The writing stopped several inches short of the end of
the page. Lorian paused a moment before placing it on the
left-hand pile. Suppose this had been (as Amy might have
said) the end of it? Suppose these meticulous scribblings were
the scientist's last words?

But these were perverse thoughts—Lorian's way of tanta-
lizing herself with the dreadful truth of why these pages,
these "program notes" as Amy called them, had been left
unfinished on the writing table. She lifted the page, and
beneath it was another. The plumbago-blue handwriting went
on. Lorian's mouth twitched sideways and she thought: Anyway, nobody else cared about the journal in the first place.
They took one look at the drawing up front and that was the
end of it. Only another woman could have understood that
something so homey, so personal, might hold the great
truths they were looking for.

Overhead the floorboards of the library shuddered as a
toppled bookshelf was set right. On the *other* hand, Lorian
thought—obliged by the laws of objectivity to amend her
last idea—there was Groby. She read on.

It's hard to understand the lack of interest in my paper. If I were reporting something trivial—like maybe I
had inserted a few genes and <u>Sorbus</u> a. was showing better
seed production despite higher toxicity in the berries—
then wow, I'd be getting published twice a year. It's the
big ideas they have no stomach for. When I say—look,
you don't have to touch the genes at all; you can access
the plant's organizing powers directly—<u>that's</u> when they
say thanks for letting us see this anyway and good luck in
your future projects. And if I ask them why, they say,
well, you didn't have enough isolation, we thought you
might be observing a spontaneous adaptation to the
environment.

I suppose what I'm really going to have to do is take things a step further and demonstrate the possibility of direct, dynamic interaction with the fields, TWO-WAY. The capacity to get in there and pull the genetic trigger. No environmental pressure. Within one growth-cycle.

Examples. I don't know. What about phalanxes and guerrillas? We can get a species that normally uses one strategy to "borrow" the tricks of the other. Acorns, say—heavy, slow, and dense in the immediate vicinity of the tree. Classic phalanx approach. Tell root cells to undifferentiate, act like apical meristems for a while. Quercus could put sappers fifty, eighty feet from the main trunk.

New species perhaps too ambitious at this point. Though McClintock thought it possible. (Quercus robinia!) Stress said to be necessary. New genus even. That would be a real hybrid—genes by god, body by Hayata.

Try to work this into my program, if the akasha is clear. The chickens are restless lately, and the last time that happened was when our friends on the Force paid us a visit. Thank God the wall's finished now.

Lorian looked up from the bottom of yet another page. She thought how strange the air smelled. The moldy sweet odor of leaf piles, warmed by the sun, clashed with cooler drafts of rust and chemicals seeping down from the loft. Was this last passage—the part about a new species, especially—worth bringing to the attention of the Crusade? She decided not. Not yet. Anyway, *she* was the Crusade, as much as anybody.

She slipped a finger under the page and wondered out of habit whether this entry was the last, the missing half of the "January to −" equation.

And this time it was.

Up in the library the business of the Crusade went on.

"No, no," said Sheldrake. "Put it *there*. His lordship wants someplace nice to sit. Someplace with a view."

Agreeably, Groby lifted the cherry writing desk in one hand and an armchair in the other. He carried them to a swept-out corner near the east wall of the dome, where broken windows looked out on the wildflower meadow.

"Is this okay, your lordship?" Sheldrake inquired officiously.

Tattersall glanced up from his contemplation of a rotted herbal. Owing to some quirk of chemistry, only its color plates had survived. Choosing one—an ice-white flower held like a cup above ground-hugging foliage—he handed it to Sheldrake. "Here," he said. "Tack this up by the desk, won't you?"

"Great Dixter," the small man muttered. "It's bloodroot."

"I beg your pardon?" said Tattersall.

Sheldrake set to with a hammer. He said between blows, "Produces visions of the long-departed."

"Ah." The Governor considered this, not entirely without approval.

Behind him Groby said, "Um, excuse me, your lordship, but I've found something. . . ."

Tattersall turned quickly, as though in alarm. The big man stood before him holding a door-sized black panel.

"It's nothing to do with the Crusade," Groby explained. "It's something electrical, I think. I just wondered if I might take some time . . ."

"Oh, by all means." Tattersall was surprised by the extent of his own relief. Didn't he *want* the Crusade to find anything? Puzzled and disturbed, he lowered himself into the armchair before the cherry table. "You've done well, Sheldrake. The view from here is very nice. I say, what has become of Thrull? Isn't he supposed to be helping us?"

"He ran off with some kind of little box," said Sheldrake. "Groby said it was all right—it was just an airfax machine."

"Ah. Well, you might as well take a break yourself, then, if everybody else has. We've gotten quite a bit done for one morning, don't you think?"

With an ancient copy of *Poisonous Plants of the World* tucked under his arm, Sheldrake departed the library.

Lord Tattersall, left alone, leaned back in his chair, admiring the view of the meadow. The swept-out corner had a tidy, comfortable feeling, as though it were indifferent to the decay all around it, or hadn't gotten the word. Tattersall liked that. If Truth was, as Lorian thought, something definite and knowable—as against the inchoate, blinding gnosis believed in by the Pure Force—then the truth of the matter was, Tattersall was enjoying himself.

*   *   *

"We're supposed to stay in the compound," said Vesica.

Tamlin brought his finger to his lips and motioned her to follow. She did so without further complaint, excited by this new mood of complicity. He led her through the gate and into the orchard of thrice-coppiced oaks, their resurgent trunks now several stories tall and centuries old.

"I think I remember this place," said Tamlin quietly. "I think I remember . . . since that night, with the music . . . I remember a lot."

Now they were going to look for the thing he did not remember, quite, but which seemed terribly important. And they were going together because Tamlin—though of course he did not say as much to Vesica—was afraid.

He led her through the meadow almost startling in its brightness, dotted with orange flower-balls. She watched his shoulders, his narrow haunches, his flowing stride. He must be getting accustomed to his limbs.

"Marigolds," Tamlin remembered.

"Marigolds," sighed Vesica. She had watered them in pots outside her stepfather's study. For what, she now wondered.

The two of them felt very far from home, far from anything like a family. In this they were united, together in their aloneness. Pretending not to notice much, they took each other's hands.

"I think it's here," said Tamlin. He stepped into the dark mouth of the path and led Vesica down the hillside blooming with mountain laurel.

"It's so peaceful," she said.

He nodded, though his true thoughts were otherwise. To him it all seemed unsettled and wrong. He had left this place a very long time ago, and not of his own will. He did not remember how or why he had left but he remembered not wanting to, not believing it was over. Thinking there had to be more.

His hand tightened on Vesica's and she looked around happily, but the tightening had not meant that.

At the bottom of the hill the path opened to a cool shady grotto. The air was damp and the ground was bare of almost everything, just sand and stones; not even ferns were

growing under the dense shade of a tree older and larger than
Vesica had ever seen before. Tamlin's breath came rapidly.
There were very large rocks bunched up before them; if they
had been smaller you might have thought, *A nice place to sit*,
but they were gigantic things. Can rocks grow? Can they
grow like trees, and can trees keep growing forever, as long
as they can find room for their roots and sun for their leaves
and water and things like that? Vesica wondered because it
really looked like these rocks and this tree had been here
forever, taking up more and more and more space, and were
still growing. Already the tree had shoved the stream out of
its way; the water took a C-shaped course around it. Even
the air here felt crowded. As if the rocks and the oak tree
were filling it up, pumping out something that filled the air
and made it heavy.

Tamlin and Vesica walked slowly. The ground was very
cool here. It was like water, the way water swirls around your
feet, cooling them more than it would if it were still. Vesica
wiggled her toes as Tamlin did when he was nervous. Both of
them were barefoot, Tamlin in patchwork pants without a
shirt and Vesica in jeans. They were very small next to the
oak tree.

Beside the rocks were two old long sticklike things made
of black wood and metal. The metal had rusted and the
wood was rotten, and they looked like something that had
grown there, where nothing grew but rocks, if rocks can
grow. Vesica naturally wanted to pick up one of the sticks
and see what it was, but Tamlin pulled her away by their
joined hands.

"What's wrong?"

He shook his head, which might have meant he didn't
remember, though Vesica was a little suspicious of that.

"Let me go, then," she said. "Just for a minute."

He let her go and she walked to the rocks and picked up
one of the objects.

"It's a gun, I think."

Tamlin stared at it wide-eyed. The thing Vesica was
innocently holding, inspecting, looking down its barrel.

"A really old one. I'm sure it doesn't work anymore."

"*NO!*" he cried without warning. And raced forward and
snatched the thing from Vesica's hand and smashed it with

all his strength against the rock, slamming it into the other weapon so they both broke apart, until there was nothing but a pile of brittle, rust-brown metal and flakes of rotten wood on the ground, and these he kicked apart and stomped into the dirt like embers.

Vesica watched all this in fear mixed with relief—for Tamlin's outburst, his tantrum, broke the tension she had felt but not recognized in this grotto. Now it was more ordinary, the air more breathable, the ground less awfully cool, and a bit of sun she hadn't noticed before worked its way down through the overarching branches.

Tamlin said, "I'm sorry I scared you," standing there with a quizzical look as though he had scared himself, too, as if a ghost story he was telling had gotten out of hand. He brushed his sun-gilded brown hair back away from his face and smiled, and Vesica, finding his smile as always infectious, smiled back. They stepped closer together.

"What's this?" she said.

She pointed at the side of a rock where something was scratched, a message once maybe, but weathered so that it was barely readable. They bent together to study it.

8 ———

Robin is 6. ——— 7

This tall → ———

"Ha!" laughed Vesica. "Some little kid must have come here every year and measured himself against the rock."

Tamlin looked very puzzled, as though he could not comprehend how or why anybody would do this. Vesica stood up next to the rock, bringing her hand up to touch herself against the ribcage where the 8-mark came.

"Isn't that cute?" she said. "There must have been kids living here."

"No," said Tamlin faintly.

"What?"

"No kids."

"Oh no? Really?" Not stopping to wonder about this, accepting it, she went on: "Maybe it was somebody's nephew or godson or something then, that visited once a year. Maybe they had picnics down here or something."

Tamlin started to say No, no picnics, but the great thing that he didn't understand and couldn't remember prevented it.

"I guess," he said. He ran his finger over the scratched-out indentation in the rock. He saw how long and large-knuckled his fingers were, as though that too were a mystery, and looked at his feet on the sandy dirt, the toes with tiny brown hairs, and turned away before Vesica could see the shadow returning to his face.

Vesica saw but pretended not to notice. Maybe it hadn't been such a good idea to come here. Maybe whatever was wrong with Tamlin just needed more time and it would straighten itself out, like waking up after a nightmare, and all of this would make sense to both of them.

"Hey," she said after a suitable length of time—not too long, so he wouldn't think she had been wondering about him. "Want to go up the stream a ways, and see where it goes? There's this place, if I can find it, I'd like to show you."

He nodded. He turned around to face her, and with a rush of feeling that neither of them expected he reached out and embraced her, hugged her tightly and she hugged him back and they stood there for half a minute, and then another half a minute, together and alone.

His arms were long and strong. Hers were long too, but thinner and somehow differently constructed. Maybe the elbows bent a different way. They were caught underneath Tamlin's, wrapped around his naked, muscular back. His were around her shoulder blades. She thought of her body again, as she had in the glass-walled manor—remembered there being one, a thing apart from herself, with its own desires and priorities—and wondered what her body was doing, what it wanted now.

For yet another half a minute they stayed that way, eyes open and staring in opposite directions, then drew as sud-

denly and unexpectedly apart. It was a startling experience—
not being hugged, or hugging, but doing both at the same
time with such intensity—and the letting go had been startling, too; the breaking of an energetic bond. They both
looked away from each other's eyes because there seemed an
awful lot to think about, and walking up the stream just
somehow happened while they were thinking about it. The
water was cold around their bare ankles, but that was nothing.

Vesica's heart raced and her thoughts were tied like a
kite to Tamlin's hand, tangled in hers, with both palms damp
from sweating. She drew it a little closer, its warmth into her
warmth, and they splashed up the stream getting their pants
wet. Her body was still there, still separate, and instead of
merging with her again it was sucking her into it, taking
over.

"I wonder where the stream goes," she said, her voice
pressed through her larynx by muscles that seemed only
partly under her mind's control.

Tamlin shrugged, which was much more sensible. They
touched each other nervously, like researchers conducting a
mutual investigation: fingers on arms and necks and faces.
Vesica's lungs filled and emptied rapidly, moving something
in and out of her that was more than just air.

She said, "Let's sit down."

He obeyed her. For the first time in several minutes they
looked at each other's eyes again, and she was surprised how
wide his had become. Their blue, which of course she remembered, had grown deeper, the blue of a sky in early
morning, but she must never have really seen how deep and
liquid they were, for she could have drifted into them at that
moment, she was sure, and never come out again. In fact she
did begin drifting into them, floated closer and closer with
her own eyes half shut and her lips half open and feeling the
way she had felt when she floated across the pool naked and
warm and let the sun caress her bare smooth body. Anything
might happen now, she thought pleasurably.

What did happen was that the sky blew apart like leaves
in a gust of autumn wind. Even after she closed her mouth
and opened her eyes the wind kept blowing and howling and
getting louder until Tamlin and Vesica held each other not as
they had before, but in terror.

"What is it?" said Tamlin as the sky filled up with a searing wail like an animal being tortured.

Vesica opened her mouth to say, I don't know what it is—but then she did. She knew it was the same sound that came when the airlorry brought her stepfather back from the city. The same but louder.

"Oh, no," she could only say. "Oh, no."

"What is it?" shouted Tamlin over the noise.

"Here," she said quickly. "I've got something for you. It was going to be a surprise. I was waiting for the right . . . Just—here, take it."

She pressed into his hands an eight-inch clothbound cylinder. The double flute she had found in the streambed; the shiny treasure that belonged to Tamlin, as she had realized that night by the fire, if it belonged to anyone.

"What . . ." he said, but she pressed the bundle into his hard warm breast and kissed him.

Of course they had to go back eventually. They stayed a long time in the woods by the stream after the noise ended, but they had to go back; they couldn't hide in the woods forever, even though they held each other and talked about it. Eventually they would have to join the others and see what had happened and if they could help.

The aircruiser had set down in the center of the compound, flattening trees and flowers and bushes like so much grassy stubble under a dog. Its wings were a dark gray that seemed less visible than black, a color that was no color at all. The air stank of exhaust.

Tamlin had stopped asking *What is it?* because by now he probably didn't want to know. Perversely, Vesica decided to tell him what it was, that it was her stepfather.

"It's got to be," she said in a voice without hope. She let go of Tamlin's hand and in her mind she said goodbye to him, wished she had done so in some more meaningful way while they were alone at the stream. But now it was too late for anything. She walked across the compound, not thinking about whether Tamlin was beside her or not. Walked forward to meet the fate she had always known was tracking her down.

Tamlin grabbed her arm.

"Don't," he whispered. "Stay here. Hide in the roses. I'll go see what they want."

She looked at him. His sad beautiful eyes. His sun-gilded brown hair and stubborn cowlick. His long arms and legs and widening chest and the down beginning to appear along his jawbone. She wanted to kiss him goodbye, but across the compound a voice snapped out and put an end to that. To everything.

"Come here, young lady," it said, not even her name. "Come here this instant."

She looked at Tamlin, not at Narthex; Tamlin receding into the green background, Tamlin getting smaller and more helpless and more distant though it was she who was walking away from him.

"And *you*, young man," the Low Commissioner said loudly. "I have a few things to say to you as well."

"NO YOU DON'T," screamed Vesica, turning to look at her stepfather. He redirected his gray stare.

And in that instant—as she had hoped he would, as she had known—while Narthex's hawkish eyes protruded at Vesica and her own stared hatefully back, Tamlin made a slight
unnoticeable move
and was gone.

Twenty-four

"LOOK HERE, LOW Commissioner," said Tattersall, straightening up a bit behind the cherry writing desk. "Enough is really more than enough."

"Get through this quickly, won't you, Tattersall? I plan to be back in Riverrun by dark."

Narthex was seated also, in a folding chair set up by an aide. The two men faced each other across the otherwise empty loft. The seconds on both sides—the Crusaders on Tattersall's, a platoon of men with red armbands on the Commissioner's—were mustered in the wildflower meadow, watching the confrontation through broken windows.

Tattersall cleared his throat, apparently undecided as to how to proceed. His eye was caught by something below, and he looked down to see Lorian holding a map at which Sheldrake was making an exceedingly crude gesture.

"Ah," he said. "Well. To begin with, you are entirely out of your jurisdiction. I am, as you know, the Governor of All the Northern Territories."

Narthex appeared to smirk. From a pouch he produced a stamped and beribboned document which he shoved across the desk. Tattersall squinted down at it, moving his lips. A few sentences in, he looked up in transparent alarm.

"Why, this is an outrage! That is to say, what can this

possibly mean? This bit about 'pending the outcome of an Official Inquiry' . . . and this 'relieved of all duties for the duration of proceedings' . . . and good God! 'Moneys frozen and held in escrow by the Exchequer'! I mean, look here, you dastard—what does this mean?"

The Commissioner returned the document to his pouch. "It means, you old fool, you're out of a job. You're being investigated for squandering official funds and abusing the public trust by gallivanting off on this Crusade while your territory is in disarray."

Tattersall continued to be 'flabbergasted. "Disarray . . . why, the territory has *always* been in disarray. The *world* is in disarray. I mean, it's the nature of life, isn't it? But squandering funds . . ."

"Just shut up, won't you? You're babbling."

Narthex said this with relatively little nastiness, his tone was purely businesslike. He brought something new from the pouch.

"What's that?" fretted Tattersall, biting his lip.

"A warrant," the Commissioner pronounced, anointing each syllable with a drop of acid, "and a contract. The former is for your arrest—kidnapping a minor child—and the latter is an agreement under the terms of which I will not serve it."

Tattersall blanched. "Kidnapping . . . ? Arrest . . . ?"

Sheldrake gestured furiously below, but his lordship was blinded. Narthex held the floor, or rather desktop, unchallenged.

"Now. This agreement, which I see you are in no state to read properly, states that you will make no attempt to retain the governorship as the investigation proceeds. Neither will you contest my own claim to the title, should I choose to make one."

"But . . ." Tattersall opened and closed his mouth like a fish. "But—I kidnapped no one. I am innocent. That is the truth."

The Commissioner leaned back with an air of philosophical smugness. "Who alive is innocent? And who shall say what is truth? I have here"—a pat on the dire pouch—"a score of sworn affadavits—and I can obtain as many more as you like—describing the precise manner in which you, so to speak, seduced my hapless stepdaughter into your vile clutches, for what unthinkable ends I do not care to guess—though I am certain the popular press will not be so inhibited."

Tattersall lowered his head into his hands.

Narthex nodded. "You *do* understand, then. Very well. Now, this contract does not obligate you to resign the governorship. I would certainly think, however, that that would be the most honorable course to take. If you care to look the documents over, please do so now, and if not . . ."

He reached a final time into the pouch and came up with a quill, but in the meantime Tattersall raised his head and stared outward, past the Low Commissioner, through the broken frame of the dome, over the bristly cedar walls, into the woods and probably beyond them, to some bright invisible plain.

"If not," repeated the Commissioner, "then please sign all copies, and I will depart with my stepdaughter and trouble you no further."

Tattersall did not hear, or else chose not to answer. He rose slowly, his body by degrees extending itself until he was taller than Vesica had ever seen him and still not quite erect. He straightened further, and even Narthex's myopic eyes sensed that something unusual was going on. The Governor pressed the last wrinkle of a slouch out of his lanky frame, attaining a height from which he could have inspected Groby's scalp for hair-lice. For the first time since Vesica had known him, maybe the first time in his life, he stood completely, commandingly, unbelievably upright, and Narthex would have been alone at the research station had he been unimpressed.

"Eat him alive," growled Sheldrake.

The militiamen stirred restively, touching the bulges in their coats.

"You dare," said Tattersall—and for some reason, perhaps the straightening of his windpipe, it came out *YOU DARE*—"speak to me of the most honorable course to take. You, Low Commissioner, to whom the concept of Honor is on a par with the concept of Clipping One's Nose-Hairs—a thing of which you have little apparent understanding and in which you do not, as far as I can see, indulge."

By the time Tattersall had dished out and Narthex digested this sentence, the air of the dome was fairly crackling.

"I shall tell you," said Tattersall, "what you may do with your Warrant and your Agreement and your Imperial Decree. And that is—"

("Don't listen to this, Vesica," Sheldrake warned.)

"—you may put them back in your pouch and take your pouch back on board your ghastly aircraft and fly hurriedly back to consult with your barristers in anticipation of my return. Because I shall return forthwith. And when I do—"

The Crusaders gave forth a lusty round of cheers.

"—when I do, Low Commissioner, you may count yourself lucky if you retain the right to walk the streets, much less aspire to public office. And as for Vesica."

"*As for Vesica,*" said Narthex, rebounding from his loss of momentum and rising to his feet (though this was a pitiful act, all too easily accomplished, and left him still a head-and-a-half lower than Tattersall), "Vesica is my stepdaughter and is coming with me, and there is nothing you can do—legally, morally, or practically—to impede me. The rest, we will attend to in due course."

Tattersall looked down as Vesica looked up. The spirit of resignation leapt the twenty-foot gap from her face to his, and he turned sadly back to the Commissioner.

"Well. I suppose in that, though nothing else, you may be right."

Narthex curtly nodded. He refilled his pouch, behaving for all the world as though he were not following Tattersall's instructions to the letter, and in all dignity and righteousness removed himself from the loft.

"Come, Vesica," he told her, storming past.

"I hate you," she said behind him.

He stopped. He started to turn. He thought better of it. It had been a futile statement—no more than a show of miserableness in defeat. He proceeded to the aircruiser. Just below the hatch he turned to one of the militiamen.

"When my daughter is aboard," he said, loudly so that everyone could hear, "you may commence the loading operation."

"What do you mean?" demanded Lorian, storming after him through the compound as heedlessly she had stormed, uninvited, through the Embarkation Ball. "What do you mean, loading operation?"

Narthex eyed her for a moment and then smiled.

"I mean," he said, "that we're taking all those things, the contents of the library, back to Riverrun. All of it. But don't worry," he added thinly, "we'll leave you the trees."

"You bastard," Lorian said, walking right up to the Commissioner's face and raising a hand to slap him. He seized the hand en route, twisted it, turned Lorian around. She kicked his shin backward. Still grappling, they danced around in collective pain.

"I think," he panted, "we may take you back too. And put you to work in the sewers."

A group of militiamen converged. Lorian tried to break free, but Narthex was evidently quite experienced in such scuffles. The gang of reinforcements was an arm's length away when an explosive clap thundered across the compound. Dirt splattered the spidersilk suit. Everyone became very still, except for heads craning wildly.

The heads homed in on the library. There, the Owl stood behind Tattersall, who stood behind a wide-barreled hunting gun.

"I wouldn't," said Narthex, composed again, "play with things you don't understand. You could hurt yourself."

Tattersall squeezed the gun, and Narthex's pouch flew out of his hand before the sound of the explosion could reach him.

"Hunting," Tattersall declared, "is one of the few remaining solaces of the mannered class."

The Owl nodded energetically. "Wouldn't have given him the gun," he called down, "if you folks hadn't done so much damage to the place here. Shouldn't have done that. Doesn't do much for a caretaker's attitude. And don't"—he turned to look at the militiamen taking up positions on his flank—"don't waste your time fiddling with those heatweapons. They don't work here."

Not at all believing this, a militiaman pulled a trigger. Nothing happened. Well, his weapon started to smoke and he dropped it cursing; but nothing else.

The Owl shook his head. "Don't know why that is. Just is. Now why don't you folks do like the Governor says and get on back home?"

Narthex, retrieving his pouch, walked over to Vesica.

When he was almost there, she stepped haughtily past him, proceeding by her own will toward her inexorable fate.

"Bye, honey," said Lorian as she went by. "Take care of yourself."

"We'll miss you," called Sheldrake.

Groby said nothing, only waited for her to turn and look back from halfway up the ladder; then he smiled. The Owl and Gerta waved, as though she were off on some pleasant afternoon outing. And Tattersall, from his desecrated loft, said deliberately, like a vow:

"*Au revoir*, dear girl. *Au revoir*."

Goodbye, mouthed Vesica, beneath the aircruiser's belly. Her stepfather waited behind her. One last time she turned to stare across the compound—in the other direction, toward the gate—and said, barely out loud, "Bye-bye."

A young male voice called out then, and Vesica nearly leapt from the ladder and fled across the compound and hurled herself into Tamlin's arms. But the voice was Thrull's.

"Not without me!" he cried, crawling out from the rhubarb patch where he had hidden all day. "Don't leave without me! You couldn't have *gotten* here without me!"

He came limping toward the aircruiser, favoring an ankle which he had injured somehow. Reaching the ladder, he paused and groveled there, or perhaps he was just catching his breath. From the hatch the Low Commissioner said, "Come on up, then, little swine." If Thrull heard this—which is doubtful, what with his noisy wheezing—he did not mind at all. He thrust rudely past Vesica, leaving only his rancid body-scent and a few drops of sweat to be remembered by, and presumably they, too, would soon be gone.

"Come, Vesica," said Narthex, his voice quiet and almost gentle now. He held down a hand.

"We are going home."

Civilization

And a sweet sense of horror,
the shivery fascination with monsters and creeping forms
that so delights us today,
even in the sterile hearts of cities . . .
— EDWARD O. WILSON

Pelargonium (hybrid)
"Geranium"

Removed from their native range and cross-bred

intensively, such varieties have lost hardiness.

Suitable for decorative use only.

Twenty-five

A̲N UNREAL AIR, thought Vesica. She thought of herself in a story, her name a word in the midst of sentences. One of the sentences read:

An unreal air pervaded the aircruiser.

But that would mean, in the story, not that there was anything wrong with the air, really, but that somehow nothing seemed real. *Air* was just another word, like *Vesica,* that stood for something else; in this case the general situation of the tale. Whereas what *she* meant, what had prompted the thought, was that everything was very real, all too terribly real, *except* the air, which seemed artificial. Artificial air, she thought. Manufactured.

Like the tomatoes. Narthex had once had a tomato machine. It manufactured tomatoes. He had found it in some ruins somewhere, or taken it away from a tenant farmer, and brought it back to Gravetye and set it up in a pasture. All it had to be was in the sun, he said. The machine would do the rest. There were all these bags of tomato ingredients as old as the machine. Even the plastic bags they came in had gotten brittle with age, which Vesica wouldn't have believed if she hadn't stuck her finger right through one.

That's all right, Narthex had told her. She was very little at the time, six or seven probably, and she didn't know him, really, and he didn't know her. She had no friends. He was at the farm more.

She slid across the long seat in the passenger compartment, closer to the duct where the artificial air came out. This brought her closer to the window, too, and she stared at the blue-green hillsides drained by silver streams a million miles below. The air was clean and sterile as it blew on her face.

That's all right, said Narthex in the story in her head. It was her own story, a true story, but she was editing it now in light of later events. It doesn't matter how old the tomato ingredients are, he said. See, you just pour them in here and hook up the water hose, and the machine does everything else. A few weeks later you come back and pick tomatoes. How about that, Vesica?

Six- or seven-year-old Vesica regarded the tubes and plastic lid and growing-tank with apprehension. In the original version of the story she had laughed and held his hand and they had walked back to the manor. Which of them had been different then? The theory was that the things in the bag and the water and the sun coming down through the plastic lid were all you needed to make tomatoes. Probably that was the theory with the air too. That you only needed so much of this and so much of that and you mix it together in a metal tank and blow it through the duct and it comes out Air. Same as the real thing. Better, maybe.

Vesica looked out the window of the passenger compartment and wondered what land that was below, lush and rolling, and what that moon-shaped thing was on the hill.

Beside her on the long seat Narthex said, "That's Biggar's Neck down there. You've seen that before, haven't you?"

She hated him. Hated her stepfather. Hated the aircruiser. Hated artificial air.

"That's not Biggar's Neck," she said. "Biggar's Neck is not covered with forest like that. It's got a beautiful lawn, with tennis grass."

"That's Biggar's Neck," he said.

The tomatoes were half orange and half yellow-green and tasted like plastic. The air smelled like metal tanks.

In the original version of the story, all you needed was a little girl and a stepfather and a big house on a farm and you had a family. But tomatoes were more complicated than the things in the plastic bag. Air wasn't just so much of this and so much of that mixed in a metal tank. It could be stale or sad or sweet, but it wasn't just something on the other side of an equals sign. The air in the cool dark grotto had been so full of things you could hardly breathe it—things that would never fit inside a metal tank. Tamlin could not live on air from a metal tank. His soft pale skin would crack and dry. His firm just-widening chest would heave in desperation. The arms that had held Vesica would go weak and slack. She was glad to have spared him that. She was glad he was gone, hiding in the woods, edited out of the story.

"There, there, Vesica," Narthex said, sliding over beside her. "Don't cry. There's no need to cry."

"I'm—not—crying."

The artificial air was dry and chilly in her face. Tears evaporated before they could cross her cheekbones. Everything in the aircruiser was clean and shiny. A million miles below, Biggar's Neck lay lush and wild and overgrown, a piece of exquisite jewelry lost in a patch of nettles, spattered with earth, its setting tarnished, its stone twinkling helplessly, abandoned by those who loved it, alone for the rest of time.

Deeping Lube, remembered as a place of great adventure, had devolved to a ransacked encampment, squalid and dull, teeming with panicky refugees and surrounded by dark giant trees. How long, only a month? And this had happened. The whole town seemed to have gotten up and moved, plunked itself deep in the forest, beyond the Blistered Moor.

"Out of the way!" the driver barked, slashing at the crowd that shuffled before the Low Commissioner's carriage. The farmers and beggars and mendicant priests looked as if they would dearly love to oblige, but there was nowhere to go. You can die in Deeping Lube, the local Press Pool said, but you can't fall down.

The Gallows Square had not been named for nothing. People camped on the periphery with their last sad belongings, small goats, sick children, watching the show. From a rooftop a fuzzy holotape of the Low Commissioner, projected too large, exhorted the populace to remain calm. Help is on the way. Foodstuffs are being distributed. Do not go to the hospital; it is already full. The inn is needed for the provisional government. Remain where you are, or go up the hill to the manor. The manor is unoccupied. Go there if you desire. Nothing else lives there; nothing grows in that ravaged soil; perhaps you will be able to.

"Out of the way!" barked the driver, slashing with his whip. The engine roared and its valves clattered. Smoke filled the air, which was already thick and malodorous. Real air, thought Vesica. She swayed in the back seat, her stomach turning.

"We'll just be a short while," said her stepfather. For a moment it appeared he was going to pat her hand, a token of reassurance, but she responded with such visceral dread, even to the subtle prodrome of this, that it must have gotten through to him. He took his hand back. Something similar had happened between her and Tamlin, but the comparison was grotesque, a reflection in a madhouse mirror. All her memories were that now.

The driver shouted. Thrull rode beside him in the right-hand passenger seat. The shotgun seat, it was called once; Vesica had heard that. Her mind was a library of things other people had said, a library of stories; but the story of her life was not among them. It was new. Thrull aimed not a shotgun but a heatweapon at a gray-green-clad pedestrian who refused to vacate their path. She remembered the militiaman's heatgun not firing, starting to smoke, back in the compound. Perhaps the disease had spread through such weapons everywhere, a contagion. The pedestrian seemed to recognize Thrull. He grinned. He waved a stenciled sign.

MAN NOT NATURE
HAS DONE THIS

The heatgun buzzed. The pedestrian's gray-green cloak opened easily, admitting the amber stream. His skin crackled. What made that sound? wondered Vesica. An electric charge passing into the flesh? Thousands of cells dying at once, each with a tiny, tiny shriek? The pedestrian's mouth opened, but it appeared that he was already dead, the mouth-opening was a last reflex, though they say you soil yourself also. So much knowledge resides in received ideas only, not personal experience. Stories kept tidy by caretakers. The pedestrian had died but he had not fallen down. The carriage ran over him.

"It will not be like this," the Low Commissioner promised, "in Riverrun."

"Riverrun?" Vesica didn't really care; just curious.

"I'm taking you back," he said smiling, actually smiling, "to Civilization."

The convoluted alley past the age-old gasworks was lived in now by a vine. It was a huge twisted thing, its skin green and smooth like a watersnake. Back and forth across the alley it wound, through rust-punctured storage tanks, over potholes, into the path of the carriage. The driver wrenched the throttle, flooding the engine with the filthy fuel they squeezed from the soil here. The carriage bumped along, running the snake down and down again. Thrull drained the heatweapon into its green hide. The snake survived this. Like many creepers it was nearly immortal. Every few feet it sprouted a tangle of would-be roots and an upright stem. Whether the roots found sustenance was doubtful; Vesica could not guess what such a thing could live on. Yet she thought she understood it. It was the forest's way of growing, even here, where no seeds could germinate nor underground creepers penetrate the compacted poisoned crust. Why would the forest *want* to come here, though? Why leave its northern home for this outpost of Civilization? The suckers rising from the body of the snake opened leaves that were flat and dusty, like white oak. Where it was bruised by the carriage it gave off a smell of dittany-of-Crete. Where the heatgun burned it, it reeked of flesh.

"This place stinks," Thrull said. "It always has."

Over the oiled door of the Hoar's Bed Inn a banner said PROVISIONAL GOVERNMENT. Sentries with red armbands stood by the door. They became agitated on catching sight of the Low Commissioner, shifted about and raised their weapons.

The common room of the Inn was the same only dirtier, and the sign over the bar was gone. There was not the troop of shuffling characters Vesica had expected; only a few clerks attending to piles of paper at the small round tables and a banana-haired woman behind the bar.

"*There* you are," Mrs Blister said when Thrull crept in behind the Low Commissioner. "Well, I've docked your wages for the time you were gone. Start mopping the floor if you want dinner."

He sneered. "You old bitch, I don't have to listen to you anymore. I've got a real job now."

"Yes," said Narthex, touching his shoulder. "You do. Your job is here."

He blanched: which is remarkable, that he could. "My . . ."

"You must go on as before," the Commissioner told him. "Here is where you are most needed. Your leader—remember I told you? —that tall young man, the Speaker, is in jail now. Inciting a crowd to raid a garden party, if you can believe such a thing. I must depend on you now. And this"—he motioned to Mrs Blister—"is where you can do the most good. For the Cause."

"The Cause!" moaned Thrull. "I don't *care* about the Cause."

"No," said Narthex, smiling. "Of course you don't. But that's all right. Do your job, and the Cause will do well by you."

As he said this he slipped a small purse into Thrull's cloak and patted it. Thrull gave a slight whimper, raising his hand to the spot. The Commissioner turned away from him, both of them knowing the matter had been settled. Thrull looked haplessly at Mrs Blister.

"We all," she said, "have to take what we're given these days. Get your mop."

Gravetye Farm from the air resembled a giant bank of anemones, mostly midnight-blue. As the aircruiser descended, Vesica saw that what she had taken for petals were forty-foot drifts, whole hillsides buried in swollen blooms. What had looked like stamens were strangled fruit trees. The leaves were forests of amaranth, swollen to the size of maples. It was like Biggar's Neck again, only here the balance between wildness and domesticity had tipped even further.

As the great craft throbbed down, Vesica saw insectile creatures boring through the leaves and flowers, and tiny jets of flame squirting yellow against the midnight-blue. They were laborers in protective clothes, doing battle with Nature, defending the farm. They were deployed in rings around the farmhouse—the outer rings, Vesica guessed, dispensable—and from the aircruiser she could only surmise, by the frantic character of their movements, their terror. They were losing the battle, it was plain. The flames they played along the trunks of the enemy ignited nothing. The anemones in particular seemed impervious. Where the flames touched them they gave forth puffs of steam that extinguished the fire-jets and nearly asphyxiated their attackers.

Those fragile, melancholy flowers. How had they learned to do that? And so quickly: who had taught them?

The aircruiser lumbered down into a paddock that, except for the singed yellow heads of cow parsley, was almost clear. The militiamen leapt from the hatch and formed a bucket brigade, passing Vesica's luggage down from the manor. Through the window Vesica could see the cook supervising this from the distant door.

"Is Meggie coming?" she asked her stepfather.

"We will have no need of her in the city," he said, scarcely giving it a thought.

"But, what will happen to her here?"

Narthex tightened his lips. "What do you imagine would happen to her in Riverrun? Do you suppose the populace welcomes new refugees with open arms? It is Chaos there, Vesica. Civilization is locked in a struggle with Chaos, a struggle for its very existence."

"She might have relatives."

"We must be firm if we are to survive. We must make Difficult Decisions." He sounded like the hologhost image of himself, presiding fuzzily over the gallows. "We must choose which path we are to take, and what companions, on that long journey. That is what we are going to do in Riverrun, Vesica. But you will see."

Boxes and boxes came out of the house. All the things Vesica had ever cherished—until a month ago. All the clothes she had ever worn and tucked away in trunks because she couldn't bear to part with them. Back to a certain age, that is. Back to the time, just this side of infancy, when she had come to live at Gravetye Farm. The last of them were coming out of the house now, being passed down the row of militiamen. Was Meggie calling goodbye at the door, or just shouting final instructions?

"Where did I come from?" she said abruptly, turning upon her stepfather. "Who was my real father? Who—"

The Low Commissioner was not easily startled. Yet Tattersall had managed it, and now so had Vesica. Narthex stared at her, then away, and finally back again with a faint (and, Vesica thought, a faintly worried) smile.

"Would you like to know that, Vesica?" he said. "Would you really like to know?"

Too quick: it was Vesica's turn to be frightened now. She inhaled a lungful of artificial air. "Yes," she said bravely.

Then: "No."

Then: "I don't know. No, tell me."

As his smile grew thinner, cooler, confident again, the Commissioner shook his head. His gray eyes glinted with momentary triumph, like those of a hawk that has just swooped down and caught
its delicate
prey.

Twenty-six

LORD TATTERSALL'S RE-treat was made to a march of windchimes. The breeze swelled warm and melancholy out of the southwest; never had the Parched Scale been·so forlorn.

"Goodbye," he said to his shriveled band of Crusaders. Groby and Lorian—who were all there were—shook hands with him.

"Goodbye." He bowed to the caretakers. The Owl and Gerta smiled.

"Come, Sheldrake," he said. His muttering aide, dribbling a last swill of Gerta's ale, fell in beside him. They lifted the few pieces of gubernatorial baggage. Everyone stood, by morning light, among the herb beds, considering the Fates' latest flip-flop.

"Easy come," Sheldrake ventured woozily, "easy go."

He had been up all night. "How insightful," said Lorian, who had been up with him. True, it hadn't solved anything; hadn't brought back Vesica. But what the hell.

Tattersall smiled. "Yes, Sheldrake has always had an easy grasp of things. He learned accounting, I believe, by mail."

"*Black*mail," Sheldrake explained. "Had to keep careful records. One thing led to another."

"Now look," said the Governor sternly, addressing himself to Groby. "You must carry on with the work of the Crusade. Until I return. Which I hope will be shortly. As soon as I've . . . gotten things back in order."

"If they don't hang him," Sheldrake qualified.

"And they *shall* thank me, when all is said and done. Well."

"Your lordship," said Groby, "are you sure you can find your way back all right? If I had a little more time, I could make you a compass."

"No more machines, please," said Tattersall. "I expect we will make it. Thank you," he told Gerta, "for your hospitality."

"It was wonderful having you," she murmured.

"So long, Governor." The Owl grinned, scuffling with muddy boots through the camomile. "Come back soon."

The eagles watched him go. The bluebirds. The orchids in the trees. The squirrels and vines and wildflowers. All the forest fell silent as this peculiar adversary passed—the man who would halt its advance.

"Let's take the road," said Sheldrake.

"I prefer," said Tattersall after some thought, "the stream. It is very peaceful."

"The road's more direct."

"We don't know that, really, do we? We don't know where it goes."

"We don't know where the stream goes, either."

"Of course we do. It goes downstream. We can build a raft, farther on. Beyond the rapids."

"*You* can build a raft."

"Do you think so? Well. You never know. Anything is possible."

"Ha," said Sheldrake glumly. But the old boy's right, he thought. Anything is.

From the Owl's lookout in the walnut tree Groby and Lorian watched them as far as the marigold meadow; then they lost sight.

"It's awfully quiet," complained Lorian. She climbed down the rungs nailed to the tree and peered around the compound, at a loss. "What do you suppose those caretakers are up to? What do they do when nobody's looking?"

Groby lowered himself carefully, conscious of being quite a sight. "They've got a lot to do here," he said undecidedly. "It's a big place."

"But you never see them doing it," said Lorian. "They just sort of, *pop up*, you know, when anything happens. Then they disappear again. They're like, I don't know . . ."

"I believe," said Groby, "I miss Vesica."

Lorian looked around at him, wondering if her lack of sleep was catching up with her. They turned back to the dome.

"I don't remember," Groby resumed, "having missed anyone before."

"Mm," said Lorian, trying to be helpful.

"What do you suppose," said Groby, "is underneath all those leaf mounds?"

She looked around in bafflement. There weren't . . .

Groby added, "I mean in the dome—you know, under the library."

There was no following the man. Or men generally. Lorian shook her head. "I don't know. Benches? What do *you* think?"

"I wonder what would be lined up in rows like that."

The danger of staying awake all night, of course, is that you will do something irrational next morning. Lorian found herself plowing through dirt and periwinkle and leaf mold, cartloads of it, to satisfy Groby's curiosity. The big man himself could not fit into the space between one furrow and another.

"It's like a table or something," she reported, her arm buried up to the shoulder. "I can feel wood. And wires. There are all kinds of wires running along— *yaaah!*"

"Wires?" said Groby thoughtfully, ignoring Lorian's shout and subsequent dance along the aisle.

"There's a live wire in there!" she exclaimed. The surprise of it, more than the electricity, had cleared her eyes up.

"Ah," said Groby, sounding pleased. "So the sunscales are working. I wasn't sure, when I plugged them in . . ."

"Wait a minute. You plugged in sunscales without knowing where the current would go?"

"It seemed like the easiest way to find out."

"You could have electrocuted somebody."

"Actually the amount of power they generate—"

Lorian shushed him. Her newly cleared eyes had caught a glimpse of something yellow-green and bright at the end of an aisle. It flickered, as though sunlight were quivering down through leaves. But there were no trees overhead; only the resurrected skeleton of the dome.

As she stepped forward to investigate, displacing more leaves, the yellow-green blur grew wider. A bird twittered nearby. She turned her head, but there were only she and Groby and the piles of leaves like burial mounds. Behind her Groby said:

"It looks like you've uncovered a hologhost projector. Part of one, anyway."

"No," said Lorian. Then, "Yes! It is—it's right here."

Her hands clawed eagerly. Leaves and dirt and earthworms spattered the floor. As the machine's glassy contours emerged, the yellow-green area grew larger, brighter, better defined.

"There are probably other projectors around," Groby suggested. "A network. You might want to look."

But the incomplete image, undulating in long slow waves as though suspended in water, was sufficiently arresting. It was there and not-there, at once. Real and make-believe. A ghost, she thought—that's why they call them that. She stared at the wavering space of the image with the awe of an apprentice before her master's conjuration.

At length she admitted, "I can't make out what it is."

"Come this way," said Groby. "You need to get the right perspective.

"It's this room right here," he explained as she moved to join him. "The way it looked when the recording was made."

Lorian saw it now. Yes, the corner of a room. *This* room, five hundred years ago. There were tables, and on the tables rows of tiny pots; in the pots four-inch pale-green seedlings, and beyond them something, a shadow, at the blurry edge of the room. The remembered room, not the real one. A bird twittered again, and this time the sound came distinctly from the speaker of the hologhost machine.

"We've got to find the other machines," Lorian murmured. "We've got to get the whole picture. See what's going on."

"It doesn't look like much," said Groby. "Maybe this is just a test of the equipment."

No, thought Lorian, irrationally sure. Amy wouldn't use good holodisks just to test her equipment. When you stay up all night you understand these things.

"Today we're going to look at the results of the last round of crosses."

Groby and Lorian exchanged looks, as though each suspected the other of being a ventriloquist.

"This will be crosses two ninety-seven through three fourteen," continued the voice that belonged to neither of them. A woman's voice. *"Series two. We're going to be looking specifically at capture of bacterial proteins by the rootmass."*

Groby squeezed forward to reach the machine from which the woman's voice had come. He found its knobs and dials rusted into their present settings. Lorian cared nothing for this. She locked her eyes on the shady blur at the edge of the projection. When the voice came again, it seemed to her that it came from there. It was that shadow, that shade, who was speaking.

"The object again," said the shadow, *"is to translocate the gene or genetic complex responsible for selectively shutting down the immune response. As in earlier implants, we are looking for evidence that these roots are able to absorb intact nuclear proteins without destroying them. Specifically we are looking for a tagged genetic sequence inserted in P. syringae v. ice-minus. Come a little closer, please."*

A chill ran down Lorian's spine. "Who's she talking to?" she whispered.

Groby studied the projector. "Voice control, probably," he mused. "I've never seen one quite like this."

The image shifted, seemed to approach them up the aisle. That was illusory—an illusion within an illusion—for in fact it only narrowed in focus and flattened in depth of field. The shadow disappeared behind it.

"Damn," said Lorian.

"This is specimen two ninety-seven-F, that's as in fuchsia."

"I don't think," said Groby, "anything is likely to happen soon. This is just a data disk. Like they used to make for autopsies and things like that. What we really need is the disk where all the data were put together and analyzed. Of course, we haven't found—"

"Be quiet," Lorian hissed.

"*. . . clipping a strand of root. Someday I'll figure out an easier way to do this.*"

Across the projection floated an alabaster blob. It hovered, changed shape like a jellyfish, and one of the overmagnified plants behind it started to shake. Rustling sounds emitted from the speaker, then a muffled snap.

"*That's got it.*"

The alabaster blob withdrew.

"That was her," whispered Lorian devoutly. "That was her hand."

"*Back off now,*" said the unseen shadow.

The image changed again: widened in focus and fattened in depth of field. As the objects within it decreased in apparent size, they seemed to grow sharper, though this, like everything else, was a trick of distance and perspective and the observer's position in the room. In reality there were no objects present at all—no plants and no tables; no neatly swept floor splashed with sunlight; no Plexiglas panels of the dome. No clipped roots. No botanist.

And yet, and yet . . .

"*Here we go,*" said the shadow, standing beside her workbench again. "*One more shot at Q. robinia.*"

She held—the shadow held—the root strand up for the benefit of the viewer. A hypothetical viewer only; not Lorian, who was standing in the wrong part of the room. Facing this imaginary person, thirty degrees away, the shadow sighed. Rather, the projector relayed an analog impression of a sigh. The shadow set down the tiny object in its hand and brushed a speck of something from the blue-black shimmer where once its hair had been.

"*Oh, I don't know. I feel like spending the day in bed.*"

The shadow's eyes flashed like onyx in the long-forgotten sun. It seemed to be waiting, expecting something.

"We're here, Amy," Lorian whispered. Her own eyes were damp and clouded. "Amy, listen to me. We're here."

Lord Tattersall stood before a wall of rock.

"I wonder what we should do," he said.

Sheldrake rubbed his head, perspiring.

"The stream"—Tattersall pointed—"just seems to end here."

"Ha," pronounced Sheldrake, his voice threatening vehemence without the strength to make good on it.

The sun slid down between the massive trunks around them. They had followed the stream all day, obeying its capricious turns and reversals, and now this had happened: the water vanished under a rock. Abandoning them. In barely penetrable woods.

"I don't believe," said Tattersall, "we came this way on the way up."

He looked at Sheldrake, expecting a rude confirmation, but the short man only sighed.

"Perhaps we should make camp, and decide what to do in the morning."

Sheldrake nodded gratefully. He set down his bags. He would build a fire.

As he turned from the rocks to look for wood, he had a deranged experience, something like *déjà vu*—a notion that he had already made the trip and was returning now with his arms full of timber. He stared at the person he took to be himself, his near-future self, standing before him. Oh, I see, he thought. It's just the boy.

"Here," said Tamlin, stepping between the trees. "I brought some wood for you."

Sheldrake opened his mouth, but the words that were spoken were Tattersall's. It was all too confusing.

"My, my!" exclaimed the Governor. "What a pleasant surprise! We missed you, my boy, at our departure."

Tamlin set the wood down beside the rocks and stood there shyly. Then he seemed to think better of his shyness, and lifted his head with the air of someone who has thought it over very carefully and is confident of having chosen the right thing to do. His large blue eyes looked tired and, somehow, older.

He said, "I was going to just follow you. But you probably don't know really where you're going. So I'll take you. Tell me where you want to go, and I'll take you through the forest and be sure you get there."

His voice came out deeper than usual and throaty, as though he wished to make it clear he was not speaking as a boy of . . . of however old he was, but as a man, an equal. This and his thoughtful pose suggested a vow taken, an alliance made. His soft features had firmed into those of the man he was becoming.

"Why, thank you," said Tattersall. "That is certainly most kind. I was just saying to Sheldrake here . . ."

"Wait a minute," said Sheldrake. He tried to imagine what Lorian would say, what questions she would ask in this situation. "If you don't know where we're going—even if we tell you, if you've never been there before—then how . . ."

He faded. "I think I've got a hangover," he confessed.

"Well, of course," said Tattersall crossly, "he's staying over. You don't expect me to send him back into the woods, do you?"

Tamlin knelt down and began arranging firewood.

"I've got some food," he told them. "I thought you might have forgotten."

From his shoulders he lowered Vesica's knapsack—abandoned in the rush of her departure. Something squirmed inside it, frantic to escape. Tamlin said, "It's a chicken."

"Splendid!" beamed Tattersall. He lowered his voice, glanced aside at Sheldrake. The little man was curled up among the baggage and appeared, already, to be dozing. "To be honest, I wasn't quite in the mood for a diet of, ahem—vegetables."

"Yeah," said Tamlin, not looking up. "Vegetables are okay for being calm. Meat is better for fighting."

"Fighting?" The Governor watched him worriedly. "Oh. Well. I suppose we do have rather a fight on our hands. A struggle, at any rate. It is all to the good to keep our strength up."

"We have to be strong," agreed Tamlin.

From a side pouch of Vesica's knapsack he pulled a disturbingly familiar device. Molded black handle, metal waveguides: It was Groby's heatsaw—very nearly the cause of his own demise. Wincing, he flipped off the safety latch and toggled it on. His slender arm trembled beneath the geyser of yellow light. With an exertion of will he steadied it, turned it down to the firewood.

To himself, it seemed, he said: "All right, then."

Then the boy slaughtered the chicken. He dressed it and

cooked it methodically, spitting it over flames that turned his
young face hot and orange. He ate his share quickly,
not waiting for it to cool,
with no more remorse
than any predator.

Twenty-seven

DOG BITES MAIN ran the headline on the Social Circles page of the *Daily Wake*.

"Can you imagine?" said Lady Widdershins, fanning herself in the sullen hour between brunch and the first caller of the day. "Heaven knows *what* kind of people write for that thing. Vesica, dear, I really don't think you should read such trash."

"I have a friend," the girl said vaguely, ". . .oh, never mind."

She set the paper on the redwood teapoy beside her on the patio, resting her hand lightly on top to keep the servants from carting it away. She looked up at Lady Widdershins expectantly, to find her ladyship looking back with an expression much the same. The two of them locked eyes for half a second and turned quickly away, taking in this sight and that around the Upper Garden. It was full summer in Riverrun and the place was deeply, almost disconcertingly lush, with splashes of color gleaming from recesses in the dank subtropical foliage. Vesica's attire was roughly consistent: a long summer dress of indigo chiffon, billowing at the skirt and sleeves, over which her long hair fell like braided goldenrod. It seemed that Lady Widdershins's younger body, and Vesica's only one, were of a size.

"What flower is that?" the girl inquired, by way of having something polite to say, pointing at a too-well-fed clump in the perennial border, whose bite-size flowerheads bore the sticky evidence of an orgy of self-pollination.

"That is a hybrid lupine called, if memory serves me, 'Poor Jerry.' It has, I believe, rather too high an opinion of itself. I have been meaning to root it out for some years now, but it is, in its noisome way, rather amusing. Do you like it?"

Yes, Vesica was prepared to say, but opting instead for honesty—why not, after all?—she said, "Not really."

"Neither do I," said Lady Widdershins.

This bit of frankness failed to break the ice between them. They tried another half-second of eye contact, and neither noted an improvement. It was too bad. In actuality the two of them, despite the wide and obvious difference in their ages, backgrounds, and social positions, approved of each other. They simply had nothing to say.

Or perhaps each had her mind on something else.

Vesica was thinking of Tamlin: wondering what had happened since she left the compound, left him hiding in the forest. It had been three weeks now. Narthex had delivered her to Marshmain, in preference to his own comfortable but hardly (as he explained it) appropriate walk-up apartment in a less desirable part of the city. The Commissioner felt strongly, on the other hand, that exposure to Lady Widdershins (who, he wished Vesica to understand, was dreadfully fond of him, in his debt for many social favors) would be . . . "improving" was how he put it, for an impressionable young lady.

An antidote, thought Vesica, to Governor Tattersall.

She had come, therefore, expecting the worst. She had sat in the cab that carried her screeching through the streets, dodging mobs and stumps and potholes, convinced that she was being sent to live with someone as horrid as her stepfather—or worse, being a woman, and therefore less tractable. She had found instead . . . something different. She was not yet certain what. Lady Widdershins was not that easy to pin down. As to her inner person, that is. As to her social self, she was freely and abundantly forthcoming.

"Thank *heavens*," her greeting to Vesica had been, "you have made it. I was so *terrified* those Pure Forceps might have snatched you right off the street. Of course the Civil Militia—isn't *that* a misnomer—are no better, but at least their *clothing* is pressed. Poor dear child, you look as though your stepfather has been feeding you whatever it is *he* eats, or rather doesn't. Let Hermione bring you some nice stew."

This memory—the first sampling of her ladyship's store of strongly held opinions—came back to Vesica this morning on the patio, and as memories often do, it had undergone an alteration of perspective, spiraled around to some new level of her mind, so that its dark underside was made visible. She squinted through the late-morning glare at Lady Widdershins's crepe de Chine-covered chaise. Keeping her tone as neutral as possible she said:

"Excuse me, my lady . . ."

"Please, dear, call me Widdy."

"Okay. Um, what do you think of my stepfather?"

Lady Widdershins reacted as though Vesica had insulted her appearance. She brought her hands up to tap lightly on the sides of her coiffure, ascertaining that it was still present, and then lowered them slowly and deliberately to parallel stations a few inches removed from either side. In Riverrun in summer, it is best not to impede circulation through the armpits. She spoke with suspicion-rousing exactitude.

"Your stepfather," she said, "and I. Have a very long. And complicated. Association."

As this pleased neither of them, she dropped the unaccustomed guard from her tongue and started over again. "*If*, my dear Vesica, you are trying to find out whether I *like* your stepfather, the answer is No. I detest the man. If, on the other hand, you are wondering whether or not I like *you*, then Yes, Vesica. I like you very much. And you are welcome to stay here for as long as your stepfather allows it. Which I *hope*," she added, fanning her bosom, "will be a very long time."

Vesica could not help smiling at this—smiling in amusement, in gratitude, in relief. And Lady Widdershins, when she was done talking, smiled primly but warmly back. For the first time their gazes crossed for more than half a second. Vesica looked away again, feeling mildly embarrassed, and her eyes settled on the folded copy of the *Wake*. She read:

The *grande dame* of the Hardy Plant Society may be the only person in town not spending the summer chasing invasive saplings from her garden. And she owes it all to her poodle.

"Have you read this?" asked Vesica.

"Of course not," sniffed her ladyship. "Moreover I can't *imagine* who could have written it. Surely it wasn't that fat reporter who came to tea last Thursday. Well, at least he got the spelling right."

Lady Widdershins, whose town home "Marshmain" sprawls over several acres north of the Faerie Sump, explained how this fortunate state of affairs came about during one of her weekly *soirées*, where this reporter managed to corner her among a fluttering pride of pansies.

Vesica giggled. Her ladyship shook her head.

"I suppose you've gotten down to the pansy part. I don't know where the man could have *gotten* such an idea. As you know, I have none of those droopy things in *my* garden. I rather suspect he is making a vulgar joke."

"Heaven knows," her ladyship declared, fondling her pet poodle who answers to the name Paracelsus, "the poor darling must have been lonely here without his mummy-jummy. Otherwise he *never* would have chewed through that nasty old pipe, would you, little pookins?"

She went on to explain that by puncturing the sewer main which transects her grounds, the diminutive saboteur had set off an inundation that ultimately flooded the low-lying land on all sides. The manor now sits in solitary splendor on a hill surrounded by an unsavory but not unattractive *ad hoc* moat. This state of affairs had made it necessary for the Civil Militia, under the guidance of the Low Commission, to erect a pontoon bridge across the Sump in order to provide Lady Widdershins's guests ready access to her frequent social and charitable functions, including the one attended by this reporter.

But the ill waters have also brought some good. As Lady Widdershins explains:

"You *see*, don't you, how the croquet lawn is just as smooth and green as ever? That is because whatever horrid weedy thing it is that is growing everywhere *else* in this city has left us blessedly alone. One assumes it must *abhor* the thought of crossing an open sewer. And who can blame it, really? But one does what one must."

As her ladyship claimed, her lawn and gardens are immaculate, unblemished by the fast-growing and hard-to-kill vegetation that has found its way, it seems, into every crack in the city pavement this summer. This vivacious invader, the reader may recall, was dubbed *Quercus rabidinus*, or rabid oak, by a spokesperson for the Secret College at a press conference last week. It has thus far proven frustratingly resilient, successfully fighting off all efforts to eradicate it, whether by pruning-blade, poison, or pyre.

Its absence from Marshmain is all the more striking in view of the fact that from the broad patio between the two wings at the rear of the mansion, a visitor can gaze across Faerie Sump and see rabid oaks establishing themselves along the Aleatory Strand in twenty-foot-tall clumps, recognizable even from that distance by their distinctive dusty green coloration. The stadium just off the Strand, once used for the monthly execution of barristers and lately a scene of frequent demonstrations by the Pure Force, is all but reclaimed by the forest that once, we are told, covered this part of Civilization. The Force has been forced out.

"And good riddance," opines Lady Widdershins. "They were making so much racket that we couldn't hear the *music* at our little dinner-dos."

A spokesperson for the Pure Force denies that his group is responsible for any disruption of what he termed the "decadent disporting of a doomed dildotocracy." He added that while the Force has rescheduled many of its public activities for sites less affected by reforestation, in his view this should be taken as a positive sign that "the final triumph of Nature over Society is at hand."

Somebody should tell that to Paracelsus. He'd nip their back-to-nature sides.

"That's pretty silly," said Vesica, setting it down.

Lady Widdershins regarded the newspaper balefully. "I'll

bet it *was* that fat man," she said. "That's the last time I let *him* eat scones all afternoon. Ooo—who's coming?"

Vesica peered down the sloping lawn, and yes: marching across the pontoon bridge was the first caller of the day. It was a thin man, coming straight across the bridge without dallying to digest the unusual view; therefore, presumably, someone who came here frequently, or was indifferent to his surroundings. These clues led to an unpleasant hypothesis, which was confirmed as the figure came close enough for Vesica to recognize the sheen of sunlight on spidersilk. She stood up.

"I'm going inside," she announced, caring little just then for decorum.

"*Brava*," murmured her hostess.

"How is my daughter?" said Narthex.

Lady Widdershins sniffed. "Your *step*daughter is in good health, if that is what you mean. More to the point, if I understand you—and I'm afraid, Low Commissioner, I understand you all too well— she has shown no inclination toward running away, and I see no reason whatever for you to keep those ruffians stationed at the end of my bridge. I am quite sure they are intimidating my dinner guests."

"I am only concerned, dear lady," said the Low Commissioner smoothly, "for your safety. And, of course, for the safety of your goddaughter."

Lady Widdershins curled her tastefully reddened lip.

"But really," said Narthex, venturing a step closer over the flagstones (as neither of them had deemed it safe to sit), "you do enjoy having her, don't you?"

"Vesica," said her ladyship, matching his step forward with two aside, "is a perfectly mannered young lady. One wonders how such a thing came to be. Perhaps it is all genetical, as Tylyester insists."

"You have been in the paper a good bit yourself, my dear."

"*Watch* yourself," she said, turning back to him. "We have made our bargain and I, for one, am keeping it. If you wish, I will call the girl down and you may speak to her. But do not—do *not*, I say—press it any further."

Narthex bowed. "Indeed, you have been most obliging. More than that: your assistance has been indispensable. Particularly in the way of that aircruiser."

"That was *very* difficult to arrange."

"And I have thanked you for it. I only wish you would believe in my sincerity."

"I believe you are *quite* sincere. I have never seen such a sincere display of greed in my life. Or such a trivial notion of what there is in life worth being greedy over."

"But, Widdy," he protested, and hurried on before she could upbraid him: "I am ambitious—I do not deny it. But you must believe, it is not only for my sake that I desire success. I have no wish to enjoy the fruits of my ambitions alone."

"*Please*, Commissioner, do not horrify me with your tales of growing up an orphan in old Earl Tattersall's fieldhouse."

"I *did* grow up an orphan in a fieldhouse," he said, momentarily bristling, as her ladyship had hoped. He recovered faster and more gracefully than she anticipated. "But that is neither here nor there, is it? It's all genetical."

Despite herself, Lady Widdershins smiled. Narthex pressed his fleeting advantage.

"I do not claim to be different from anyone else," he said. "I merely want what we all want. What *you* want, Widdy, as well as I. I want to be secure in the material necessities of life. To have a voice in Society. To know the comfort and companionship of a family. Isn't that what you want, my dear? And aren't you happier now, when you have *all* those things, and not just some of them? Wouldn't you like—"

"Stop it," she warned him. "This is mawkish and vulgar."

"—*to keep them?*" he pressed her. "Have them with you all the time?"

"Get out," she said.

For several moments he remained absolutely still. The first part of him to quiver was his lips—into a narrow smile. "Perhaps I *will* see Vesica," he mused.

And only after this had had its effect did he shake his head and say, with poorly feigned regretfulness, "No, not this time. Next time, perhaps. After you are better used to having her around."

He departed with a bow, leaving Lady Widdershins to retreat into her sunroom and brood there among the speckled pelargoniums.

Vesica knew nothing of acoustics, but she knew that every word spoken on the patio could be heard quite plainly from the bay window of the second-floor music room, which incidentally offered a splendid view of Faerie Sump and the untamed city beyond. She had not availed herself of the opportunity implicit in this knowledge before—perhaps because she wished, truly, to live up to Lady Widdershins's image of a perfectly mannered young lady—an image so different from her own—but today she was tired of this. Besides, if her stepfather *had* wanted to see her, she would have needed a few minutes' warning so as to render herself convincingly indisposed.

Now she halfway wished she hadn't listened in, for there were so many new things to think about.

Her thinking led her to pace energetically around the music room, to tap on the piano there (which proved much less satisfactory than the junkyard gamelan), and finally, after determining that Lady Widdershins was safely preoccupied, to succumb to the urge that she had known all along she was going to succumb to, ever since she heard her hostess report that she hadn't yet done it.

First she changed her clothes. The indigo summer dress was cast aside in favor of a one-piece romper, whose skimpy construction left her long, cashew-tan limbs exposed to anyone who happened to be watching (though she hoped no one was), but had the compensating advantages of being cool, and of freeing her to maneuver as necessary to make her escape.

She accomplished this not by way of the footbridge, which she understood to be under constant guard, but by another path that as far as she knew she was alone in having discovered. It was not a path, really, any more than the winding way through the forest had been one. But with eyes schooled by that earlier journey, Vesica was able to spot a felicitous alignment of rocks and weeds and cypress knees leading away from the dark passage between rhododendrons that Lady Widdershins called the Gnat Walk. And since the Walk itself was accessible from the shadowy Low Garden via a dense clematis arbor, which in turn led directly to the french doors of Vesica's bedroom, slipping away for an afternoon was not only a constant possibility, but in the end—today—irresistible.

In ten strenuous minutes (creeping, hopping, sloshing through muck, swinging from low-growing willow limbs) she was across the Sump—not much more slowly than Narthex taking the footbridge. Unlike the footbridge, though, the path led her not to the Aleatory Strand but to an adjacent peninsula of crushed stone shaded by mulberries, whose bright green leaves made the dark alleyway beneath them doubly inconspicuous. Vesica scrambled up the rocks and ventured into the alley with a caution she had learned in that other wilderness—the cooler, gentler one.

This was not misdirected. She had scarcely passed between the sagging brick buttresses when Low Commissioner Narthex himself entered the alley from its opposite end, fifty paces ahead, where it opened on a sunlit square.

His attention was devoted to a large wooden plaque, which took both of his bony arms to carry. Vesica had just sufficient time to press herself into a twisted trunk of mulberry before he set the plaque against a wall and glanced around the alley—making sure he was in the right place, perhaps, or that he was completely alone. He fished out his pocketwatch. He scuffed the rubble.

"Hurry up, old fool," he whispered, or something like it. Vesica had gotten pretty good at eavesdropping. Narthex repocketed his watch and began to pace again, in a nervous, roving manner that brought him nearer and nearer, with each lap, to Vesica's tree.

She saw what she had to do. At the next moment that her stepfather's back was turned, she stepped back from the mulberry, appraised its contortion of limbs and seized one at outstretched hand-level. She scrambled up the trunk, and by the time Narthex turned to repeat his tour she was frozen with one leg hitched just above his line of vision, trying hard to wish her other leg, straggling beneath her, into invisibility.

The wish worked once. Narthex spun away from her, facing a door that swung out from a recessed portico.

"Ah," said Narthex, not in satisfaction.

Out the door came a fat man and a younger, slimmer companion. Their strides were unsteady. They recognized Narthex with little apparent joy.

"Commissioner." The fat man nodded. "Anything for us today?"

His younger colleague, less laconic, came forward with: "Is it true you've brought charges before the Low Commission against Governor Tattersall? Aren't you worried about an adverse public reaction?"

Narthex wore a smile that would have comfortably adorned the mouth of a snake. He said, "Nothing today, I'm afraid. But ask me next week—there may be something then. Something dramatic."

The young man looked ready to continue his inquiry, but his weighty companion, in the spirit of hard-hitting journalism, gave him a punch in the kidney.

"See you then, Commissioner," the fat reporter said.

Narthex smiled again, this time more convincingly. From the direction of the street appeared a man wearing the gray robe of an academician. His dark-browed eyes looked downward, and a bulky sheaf of papers was clutched beneath his arm. He proceeded inattentively toward the door from which the journalists had emerged, and would have entered had not the Low Commissioner blocked his path.

"No, thank you, I've already . . ." the man began; then, recognizing Narthex, squared the broad shoulders beneath his robe. "Sir, I believe we have nothing to say to each other."

Wow, thought Vesica. Nobody *ever* talked to her stepfather that way. Nobody but Tattersall. She snuggled against the mulberry limb, assuaging an advent of sadness.

"But we do," Narthex was saying. "We have a good many things to discuss. We might begin with your Crusade."

The other man (whom anyone but Vesica would have recognized, from his frequent appearances in the *Wake*, as Professor Tylyester) betrayed himself by a shifting of wrinkles and woolly brows.

"I have *been* there," Narthex went on heartily. "I have been to Balance Act, and I have seen your pitiful Crusaders.

And I can tell you, Professor, there is not one chance in a thousand that anything will come of that misbegotten project but a costly—and well-publicized—waste of time."

"You have . . . Balance Act . . ." Tylyester's face grew very dark. "I don't believe you."

"I'm not surprised. How lucky, then"—Narthex crossed the alley to where he had propped the wooden plaque— "that I thought to bring back a little souvenir."

He held the plaque, with some difficulty, so that Tylyester (and, obliquely, Vesica) could read its inscription: **Reporting Station #12.**

"Anyone," snorted Tylyester, "can manufacture a sign."

"But can anyone make dead wood bloom? Look more closely, Professor."

Of course, thought Vesica with bitterness. He can take even wonderful things, miraculous things, and twist them around to his advantage.

"But why," demanded Tylyester, straightening from an inspection of the sign, "was there no signal? I have been waiting . . . I programmed the equipment . . ."

"There was a signal. Not on the frequency you were monitoring, perhaps. Though *I* received it plainly enough. But there will be no signals anymore. The only way to reach Balance Act now is with my blessing—and my map."

Tylyester's face performed a series of slight contortions, as though the mind it mirrored were raising and demolishing a series of objections to the things Narthex had said. At length the face grew still again, and the Professor asked quietly:

"What is this all about, then? What is it you want?"

"I want to be Governor of the North," Narthex replied calmly. (After all, there was nothing to gain, in this instance, by a lie.) "And *you* want, I presume, for your Crusade to be successful. Or at the very least—"

"It is not what I want, but what is necessary for Civilization."

"—at the very least," Narthex pressed on, oblivious, "to avoid the disgrace of a public failure. And it *would* be public, let me assure you. I am very well connected in the Press."

Tylyester had become immobile.

"What I propose, then," Narthex went on, in the neutral and businesslike tone he had used to threaten Lord Tattersall, "is simply that your interests and mine should serve each other, rather than continuing in opposition. You need my help, Professor—either to salvage something of your Crusade or to shift the blame for its failure. For my part, I require only your silence."

Tylyester gave him silence aplenty, at least for the moment.

"What I intend," said Narthex, "is to have Governor Tattersall removed from office, and myself installed as his successor. This will be accomplished on grounds of flagrant mismanagement of the Crusade, wrongful use of the property and funds of the Hardy Plant Society, and general abuse of the public trust in this time of crisis. These charges will be heard by the Low Commission in a special session, convening after Saint Swithin's Day."

"Only two weeks," murmured Tylyester, as though at a loss for any more substantive response.

"Time enough. My case has been thoroughly prepared. The only way it can be effectively refuted—as I'm sure you are clever enough to deduce—is by yourself, as the planner of the Crusade, or the Hardy Plant Society, whom you somehow obliged to cough up the money."

At this, Tylyester appeared to brighten. The idea of trying to keep Lady Widdershins quiet must have seemed quite preposterous to him.

"You may doubt," said Narthex—nurturing the impression that he had, indeed, anticipated everything—"that I can succeed in this. But I tell you, Professor, you can put such thoughts to rest."

However that may have been, Tylyester appeared to have rallied. He straightened himself before the Low Commissioner. "If you will excuse me," he said, "I have come here to dine, not to be coerced."

"By all means," said Narthex, stepping aside. "Enjoy your dinner. Only bear in mind: a few words from me to the Press, and *that*"—he pointed at the bundle under Tylyester's arm—"will have come to nothing."

The Dean of the Secret College gathered up his compendious study of the life and work of Amy Hayata—another tragedy, there—and stalked through the door of a crumbling brick warren.

Narthex seemed to think little of his abrupt departure. Or else he had already turned his attention to something else, some further complication of the plot. He set the Balance Act signboard down again and appeared to search for something in his spidersilk coat. Vesica inched her way out onto the limb. She could, if she wanted, have spit on his back. She had never been good at spitting, though. She should have gotten Tamlin to teach her.

Or Narthex, by the same token, could have reached up—

reached up and grabbed her by the leg. She screamed—so fast, so startling was the movement—and kicked until Narthex released her.

But that was stupid. There she was in the tree in her legless cotton jumper and there he was, her stepfather, staring up at her. Narthex was so dumbfounded, so perfectly astonished, it was almost worth . . . but that was stupid too. There was nowhere to go now. She gave him a helpless, would-be comical shrug: *The game is up,* it said, as though by saying it she might fool him into agreeing, Yes, it was only a game, it's time to go home now.

"Vesica?" said her baffled stepfather. Inviting her to speak, to do anything. But there was nothing to do.

"Come down," he commanded, reverting to a more familiar mode of behavior. "Come down at once."

She clung to the mulberry. "What are you going to do with me?"

"We'll discuss that," he said, glancing aside, "when we get home."

"Home?" she said, daring to hope—

"A new home," he said. Adding, evidently to himself, "Do you know, this may be all to the good. Things may work out more easily than I had thought."

Hopeless, more alone now than ever, Vesica stared at the doorway sunken in the wall. Above it she could see a faded logo, of whose lettering there remained only

lent art rs C

—and beneath it, etched into the facade, a graffito whose wheels-within-wheels motif reminded Vesica vaguely of a fortune card,

THE RANDOM WALK.

Twenty-eight

"COME BACK TO the raft," called Tattersall. "Tamlin, where are you?"

There really was a raft. They had felled the logs for it with Groby's heatsaw just downstream of the falls, and lashed it with vines and clothing. There were plenty of these to spare; as the stream carried them down to the Moor, the full weight of summer fell on their unscreened shoulders. The countryside was different, too, from the one they left, and even more so from the one they remembered—the Moor as it had been a few weeks ago. The expanse of yellow soil was a farm of waist-high saplings; not a moor now but an oak barren.

Tamlin was down in the water, out of the heat, diving for fish. His patchwork clothes, torn off at the knees and shoulders, lay discarded on the timbers of the deck. The Governor and Sheldrake prodded the shallow stream with birch poles, keeping the raft from drifting away from him.

"Tamlin!" Tattersall cried again.

The boy appeared in a swoosh of upflowing water. Wide-eyed, he hooked an arm across the bow and laid a fishing spear on his clothes.

"I almost had it," he panted. "A big bass, *this long*. But it got away."

"Sure, sure," said Sheldrake.

"Come on out now," said Tattersall kindly. "We must be getting along. And we've plenty of fish, anyway, for supper."

Tamlin clenched his teeth in a show of frustration. In truth he must have been grateful for a rest, for his face was weary and his eyes had lost a bit of their shine. Declining Sheldrake's hand, he hoisted himself from the current. He stood, bracing his feet against widely separated timbers, and shivered as the water ran down his back and between his thin buttocks. The late afternoon sun made his skin look tanner than it really was. If anything, he had grown paler. Tiny blue veins could be seen through the hairlets on his legs. He seemed to sway, yielding to the motion of the raft instead of resisting it, and after a moment sat down.

"Are you feeling all right?" asked Tattersall.

"I'm . . . tired. I guess. A little dizzy."

"With all that swimming I shouldn't wonder. Well, just lie down, and Sheldrake and I will pole."

Running Water, they called it. The thin river that drained the Moor and rendered Deeping Lube livable. Well, no longer: it no longer drained the Moor, for the million thirsty saplings there had no water to spare it. And just northwest of Deeping Lube, that less-than-ever livable outpost of Civilization, it narrowed to a creek and then a trench and then dribbled out altogether, its last drops turning to steam in the late June swelter. The Crusaders were obliged to beach the raft and pick their way down the empty bed until it aligned itself like a rifle-sight on Tattersall's huge and decrepit home.

As was his habit, on catching sight of it, the Governor sighed.

As was not his habit, he took a second look at the place. He said, "What's that?"

Sheldrake and Tamlin squinted to follow his sharp-eyed gaze, though only Tamlin succeeded.

"It's some kind of factory," the boy said.

"No, no—flying there from the catwalks."

"Um: a flag?"

Tattersall frowned. "There's never been a *flag* before. And there beside it—isn't that some sort of power-cannon? I wonder . . ."

Before they could find out, they had to trudge up the oil-black escarpment on which the manor stood. As they came nearer they could see more clearly the rest of the town, spread like litter on the opposite hill. It looked at first glance to be deserted. At second glance it was not deserted, but its few inhabitants had abandoned their homes—wretched huts and lean-tos, well worth abandoning— and fallen back around the Gallows Square and the Tanks.

On third glance its inhabitants were not few but many: a wretched teeming horde.

"My goodness," said Tattersall, feeling weak. Something about the vista sickened him: perhaps a taint of illness along with the usual stench in the air. As they stood uncertainly halfway up the slope, a loud sucking noise came from behind them, like air being drawn into a fireplace. They turned to find the hunk of earth on which they recently stood hurled up in a flaming geyser. The flames rose, delicate lavender, in a twenty-foot column; this lasted only a second or two, then dissipated into the cloud of dust the explosion had hurled in the air, leaving the soil to stink and smolder.

"Great gods of butane," cried Sheldrake. "What was *that?*"

The power-cannon pivoted on the roof of the manor, wagging its barrel at them. The Governor's shoulders firmed. "I don't know. But I mean to find out."

"Wait!" said Tamlin. "Look!"

From the direction of town, a bashed-in motorwagon sputtered up the winding road. A humble truce flag—someone's soiled white shirt—flapped madly from its aerial. On its flank a hand-lettered sign proclaimed PRESS.

"Ah," said Tattersall.

At the wheel was a shirtless journalist whose excessive flesh quivered as the vehicle lurched to a halt.

"Hello, Governor," he said, adjusting the placement of a cigar between his yellow teeth. "Have I got news for you."

"Why, how nice. I wonder if you would be so good—"

Sheldrake, unable to endure his lordship's time-consuming courtesies, burst out: "What in the Serpent's name is going on?"

The fat journalist rolled his eyes. "Better hop in," he said, "before those fools start shooting again."

As the wagon bounced and backfired its way back to town, he went on: "Big doings up here. Flew up from Riverrun yesterday, when I heard. Working for the *Wake* now, you know. Some broad's old job. Society stuff, mostly. But up here, see, there's this rebellion going on. The works: bombings, hangings, Provisional Government smashed. Commissioner Narthex tipped me to it."

"But what," Tattersall wanted to know, "is that banner flying up there?" With a hint of pique he added, "From my roof."

"Reminds me," the journalist said, slamming the wagon in gear—"Narthex thinks he's got a lock on your job."

"We know that," said Sheldrake, as the Governor sat glumly.

The wagon belched. The fat journalist bit his cigar and wrestled the vehicle around a corner. They were into the town now, and the sight was not uplifting. Citizens who once—out of sheer irascibility, if nothing else—would have crowded around the wagon, examining the passengers and if possible the contents of the trunk, now lay beside the road, whether disconsolate, dying, or decomposing it was difficult to tell. The fat man said:

"It's the Pure Force. Their new logo. You can't really appreciate it from here: white fleur-de-lis rising from an infinity sign, background loden green. High concept—a real professional job. Kind of makes you think, doesn't it?"

Tattersall frowned, not quite sure what it made him think of.

"Only good thing is," the fat man went on, "with the Provisional Government gone, the Hoar's Bed's open again. First time in months you can get a decent meal around here."

"Ah," said Tattersall. "I wonder if you would mind—"

Mrs Blister regarded them skeptically.

"A fine time," she told Tattersall, "*you* picked to leave town. First some thin man with a little pointed chin—"

"That would be Commissioner Narthex."

"Right. Came in here, putting up notices saying you weren't Governor any more. And now *this*."

"How about some stew?" said Sheldrake. "Look here, I'm starving and the boy's not feeling too good."

Mrs Blister scowled and seemed inclined to ignore him, but a glance at Tamlin made her reconsider. The boy sat silently at the end of the bar, from where he could survey, with baffled or terrified eyes, his new surroundings. It occurred to Tattersall that, as far as anyone knew, Tamlin had never seen a town or village before—much less a disease-ridden encampment like Deeping Lube.

"Sheldrake's right," he said quietly. "At least, about the boy. But keep talking," he called after the proprietress, who disappeared into her kitchen. "We may not have as much time as we would like."

She came out lugging a stewpot. Great dollops of its contents were disbursed into clay bowls.

"We had better tableware in the woods," Sheldrake complained.

Mrs Blister ignored him now. "*Anyway,*" she said, "whatever's going on around here, that shiftless boy of mine has run off to join it. Maybe it's a circus."

Tattersall frowned thoughtfully. "Your boy . . . ?"

"Thrull," she said sourly. "Never was worth a damn, and lately he's been worse than ever. I don't know why I never fired him. I think I *did* fire him, but he wouldn't leave. Kept whining that the Commissioner had told him he had to stay here. Anyway, he's gone now."

"The Commissioner . . ." Tattersall stroked his chin. He looked around the room—empty, except for the fat journalist drinking in a corner—as though surveying what remained of his dominion. "I suppose the first thing to do is to raise a force and take back the manor."

"You'll have trouble with *that,*" said Mrs Blister decisively.

"He sure will," said Sheldrake. "He can't even raise his own flagpole, if you know what I mean."

"Shut up and eat," she told him. "What I mean is, nobody in this town is strong enough to fight. *I'd* be happy to throw in with you, but we wouldn't get very far, just the four . . ." With another glance at Tamlin, who had laid down his spoon and lowered his head to the bar, she amended quietly: "The three of us. You want me to put him to bed?"

"A little young for that, isn't he?" said Sheldrake.

Hearing or sensing himself being talked about, Tamlin

raised his head. He blinked at them. His eyes were cloudy and gray.

"I'm all right," he said: with effort, but also with a certain underlying strength.

"We believe you," said Tattersall. "We just want you to rest. I think we may have a bit more traveling to do, Sheldrake and I, and—"

"Traveling?" said Sheldrake. "Maybe *you're* traveling, but I just got here."

Tattersall brought his palm down onto the bar. It did not strike loudly, but the effect was comparable to that of a gun going off. Suddenly everyone seemed to remember that the Governor was two heads taller than the rest of them. They all looked up.

"We," he said quietly, "Sheldrake and I, are going to Riverrun. We are going to hire a brigade of mercenaries. There should be plenty of unemployed farmers ready to sign on. Meanwhile we are going to initiate certain inquiries into the activities of Low Commissioner Narthex. Then we are going to return and liberate Deeping Lube. *Then* we are going to resume the Crusade. I am tired"—he stared meaningfully at Sheldrake—"of being interrupted."

The short man was cowed only momentarily. "There's just one problem," he said when the moment was over. "You don't have any money."

Tattersall faltered. "Ah," he said. "Well. I suppose you're right."

Mrs Blister drummed her fleshy fingers on the stewpot. "What about that old woman?" she said: "The one that used to have that place, what was it called, somebody's neck?"

Tattersall stiffened his spine. "Lady Widdershins," he said, all dignity, "is not *old*. She is a dozen years younger than myself. And *I* am not old, either." He frowned, trying to remember his age. "At least I don't think so. However," he said with a nod to Mrs Blister, "that may be a good thought. We will look into it. Now hurry up with your stew, Sheldrake. We have an adventure ahead."

As Sheldrake lowered his mouth to his bowl and resumed shoveling food in, Tamlin gamely lifted his own spoon and, in smaller quantities and with better table manners, did likewise.

"I'm glad to see your appetite has returned," Tattersall noted.

Tamlin nodded. "I'm okay," he said.
"And I'm coming
with you."

Twenty-nine

THE SILENCE OF the dome was overlaid by a hiss of electric speakers as Amy Hayata strolled between the tables in her laboratory. It was about four o'clock in the afternoon; the sun threw golden spears from left to right, as seen from the cherry desk in the library above. The tables were covered with seedlings. Their leaves were April green, smaller than thumbnails. Amy wore a baggy cotton sweater and carried a notebook in one hand. (Did its cover read *Program Notes*? Lorian couldn't tell.) The other hand prodded seedlings as she passed, either randomly or according to a pattern submerged beneath the surface tension of events, a deep game. The sweater had lilac-blossomed wildflowers embroidered around the neck. Its sleeves were damp from the automatic sprinklers and spotted with dirt at the elbows, from Amy's habit of propping herself on the lab tables whenever the notion struck her, to scribble. In the loft, Lorian turned the pages of the old notebook on the cherry desk. She had read them all several times now. Amy was humming a tune, repetitious, stopping now and then while she studied a seedling; embellishing the notes with snatches of words when she remembered them, or when she felt like it on some other account. Another deep game.

"Trip away:
Make no stay:
Meet me all by break of day."

Nearby, Groby fingered a newly oiled knob on the number 3 hologhost machine. The wildflowers on Amy's sweater slid down the spectrum from lilac to magenta; the April-green leaves crimsoned at the edges; the sun turned from spring-pale to autumn-dusky. Lorian looked up from the notebook, noticed the change and saddened. The season of growth, of possibility, was over. Amy's tune grew wistful, or perhaps it was another tune altogether. Lorian did not have the ears to be sure.

"And the blots of Nature's hand
Shall not in their issue stand:
Never mole, hare-lip, nor scar,
Nor hmm mm mm, hm—"

Late-June sun, already hot at ten in the morning, shone from left to right through the repaired roof of the dome and warmed the pages of the notebook. Momentarily it washed out the more delicate coloration of the remembered sun below; then Groby turned up the BRIGHTNESS and adjusted an awning. Amy was occupied with a particular seedling on the far side of the dome, under the windows.

"Hm," she murmured, segueing out of her song, then spoke up for the microphones. "The disappointment here is that the F-three stock show no inclination to hang on to the transposition we induced at the beginning of the line. It's like they don't recognize it's an addition to their bag of survival tricks, and they just let it go. If we could only, somehow, *get their attention*." She rapped on the table-top, as though to call the saplings to arms. "Oh, well . . ."

Oh, well, thought Lorian. This disk must be one of the later ones; the wistfulness was creeping in. Amy went farther down the aisle. Lorian closed her eyes a moment, rubbed them, lifted an ancient page.

. . . about the peculiar arrogance of science. How it presumes—this is what brought the thing to mind, that article—to descend upon a Tibetan monastery with fancy theories and field-sensors and examine in a period of weeks a 3,000-year-old tradition, then pronounce upon its ultimate validity in the next issue of <u>Nature.</u> It's as maddening as that literary critic that made his name by vivisecting beautiful stories older than the language and pronouncing that the color of the riding-hood refers to menstruation. (!!)

But of <u>course,</u> if you're going to be so gross about it. You can argue that EVERYTHING refers to EVERYTHING. All statements are context-sensitive. To understand anything, you have to consider it in light of everything else. Chromosomes, equations, fairy tales—they're all made from the same pieces, the same bag of goodies. Now and then something <u>really</u> new comes along, but mostly it's the context, the combination. In nature, meaning arises out of all these cross-references and self-references, but you can't really grasp that by thinking about it. You just have to <u>get</u> it. All at once.

But something as refined as a fairy tale—to return to the Red Riding-Hood thing, which is <u>not</u> a trivial example— has acquired so much resonance with reality over the centuries that it's incredibly solipsistic to think you can say it means THIS, if THIS is some little thing you've just thought of.

The author of these lines looked up, attracting Lorian's eye. Something had drawn her attention across the lab. She moved quietly around a table.

"Where'd she go?" Groby called up. "I can't see her."

"There"—pointing—"behind the potting trays."

"What's she doing?"

Amy reappeared for a moment, glanced around the lab, ducked out of sight again.

"Got you!" her voice crowed.

"Got what?" wondered Groby, struggling for a better vantage.

"She's under a table," said Lorian. "I don't know."

"Come on out now," Amy coaxed. She reappeared, her eyes trailing low behind her. "Come on, it's time for Mommy's program."

Lorian snapped to alertness.

"Mommy's program," mused Groby. "Television, do you think? I'll have to ask the Owl if there's a set around."

"Robin!" Amy spoke more sternly. "Come *on* now."

Groby said, "Robin? What's that? Did she have a cat or something?"

"I don't think so," said Lorian faintly.

"Oh, well," said Amy. "Suit yourself. I'm going anyway."

The three of them dispersed. Groby went off looking for the Owl in the late June morning. Amy left the lab to attend to something called her program on that April or September afternoon (depending on the TINT setting; it was so hard to know). And Lorian turned another page of the notebook.

> Things went very well today. I felt while I was in the silence that I was really getting to know it. Really getting to feel what it's about. There was this great sense of meaning, and I kept thinking, <u>this all makes sense.</u>
>
> Now I'm more sure than ever that I disagree with the mechanist types who say—well, you know, you've got these biomolecular processes going on and all you can say for sure is that this kind of measurement yields this kind of numbers. But if you press them for what it <u>looks</u> like, what it <u>feels</u> like, they hem, and haw and end up muttering that Bohr had a better handle on this than anybody else, and it's none too clear exactly what Bohr had in mind here.
>
> I mean literally they don't <u>know</u> what they're talking about. Though they can talk about it with great precision. They'll even (if you get them pissed off) argue that it <u>can't</u> be known, in the sense I mean—that "knowing" is not intrinsically permitted by the structure of reality except in certain classes of phenomena. And so forth. They think a complete description of any system—of, say, the organization of an oak tree—is going to lead you into paradox; that you're going to end up describing your own description.
>
> But paradox, I think, doesn't really exist. Not in actual time. We know Achilles is going to catch the fucking tortoise if he hustles.
>
> It only looks like a paradox if you freeze it, if you try to remove it from the context of Time. But in real life you can't do that. Before your paradox can twist around on itself, Time has gone by, so you're dealing not with a circle but with a spiral. Different levels of meaning. A whole new story.

The helix is really a great symbol of that, isn't it? God's
big hint.

"Hm," said Lorian, wondering if she, too, were beginning to understand. She glanced down into the laboratory,
where it was about four-thirty in the afternoon; and then,
adjusting her eyes, into the other laboratory where it was
ten-thirty in the morning. Both were empty. Their distinct
lighting and coloration, juxtaposed so arbitrarily, were jar-
ring to the mind, but somehow the combination was more
meaningful than either version taken alone.

"Groby?" she called. "Would you run the disk forward a
half hour or so? She's disappeared again."

But she got no reply, and finally resigned herself to her
position: stranded there, on her slightly elevated perch, between two worlds.

Groby loped through the low-lying grove at the shaded
western bulge of the dome called on Amy's chart the Bog
Garden. It was home for several hundred wet-loving species,
a pile of metal scraps, rusted to the color and texture of old
manure—which, come to think of it, may not have been
scraps but someone's attempt at sculpture—and a bench. The
biologist's path that had kept the place open for inspection
was barely discernible between rival clumps of marsh marigold and cattails: a score of rocks turned up in the excavation
of the dome's footings and dropped here to allow a chain of
walkers, lastly Groby, to cross the bog without specialized
footwear. The rocks were large and firmly planted; they did
not discernibly yield beneath his weight, and the cattails
barely chattered.

The Owl sat placidly on the bench, where for unclear
reasons Groby had expected to find him. Well, it was cool
here, and the sun filtering down through the golden leaves of
Robinia pseudoacacia 'Frisia,' splattering into puddles from which
rose little purple fists of opening fronds, was certainly restful.
And the Owl seemed the sort of person who liked his rest.

"Hey," he said, eyes half open, as Groby approached.
Nothing surprised him. "Been looking for you."

Groby frowned. "I was in the lab."

"Know that," said the Owl.

"How old are you?" asked Groby on a whim.

The Owl smiled. "Not as old as some. Take a load off?"

Groby accepted. The bench sagged slightly at his end, though springily, as though its peaty underpinnings would rise again when he did. "Lorian and I were watching one of the disks . . ."

"Never going to get through them all that way. Even the ones that still play. Amy was here for *years*. Other people before that. Some after."

"Some after?"

The Owl wriggled his shoulders. "Well, there's Gerta and me."

"Oh. I see. Anyway, Amy mentioned something about a program—'time for Mommy's program,' was what she said."

"Ah: Mommy."

"Right. Do you know what she was talking about? I thought maybe television . . ."

"Television?" The Owl gave his not-connecting frown. "Don't think she'd want to watch TV during her program. Well, maybe—but no, don't *think* so."

Groby stared at the man. Was it devilhemp, he wondered, that had done this? Then a notion struck him that for some reason seemed very obvious then but, if indeed it was obvious, had strangely never occurred to him before.

"All right," he said, striking a no-nonsense tone. "Do you want to tell me about it?"

"Sure," said the Owl. "Why I was looking for you."

"What?" said Groby.

"Show you Amy's program. Never going to understand all that stuff without it."

Groby thought very hard about this. It took a couple of minutes. At last he said, "You're going to *show* me Amy's program?"

The Owl wore a patient look, as though waiting for all these questions to die down and the Bog Garden become quiet again. His eye seemed to have been snared by a lady's slipper orchid.

Groby sighed. "All right," he said.

"Close your eyes," smiled the Owl.

*   *   *

A white blur. Lorian fiddled with the FOCUS controls, but the white blur persisted. She could hear noises coming, as it were, from the other side of it—footsteps, Amy's voice, the businesslike clatter of laboratory equipment—but the blur remained blurry.

"I don't know," said Amy. "Maybe I should have done a sort of numinous impact assessment before I started all this. Some of these seedlings are coming out pretty weird."

Another bad disk. There seemed to be thousands of them. At least the audio still worked. Lorian listened half-mindfully while she experimented with SPATIAL DEF, SYNC SET, TRACK ALIGN, and SCALE.

"Here's another one," Amy announced. Her voice was indistinct, as though she were bending over a table. "They're showing a moderate increase in vigor, but nothing like I hoped for. And I socked the field good this time. I mean, I must have been sending out pure panic. I really hoped for something . . ."

There was a bit of silence as Amy repeated whatever operation she was performing.

"Golly," she said, "this is odd. This one here—which would be, um, four twenty-nine B, that's baby—this one displays, and I mean unmistakably, the rhizome-forming pattern induced in the *previous* series. Like the trait has spilled over from one physically isolated population to another. Hundredth monkey type of thing."

Lorian gave up. No video, and the audio was incomprehensible. She slapped the hologhost control with the flat of her hand. The white blur jiggled a bit; colors moved within it, but nothing definable.

"Maybe I should stop for a while," mused Amy. "Stop my program, I mean. I don't know, maybe I'm causing these aberrations myself."

Don't blame yourself, thought Lorian. She wished the picture were working; felt irrationally that Amy would feel better if she weren't lost in this shimmery fog.

"I wonder," Amy said, "if screwing around with the fields has made them more susceptible to genetic corruption. I don't know. I've been pumping a lot of stuff *out* there. Maybe it's not going to the right place. Maybe it's going *everywhere*. I really should have thought about this before."

Lorian sighed. This self-criticism was making her despondent. She started to pull the disk, start again with another one, when a small voice called out:

"Mommy!"

Lorian's fingers froze.

"What is it?" said Amy.

"Look!" the little boy's voice commanded. "Look what I did."

"What . . . ? Oh, no."

There were rapid footsteps. The unseen child giggled.

Well, thought Lorian. That's certainly no cat. She wondered where Groby had gone.

"Robin!" said the weary mother. "Come here right now. What have you done to the recorder?"

Lorian heard small feet scuffling under a table, very nearby, fingers tapped on plastic knobs. Robin, she thought. Somehow she had expected it to be a girl. Or something.

"I'm invisible!" Robin proclaimed from his hiding place. "I'm a ghost!"

"You're a mess," said Amy, sadly, fondly.

Lorian felt ridiculous, eavesdropping on this domestic scene through a white blur.

"I'm haunting the dome," the little boy declared. Then ghost-noises: "Woooo, woooo, woooo!"

"Oh, I see," said Amy. Her roughened fingers (*so dry*, thought Lorian) brushed against the console—the very console beside Lorian. Far away in time a knob was rotated. The white blur altered, became a metaphor for creation out of the void; it fractured into a hundred colors; the colors swam together, resolved into objects, tables, seedlings, Amy's hand. Lorian stood up, looking for the boy, but he was expertly hidden. Invisible.

A ghost, she thought. For sure.

"All right, Robin." His mother was standing too. Amy and Lorian: three feet and five centuries apart. "You can stop being invisible now. I've fixed the machine."

How old is he? Lorian wondered. Pretty young, the way she talks to him. Lorian's experience with children had been sparse, and mostly aggravating, involving the older kind that haunted the trash-strewn streets of the city.

Children must be very expressive, she thought. Even the

little foot-dragging sounds Robin made emerging from his hiding place among bags of potting soil conveyed a playful reluctance. Small bare feet slapped the floor. Amy and Lorian turned their heads; their gazes converged on a soft sun-gilded cowlick of brown hair, just visible above the table-top.

"Come here," said Amy. "Let me look at you."

The silence of the field. A phrase of Amy Hayata's. Groby remembered it from somewhere in her rambling notes. Program Notes. Ah—he smiled. Everything felt very clear.

He opened his eyes in the Bog Garden where the Owl had left him. Left him some unknown time ago to be by himself and follow the quiet private ritual he had learned. The program. He took a deep breath, feeling the air, the real air full of many more things than gases mixed together, enter his lungs. Amy's phrase came again, of its own accord, to his mind.

The silence of the field.

"Think I've heard it called," the Owl had said, "the Perfections."

"By whom?" asked Groby. As he imagined Lorian would have done.

"Don't know for sure," said the Owl. "Lots of folks. Just a few at a time, but that's a lot if you add them up over all these years."

All how many years? Groby's great long-slumbering spine tingled. Five hundred? Three thousand?

A long, long time. Lots of folks have studied the Perfections, practiced Amy's program, gone into the silence of the field.

Groby studied the patterns of bark on a willow stump. Who could have designed that? he wondered. What engineer's hands could have shaped that living substance? Morphogenesis: the birth of form. The word made palpable. Groby stared at his own callused palms.

It was so easy, he thought. Such a simple technique—a trick, like the right-hand thumb rule, or sticking to one side of the color wheel in planning a garden. Yet had the Owl not taught him, not taught him the quiet ritual, he never would have known. It wasn't like an answer to a problem, that you might just stumble over. You had to be *given* it, all at once. The willow roots, the parade of ants across the rocks, his bare feet planted on the ground, all wove themselves like colored threads into a vast and coordinated tapestry. Yet Groby never would have noticed that. Or only intellectually. Never would really have *known*.

He closed his eyes again, meaning to continue. But before his mind could begin again that effortless effort of thought—riding the horse, the Owl said, the way the horse is going—another phrase of Amy Hayata's drifted up to distract him.

The presence.

He stared at the garden around him. It was a wild place; calling it a Bog Garden seemed a kind of gentle irony, Amy's lonely joke. Untameable, it surrounded Groby, made him complicit in its moods. Its presence.

He stood up. An unformed notion had settled at the back of his brain, a sense of deviation from a guiding pattern like that which had made him recognize—such a short time ago—that the black object hulking in the field was going to carry him away to misadventure. It was a vague idea, a movement below the surface, and he struggled to capture it. What pattern had changed, he wondered. What pattern and what change and what new element was he feeling?

The Presence.

The change was in the Bog Garden around him. Not just his mind: he was sure of that. His awareness of the garden had changed, *and the garden had changed with it.*

Groby felt a triumphal sense of having made a distant, difficult connection. Yet he felt, too, a certain eerie familiarity. The garden had made a subtle adjustment to his shifting awareness, and it seemed to Groby that he recognized what it was changing from, and what it was becoming—something he already knew, though he couldn't give it a name.

The Presence, he thought. Stirring, waking, coming to life in the silence of the field.

I've got to tell Lorian.

The ghost boy scampered down the aisle and turned around the corner of the table. He beamed up at his mother, proud of the trick he had played, happy to have been caught at it. He was eight years old. He was wearing clothes that had been tailored down from something else. Probably there was no child-size clothing here; this was no place, no life, for children.

"You're a mess," said Amy.

Pleased with the mess he was, he smiled up with wide azure eyes.

My God, Lorian thought.
It's Tamlin.

Transpositions

We're going to have a completely new understanding
of the relationship of things to each other.
— BARBARA McCLINTOCK

Kalmia latifolia
Mountain laurel

A plant of contrast and deception. All its parts —
glossy leaves, blush-pink florets, pliable wood —
are graceful, refined, and poisonous.

Thirty

~

THE DEEP GAME room at
the rear of the Silent Partners' Club might have existed for no
reason other than to perfectly fulfill one's most paranoid
ideas about Society: that it was an exercise plotted out
behind closed doors by a select and secretive group of people, mostly men, past middle years, shadowy of mien and
habit, chummy, prone to dozing during the evening news or
glancing wryly among themselves as what minor catastrophes
they had engineered that day were at once made too much of
and trivialized by the Press.

Perhaps this fantasy was no less than the truth. Perhaps,
as the founders of the Silent Partners' Club believed, there
are only a handful of people in any era who truly make any
difference, who perceive clearly the direction of events, who
have the wit and grace and decisiveness to know when to
trim the sails, when to hold fast, when to tack radically. At
any rate it was on this assumption that the Club was founded,
its rooms carved out of the brick warrens of a then-
unfashionable quarter of the city, and its symbol—based on
the wheels-within-wheels motif of a fortune card—etched in
the brick facade.

Unfortunately, whatever virtues the Club's original members might have had, these did not include enough money.

Perhaps they were *too* virtuous. The Club fell badly into debt within a few years of its founding—owing, in part, to its founders' excellent eye for real estate, which enticed the civic authorities to reappraise, frequently and upwardly, the tax burden upon its headquarters. Long before the first saplings of *Quercus rabidinus* sprouted among the mulberries outside the Club's recessed portico, the luxury of exclusiveness had been surrendered. Bellying up to the long maple bar could now be seen such eyebrow-raising *arrivistes* as barristers, journalists, diplomats, even legislative aides. As an organization whose original mission had been to recruit only persons qualified to chart the course of society, the club had been conspicuously unsuccessful.

Yet even now, a generation after this comedown, not all standards had been forsworn. As a mariner beset by a storm may find the resolve to steer a steady course, transcendentally certain that the winds will change, so the founding members of the Club had fallen back on the one refuge that remained to them. They became stubborn. They retreated, licking their wounds, into the Deep Game Room—a sanctum just off the main bar, once reserved for the playing of snooker. They sealed it with an electronically operated door. And they caused a hole to be blasted through the bricks of the Room's rear wall, bringing to that hallowed preserve an unusually depressing view of Faerie Sump and a means of exchanging the stale, cigar-soused, and usually overheated air.

Here they gathered, some of them nightly, some of them twice-yearly, some of them once a generation, to dine.

They were admitted, or not, by Evergrey, the aged bartender. He was a fixture of the Club. Like as not he was included in the annual tax appraisal. He knew all the members, founding and lately arrived, and was the sole guardian of what in a less exalted situation would have been called a pecking order. Before a member of the Club could be admitted to the Deep Game Room, it was necessary for Evergrey to approve the applicant's entry by activating, from behind the bar, an electrical switch disguised, for reasons no one but he remembered, as a bottle of Old Juggler. This switch did not, as was generally believed, cause the doorlock to open. It was supposed to. But what it actually did was turn on a servo-motor too weak to pull the rusted bolt, but strong enough to scrape and whine and make ratchety sounds so annoying to the occupants of the Room (and there were always some of them around, one or two were believed to live there) that in due course the door would be unbolted, manually, from within.

Late in the afternoon of Saint Swithin's Eve, the servo-motor began to scrape and then to whine and then to ratchet. The three people present in the Deep Game Room looked up from their solitary pursuits—an eminent cartographer from his topological survey of Faerie Sump, Professor Tylyester from a glum revision of his compendious essay, and a poet of justifiable obscurity from his moony examination of the latest round of cracks in the plaster ceiling—following which there was the usual period of uncertainty over who would be sufficiently annoyed by the racket to get up and open the door.

The answer was Tylyester. He had been restless to begin with, and in any case the task of editing out of his monograph all references to the First Biotic Crusade was not a happy one. He rose from the armchair he had pressed into conformity with the curvature of his spine, frowned a moment through the oily peephole, then threw the door open with, for a normally restrained academician, great excitement.

"Tatty!" he exclaimed.

"Hello, Ernest."

Tylyester frowned at the rare employment of his given name. But what the hell: once a generation was not too much to live with. He stepped aside, beckoning happily, and into the room strolled the tall and gaunt and remarkably resolute form of the Eighth Earl Tattersall.

"Look, everyone," said Tylyester, dragging the door shut behind them. "Look who's here! It's old Tatty!"

Tattersall had come lately to feel about "old" much as the professor felt about "Ernest." But he was not inclined to fret about this just now.

"How have you *been*, Tatty?" said the cartographer. "We've been hearing . . ."

"*Where* have you been, Tatty?" wondered the poet, who hadn't read a newspaper in months. "Still living up north?"

And Tylyester, realizing how awkward this meeting might

turn out to be, said more soberly, "Is it true, Tatty? Did you really find Balance Act?"

"Hello, hello," Tattersall told them, told them each individually as he came slowly, shaking hands, into the room. (He *would* have thought someone might have dusted the furniture since his last visit. Oh, well.) "Yes," he told Tylyester, "I was there. Everything was exactly as you described it.

"As to myself. Well." He moved past them to the broad window, open a crack, where the stale air of the room competed with the fumes blowing off the Sump. "I've been having just a tiny bit of difficulty of late. As you may, I suspect, have heard."

The circle of Deep Gamers nodded sympathetically.

"But at least," noted the poet, whose profession had taught him to make the best of an intrinsically bad situation, "you can move out of that godawful manor."

Tattersall clucked his tongue. "Now, now," he said, "one shouldn't lose hope prematurely. I'm still the Governor, as far as I know."

"For a day or two," agreed the cartographer.

"But don't worry," insisted the poet. "Things will brighten up."

And Tylyester, for all that he wanted to ask and hoped to learn, said nothing.

"Come along, Tamlin," said Sheldrake. The gruffness of his voice was a poor attempt to mask his concern for the boy's well-being. Whatever infirmity had come over the youth during the raft ride to Deeping Lube, it had gotten worse as they came on to Riverrun.

"Ahhnun," Tamlin seemed to say. His face was as pale as if all the blood in his body had turned the color of phlegm. He tried again. "I don't . . ."

"What's that?" said Sheldrake. "Look, if you can't speak any more politely than that, there's no use taking you to see Lady Widdershins."

This had its effect. Tamlin jerked his body erect and labored to pull abreast of Sheldrake as they walked together, far from briskly, down the Aleatory Strand. The crowd of pedestrians, loiterers, pickpockets, rabble-rousers, and variously

uniformed guards was so thick that—though Sheldrake tried
to shove and elbow for the both of them—they were barely
able to keep themselves on the road and out of the sapling
trees that grew like rushes in the gutter.

"Gods of spray deodorant," the ex-tree pollard muttered.
"Where do they all come from?"

Tamlin made a small sympathetic noise, in the manner
of one who detects a pause in a monologue to which he has
not been paying attention.

Sheldrake turned to address him forcefully. "Look now,
boy—can you make it or not? We're Lord Tattersall's repre-
sentatives, now. We can't be embarrassing him. Passing out
on her ladyship's carpet, for example: it just wouldn't do.
Now what do you say—would you rather rest here in this
little park while I go across the footbridge?"

This little park was, in fact, the site of the civic arena. It
was impossible now to form any picture of the place. Ten-
foot trees with dusty leaves grew as close together as fence
slats. Many bore ax marks or other scars, none of which
evidently had been effective. The trees were still growing.
Tamlin ran his hand along one of them, then drew back with
worried eyes, puzzled by its leathery texture, its unwoodlike
resiliency.

"I'm staying with you," he said hoarsely.

"Ha," said Sheldrake. "Let me feel your forehead."

It was cool; the faded blue eyes were cool; the breath
emerging from the fallen chest was cool. The boy didn't
seem to be sick so much as to have left the better part of his
vitality behind.

"All right," Sheldrake conceded. The truth was, he would
not have left the boy to fend for himself in this unruly city.
Unlike the wild places Tamlin was used to; here the laws of
survival were enforced not by strength and speed but by
blade and gun and truncheon. "Just let *me* do the talking."

Tamlin said, "Uhmum."

They came in due course to Faerie Sump, and the footbridge leading across it. Marshmain stood on the other side:
stately, lush, bejeweled with summer flowers. On the near
side stood a platoon of armed and armbanded militia, nomi-
nally supervised by a token terrified Home Guardsman. Be-

fore their eyes—and, most likely, for their benefit—a
demonstration was being staged. Two hundred young people
ambled about thumping drums and chanting three or four
simultaneous slogans that created an interesting polyphonic
effect but were, from an ideological standpoint, ineffective.

"Free   Held Without
"   the Curse of the   Triumphant
"   Nature's Final
"Let the   in their Filth!"

—they seemed to be saying. There must be a shortage, Sheldrake noted, (along with food and water and money and
decent public housing) of gray-green robes these days. More
than half the demonstrators were wearing nondescript ap-
parel that resembled, if anything, the work-suits handed out
to refugees who signed up for the Low Commission's resettlement program.

"Hey, you!" he greeted a sitting militiaman—more cour-
teously, he thought, than the miscreant deserved. "How
about sleeping somewhere besides the footbridge? Me and
my friend here are on our way to Lady Widdershins's."

The surly individual rose to his feet and glanced aside at
his colleagues.

"Do you, uh," he said, "have a pass?"

"I have something better than that," Sheldrake said, not
showing (he hoped) the slightest discomfiture.

Three or four other militiamen congealed around the
first, forming a human—or at least protohuman—barricade
between Sheldrake and Tamlin and the shining manor across
the Sump.

"I have," Sheldrake pronounced, "Credentials, attested to
by a Person of High Authority."

He produced a document and waved it in the air.

The militiaman grabbed for it with an eagerness that
suggested that this was a ruse he had been instructed to
watch for. The thick parchment crackled as semiliterate eyes
scanned rapidly down the page, settling on the signature at
the bottom. "What's this name?" The man frowned. He began
to spell: "T—"

"*Tattersall*," said a voice, sharp as a tax appraiser's eye,
behind them.

Sheldrake winced. "Fish lips," he muttered.

"Are you visiting our fair city alone?" Low Commissioner Narthex inquired. "Or in the retinue of some disgraced personage?"

Narthex stepped smartly up to the footbridge. The notorious satchel of warrants and summonses and affadavits bulged beneath his arm. An armored carriage stood grumbling in the street behind him.

"Ha!" Sheldrake said defiantly, making himself as tall as possible, which required a bit of help from the bridge-planks. "You can't bully *me*."

Narthex displayed his snakish smile. "Nor do I need to. I can simply have you thrown into jail."

"Not unless you've bought off the Home Guard and all the newspapers too."

Sheldrake waved his credentials before the Commissioner's face, indicating at the same time the lone guardsman and a small pack of journalists, distracted from their dutiful coverage of the demonstration by the arrival of the angry-looking carriage. Narthex studied each of these in turn.

"You have no shortage," he observed, "of feeble allies. Unfortunately, this bit of paper will do you no good. Your Governor, if you remember, has been relieved of the powers of office. Pending, of course, official inquiry. Meantime, Marshmain is strictly off limits. As you may know—or perhaps not, with your debased standing in Society—tomorrow Lady Widdershins will be hosting her annual Saint Swithin's Day Bull Roast. *All* the notables of Riverrun will be there. For security reasons—what with all this civic unrest—the grounds of the manor have been closed to all but invited attendees."

Sheldrake set his chin. "What civic unrest? All I see is a bunch of shills you hired from the refugee camps—right in Deeping Lube, I'll wager."

"Nonsense," said Narthex (with an unclockably quick glance sideways at the Press). "These demonstrations have been going on all summer. Though I must say, your lordship's bungling of the Crusade does seem to have egged them on."

"I bet," Sheldrake growled. "Well, see you at the party."

"Sadly," Narthex smiled, "all invitations were *personally*

delivered, two weeks ago. I have here"—patting the satchel—"a complete list. So you *needn't* think of forging one."

Sheldrake decided not to expend the energy required to glower. It was unlikely, this late in the day, that he would be getting any more of it.

"Come on, Tamlin," he said, turning haughtily, "let's get some fresh air."

But the boy was—

"Gone?" said the Low Commissioner. "What exactly do you mean, *gone?*"

"I should have thought I hadn't begun to stutter at *this* stage of my life," said Lady Widdershins.

"Do you mean to tell me—" The Low Commissioner paused, gathering wind.

"Yes, that is what I *do* mean," her ladyship told him crossly. "She vanished on the very day of your last visit. An intriguing coincidence, I thought."

"Now, Widdy," said Narthex, "you needn't misdirect the blame for your own lapse—your own *shocking* lapse of responsibility. Just think of all the things that could happen to her, wandering about in this city."

"I have—"

She cut herself off and turned her head in the other direction, staring at the untouched keys of the old piano. Vesica had loved the music room, she remembered. Its pink wallpaper, its window boxes, its view of the Sump . . .

"I have been thinking," she continued resolutely, dabbing at her eyes, "of nothing else, Narthex, since the day she left. Nothing, nothing, nothing else. Oh, my poor darling Vesica!"

"Why—Widdy." Narthex took an uncertain half step forward. He was as astonished by the spectacle of Lady Widdershins in tears as by his own instant and inexplicable empathy. A bony hand went out, but it hovered just short of her quaking shoulder. "It's . . . there's no need . . . I'm certain she's all right."

"Oh, but *how?*" She was sobbing audibly now. "How can you be sure? *Anything* could have happened."

It occurred to Narthex that this was more or less how *he*

had felt, in his own less dramatic fashion, when his step-daughter vanished from Gravetye Farm. The anxiety; the shock; the sudden sense of aloneness—compounded, in his own case, by the startlement of realizing that it was possible to feel anything *other* than alone, and that he had felt it, he *must* have, before Vesica was gone. It's really true, he thought. You never realize what you have.

"Oh, Widdy," he said, insensibly sorry for the poor woman, wanting to comfort her—but it was an overture with no opera. What could he say, after all? *Everything's quite all right—I've got her safely tucked away in my apartment. I'll let you have her back as soon as you promise* . . .

"Don't you worry now," he began instead, adopting a strategy markedly different from the one he had intended. "I will search the entire city. I will personally comb the Epicene Pits, if that's what is required."

"Oh!" she gasped. "The Pits!"

"No, no," he said hastily. "That's not . . . I just meant, I am ready to do whatever is needed. Whatever is required. To have our daughter back again. And I hope you are likewise."

"Our . . ." Lady Widdershins stanched her flow of tears long enough to consider the nuances of this. "She is *not*—"

"I know, I know. Of course. It was just a manner of speaking. Although you know, my dear lady, that I would *like* it to be more than that."

The great lady drew herself together. She had needed a good cry, she now saw; but in front of Low Commissioner Narthex was not the place to have it. She disconsolate, he the consoler; she powerless, he in firm control: no. It would not do. There were quite enough distorted roles, time-blurred identities, grotesque transpositions of person and place in this tragicomedy, without *that*. She sniffed, a final time, and lifted her head.

"Yes," she said, "do search. Comb the city. Do what you can—whatever it takes—to find her."

Narthex nodded, drawing nearer. The chilling gleam had not left his eyes.

"And bring her," she told him, very carefully, knowing who it was she dealt with, knowing the object of their dealing, "bring her back."

"I shall, Widdy," he said.

And don't, she started to say, but stopped herself. One must not antagonize him now. One must endure him a while—perhaps a great while—longer.

Narthex was about to say something more, too, but like his hostess he checked himself.

The unexpected avalanche of emotion had left them both feeling a bit vulnerable. Neither thought it becoming.

The Commissioner bowed slightly from the waist. "Until Saint Swithin's Day, then," he told her.

Vesica languished in her room.

That's how she thought about it, how she described it in the story.

It was a long story, though it had lasted only a couple of months now, from spring till summer. And it wasn't a simple story anymore; it wasn't *The Girl and her Wicked Stepfather,* nor was it *The Enchanted Forest.* And for sure it wasn't *Fair Janet and Young Tamber Lane,* because that had a happy ending. It was more like *The Young Pucca,* where the end was confusing, or you didn't know how it really ended at all—where the story just stopped when things were happy, after the boy and the girl went off together into the woods, and you didn't have to know what happened after that.

The heroine languished in her room. The room where her stepfather kept her night and day. The room with one small window with bars on it in a comfortable but hardly ostentatious walk-up apartment overlooking the Tomb of Artists in the sewer-moated city, eight hundred and forty miles southwest of Balance Act, a million million miles from Tamlin, a lifetime away from anything like a home.

She wore a cotton dress her stepfather had given her—a little-girl dress that didn't fit right—after he had brought her here and sat her down and smiled and talked to her. He said We're going to be together now, Vesica; we're going to be together from now on. And soon it won't be just you and me—soon, just as soon as I can do what must be done—and if everything goes the way we want it to—then there will be three of us, Vesica, and we'll all be living together; we'll be a regular little family and I'll be an important man, the most important man in the North, Vesica, and you'll be my daughter, and Lady Widdershins will be your mother, and don't you want that, Vesica?

Vesica languished in her room. What she wanted was to die.

No. She backed up, edited that out. You can't leave out hope from a story, even one that ends sadly. You must leave your heroine some room for hope, however small, some possibility of final happiness.

The heroine languished in her room, where her stepfather kept her night and day, yet even now she had not given up hoping that someday the enchanted prince, her beloved, would come to this sewer-moated city and . . .

But maybe it was better not to think about it. Just to hope, but for nothing in particular.

As if to confirm this, a door opened and closed somewhere below, and the sharp-heeled stride of her stepfather ascended the staircase. It was late afternoon; there was no clock in Vesica's room, but through the bars of the window she could see the sun tumbling like a catapulted fireball behind the western battlements. Soon it would be eclipsed by the half-deflated ball of the Observatory that stood against the sky as the dome at Balance Act had stood against the trees. Vesica was so sad and so angry that at times the story was her only refuge, the only place she could flee to escape this wretched little room.

(Actually it was a spacious, thoughtfully furnished room; but it was tiny and wretched and cheerless in the story.)

The footsteps came up the hall. They paused outside her door, their cessation thoughtful. Then, after a minute or so, they resumed; clack clack, clack clack, down to Narthex's study. In this apartment, as at Gravetye, he had a study in which he spent most of his time. If he ever ate, or slept, or did anything normal, he did it secretly, or when Vesica was asleep, and these days she was sleeping very little.

She heard his voice. Just audible, a thinly articulated string of syllables, none receiving more emphasis than the last. He must be at his airfax machine again. It was the only thing he did in his study that made any noise. Just to be doing something, rather than out of any particular interest, she moved from the narrow coverless bed where she hardly

slept to the door that was locked almost all the time, except
when he invited himself in to feed her. She would rather he
not do even that, that he leave her to—

No. Edit that out. She pressed her ear to the door,
which was hollow, sculpted from thin panels, and tried to
make out what he was saying.

"Hmm time tomorrow," it sounded like, "uhll be gmming
ohrrww the final tape. Wwrlll set them off. Just about noon-
time murm the hmm tnn ss tp."

More of his plotting. Wouldn't you get tired of that, she
wondered, after a while? Still it made for some interesting
eavesdropping, when she could make it out.

"The old fool," she heard clearly. "I'll be glad when . . ."

Some kind of noise outside the window got in the way
of what came next.

". . . in all the papers the next day. Let them *see*
what . . ."

There was more noise outside. *Shh*, thought Vesica. It's
just getting interesting.

But that didn't work and the noise got louder: some kind
of tapping. Just my luck, she thought. She stood up; her leg
was getting cramped anyway, and what was all that tapping
about?

You should never lose hope. In a story, if you're the
heroine, you should never lose hope nor ever cease to believe
in magic or think miracles are going to happen. Because if it's
a real story, and you're really the heroine, then somehow,
someday—

You'll turn around in your room—

And there outside the window will be the hero of the
story, the Enchanted Prince, balanced on the ledge with his
pale face pressed against the window, holding on to the bars
with one hand and tapping on the glass with the other.

"*Oh, my God,*" said Vesica, at about the same time Lorian
said the same words eight hundred and forty miles away, and
for about the same reason.

Tamlin tapped again and beckoned for Vesica to come
to the window. She could hardly move, hardly breathe in her
excitement. Her limbs were made of something other than
flesh, something magical, and she couldn't quite control
them. She had to will herself, to *imagine* herself moving across

the room and standing before the window and looking out at Tamlin—

Really Tamlin—

Inches away, pale-blue eyes wide and imploring, long fingers gesturing, soft lips moving, forming words.

"What?" she said.

He frowned, shaking his head: *Be quiet.*

"What are you doing here?" she whispered.

His lips moved: *Can you open the window?*

She shook her head. Helplessly, pointing at the bars.

Tamlin's hands gripped them, tugged at them, but they were as strong and wide a barrier as the million million miles had been. Tears formed at the corners of Vesica's eyes. All this, she thought, this miracle, for nothing.

But remember to hope, because in a story everything will be provided for. Everything will have been foreseen.

Tamlin reached into the knapsack—Vesica's knapsack—hanging from his shoulders, and pulled out Groby's heatsaw. As Vesica blinked in disbelief he thumbed its POWER button and trembled to control the sputtering blade. Sparks flew crazily from the old iron of the bars. And the heat—Vesica could feel it even from inside—turning the bars red and then white and then dissolving them, the metal running like honey, Tamlin squinting in the brilliant glare, and the heatsaw turning his skin from white to scarlet.

Then the last bar fell away, struck the ledge and bounced off, falling to the alley below and landing there with a loud and ominous *clung.*

Quick, said Tamlin's lips, *open the window.*

"Now hurry," he said when she had done it. "Somebody's going to figure out what I did to the carriage and then we're done for."

The iron was hot through the cotton dress as she clambered out the window, onto the ledge with him, but she didn't care—about that, or the need to hurry, or the danger of falling from the ledge or, as seemed more likely, off the edge of the world. She hugged him and cried and laughed and ignored his efforts to shut her up, and finally he figured out he was going to have to kiss her.

The sun was a dull red glow behind the Observatory. For a long time they held the dangerous kiss on the ledge.

"Damn it," he whispered, breaking away and grabbing her hand, "*come on* or they'll catch us for sure." He turned around. A rusty drainpipe that only a character in a story would believe, or trust, led down from the ledge to the alley. Tamlin turned back.

"Vesica, I love you," he said.

And she said . . .

But everyone must
know that.

Thirty-one

"THE CRUSADE IS over," Professor Tylyester declared. "That much is certain, no matter what happens the day after tomorrow. Even if the Low Commission rules in your favor. Narthex will never allow us to return to Balance Act."

"*Narthex*," uttered Tattersall. "Do you know, I'm getting just a bit tired of hearing that man's name. I suppose it's easy to lose sight of, when one lives in the city, but there *are* other things in the world besides the Low Commission. By the way," he added, having wondered this for some time, "is there a High Commission somewhere?"

Tylyester trod the threadbare carpet of the Deep Game Room. It was hours past suppertime, and the two of them were alone, except for the poet of justifiable obscurity, who had no place else to go. The Professor said:

"Oh, it isn't just Narthex—though I agree with you. There is a public outcry. Trees are growing in the streets. Commerce has become well-nigh impossible. The Press is all over it, fanning the flames, and everyone is looking for a scapegoat. And *you*"—he lowered a lecture-hall gaze at the Governor—"are the likeliest candidate. You or I. Our names have somehow gotten attached to this whole mess in the popular mind. Not just the failure of the Crusade. The entire

ecological crisis. I don't know how they got the idea . . ."
He reflected. "It's a wonder they've overlooked poor Widdershins."

Tattersall frowned. "Why do you say 'poor'? Surely she
hasn't lost all that money . . ."

"Oh, no, no. Just, you know, the Crusade was very dear
to her, too."

"Ah." This was a substantial relief, though Tattersall did
not like to admit it. "Still, I can't help thinking you're being
overly gloomy."

"Gloomy?" Tylyester's brow was as dark as a thunderhead. "I should say so. And the worst part—what truly
worries me—is this resurgence of the Pure Force. I had
hoped it would all die down when they arrested that young
speechifier, that fellow that calls himself the Speaker. But if
anything, they've gotten more strident since then. I'm just
terribly afraid this furor over the Crusade will turn into a
wholesale rejection of scholarship. Because if that happens, it
will be the end of the Secret College. It will be the end of all
my work. And it will be the *very* end," he rumbled, glaring
down at his blue-penciled monograph, "of *her*."

Tattersall nodded, though in truth these high-flown matters were not his immediate concern. "The Pure Force," he
said, "is camped out in my living room."

This got even the obscure poet's attention.

"Well, then," said Tylyester, "so you see."

"I see quite plainly, thank you," said Tattersall. "And one
of the things I came here to look at was Lady Widdershins. A
little chat with her, it seems to me, might straighten quite a
bit of this out. If the Press is our problem, then perhaps we
should persuade her to buy up all the newspapers. If it's the
Pure Force, then perhaps she could buy *that*."

Tylyester—whose academic background had not accustomed him to thinking in such terms—could not tell if the
Governor was joking. Hedging his bets, he said, "I shouldn't
count on too much help from Lady Widdershins. Narthex
implied the other day that he's got *her* in his corner too. In
any event, the Home Guard or somebody has sealed off
Marshmain until after her big party tomorrow. And by then,
you know, the Low Commission will have begun its inquiry.
It will be too late."

Tattersall remained unconvinced. "I shall think of something," he vowed. "Meanwhile, I must go find Sheldrake and Tamlin."

From the damp recesses of the room, the poet said, "Did I hear someone mention a party?"

Careening through the dark streets.

Night had fallen on Riverrun and besides the stars there were only the lights of explosions and firearms somewhere near the Fish Market. In the stolen armored carriage Tamlin and Vesica were careening through the dark streets.

"Do you know where we're going?" she asked him. Her hand held one of the arms, thinner than she remembered, that clutched the wheel.

"No," he said. "I've never been here before."

She didn't care. Tamlin rounded a corner, angling the carriage at a mob of Pure Forcers who stood drinking ale and smoking devilhemp after a tiresome day of provoking unrest in the sun. They looked up at the screeching carriage, and Tamlin and Vesica looked back, nobody quite certain what was going to happen.

"Tamlin!" said Vesica. "Look up there."

He strained at the brake cord. Another second or two and he would have killed somebody. But everything had been provided for.

Projected twenty feet over their heads, its colors confusing against the orange explosions in the sky, a hologhost hissed and shimmered. The young Pure Forcers, who had been ignoring it anyway, ambled over to where the carriage growled to a halt. They peered through the windows, curious but essentially indifferent: catlike. Some rich kid, they thought, out with his old man's car. Hey, look at the cute little chick.

"Look," asked Vesica. "Can't you see it?"

Tamlin squinted. His vision seemed feebler, now. "It's . . . somebody."

Vesica squeezed his arm impatiently. "Don't you—no, I guess you don't." She took a breath. "It's *Thrull!*"

He blinked. The hologhost was speaking in a monotonous electric whine.

"Soon," it said, "the last great stronghold will fall."

"Hey, little chickie—"

Someone grabbed the door of the armored carriage—Vesica's door. She turned in fright, but her fright quickly dissolved to exasperation. Maybe the sight of Thrull had done it.

The door opened. An arm reached in. The sputtering blade of Groby's heatsaw lashed out.

"Yeow!"

Vesica waved the stream of fire before the gray-green cloak. "Let's go," she told Tamlin.

The armored carriage snarled, and they were careening through dark streets again.

The Aleatory Strand made its random way through all the quarters of the city, so it was foreordained that they should come to it eventually. When they did they found it empty, except for saplings growing from cracks, and refugees sleeping in the open, or dead.

"Which way?" said Tamlin wearily.

Vesica sniffed the air. "There." She pointed. "Toward the Sump."

He nodded. A series of small explosions lit his face like a slow-moving animated film; in those moments he looked successively paler, weaker, less confident at the wheel. When the last explosion had faded he throttled up the engine and made a long, wide-angle turn. Slowly they built up speed.

The narrow alley that led past the Silent Partners' Club was recognizable chiefly by its darkness, and by the vague feeling that something grand might once have resided here, or at least passed this way. Also of course there was the worsening smell of the sewer main.

"Slow down now," said Vesica. "We're almost there. See, the path to Marshmain starts at the end of this alley."

At the wheel of the carriage, Tamlin appeared to nod.

"Hey, slow down. We're going to miss it."

Maybe his ears were failing too. Vesica tugged his arm to get his attention.

The arm fell sideways, dragging the wheel. Tamlin slumped behind it.

Oh, no, thought Vesica.

The carriage, without slowing, spun into a shrieking turn. Gravel flew from its wheels, the stars skidded from one side of the windshield to the other, and Vesica might have screamed but she was so frightened for Tamlin that she just held him instead, determined that whatever horrible fate they met, it would be the same fate for both of them.

The Club's brick facade was rotten a generation ago. The armor of Narthex's carriage was newly forged. The right front fender, which struck first, was seven feet into the building before the massive quantities of inertia involved finally canceled each other out and the ceiling of the main bar fell in. Fortunately that was rotten too. It crumbled into bits of moldy plaster with the consistency of cheese. Candles, displaced, set fire to table linen, and the dozen dazed patrons lingering at the bar set about dousing the flames with wine.

The commotion did not go unnoticed in the Deep Game Room.

Tylyester, huddled with the obscure poet over a large brown chart, frowned at what he took to be another retirement party getting out of hand.

"This is intolerable," he pronounced. "I've half a mind to go complain."

"Do it," said the poet, an admirer of those whose temperaments inclined them to action.

"I was on my way out anyway." The professor rolled up the piece of brown paper and tucked it into his robe. "I promised Tatty I would drop this off at the Observatory."

With a nod at the poet, Tylyester drew back the bolt on the electronically operated door.

"Great stars," he exclaimed, confronting the outer wreckage. "What has *happened*?"

Evergrey, the aged barman, bent over two small forms lying inert on the rubbly floor, beside what looked very much like the front end of a motor carriage. The other patrons—a bungle of legislative aides—stood well back, discussing among themselves Evergrey's bad mismanagement of the situation. (The children might be dead, for all anyone knows. Why doesn't the fool call a doctor?)

"Out of the way!" cried the professor, quite needlessly. He hurried across the room and bent to touch first Vesica's cheek, then Tamlin's.

"They're alive," he decided. And after a bit of further

examination: "There seem to be no broken bones. They are probably winded. Or in shock!" He turned to the crowd of onlookers. "Does anyone know whom they belong to?"

The legislative aides conferred among themselves. It was decided that, since this was a subject about which they clearly knew nothing, they should speak up.

"Now, Professor," one of them said. "Consider the legal consequences of touching those children. The parents could argue in court—"

"To hell with that!" He studied the two battered forms. "I'll take them back to the College. Here, some of you help me."

None of the legislative aides showed any inclination to move.

"I need," explained Tylyester, sizing up the situation, "some expert help here. It's a tricky situation. Only those with expert qualifications and lengthy experience should attempt to handle these children."

After a bit of consultation, half a dozen aides stepped forward.

"Grab them by their heads," one of them suggested.

"I've heard you should elevate the glands," attested another.

"By all that sweats in the summer," Tylyester murmured. "Maybe the Pure Force has a point. Evergrey! Call a cab!"

Thus, after many delays during which meaningful and substantive evaluation of their situation was conducted, followed by discussion and rejection of several alternative courses of action,

Tamlin and Vesica, still unconscious, were bundled off
by incompetent hands
into the night.

Thirty-two

THE SECRET COLLEGE was more accurately Inconspicuous, or Ill-lit, but the name was purely historical. Professor Tylyester, its Dean, directed a cab between its rows of blockish buildings, nervously glancing from the tan slender girl on his left to the pale, famished-looking boy on his right. Of the two the boy was more unnerving. During the ride his eyes popped open, to stare unseeing at the midnight city where the mortar battle had been won or lost at the Fish Market and the sky had fallen dark. Yet despite this sign of consciousness, the boy did not react in any way to Tylyester's efforts to communicate—even to being prodded in the bony ribs—and his breathing grew ever more shallow.

"Here," said the Dean, directing the driver's attention to his black-porticoed townhouse. "Now if you could just help me . . ."

The driver, like many of his profession, was a person whose diurnal body rhythms were severely distorted. As chipper as though it were midday, he leapt from the cab and offhandedly hefted the stricken children into the house.

"Nice place," he ventured, possibly angling for a tip. "Anybody famous buried here?"

"Here you are," said Tylyester sternly. "I will take them now."

Dispassionately the driver examined the handful of coins. "Hey, Prof," he said as Tylyester moved to close the door on him. "Aren't you going to call a doctor?"

The Dean grimaced. There were, of course, several learned physicians on the faculty of the College. This fact had given Tylyester frequent cause to be thankful for never taking a wife, lest the union have produced a daughter who should want to marry one. The current medical orthodoxy, if he understood it correctly, was that the key to health lay in frequent injections of organically produced insecticides.

"No, thank you," he said.

The interior of the townhouse provoked a considerable impression of *brownness*. The spines of books, the wood of shelving, the skin of globes, the nap of carpets, the leather of chairs, the shades of lamps, the veneers of ancient *objets*—everything came in graded degrees of brown. Even the matched love seats on which the driver had laid the boy and girl were upholstered in old fabric whose once-florid pastels had faded to papery tans. The children, in contrast, were pink-tinged amber (in Vesica's case) and white with yellow undertones (in Tamlin's). Their dreamy, unblemished, slightly dust-powdered faces were heartbreakingly poignant by the light of candles Tylyester placed on xanthée tables before them.

The tender tableau was short-lived. The boy's eyes, formerly open, fluttered shut, and his limbs began to move like those of a very small child trying to wake from a nightmare. The girl, a few moments later, sat up without any sort of prelude, blinked her eyes, and said quite forwardly:

"Who are you? What are you doing to him?"

Tylyester introduced himself. "I am quite afraid," he said, "this boy may have been injured in the crash."

She shook her head. "He was that way before. Sort of sick, like. His name is Tamlin. I'm Vesica."

Tylyester shook her proffered hand. "And is this, um, your . . ."

"My brother," said Vesica readily. (She had been thinking this out while pretending to be unconscious.) "We're, see, just visiting the city here, staying with this lady near the Sump. A friend of the family. We got lost, and some man in a car offered to give us a ride, but then he got out for a minute to buy a paper and the car started rolling—"

Tylyester nodded distractedly. Vesica's elaborate forethought may have been unnecessary. "Come here, then, Vesica, if you are feeling all right, and help me with your brother. What he needs right now, I think, is a good hot bath. He seems unnaturally cool. Yes, that's good: by the ankles."

Tamlin was as light as a boy of eight or nine. His feet were uniformly callused, from never having worn shoes. (Suppose the professor asked about that? There were so many things to think about.) They carried him down a corridor, lined with shelves, that ended in a chilly, marble-floored bath.

"Is he older or younger?" asked Tylyester, propping his end of Tamlin against a towel rack and turning on the hot water.

Vesica was ready for this one. "We're twins," she said quickly. "I mean, not the identical kind . . ."

Tylyester smiled indulgently. He unbuttoned the patchwork shirt. Tamlin's chest was thin and pale, faintly heaving. The diagonal scar, his second navel, was starkly shadowed by candlelight.

"Hm," said Tylyester, "appendix? Or no, that would be lower."

"No, he, um . . ."

Vesica stopped, partly because she couldn't think of anything and partly because Tylyester was untying the drawcord of Tamlin's torn-off pants.

"Here," he said. "If you could just lift his legs while I slip these off."

Vesica bit her lip. She hadn't, she saw, thought of *everything*.

"Well, come on," said Tylyester, sounding impatient. "You have, I presume, seen your brother without his clothes on before?"

Well, when you put it that way, yes. Vesica had. The first time ever, when Tamlin had stood before Wild Turkey Pool in the thrumming silence, naked and ghost-white. Of course she hadn't really had a chance, then . . .

Dutifully she lifted his calves. How smooth his skin was—how long and thin and fragile-seeming his legs!

The patchwork clothes, which she had made in such a hurry from a baby's blankets and shirts, fell to the floor. The long limbs they were made to fit were lowered into the steaming water. Despite her unclear intention not to embarrass Tamlin by looking at him while he was helpless this way, Vesica allowed her eyes to straggle up his sad and weakened frame. The muscular youth who had held her in the forest was a make-believe person now. Beneath the swirls of water, his body seemed to waver like a hologhost. The hero of the story had become a sickly child.

But no, not a child, either. The willowy, almost feminine delicacy of Tamlin's frame was given the lie by the (to Vesica) astonishing virilia that bulged from its tangle of hair at the juncture of these suddenly sprouted, still half-formed legs. Not a child, but an ailing faunlet.

"Oh, make him well," she whispered—not to Tylyester, not to anybody or any deity in particular, just a petition to the Hidden Causes that determine such things, that make up the stories and decide the way they come out.

"He was this way," said Tylyester, not in answer to her either, pondering aloud, "before your . . . accident?"

"Before the carriage started rolling," Vesica clarified. "He's normally not this pale, see. This, um, limp."

"Aha," said the Dean.

They stared down at the object of their discussion, Vesica willingly now, more frankly curious, until the heat of the bath brought a bit of color back to his cheeks.

"Unfortunately," said Tylyester, reaching for a towel, "there is little more we can do tonight. It will be best for us to rest—all three of us—and see how things are in the morning."

Vesica nodded, as Tamlin took a pitifully shallow breath and released it with a sigh. She took an arm and Tylyester took the other, and together they lifted him and dried him and wrapped him against the chill.

"I can show you," Tylyester offered, "to an empty room."

"I'll stay with my brother," she said. "Wherever you put him."

The professor gently smiled. "Very well. Shall we dress him, then? My nightclothes would be rather large, but . . ."

"Just bring a blanket." She nodded, more sure of herself now. "I'll put that over him. I think he might feel more . . . natural this way."

Saint Swithin's Day dawned with the subdued glow of a rosebud, promising greater brilliance ahead. A whisper of that promise made its way through the tall damask curtains of the guest room and wakened Vesica. She stirred beneath the sheets for only half a second before the realization of where she was, and who she was with, and what she had to do now, erased all memory of the tossing and turning and trembling limbs that had marked her passage of the night.

Tamlin, inches away from her, lay pale and still beneath the bedcovers. His face was pure yet clouded, a paradox perhaps, but characteristic; one arm had crept out of the sheets and lay across the pillow, barely touching her shoulder. Imperfectly reflecting this, one of Vesica's legs made a gopher-mound through the blankets and pressed against his shin. She rubbed it against him, cautiously. He sighed, and then with a sudden access of energy he rolled over and opened his eyes.

"Vesica!" he whispered hoarsely.

"Shh." She moved closer, sharing his pillow. "Are you okay?"

He reached over to hug her. There was a confusion of cotton sheets, a bit of thrashing, and his arms broke free to slide around her back.

He tensed as his fingers caressed bare skin. In the next moment he seemed to become aware of his own nakedness; in alarm or confusion he pulled away. Unwilling to let him go, just yet, Vesica pressed herself against him, felt for the first time the electric warmth of her breasts being flattened by the firm chest of a boy. Their thighs interlocked like the fingers of opposite hands. Through the unseen silken shield of her underpants Vesica felt something warm and mysterious: the faunlet arising; and that, finally, frightened her. A little.

"I just thought," she explained (letting him go, sisterly

now), "that since *you* didn't have any clothes on, I would . . . you know, myself."

Tamlin nodded, baffled and abashed but at least awake, which made things easier.

"What happened," he said, his voice feeble, "last night? What are we . . . ?"

She did her best to explain while they dressed demurely, on opposite sides of the bed, with their backs turned. As demurely, too, as possible, they investigated the availability of plumbing, finding only a chamber pot behind a screen in a walk-in closet. Well: they were certainly getting to know each other.

"Now what I think we should do," said Vesica, "is, you should stay in bed and pretend to be real sleepy—I mean, I guess you *are* real sleepy—and I'll try to figure out what he's going to do with us. If I can, I'll get him to take us to Lady Widdershins's. If not, we'll have to make it there on our own. But either way we've got to get out of here, because for *sure* my stepfather's going to be all over town, looking for me."

Tamlin nodded. The very thought of making their way across this unruly city, just the two of them, caused his face to grow paler again. A night's sleep had partially restored him, but it was clear he was not the old Tamlin anymore, the Tamlin of the forest.

"Okay," said Vesica, putting the best face on all of this, "I'll go out now and see if the professor's awake."

"Bye," said Tamlin, gamely but weakly. Without need of prompting, he climbed back into bed.

The bed we shared together, thought Vesica. She didn't know what story she remembered *that* from, but she had never imagined it, if indeed she had imagined it at all, quite like this. She wanted to kiss him, but she was into her sister act now. Smoothing her little-girl dress, she stepped primly and quietly out the door, and almost collided with Professor Tylyester.

"Excuse me," said the startled Dean. He showed less concern for the girl, whom he had nearly knocked to the floor, than for a stack of finger-smudged papers under his arm. "I didn't know—"

"I didn't know you were up," said Vesica, completing the thought for him.

"Up and out. It's Saint Swithin's Day, you know. How is your brother?"

Vesica raised her hand to her mouth, ladylike, and cleared her throat. "A little better," she said cautiously.

"Good, good," he said, sounding grateful not to be troubled by this right now. He edged down the hall. "Will you be all right here, just the two of you, until I return? It will be an hour or two. You see, I have an errand—something I forgot in the excitement . . ."

"Sure," said Vesica. "We'll be fine. I mean, I'm sure my brother can use the rest and all. Don't worry."

"Oh, good." The professor arrived at an escritoire just inside the front door, where a roll of brown paper lay crinkled.

"Hey, listen," said Vesica. "Thanks a lot for bringing us here. Especially Tamlin—my brother. We really appreciate it."

"Oh, that's quite all right, dear girl. Vesica, isn't it?" He scooped up, more or less simultaneously, the roll of paper and a cloak. This left him with no hand for the manuscript, which he laid on the escritoire. He started to pick it up again, but this would leave him no hand for the door.

She said, "Vesica, that's right."

"Lovely name. Architectural. Well, I've got to—"

She held the door for him. He smiled and stepped out into the bright and already sultry morning. The door closed behind him. A pendulum clock on the escritoire said seven fifty-five.

"He's gone," she called back to Tamlin.

There was no reply but the stillness of the black-porticoed townhouse.

"Are you okay?" she called, and started back to him, when her eyes fell on the stack of papers the professor had left behind. She said, "Oh, gosh," and opened the door in time to see him entering a cab. The driver, recognizing him, tried to escape, but Tylyester already had a foot in. Swerving, the cab receded up the cracked and littered street.

"Oh, well," she said. And only then—after she had tried, honestly, to catch him—did she notice the title of Tylyester's manuscript:

NOTES TOWARD A CRITIQUE OF HAYATA'S COMMENTARY
ON THE "ORGANIZING PRINCIPLE" OF GENETIC TRANSPOSITION,
WITH EMPHASIS ON THE HISTORICAL AND BIOGRAPHICAL CONTEXT
AND HER EFFORT TO END THE CRISIS OF INDETERMINISM

—and having seen that, what could she do? But go back to
the bedroom to show it to Tamlin, who she thought might
be interested; and finding the boy asleep, so weak and pale it
was heartbreaking even to look at him—what could she do
then? But sit down beside him, hovering close, hoping her
warmth might communicate itself to his enfeebled body, and
choosing a place in the middle of the stack, begin to read.

Of course such efforts are so often foredoomed to
frustration. They require too long a season to bear fruit.
Most often the outcome is not apparent until after the end
of the investigator's career. Or indeed life. Which is why,
during that era, these matters were considered to fall within
the purview of Religion. Which, if not intrinsically more
patient than Science, has at least traditionally taken a more
lenient view of what constitutes "proof."

Vesica frowned. Wasn't this supposed to be about Amy
Hayata? She scanned down the page and the one after it,
until at last she spotted the woman's name.

Things only got worse, however, as Hayata attempted
to "clarify" her position. More and more, with each succes-
sive draft, she came to rely on terms like *Organizing Principle*,
which she apparently made up herself, yet which nowhere
in her paper did she adequately define. We can only understand such terms in context. And in the specific case of
Organizing Principle, this is far from being a straightforward
task, for the context in which she uses the phrase is highly
variable.

We do not encounter the term at all in the version of
her monograph generally held to be the earliest.[231] Its first
occurrence is in the "Dun, Crinkle-cut" [DC] draft, probably dating from two or three years later. Here she uses
it—in lower case—in an unremarkable reference to genetic
engineering. Thus:

"Attempts to introject the attributes of one species into

the genome of another have often failed on account of failure to take into consideration the often sharply distinct organizing principles involved." [The reader will note, I trust, the stiff and somewhat fusty tone of the quotation—so different from her later, more colorful style.]

In this instance, *organizing principle* seems to refer, in a very general way, to the underlying genetic or morphological structure of the respective organisms. The writer's point seems relatively clear.

Now consider, if you will, the following passage, from what may have been [232] Hayata's final draft:

"[It is not] enough to direct the transmissions to some fuzzy form-image of the species. You've got to achieve what McClintock called 'a feeling for the organism' and then, when you've got that, to aim the emanations right at the Organizing Principle itself."

The difference could not be more striking. And yet the rough similarity of contexts—altering the form of a species through mentalistic means—suggests that whatever this mysterious *Organizing Principle* might be, it is the same thing in both cases.

The later draft contains several other usages of the term. None provides a clear definition, but one at least, from the appendix headed TECHNICAL NOTES, is worth citing on the grounds of peculiarity. The appendix deals largely with a self-hypnotic or meditative discipline Hayata calls "the program." It does not do, she informs the reader, when one is practicing this program:

". . . to go in and try to boss the Organizing Principle around. You've got to remember who's running the show here. Remember that your own goals are only destinations, not specific paths to attain them. They should be presented just as what they are, as ideas, and not as orders or instructions. Upsetting the Organizing Principle at this stage is only going to destabilize the entire program."

All of which sounds more like advice on getting one's project approved by the Department Chairman than anything to do with impersonal forces or laws of Nature. Indeed, the rather eerie way in which Hayata seems to personalize her *Organizing Principle* has led some scholars to suggest that the years alone in the wilderness were catching up with her, that "she was seeing pucks and goblins behind every tree."[233] I think it more likely that Hayata wasn't sure quite *what* she meant—that her use of the term was a kind of mental shorthand, on which she might have elaborated later, as her ideas matured.

In any case, it is all rather strange.

The rest of the paragraph had been struck out, though Vesica had no trouble reading it.

. . . This is, after all, the very crux of Hayata's work. It is as though she had devoted her life to the study of this thing, this Organizing Principle, but had never dared to approach it too closely, to recognize what, exactly, it *is*. Or, to draw an analogy, as though one were studying the life of some historical figure, yet had confined one's investigations to the superficial aspects of that person's career— never coming to know who that person was, as an individual, at all. Which brings us to the First Biotic . . .

Vesica's attention was stolen by a shuddering sigh beside her on the bed. She looked down to see Tamlin lying wide-eyed, staring up at her.

"Thfl," he seemed to say.

She ran a finger across the boy's forehead. It was cool. The pale skin was almost transparent. *He's fading*, she thought: another phrase from another story.

"What is it?" she whispered, bringing her ear low.

More carefully he managed: "In your knapsack."

The knapsack he had carried all the way from Balance Act lay on his side of the bed, beneath the towels Tylyester had wrapped him in. Vesica reached across his unmoving form to grab it.

"Do you want anything?" she said. It was so much like talking to a child—or to a wild thing that couldn't talk back.

When she opened it she understood. There, protruding from the torn-off ends of his clothing, was the tiny double flute: her gift to him, the forest's gift to her, and very much longer ago someone's unintended gift to the forest. She took it out, as shiny as brand-new, and placed it between Tamlin's fingers.

Something confusing happened next. Only, the confu-

sion came later. After Vesica thought about it, trying to get
the story straight. Not just then.

Just then, Tamlin raised the flute to his slightly blue-
tinged lips and started to play. She recognized the melody,
though it was a thin and halting one. It was the only song
they both knew, probably—Gerta's ballad of Young Tamber
Lane.

"I figured it out," he told her proudly, pausing halfway
through the verse to rest, "on the way down"—and seemed,
for someone who looked ready to expire at any minute, quite
pleased with himself.

And that was the first confusing thing: how he managed
to play it at all. His lungs were so empty that he could only
blow a few notes at a time—at the most, a couple of very
soft bars; then he had to stop and take a slow indrawn breath
before going on. Yet the rhythm of the song established
itself, as surely as when it was tweeted out by the Owl on his
reedy horn. And the notes themselves—barely strong enough
to be heard above the wheeze of air moving past the twin
rows of finger-holes—were as round and full as the chords of
the whole Crusaders' band. It was the same song; and more
than that (another confusing part), the experience of hearing
it was just the same, as happy and as heartrending as when
Tamlin had played it not on this tiny flute with feeble lungs
but on the strange old harp with the whole of his being.

Well, perhaps there is nothing magical about that. Perhaps that is the nature of musicianship. But the thing was,
the final confusing thing, that as Vesica listened she forgot
that Tamlin was weak and ill and possibly dying, and she was
alone, unable to help, in a stranger's house in a great and
dangerous city. She didn't exactly think they were anywhere
else; she just didn't think about that at all. She just listened.
Tamlin just played. And the song went inside of her and
filled her up.

So what did they do then? Tamlin's playing went on or
seemed to go on for a very long time. It stopped being,
somewhere along the line, just a song about Fair Janet and
became something else much simpler and yet much more
difficult to understand. It was something really important,
Vesica could tell that. Something fundamental. Like the cry
of a baby—a sound that pierces all the layers of inattention,

gets its urgent message through to whoever is listening, whoever is able to help. The thing the song became bound her and Tamlin together like a dream they were both sharing, the way they had shared the bed: twined together, intimately exposed, blissful and (at least while it lasted) safe.

So maybe it *was* a dream. That's what Vesica decided later, tentatively: that the song had soothed her and put her to sleep with her head on Tamlin's chest, and that the magic or musicianship, whichever it was, had occurred not implausibly, in the real world of sickness and loss, but quite naturally in the fairy-world of dreams, the one where Janet and Tamber Lane lived happily ever after.

Anyway, she went to sleep. Somewhere along the line she put her head down and Tamlin wrapped his arms around her and they slept like innocent children, while the sunlight coming between the damask curtains crossed the room. And they were still asleep, deeply and without care, when the door of the bedroom opened and footsteps entered the room and paused a few feet away from them, with someone's eyes looking down.

"Hmm," Vesica murmured languidly, adjusting her head on Tamlin's chest and turning her eyes away from the light.

"I'm sorry," someone's voice said, "to disturb you . . ."

She opened her eyes. Professor Tylyester stood in the filtered midday light before the bed. Tamlin breathed evenly in her ear.

"I just came back to look for— Ah!" He reached down, gathering up the scattered pages of his precious manuscript.

"Oh," said Vesica, struggling against what seemed an insuperable state of confusion. "I'm sorry. I just found it—"

"No matter," he assured her, then lowered his voice in consideration of the still-slumbering boy. "It is intended, after all, to be read. I was just worried . . . but it's safe, so no harm is done. Is your brother all right?"

"I think so." Vesica nodded, not sure why. She propped herself on her elbows, looking around at Tamlin. As she did so, the double flute rolled out of his fingers and came to rest where Vesica had lain, across his narrow chest.

"My, my," murmured Tylyester with interest. "What's that? A rather unusual instrument, I should say."

She nodded sleepily. "We found it— I found it in the woods."

The professor frowned. "Might I take a look?"

She didn't want him to. Yet having read his manuscript, she didn't think she could decently refuse. Reluctantly she took the flute from Tamlin's chest.

True to his academic temperament, Tylyester immediately became absorbed. He ran his fingers gently along the finger-holes, examined each of the twin pipes in turn, finally turned the instrument over. His eyes lingered over the inscription below the mouthpiece.

GOODFELLOW, his lips spelled out.

"And you found this . . ." he said.

"In a stream. In the woods."

"In the woods. What woods would those be, Vesica?"

She didn't realize right away that she was being, not just talked to, but *questioned*. When she did, she made a rapid and clumsy attempt (such things are so difficult when you're just awake) to tell him something besides way up north, or the Carbon Bank Forest, or the stream below Balance Act. She ended up telling him nothing. Only sitting there on the bed feeling like someone with something to hide.

"Vesica," the professor said gently. He was not an unkind man, she knew; he had brought them here, after all, to his home, not knowing who they were, because they were helpless. Still she cowered like someone being threatened by, say, an angry stepfather.

"You haven't," he said, "told me *quite* everything, have you?"

She slowly shook her head. "But see," she said quickly, "we were afraid. We're being followed, see, by my . . . by this awful . . ."

"Are you really in town, as you said, just visiting a friend?"

She let her breath out. "No."

Tylyester nodded. "And is Tamlin," he said, driving right to the heart of it, "really your brother?"

She turned away, embarrassed. The bath; the bedroom; sharing the bed . . .

"It's all right," he told her. "I'm not trying to pry. . . . But this flute, you see . . . Who *is* he, then, actually?"

Oh, all right. She told him. The whole story, or at least the main chapters—Deeping Lube and running away from home, the Crusade and Biggar's Neck and entering the forest, the sky-blue orchid and Wild Turkey Pool, finally meeting Tamlin, making clothes for him—the whole story up to Balance Act. And then Tylyester interrupted.

"Go back," he said. Vesica was startled to see that the Dean had lost, or nearly lost, his air of avuncular calm. His lips moved, forming hastily chosen words. "Tell me again: he just *appeared* to you?"

She narrowed her eyes, at once trying to remember and wondering why he was asking this. "I don't know. I mean, I turned around, and he was there."

"And was it then he told you his name was Tamlin?"

"Oh, no. I mean, he never told me that at all. Tamlin's just a name I made up for him. Or I didn't make it up but, see, I got it from a fairy tale, but see, Tamlin—when I met him, and even after that—he couldn't remember his name at all."

"He couldn't remember his own name?"

She shook her head. "At all."

Tylyester was transparently excited. It was remarkable in such a sober, dark-browed man. He stared at the flute and paced across the floor. Tamlin still slept beside Vesica, but Tylyester cared nothing for that, or had quite forgotten. When he spoke again it was loudly, energetically:

"And then, Vesica—what then? What about later, at Balance Act?"

Well, what about it? She couldn't tell him everything; didn't want to, and didn't understand all of it well enough to tell. So she told him about the evening before the pale fire—the instruments, the singing, Tamlin strapped into the old leather harness and going into a kind of trance, playing the song.

"It was the ballad," she explained, "of Fair Janet—"

"A chthonian harp," breathed Tylyester. He was squeezing the silver flute so hard that Vesica was worried he might bend it. Gently she eased it from his hand. Tamlin, disturbed at last by the racket, showed signs of waking. The professor murmured: "GOODFELLOW.

"—Don't you realize," he said, spinning around and nearly shouting now, "what this means?"

While Vesica was thinking: No—she couldn't imagine what it all meant or else she would have figured out how the story was going to end a long time ago—Tamlin sat up in bed. They turned to him in surprise, Vesica and Tylyester, and in greater surprise they saw the look of new vitality that had come into his eyes. They were not the eyes of a sick boy any longer (or yes, they were, but not *just* that); they were the eyes of someone very much older and very much sadder and very much, incredibly more wise.

Looking from one to the other at first, then taking the girl's warm hand in his cool one, Tamlin softly and slowly said, "I think
I'm finally
awake."

Thirty-three

THE CLOUD THAT HAD
filled Lady Widdershins's sky since—now that she thought
about it—the departure of the First Biotic Crusade, reached
its darkest on the steamy morning of Saint Swithin's Day, as
the carefully screened attendees began oozing in for her
annual Bull Roast. Needing little excuse to celebrate in that
hot and bewildering summer, the partygoers arrayed themselves in a circle on the croquet lawn, raised their watermint
juleps to the torrid mid-July sun and paused expectantly,
waiting for someone to propose a toast. Their patience was
rewarded when a voice from the Upper Garden sliced the
sultry air.

"*To Tylyester's house.*"

"To Tylyester's house," the partygoers concurred, and
drank. Three dozen watermint juleps and several cobalt crystal glasses vanished in a matter of seconds. Only after the
sugared liquor had had its effect did the partygoers think
what an odd sort of toast this was to begin a Bull Roast with;
but by then it had ceased to matter much.

Low Commissioner Narthex stormed down from the
Upper Garden with Lady Widdershins in tow, the skirts of
her plum-colored dress billowing like the sheets of a schooner.

"Are you *certain*," she implored, in a tone that none of the partygoers had heard her use before, "you are not acting rashly? I mean to say, the Dean of the Secret College . . . !"

"That criminal," snapped Narthex, not bothering to look at her, hurrying on across the lawn, "has engineered the kidnapping of our—"

Lady Widdershins caught the Low Commissioner by a spidersilk sleeve and spun him around, boring his heels two inches deep in the soggy lawn. "You had better," she told him sternly, "know what you're talking about. Libel does not go down lightly among the sort of people you're trifling with."

"Nor does kidnapping, with the courts."

He gave her his very thinnest smile, but she sensed that the gesture was reflexive. He really was rattled this morning, in a way he had not been heretofore in their rounds of emotional fencing. This disturbed her even as it lent her a vague sense of hope. The former, on Vesica's behalf; the latter, because she could not help feeling that if Narthex was unhappy, there must be *some* reason to rejoice. And she desperately needed grounds for rejoicing on this awful holiday.

He snatched his arm away from her. "You are only," he said curtly, "delaying the search for Vesica."

She sighed. She nodded. "Go ahead then. Send your little henchmen out and arrest everyone who's ever snubbed you, if that's what you've made up your mind to do. Just bring her back. That's all I really care about."

Narthex's farewell bow contained a touch more satisfaction—as well it might have. She had delivered herself up to him, she knew, as surely as she had once delivered another, infinitely more helpless. One does not think, when one sets events in motion, that Fate will come around again; nor that, like a spiral staircase, when it does it will have jumped to a different story. Or maybe it is the same story, and Fate just wanders from room to room in it, as one used to wander through the succession of rooms that were really a single room in one's happier, brighter, forever abandoned manor at Biggar's Neck.

The Commissioner reached the footbridge, which had begun to float lower on its pontoons. The broken sewer main had been capped off and the waters were slowly receding. Lady Widdershins returned to her guests.

"Widdy!" they cried, waving their glasses at her. "Do join us!" "Who was that horrid man? He looked like a politician." "Your garden is *magnificent* this year." "Want a drink? You look like you need one." "We were just admiring your dahlias. Isn't that one called 'Bertie's Blush'?" "(No, Tussie, I think it's 'Poor Dorcas.' Don't you see how it's starting to fade, even before the climax of the season?)" "It's dreadful, isn't it, all this horrid publicity about the Crusade. I personally don't believe a word of it." "Tatty must have been worse off than one suspected." "Have you seen those two enormous things they're building in town? I can't *imagine* . . ."

Out of habit, mostly, Lady Widdershins smiled in an insipid parody of the Ideal Hostess. She turned a vacant gaze across the croquet lawn toward the large muddy pit where a squad of servants was preparing to light a fire.

"I don't think we ought to talk about politics," a guest was saying. "This *is* a holiday, isn't it?"

The Brigade of Irregular Poets assembled in the dank confines of the Observatory. Its four dozen members shuffled in and out of ranks, sipped xanthée, hummed little-known tunes, chatted, worried about rats, and yawned. Few of them were used to being awake this early.

Before the Brigade a short man with a very large mouth paced to and fro energetically. Those poets who were seeing clearly enough to notice him assumed that he was some sort of gnome or undergraduate assigned to toil in this unhealthy place, tending the arcane machinery of Observation. (Not many poets have a very clear understanding of the function of observatories, nor of undergraduates.) In reality the short man was a person of some importance, and was trying to get their attention. His large mouth opened and closed repeatedly, but such were the acoustics of the Observatory that only an indistinct roar, like that of the ocean, came out of it. Those poets who were hearing clearly enough to notice this assumed that it was the natural product of being awake before noon, and would go away if they ignored it.

At last the short man saw someone he recognized, shuffling in and out of ranks with the rest of them. "Ha!" he cried. "You there! Sergeant-at-arms!"

A poet of justifiable obscurity looked up on hearing his newly bestowed title.

"Hi, Sheldrake," he said amicably.

"Call your men," said Sheldrake crossly; then, taking a more comprehensive look at the Brigade: "Call your *people* to order."

The poet beamed with pride.

"Hey, folks," he said quietly. "Soup's on."

At the mention of food, the dank confines of the Observatory fell silent. The Irregular Poets fell into line and stared forward expectantly. The Sergeant-at-arms smiled.

There were several problems with assembling a brigade of poets, not the least of which was identifying potential recruits. Poets cannot, as it develops, be counted on to realize who they are. Moreover they are virtually impossible to contact, owing to their proclivities toward keeping unusual hours and residing at addresses not shown on any streetmap. On the other hand, there had been the challenge of raising a troop of veteran party-crashers with no fixed loyalties in a city where everyone seemed already to have been conscripted by one cause or another, to join an undertaking probably foredoomed, at the very least, to absurdity, and more probably to jail, on twelve hours' notice, with no money. Where in the world, Lord Tattersall had wondered, could you find anyone like that?

There was only one answer.

A complicated rumor had been introduced into certain watering holes near the Epicene Pits, involving a party and lots of food and an open bar and a large swimming pool and many small pieces of valuable tableware. How, exactly, the rumor had been adapted so as to stress the necessity of arrival by noon at the Observatory of the Secret College, the poet of justifiable obscurity could not presently recall. He was unused to being awake at this hour.

"Very good," Sheldrake forced himself to say. "I'll go tell his lordship that the Brigade is present and accounted for."

At the mention of someone called *his lordship*, the poets smiled and nodded and ran their hands around inside their roomy pockets and shoulder bags. Their Sergeant-at-arms looked smug.

Lord Tattersall stood outside by the balustrade that circled the dome, conferring with a graduate student in Astrology.

"What do you see now?" he wondered, sounding fretful.

The graduate student squinted again through elaborate
and slightly out-of-focus optics. "It looks like a bunch of
terrorists—no, wait: they're musicians; I mistook the lutes for
. . . Hey, there's some kind of big animal. Wow! They're,
like, turning it over or . . . there's smoke everywhere . . ."

"Yes, yes," said Tattersall. "That would be the bull."

"Wow." The student nodded appreciatively.

"Who else?" said the Governor, biting his lip.

"Hmm. Lots of skinny guys in pink shirts, and some
ladies, and hey, there's this big lady with, wow, the most
gigantic—"

Sheldrake tapped his lordship on the shoulder. Tattersall
jumped, slamming against the rusty railing. The ancient metal
of the balustrade groaned.

"Damn," exclaimed the student. "It's messed up again."
He eyed Sheldrake accusingly.

"They're ready," the little man told the Governor.

At their feet, the great city of Riverrun lay flat and
bedraggled, as though the unrelenting heat of yet another
July were getting it down. Some relief was promised, however, by the purplish welt of a thunderhead in the western
sky. The Governor, who had been here before, though a
generation earlier, remembered the view as being predomi-
nantly gray and brown. This had changed. Now much of the
city was hidden under the dusty green boughs of rabid oaks.
In some, unbuilt-up places—the Fish Market, the stadium,
the llama stalls—the prospect was more rural than urban;
except that, unlike a natural landscape, this one showed a
disturbing lack of diversity. Everywhere the eye fell, with or
without the aid of elaborate optics, it found the obsessive
sameness of that lately arisen species, *Quercus rabidina*.

"Keep looking," Tattersall told the graduate student.
"And be particularly watchful for a teenage boy with odd-
looking clothes on."

The graduate student nodded, as though this description
might apply to any fewer than the seventy-nine thousand
teenage boys in the city.

It took the Governor a few moments to reacquaint himself with the interior gloom which, for the poets, was a congenial milieu. The Brigade maintained a respectful silence, or its equivalent.

"Well," said the Governor at last. "Good morning, everyone."

"How's it going?" said the poets, in trochaic chorus.

Tattersall turned to one side; the wrong one. Sheldrake unfurled a roll of brown paper behind him. It turned out to be—as absolutely no one but poets could possibly have discerned in that light—a map of the city. If the Governor had trouble finding this, however, he had a good fix, as usual, upon his audience.

"So good of you to join me," he told them, "at this hour of the day. You will be happy to learn that there are, at any rate, clouds out."

The poets murmured gratefully.

"Yes. Well. The fishflies are terrible, aren't they?"

Now, poets, who are widely assumed to have their minds on higher things, are actually a down-to-earth ilk. So few people appreciate that.

"And the heat!" the Governor went on, "is enough to make one wish for a large cool drink."

The poets fervently wished for large cool drinks.

"I will be brief, then," said the Governor, knowing how his audience esteemed brevity. (Few of them had written more than a dozen lines this year.) "You must travel across the city—without, by the way, attracting undue attention—and then you must, ahem, gain entrance to someone's party. Can you manage that, do you think?"

The poets smiled. So far, what this tall and kindly gentleman proposed was not unlike a typical day's occupation.

"Good," said Tattersall. "Well. What you must do at the party, the whole purpose in fact of your going there, is to deliver a message. You must each of you memorize the message, so as to be certain that *somebody* will remember it at the party, and you must deliver it to everyone you meet, so as to ensure that the right person eventually gets it." He glanced nervously aside. "Have I forgotten anything, Sheldrake?"

"The message," muttered his aide-de-camp.

"What? Ah—very good. The message is this: *Without Lunaria, the deep game is lost.* Is that clear?"

"No way," said the poets in spontaneous spondee.

"Good." The Governor smiled. "Now let me just add. Today's little party may not be entirely devoid of, to put a blunt face upon it: danger. But," he was quick to conclude, "there may also be a bit of, ahem, money involved."

"Money?" the poets declaimed. (Their vocation had conditioned them to be leery of activities for which payment was promised.) This reaction puzzled Tattersall, being so different from his own.

"Not my *own* money," he added uncertainly.

Ahhh, breathed the Brigade. Everything was clearer now. Danger . . . crashing parties . . . other people's money: the things of which Life was comprised. And though commonly supposed to revere only Art, poets are also great admirers (though often from a distance) of Life.

"Very good," said the Governor, turning at last the proper way to bear upon the chart. "Well. To begin with, we are *here*."

And so they were; and so was the graduate student in Astrology, who stood blinking at the entrance of the dome, adjusting his eyes.

"Hey, Governor!" he called to the darkness. "Come quick, your lordship! There's something you might want to see."

Above the feverish city rose a pair of great and spindly towers. Three hundred feet tall, still being fitted with topmasts, their exoskeletons had been gutted from fallen airships and painted featureless gray. Holding them aloft were miles of the same steering cable that figured so prominently in Vesica's fate; her permanent MacGuffin.

"What *is* it?" the girl said in wonderment, staring at the nearest tower through the window of the black-porticoed townhouse.

"What are *they*," Professor Tylyester corrected her, reaching across her shoulder to point out—further west, toward the Observatory—its companion.

"Gosh," she said.

"If you children will excuse me," he added, "there are many things I must think about."

He released his half of the damask curtain. Tamlin, standing in the window next to Vesica, caught it. He said nothing at all.

For the hundred and eighth time since the playing of the double flute, Vesica cast an apprehensive glance at him.

Color was back in the boy's face, but not a normal color; more a desperate flush, as though he were burning off whatever store of energy was still untapped in his wasted frame. His thin chest bellowsed rapidly, consuming the stale air. His limbs, though they moved him around the bedroom with a certain dispatch, had lost their springiness, become like alien appendages again. Only his eyes had staged a recovery, and even that was an odd one: blue and sharp, they tirelessly explored the window-framed expanse, as though at the behest of some distant or disinterested awareness. They fell now and then on Vesica, but never sought out her own—didn't avoid them either, but only *just* didn't avoid them.

Vesica, for her part, didn't *quite* wish that the boy were sick, but at least himself, again.

Up the scaffolding of the towers scrambled dozens of small figures dressed in the coveralls of the Guild of Refugees. They reminded Vesica of the laborers trapped at Gravetye, running like insects while the forest closed in around them. And the towers reminded her of windmills, overgrown cousins of the ones at her stepfather's farm, only without the blades, without any clue to their purpose—beyond just being there, looming over the city, which must mean something.

The blue eyes flickered beside her. They had caught some movement, some change, outside the window. Vesica, noticing this (noticing everything about the boy, and understanding none of it, any more than she understood the deathly gray towers), followed Tamlin's gaze along the street. She saw only a blur of moving bodies: students, mostly, on holiday from the Secret College. They were slightly older than Tamlin and herself and much more glumly attired, in clothes that seemed principally designed to disguise all sexual characteristics. Vesica thought how conspicuous they would be—Tamlin in his patchwork clothes, she in her little-girl dress—among them.

"We've got to go," said Tamlin quietly.

"What? Wait—"

He took her hand in a surprisingly strong grasp. By it, he led her away from the window, back through the bedroom, not even slowing down while he scooped the knapsack from the floor and the flute from the rumpled sheets where she and Tamlin had lain such a short time ago, together.

"Wait," she said. "Tamlin, hey—what are we doing? What's going on?"

At the moment his reply would have come, had he opened his mouth to make one, a vigorous pounding echoed through the townhouse from the stout persimmon door. It came again: *rump rump rump*, before anyone could think of answering.

Something about the sound drew cool fingers of fear tight around Vesica's throat.

Rump rump rump rump bump bump bump.

"Damn you, just a minute!" shouted Tylyester from a distant chamber. "I do not employ a butler, you know."

"Come on," said Tamlin. "There's a back way, I think."

The fingers of fear worked their way down Vesica's throat and into her stomach, where they churned the remains of a bachelor's breakfast into acid-tainted soup.

"Who could this be?" muttered Tylyester, passing them in the hall. He paused. "Are you children going somewhere?"

From outside came muffled shouting. The door was very thick.

"Thank you," said Tamlin, facing the professor. (The skin of Vesica's wrist had turned white beneath his grasp.) "You've been really kind to us. I hope he doesn't hurt you."

"Who?" whispered Vesica, as Tylyester only frowned. Pulling her away again, Tamlin said:

"Goodbye."

—And the persimmon door was replaced by a blinding, crackling, yellow-white sheet of flame. And then by smoke and moving shadows.

"No one will be harmed," said a familiar voice, "if you just come forward peaceably. And bring my stepdaughter."

"Narthex!" whispered Vesica. "It's my step— Ow!"

Tamlin dragged her down the hall toward the rear of the townhouse as Tylyester remained stiff with astonishment and indignation before the wreckage of his front door, which had withstood generations of student riots.

Just past the large and chilly bath, Tamlin turned into a side hall where a door offered a cobweb-clouded view of what was once a kitchen garden, now a thriving stand of rabid oaks.

"You down there!" the Commissioner called behind them. "There's no use in running. The Civil Militia has surrounded the house."

The door was unlocked. As narrow heels clomped down the hall, Tamlin pushed Vesica through it, into the garden. By the time she regained her balance on the marble stoop, she had more or less brought herself up to the speed of these whirling events. Tamlin, still clutching her wrist, stepped through the door beside her.

She slapped him hard on the face.

He dropped her hand. He blinked, as though struggling to recognize who had hit him. Narthex's voice shouted something behind them.

"All right," said Vesica, softly and quickly. "I've got the picture. Now I think I can do this on my own."

Tamlin nodded. He didn't bother, any more than she, to say he was sorry. He looked straight into her eyes for the first time since his awakening.

"Just follow me," he said. "Do what I do."

"Well, sure," she said, "that's okay. Only, you could at least—"

But Tamlin wasn't speaking in general. He meant, really, *right now* she had to follow him. Leading her gently but no less firmly he walked into the oaks.

"Here they are, Commissioner!" someone shouted from the house. "Out in the yard—it's two kids, I think."

"*Two* kids?" said Narthex.

Vesica saw them, shoving into the doorway. Saw her stepfather seeing her. Saw the grin moving up the hawkish face.

"*Well . . .*" he said, and she knew what was going to come next.

Or thought she did.

"Here," said Tamlin. "Right here . . . Can you feel it?"

"What . . ."

Baffled: pressing against Tamlin: her stepfather closing behind them: another step: and

"Vesica!" cried the Low Commissioner. "Damn it, where *are* you?" So surprised, it was a moment before he thought to add more calmly: "Hiding won't help, Vesica. I've got a hundred men out here. Just come out, now. It's all right; nothing is going to happen. And bring your friend."

But . . . he was *right there*. And she and Tamlin were *right here*, just a few paces away from him, standing among the trees. Just *standing* there. Not hiding. Not invisible. Though certainly, for the moment, unseen.

Tamlin had always been good at this. He took a deeper-than-usual breath and gave it back slowly. "Okay," he murmured. "Let's get going."

This time he led without dragging her, and this time she followed without wondering why. They stepped into a narrow space, less a path than a channel, between the head-high leathery branches.

"Feel what?" whispered Vesica behind him. "What did you mean, could I feel this? What is *this*?"

He didn't turn. He said, "The dragon path," and kept walking along it.

And not knowing why, nor definitely recognizing the term from anywhere, she said, "Ah."

She walked, not thinking about much but the coolness around her ankles and the boy's narrow haunches moving ahead of her. After several minutes she said, "Do you know where we're going? I mean, do you know where it goes to?"

Pausing, taking her hand again, Tamlin shrugged.

In the heart of civilization there are wild places, pockets of Nature that architects and urban planners and citizens obsessed with tidiness somehow overlook, which retain their air of genteel dishevelment while around them upheaval gives way to atrophy, urban arteries harden, the cityscape becomes as moribund and dry as revolution stiffening into bureaucracy. How this happens, and continues to happen everywhere, is mysterious. Maybe there is something in the collective mind that refuses to abandon Nature altogether, though it may consign her to the land along a drainage ditch. Or maybe there is something in the earth itself, some dark pattern woven in the fabric of the ground, that finds expression not in being noticed but in being inexplicably ignored. The threads of this pattern might, for all anyone knows, lie coiled across the land like a very old serpentine footpath. For anyone who can to follow.

"Whoops," said Vesica. Tamlin had stopped and she, distracted, bumped into him. "Sorry."

He half-smiled back.

"Do you feel okay?" she asked him. "Do you want to rest?"

He sat down without admitting anything, at the edge of a slight incline. From the bottom of the slope came sounds of gurgling water. Vesica sat beside him. Lightly she touched his knee, running her finger along the taut pale skin and tiny hairs that covered the sturdy bone there. He suffered this with reasonable grace. She said, "I wonder where we are."

Tamlin nodded downhill, toward the water.

"I hear it," she said. "You mean, we should keep going and see where it goes?"

He shrugged.

He wants *me* to decide, she thought. "Yeah," she said, "it smells bad enough. It *might* come out at the Sump."

She didn't bother to add that it was probably no use; that wherever it came out, Narthex or his hirelings would be waiting there.

Tamlin stood up, leaning on the twisted trunk of a linden. Much of the tree's upper growth had died back under repeated attacks of city air and relentless scorching summers. Tamlin looked—for a moment, in silhouette against the gray-green cloud that had swept across the sky—as weary as that decrepit specimen, and as old. Or anyway, a lot more than fourteen years old or whatever he really was. (Had she ever asked him that? Would he remember?)

"Maybe you shouldn't have come here," she told him. Meaning to add, he had been better off in the woods, safe and sound, and she would have gotten away from her stepfather someday, somehow, and they would have been together—but he didn't give her a chance.

"No," he said unhappily. "I don't belong here. With all these people. I belong with . . . the forest."

"Oh, Tamlin," she said, rising to embrace him.

But the gray-green cloud grew darker over their heads,

and as they stood together, sadly touching, the darkness spoke.

"It's the end of the world," muttered Sheldrake, cowering behind the elaborate optics of the Observatory.

"It is in exceedingly poor taste, whatever it is," declared Lady Widdershins, declining to rise from her chair in the upper garden though all around her the guests were on their feet.

"It must be," said the graduate student in Astrology, "some kind of holographic matrix, you know—put together with, like, I don't know, a hundred projectors or something. And gigantic amplifiers."

"It looks like," suggested the poet of justifiable obscurity, "a vast display of unpleasant bodily processes."

"It's working," said a tall youth wearing the gray-green clothing of the Pure Force. He spoke into a portable airfax machine.

"IT IS THE DAY OF, UM, RECKONING," boomed the shadow in the sky.

"It's all right, little poopykins," Lady Widdershins cooed to Paracelsus, her poodle. "I'm sure it will go away in *no* time."

"IT IS T-TIME," stammered the shadow, in which a yellowish blob floated, badly out of focus, and a black circle opened and closed, "FOR THE, UM, NOOSPHERE TO TAKE ITS REVENGE. FOR CENTURIES OF MALTREAT-MENT. BY, AH, VERMINOUS. MAN."

"It sounds," said Lord Tattersall, "like some illiterate reading from a script."

"It's . . ." began Vesica, stumbling through mounds of trash and rotten mattresses in a small rubbly clearing.

"IT IS THE DAY OF THE FOREST," concluded the shadow. "THE GREAT CONQUERER HAS ARRIVED."

And Tamlin said disgustedly:

"It's Thrull."

Thirty-four

THE SHOOTOUT AT Faerie
Sump, as next morning's *Wake* would waggishly declare it,
began with the cracking of a mirror.

No ordinary mirror. The eighty-inch parabolic reflector
at the heart of the Observatory was so often polished that its
silver coating had worn thin. Over the centuries it had been
subtly but irreparably warped by the oscillations of an im-
moderate climate, so that it now reflected imperfectly, adding its own bias or coloration to whatever portion of reality it
was pointed at. Ah, but this only enhanced its stature as a
symbol, and made its cracking more portentous.

No ordinary crack. The schism that zigzagged its way
across the silvered glass, like a lightning bolt, was caused by
an explosion that ripped open the Observatory's door, admitting sunshine into those dank confines for the first time since
its construction; admitting also a gray-green swarm of unusually well-fed Pure Forcers, and terrifying the graduate student
in Astrology, who was picking up discarded xanthée mugs
from the floor.

"Where *are* they?" demanded the tallest youth, who led
the charge.

The graduate student gawked. Aftershocks of the explosion were reverberating through the floor, and a sickening

noise like an immense slow-motion crow-caw came groaning out of the old machinery.

"Oh, God," the graduate student moaned. "Not that."

(He was two-thirds of the way through a dissertation on the possible existence of artificial stars. Now he might need a new topic.)

He said, "I hope your Speaker gets you bastards *good* for this one."

The crack continued to widen. As the twenty-three-ton block of glass broke apart, its weight shifted inside the rusty mounting. This intensified the structural tension on the age-worn foundations of the dome. The zigzag motif was picked up by a network of cracks spreading across the concrete floor. The tall Pure Forcer got out his transmitter again.

"They're not here," he told it. His comrades amused themselves by pulling astrological charts from the walls and making random turns on the wheels that determined what conical portion of reality the telescope was concerned with. Slowly the great barrel pointed down.

"Very intelligent," said the graduate student. "A few more inches and you'll unbalance the whole thing."

"I don't *know* where they are," said the tall youth. "There's only this one skinny kid here now. You want me to break his arms or something?"

The graduate student picked up his notebook and his favorite xanthée mug and stepped to the blown-out door. The vandals played at their new game of tilt-the-telescope. They now had it aimed at a festively decorated estate where a lot of smoke was issuing from a muddy hole. The tall youth snapped off the airfax.

"Stop him!" he cried, pointing at the student by the door.

"Go to hell," the student said.

In that instant the floor of the dome opened with a great hollow noise like a gunshot in a cavern. For a few tenths of a second the obstreperous youths enjoyed the distinction of being the first people in half a millennium to see the inside of a low-level radioactive waste containment vessel. The graduate student sucked reflectively at the inside of his cheek.

Crk! Crk! was the sound it made.

*   *   *

Midafternoon. Low Commissioner Narthex turned from the picture of his stepdaughter on his desk to pick up the squawking airfax receiver. He listened for a minute or two in silence. Even his breathing—if he was breathing at all—was inaudible.

"If you'll pardon my saying so," he remarked at last, "you appear to be letting things get *just* a bit out of control."

He did not sound unhappy. It may have been that things getting out of control was precisely what he had in mind. He toggled on a speaker, allowing a militiaman's voice to come rasping into the room.

". . . still missing," the voice said. "But don't worry. They can't make it across town without being seen by *somebody*. By the time they pop up we should have everything in order. As for the College—"

Narthex leaned forward, twisting his bony fingers into knots.

"Shut up," he said softly.

"—in flames . . . Did you say something? This equipment isn't working too well."

"I expect you," said Narthex, "to keep my stepdaughter from harm."

"Sure, sure, I promised you that already." There was a pause during which the speaker relayed sounds of an elaborate demonstration of firepower.

Narthex said, "Very well. Go on."

"Right. Let's see. The College burning, ah: the markets. The markets are in turmoil. Xanthée futures have collapsed on rumors that the plantations are overgrown."

"Are they?"

"Who knows? Probably. Everything else is. It suits your purposes, doesn't it?"

Narthex tapped the surface of his desk. The picture of his stepdaughter, taken when she was six or seven, before she learned to despise him, smiled back in innocent reproof.

The militiaman said, "Let's see. The killer virus rumor goes out at three, unless you want to save it for tomorrow."

"I don't care." Narthex leaned back, wishing he felt more of a sense of imminent victory. "Do you understand? I don't care what you do, or how you manage it. All I want is a reasonable degree of turmoil—enough to keep the Press busy—until the inquiry is over. That, and my stepdaughter back."

The militiaman could be heard to grunt. "I told you, we'll find her."

"Good," said Narthex. "And don't bother me again until you do. I have a Bull Roast to attend."

The monstrous hologhost of Thrull continued to snivel at shattering volume and to slouch grotesquely above the town. If it was possible to be fearsomely huge and still evoke the adjective *puny*, the apparition had managed it.

"DON'T LET THEM STOP YOU," the image whined. "DON'T BE AFRAID OF THEIR GUNS AND THEIR HEATWEAPONS. THEY ARE POWERLESS AGAINST THE GREAT DRYAD. NOTHING CAN HARM THOSE WHO FIGHT FOR THE TRIUMPH OF THE FOREST."

"If nothing else," noted Lord Tattersall, ensconced again in the dank sanctuary of the Deep Game Room, "his enunciation has improved. I suppose with practice one gets better at everything."

Beside him at the window, the eminent cartographer turned. "Did they like my map?" he asked, sounding eager that they should have done so. "It was color-coded, you know, to highlight the topography. . . ."

"Oh, they thought it was splendid," Tattersall assured him. "Couldn't wait to get out there and follow it."

The cartographer beamed. "What happens now?" he wondered. "When will we know?"

Tattersall sighed. What happened now, of course, was sitting here in moldy armchairs while a party raged across the Sump.

"I wonder what's become of Ernest," he said distantly.

The cartographer, watching Thrull's apparition, had no reply, so the Governor settled back to waiting. As he had been waiting all his life. In wan but never dying hope. For friends, and money, to arrive.

The Brigade of Irregular Poets paused in its march across town to enjoy a disturbance near the Progressive Brothels. Several persons employed in the area were fending off a sanctimonious assault by the Pure Force, which appeared intent on depriving them of their places if not their actual physical means of livelihood. Sensing front-page material, a sizable crowd of journalists gathered around.

"CLEANSE THE EARTH," urged Thrull's amplified voice from above. "CLEANSE IT OF ALL THAT IS IMPURE."

The Force pressed in to do his bidding, and the local employees used ingeniously unscrupulous techniques to prevent them. It was a close match.

"I'll take five-to-eight on the hookers," a fat journalist proposed.

"You're on," said a younger colleague.

The stakes were collected for safekeeping by a woman poet standing nearby. Seeing that, as usual, no one was paying her the slightest attention, she went on to collect the journalists' credentials. These had been stamped with verification-seals by the government, the Pure Force, the Civil Militia, the guerrilla movement in the South, the eastern barons against whom a war was currently being conducted, and the Guild of Barristers—to be certain of recognition by whoever should come out on top. The poet rejoined her colleagues, who were also smiling and patting their roomy pockets and shoulder bags, and the Brigade moved on.

Arteries of forest spread and divided through the city, breaking into smaller channels that zigzagged away like shafts of verdant lightning. They spread from the cracks and alleys and sandlots that had spawned them into carefully tended lawns, porches set with flagstones, cluttered sidewalks, and crowded avenues. Over the quartered grid of the city they imposed an accidental pattern of shattered hexagons. One piece of this pattern—a dusty green finger crooking southward toward the Sump, where it scratched the backs of brick warrens—emerged from the drainage fields below the Secret College to reach across the Aleatory Strand, where it was cut down to stubble by persistent vehicle- and foot-traffic. Tamlin and Vesica, who had traveled unseen within this narrow band of woods for miles through the belly of the city, stepped onto the Strand and halted there, staggered by the heaviness of the sun.

Before them, a jailbreak was in progress.

The Municipal Treatment Facility, a combined prison

and sludge processing plant, stood across the Strand. It was
surrounded by a hundred members of the Pure Force—long-
standing members, from the look of them, their grey-green
robes so old and so long unlaundered that they hung from
the malnourished young frames like shriveled gonfalons. Urged
on by the unseeing hologhost above them, these youths had
set their hearts and minds and fingernails to tearing the
Facility apart at its foundations. They had been at it for more
than an hour now—opposed only by a token contingent of
Guardsmen who roved the parapets clicking the useless trig-
gers of their heatweapons, which didn't seem to be working
anymore—and were just, as Tamlin and Vesica appeared, at
the point of succeeding. Great clumps of moldy brick were
heaved out of the ground and slung across their shoulders.
Cracks opened and multiplied along the looming wall. Finally, to an accompaniment of sobs and sighs and laughter,
the Facility split open like an underdone egg, oozing its
human and exohuman contents. Among these, borne on a
dozen shoulders, was a wide-shouldered and seemingly weightless youth whose brow shone (as Tamlin and Vesica could
see from the other side of the Strand) with an odd but
unmistakable radiance. The crowd began to cheer.

"THE MOMENT HAS ARRIVED," Thrull intoned na-
sally, "TO DEFEAT THE LAST, UM, RETROGRADE
FORCES OF THE FOE."

This go-ahead was received gladly enough by the young
members of the Force—who, if they were tired at all, were
too frenzied to tell. The mob turned into a two-hundred-eyed
body, and the first thing it found to focus on was a pair of
oddly dressed teenagers. Tamlin's patchwork cut-offs and
Vesica's little-girl dress could not have looked more glaringly
alien to those wearers of rags.

"SPARE NO ONE," Thrull commanded. "I COMMAND
YOU—THE GREAT DRYAD COMMANDS YOU—THE IN-
CARNATION OF NATURE ITSELF COMMANDS YOU—
SHOW MERCY TO NONE OF OUR ENEMIES. LET ONLY
OUR FRIENDS LIVE TO SEE THE BRIGHT NEW DAY."

The crowd shuffled uncertainly, its attention divided
between this giant blurry leader in the sky and the smaller,
only slightly more corporeal leader they had freed from his
weeks of captivity. The bright-browed young man slid from

the shoulders of his rescuers and moved between them into the street. He looked at Tamlin and Vesica—and again at Tamlin—without surprise.

"ATTACK!" wheedled Thrull. "NOW, ATTACK!"

The crowd made an intoxicated surge.

"Come on," said Vesica, grabbing Tamlin by the arm. He resisted crankily, as though too tired to move. "The dragon path!" she implored him. "We've got to find the path again, so we'll be safe."

Tamlin raised his arm, pointing toward the crowd. "It's there," he said. "It goes right through them. Not back."

The Force came forward with wild, unreasoning eyes. The radiant youth was in front of it, allowing himself to be pushed along.

"KILL THEM!" wailed Thrull.

Tamlin stepped forward to meet the approaching mob. *"No!"*

—Vesica screamed, and at the same moment, the tall and oddly glowing youth held up an open palm. The crowd froze as though it had heard a beautiful melody playing somewhere softly, and strained toward perfect silence so as to be able to hear more.

Tamlin kept walking. He covered the space between himself and the older, taller youth in several unhesitating paces. Vesica, feeling blinder and more befuddled than usual, scampered after him, weighing the option of tackling him from behind and dragging him to safety before this strange silence was shattered.

The Silence itself interrupted her.

It was the same throbbing no-noise that surrounded the dragon path: the magical stillness of the forest. The gray-green cloud still bleated overhead, but no one noticed that anymore.

No one looked at anything but the small bright spot where Tamlin stood before the youth with the radiant brow, or the youth stood before Tamlin. They stared at each other with puzzled, friendly, slightly nervous smiles. A mood of companionable curiosity went out from them, communicating itself to the members of the Pure Force and even to Vesica, who drew closer while still holding herself, or being held, a half-step back.

With no warning, the tall young man lowered himself to one knee. A quiet gasp spread among his followers.

"These people," he said—looking up, his voice soothing and fey—"aren't like the ones that hurt you. Like *that* one." (A glance at the sky.) "Or the old ones, that didn't believe."

"Believe what?" said Tamlin. "Here, get up. What do you mean?"

The youth obeyed him. "The Seer said, 'All stories are the Story.' And we believe the Story is true."

"What story?" said Tamlin. He shifted from one bare foot to the other. Vesica moved beside him, protectively taking his hand.

"*Your* story." The tall youth smiled; then he turned to Vesica. "She knows it," he said. "She can tell you."

Tamlin looked at her in surprise. *No,* she started to say, *I don't* . . . But then again, Yes. She knew lots of stories, and somehow Tamlin seemed to be in all of them.

The tall youth took their two hands where they joined together. He raised them in his own. An electric tingling seemed to pass through the tangle of fingers. Thrull's voice overhead grew staticky, as though the stormcloud were garbling its transmission. Thunder rumbled along the western sky.

"Are you," asked Vesica uncertainly, "some kind of priest?"

The tall youth frowned. The radiance of his brow had diminished; or maybe they were standing too close to it. He said, "I don't *think* so. . . . Well, maybe. I just tell people things I've heard."

"Like what?" said Vesica. "Are you the leader of the Pure Force?"

"Like this," the youth said serenely.

> " 'To the best bride-bed will we
> Which by us shall blessed be;
> And the issue there create
> Shall be ever fortunate.' "

"*What?*" said Vesica.

He released their hands. "Go now," he said. "It isn't over yet."

"What isn't?" Vesica demanded. *Something* was over, she thought. Some kind of ceremony had ended. Tamlin stood calmly next to her, as though he understood it all.

The crowd of youths began moving around them, brushing them like waves, heading off into the city.

"Goodbye," said their leader—and as he stepped away, Vesica thought that some of the radiance that had left his brow had attached itself to Tamlin's. The boy looked brighter and stronger than he had since they parted at Balance Act.

"Goodbye," Tamlin said. And taking Vesica's hand, he led her across the Strand into the rapidly growing woods.

They were out of sight by only a few steps when Professor Tylyester emerged from the wreckage of the Municipal Treatment Facility, sniffed the air, brushed off his borrowed robe, and set off down the Aleatory Strand in search of a cab.

Narthex uncoiled the chains with which the door to his walk-up apartment was secured. He descended the narrow stair and stepped out into the alley. A drainpipe overhead looked ready to collapse. His driver awaited him in silence.

The armored carriage still bore a scar or two from its run-in with the Silent Partners' Club, but on the whole the Club had gotten the worst of it. Narthex slithered into the passenger seat. The carriage entered a snarl of panic-stricken traffic, among which one bellowing horn more or less made scant impression.

"Where does everyone think they're going?" the Low Commissioner wondered.

The driver spun the wheel, knocking two lesser vehicles into a drainage ditch. "Out of town for the holiday," he suggested.

The gangs of youths that roamed the city were less a problem than the trees. Those already in place seemed to have grown another three feet overnight, and new ones had sprung up everywhere. The carriage hammered them down with a noise like a repeating-gun, but as soon as its chassis had scraped over them the saplings sprang back up, stronger if anything for the encounter. In places they were too sturdy for even the armored carriage to subdue. The driver altered course a dozen times in the mile and a half of their journey.

"Look up there," said Narthex. He directed a bony finger at one of the towers. From its three-hundred-foot topmast flapped the loden-green banner of the Pure Force. "What are *they* doing up there?"

The driver shrugged. "It's their day, isn't it? They think it is."

"Well, but . . . you don't suppose they've lapsed back to that idealistic nonsense, do you? Even with their little Speaker in jail?"

The two men frowned a moment, thinking. "I can't imagine that," said the driver at last.

"Nor I," said Narthex.

They finished the drive in comfortable silence.

The bull was roasted. Storage tanks of champagne were poured. Acres of hors d'oeuvres were served on gleaming plates. An armory of fireworks was readied for launch. Several local musicians' unions were employed, drained of creative energies, and reassigned to the bar. Forty-seven xantheé table-size volumes of photographs were snapped. One hundred and twelve new laws were conceived by legislative aides observing the unsafe practices around the pool; fortunately these were forgotten, or the aides were drowned. The pool was dragged for bodies. Thrull's hologhost, slurring its words in the heavens, was mistaken for part of the decorating scheme: a "feature." The grounds of Marshmain were bright with the cattleya-pink blooms of the old once-blooming rose 'Chunga's Revenge.' Clouds were gathering like crepe over the sun.

It was, everyone would agree, a splendid Bull Roast, the best in years.

Lady Widdershins was distraught beyond description.

"Ooo, the poor puppykins," she said, worrying the painfully dekinked hair of her poodle. "Does him miss his little friend Vesica?"

Paracelsus did not particularly give a damn. However, he turned his brown eyes upward and waxed forlorn because he had learned that this was a dependable way of obtaining sweets.

"Poor ittle-bittle thing," her ladyship declared. "Here's

some candy-poo to cheer hims up. Now run and play and let Mommykins get back to her party."

Paracelsus trotted off looking for some new object of torment. En route he nipped the calf of a corpulent barrister.

The barrister screwed his eyes shut in pain. His partner in conversation, an unnoticeable young woman, relieved him of his tiepin. She dropped this into a shoulder bag and moved on to a thin-boned man with gray, protruding eyes.

"Hi there," she greeted him.

"Mm." The thin man looked distracted.

"Without Lunaria," the woman remarked, "the deep game is lost."

"I don't follow sports," he said crossly.

"Don't brush your teeth either," she noted.

"What?" By the time the man got his myopic eyes redirected he wasn't sure which of the young ladies in the vicinity he had been talking to. He reached irritably for his pocket-watch, but for some reason couldn't locate it just then.

The woman found someone she recognized—a poet of justifiable obscurity.

"Any luck?" He smiled, raising his drink.

"Lots. But I feel like half my brain cells just exploded. How do these people *survive* all this?"

Her friend chuckled. "Well, they only do it once a year."

"A midsummer afternoon's dream."

"Oh, it lasts longer than that. Wait till you see the fireworks."

"Spare me."

If the truth be known, the woman was tremendously enjoying herself. She wore her air of ennui rather as the highly paid musicians wore dirty cotton: from a sense of professional identification.

"Ta-ta," said her fellow poet affectedly. They exchanged ironic rolls of the eyes and wandered cheerfully back into the fray.

There was a series of percussive outbursts from the band, or from not-too-far-away firearms. The smoky effulgence of burning buildings, projected against the clouds, competed with Thrull's hologhost; the falling sun backlit both of them in tinges of orange; and the whole tableau was imperfectly reflected by the waters of the Sump. If the world was ending, it was ending robustly.

Like a spiral staircase, Fate brought Vesica back to the over-grown alley outside the Silent Partners' Club. But it was a different alley, a scene from a different story. The mulberry trees were taller, their branches contorted more baroquely, than when Vesica had climbed them two weeks before. The armored carriage had destroyed the brick facade and its wheels-within-wheels graffito. In its place was a plywood partition, through which came sounds of the Club settling down to dine.

"No, by Gog," someone was saying, "I don't want to become a member. I've seen pigs fed better than this. I've seen *reporters*—"

The voice sounded familiar, but Vesica was very tired. She was imagining things. She imagined a change coming over the alley as she and Tamlin passed by. A difference in the quality of its silence.

"Come on," she whispered to the boy, who had stopped before the patched-up portico. She tugged gently at his arm. "Hey, I'm tired too. But look, see those rocks? The path to Marshmain starts right there, at the end of the alley."

Tamlin continued to stare at the plywood partition. "But, it's . . ."

"I know—we were here last night. Come on."

The dragon path ran straight down the middle of the alley. Vesica could feel it now, or imagined she could. An electric chill, swirling around her ankles. And more than that: She could feel other patterns of energy laid across the path, or trapped there. Impressions left like fingerprints by people who had passed this way. Scraps of time that the path had snared the way brambles tear off pieces of your clothing. Moments imprisoned in amber.

Was that crazy?

Vesica felt, or maybe imagined, her own past self, creeping along here. Halting at the sight of her stepfather. Climbing the tree. She trembled, reliving her own fear. In this strange state of mind she half-expected to glance into the shadows and see Vesica, an earlier version of Vesica, wearing a legless cotton jumper, still uncaptured, innocent, though it was only a few days ago. Everything was happening so fast now. Spiraling by.

"Tamlin," she said, reaching out for him, "I feel dizzy."

"It's all right," he said.

Taking her hand. As she looked back, surprised, at him. A different Tamlin, as this was a different alley. But of course also the same. His eyes shining brightly. And the radiance that had come from the brow of the tall peculiar youth was now everywhere, glowing from Tamlin's skin, surrounding him like a halo. It gave him a look of being two things at once: a mysterious being in a garment of light, but also a teenage boy in torn-off clothing. A stranger, and also himself.

Vesica remembered the glow she had seen once, near Wild Turkey Pool, that seemed to emanate from the leaves and fronds around her. While the vibrant Silence of the forest pressed against her ears. And she thought: That's what it is. The difference in the alley. And the difference in Tamlin.

It's the forest.

The forest is here.

Tamlin led her in perfect easeful silence between the mulberry trees, and Vesica noticed that they weren't really mulberries after all. Or not quite. Or not anymore. She saw with a kind of vision sharper than mere acuity the greater roughness of bark, the dusty surface of leaves, the upturning of twigs that had once hung weeping—all the subtle adjustments that in just a few days had turned these trees into something very different from what they had been, making them increasingly resemble the lately arisen and little understood hybrid, *Quercus rabidina*. And looking more closely still, she thought she glimpsed for a moment—or somehow perceived directly, without the mediation of her eyes—what was going on. What had changed these trees so quickly. And was changing them still. As she moved past them. As she and Tamlin, whose skin now glowed quite visibly in the dusk, followed the path of swirling energy beside which these mulberries crowded like thorntrees by a stream. Soaking up like water the path's numinous swirling energies. Of which

Vesica herself was somehow, just by being here, a part. Just by holding Tamlin's hand. Just by—

"Vesica."

The boy stared at her. His eyes were miraculously blue. His mouth was moving, but that seemed the smallest, the most insignificant channel of their communion.

"There are some men up ahead, Vesica. Don't be afraid."

Vesica wasn't afraid of anybody, but he didn't mean quite that. What he meant, what he had left unsaid but still somehow relayed to her, was more troublesome. She moved forward with no awareness of her own footsteps, as though the dragon path were holding her like a strong etheric flux, sweeping her along.

And then she saw. Faerie Sump. Its waters receding. The secret path she had taken here, boggy mounds and cypress stumps, a secret no longer, quite visible in fact as it stretched like a soggy arm across the waters. Marshmain at its other side. And if she could see this, with her just normal eyes, then so of course could her stepfather, with his eyes that bulged like a hawk's. And a squad of Civil Militia had been positioned accordingly. There just ahead. Hunched down squarely in the middle of the dragon path. At the end of the alley.

"Vesica," said Tamlin. "Are you ready?"

Ready for what, said the tiny facial muscles around her eyes.

No, wait, said her glance up the alley—back at the Silent Partners' Club, as if telling someone goodbye.

But *Yes*, said her hand in Tamlin's. Happy to hold it for the rest of time.

As a militiaman called out, *Hey you there. You two kids.*

And Tamlin's ancient mind whispered, *Follow me.*

And then.

The great connective, the thread that binds the patchwork fabric of stories. And then. And then this happened. And then that. One thing and then another, until the end of the story. And then it stops. And then everything stays the same forever and ever, because a story once told becomes unchanging, everlasting. Imprisoned in amber.

As if life was like that. One thing after another. When actually, as Vesica now quite clearly saw, life was everything together all at once. Not this and this and this, but all of it. Everything you could think of and then everything else too. All the stories going on forever and ever. None of them ever ending. And none of them the same.

Because each time a story is told, some little thing has changed. Some detail has been forgotten, something new added in its place. The story is the same, but different. An imperfect reflection. An errant child.

And then.

And then all the versions of the story exist together. All the different realities. Each enfolded, as a possibility, within every other. Tucked in at the places where the story might have turned. At every *and then*.

It was funny, Vesica thought. How she had never thought of this before. And funnier still that she was thinking of it now, in spite of all that had happened. All the things that ought to be on her mind.

And then. She began to wonder. Where was she thinking this from? What unexpected turning had her story taken now, and up what dark alley had it led her? What kind of story had it become?

And then, she thought. And then what.

And then, in some earlier version of what truly must be the same story, despite all the things that are different, *the girl became a fairy and went with the Young Pucca into the forest. And they lived there together for a million years.*

Had Vesica been thinking of that? Had she remembered it, in the moment when she thought *Yes*, and squeezed more tightly on Tamlin's hand?

Had she really believed when she followed him that they would live happily ever after? Or did some sadder, grown-up corner of her intellect know that happy-ever-after is impossible, except in fairy tales? Could she have known that and not cared and followed him anyway?

Or was she just so tired, so bewildered after all that had happened, that she no longer quite believed in her own free will at all? Had she surrendered, even before Tamlin took her hand and said *Follow me*, to that sense familiar to us all of being no more than a character in a story, a kind of animated metaphor? Did she truly follow Tamlin because she loved and trusted him? Or because *all* heroines love and trust the heros of their tales?

Follow me, said Tamlin. And then.

And then of course, Vesica did.

And *then*—

"Without Lunaria," the young poet remarked, handing over the poodle, "the deep game is lost."

"Oh, good heavens. Is it *that* late?" Lady Widdershins's jaw clamped shut as she examined Paracelsus for signs of damage: spilled punch, tangled doggy hair, puncture wounds from fashionable heels. Her jaw then slipped an inch or two open again.

"Young man," she called sharply.

The poet had turned away to investigate a pile of bodies in the corner of the patio. He turned back to find his hostess bearing heavily down on him.

"Without *what* did you say?"

The poet, pleased at last to have found a receptive listener, gave it to her again. The jaw collapsed entirely.

"*Lunaria,*" she repeated. "Do you know what *Lunaria* is, young man?"

The poet grinned. "A famous actress? A mental disease?"

"Mental . . . I should *say.*" Her ladyship gave considerable evidence of becoming agitated. "And *where,*" she demanded, "did you *hear* such a thing?"

The poet was just starting to reply when she said, "Never mind, it's perfectly clear. Paracelsus!"

The poodle, freed from the depths of her bosom, bounded off in the direction of the Rose Court, with Lady Widdershins, in a veritable tide of flesh, close behind.

"Not a soul," said Evergrey, the aged barman, "except the Founding Members of the Club, may be admitted to the Deep Game Room."

"Damn your suspenders," declared Sheldrake, "I don't *want* to be admitted to the reeking Game Room. I just want you to knock on the door and ask somebody to come out."

"The Founding Members," sniffed Evergrey, elevating his nose as far as possible above the source of this outpouring—then interrupted himself to call out, "Good evening, Professor."

Across the chamber came the cowled and scowling figure of the Dean of the Secret College. He seemed slightly off balance, perhaps on account of the absence of the bulky manuscript from under his arm. In addition he smelled very badly.

"Extraordinary," he was murmuring. "Quite remarkable. In just *hours* . . . Why, hello, Sheldrake. Glad you're here. Is the Governor around?"

Sheldrake hopped down from his barstool. "I don't know," he said, glaring at Evergrey. "This busboy here—"

The aged barman, sublimely assured of his position in life, even if no one else was, gave an indifferent twist to the top of a bottle of Old Juggler. The dysfunctional electric door-lock began to make its customary racket.

In short order the door of the Deep Game Room fell back.

"Ernest!" exclaimed the Governor (for at least the next day or so) of All the Northern Territories. "And Sheldrake!"

Professor Tylyester rankled. "Would you *please* not call me that," he said. "I've had a truly awful day. And I haven't the faintest idea what's become of the children."

"Children?" said Tattersall, his expression becoming thoughtful. "What children?"

"No time for that," broke in Sheldrake. He bustled between the taller men like an impatient referee. "You've got to come outside. You've got to see . . ."

And to Tattersall's surprise the Professor nodded in concurrence. "He's right, old man," Tylyester said (taking subtle revenge for "Ernest").

The alley outside the Silent Partners' Club was a different place. It was, to be more precise, no longer an alley at all. No longer an overgrown patch of glass-strewn paving walled by crumbling brick and ending in a rocky promontory over the Sump. Not anymore.

Where the alley had been was now a narrow copse, a short arm of a great towering body of woods. Where once mulberries had twisted up from cracks there now soared mighty oaks. Their trunks bulged as wide as two men standing abreast. Their roots laid open the pavement. Their limbs interlocked in a canopy whose lowest leaves were fifty feet above Tattersall's craning head. And in their highest branches, scattered with artful randomness like a spangling of jewels, orchids bloomed in a hundred brilliant colors against the gray-green hologhost and the cloudy sky.

"Good *heavens*," breathed Tattersall, as Sheldrake performed a series of rapid ritual motions, culminating in two fingers being brought to point at the ground. Whereupon the short man said:

"Look!"

And they looked. And what they saw there was perhaps the most remarkable thing of all. For between the trees that must have sprung from the earth that very hour wound a natural-looking and, to all appearances, often-trodden little path. It looked on the whole as though it were more integral to the woods than were the trees themselves, and had been there longer. The sort of path that fairly begs to be followed.

"Well . . ." said the Governor. His native caution struggled with the lure of the trail.

The Dean, a more inquisitive man, strode to the nearest tree and delivered a solid kick to its base. His boot rebounded smartly.

"I refute him *thus*," he said, seemingly to himself, then turned to make this pronouncement: "If these trees are here in the morning, that young Speaker fellow has got himself a job."

"Fine, fine," said Sheldrake. "He's got a job, and we're out of work." He pointed down the narrow winding trail. "Now can we see where it goes?"

And then there were fireworks. They leapt into the air and exploded, pocking Thrull's projected face with glowing lesions.

"THE BATTLE IS WON," he obliviously proclaimed. "WHILE THE MEMBERS OF THE DOOMED, UM, IG-NOBILITY, HAVE DRUNK AWAY THEIR FINAL HOURS AT A DECADENT BULL ROAST"—pause for a wheezy breath—"THEIR DOMINION IS COMING TO AN END."

"Is he referring to *us*?" fretted a nervous little envelope-licker from the Hardy Plant Society.

"*It*," huffed Lady Widdershins, setting a determined course for her patio with Paracelsus in hand, "is referring to things it has no understanding of."

"THE ANCIENT ENEMY OF CIVILIZATION," the tape blabbered on, "HAS ARRIVED."

From the other side of the patio, stepping carefully over fallen or otherwise recumbent bodies, Low Commissioner Narthex sauntered on an intersecting course. His face was alternately bright against the dusky green backdrop and silhouetted against the splatter of pyrotechnics in the sky. The band played an atonal waltz behind him.

"My lady," he said, bowing formally, "I wonder if I might have a word with you." He glanced purposefully aside, allowing his eyes to linger on the stalwart partygoers—many of them, curiously, displaying Press credentials on their lapels—who stood around swilling iced nepenthe and examining the crystal glassware. He added:

"Alone."

His hawkish eyes gleamed with an unsettling—one wanted to say *unnatural*—intensity. If one's teenage daughter were at home (and not lost, perhaps forever, in the violent city) one would wish her kept well away from eyes like that.

Lady Widdershins sighed. "What more do you have to say? You know there is only one thing I care to talk about."

"Then we shall talk about it. And more besides."

She sighed again. She was little better than his servant, as she well knew, no matter what this *Lunaria* business was about—though she meant to find out, regardless. Without a word she led him from the balcony to the sunroom, where her speckled pelargoniums were looking a wee bit overwrought.

"Widdy," he said, drawing much too near, "I have great news to impart."

"You're sounding melodramatic," she told him, looking away.

He seized her arms. "Momentous news," he said, "and I want *you* to hear it first."

"I suppose there is nothing I can do but listen."

This was a mistake. It only sharpened the covetous look on his face, brightened the gleam in his eyes. Narrow fingers constricted around her biceps.

(It was too, too grotesque. But now that it had started—started, really, a long time ago—what could she do to stop it?)

"Widdy," he said, "a great hour has arrived."

"You sound like that horrid thing in the sky."

"The thing in the sky sounds like *me*. Those are my words it is reciting."

She showed none of what very slight surprise this occasioned.

"All of it," he declared, "all of the, shall we say, little disturbances are part of a plan which I am about to bring to fruition."

"Is that so?" The nearness of this concentrated body of self-esteem was making her feel unbalanced. She struggled to preserve her equilibrium. "Was it you, then, who told those horrid oaks to start growing in people's lawns?"

"Don't be frivolous," he snapped. "No one is responsible for acts of Nature. I am referring to matters under human control. Such things," he added, recomposing himself, "as the governance of the Northern Territories."

"Oh, that old thing." Lady Widdershins longed for a fan, for anything to enliven the air. "Everyone knows you hate poor Tatty, and want his job. Tatty knows it himself, as well as anyone."

The grip on her arms grew tighter, which she would not have thought possible. "Well he may know it," rasped Narthex. "But there is nothing he can do about it. Anymore."

"If you are going to bore me," Lady Widdershins sighed, "with another of your interminable plots, I simply shall not listen. I have *told* you there is only one thing I wish to talk about."

The look in the Low Commissioner's eyes had taken on all manner of unseemly overtones. The next moment one expected him to grow fangs and drool. "It is not a matter of plotting," he said, all dignity now. "It is a matter of Fate. My fate and your fate. And Vesica's."

Oh ho, thought Lady Widdershins. You have to be careful of this Fate business. She flexed her arms, keeping the muscles awake. "And just how is it," she said, "that you can speak of Vesica's fate with such . . . assurance?"

Narthex ignored her. He was almost panting now. "Soon, Widdy—very soon—tomorrow perhaps—our fate—all our fates—will be decided."

Heaven, she thought, forfend.

"But, Widdy," he said, his voice frightening and low, "I do not want to succeed in this only for myself. I would not want to win the world and have to live in it alone. *Do you know what I'm saying, Widdy?*"

She was having a bit of difficulty breathing, and this seemed to further excite him.

"Must I *show* you what I'm talking about?" he panted. "Is that what it will take?"

Air, was all she could think of. Room to breathe. And time. She struggled against his grasp as though—right there in the sunroom, with the speckled pelargoniums looking on—she were in the act of being devoured.

"I see," he said, "you *do* understand."

She took a gasping breath. "Oh, Narthex," she said, "I just . . . it's all so sudden. So . . . *overwhelming.* I just need time to think. To *prepare.*"

He relaxed his death grip on her arms. "Yes," he said, "of course. Of course you do."

He smiled like a snake that has trapped and is about to swallow a delectable rodent.

"Could we," she said, "just step outside for a few moments? Just . . . walk around a bit? I was so terribly looking forward to the fireworks."

His smile grew more settled-in, as though the rodent were already decomposing in his gut.

"So," he said, "have I."

Back on the patio, an unsteady guest overshot the punchbowl and lurched in their direction. Narthex caught him by the shoulders and turned him around.

"Without Lunaria," the man slobbered, "the deep game is lost."

"That's quite all right," said Lady Widdershins quickly. "I'm glad to see you're having a good time."

Narthex's smile disappeared. "Did you say *the deep game?*"

The drunken poet repeated himself. Narthex turned to Lady Widdershins. "That sounds," he said, "like some kind of code."

"Oh, I don't—"

"The deep game," he rumbled. "The Deep Game." His face was growing dark.

Why, she wondered, can't they just go ahead and *grasp* things without all this building-up?

"That's right," said an urbane voice behind him. "*The Deep Game.*"

Lady Widdershins's heart boomed in the great sounding-board of her breast. She turned to stare across the patio, and except for the broken glass all over the flagstones might have dashed over and thrown herself into . . . well, *someone's* arms. There were plenty to choose among. Tattersall's, and Tylyester's, and the stubby arms of little Sheldrake—even the short and frantically pumping limbs of Paracelsus, scuffing at the Professor's boots.

"Oh!" she exclaimed, too weak with relief, finally, to throw herself anywhere. "Thank *heavens.*"

"Hey," said the drunken poet. "That looks like a gun."

The object in the Low Commissioner's hand certainly did look like a gun—a small and very evil-looking gun. Narthex's expression was its facial equivalent.

"IT'S TOO LATE," cried the firework-splattered hologhost. "TO REVERSE THE FLOW OF HISTORY."

"Yes," Narthex said.

"THE STORY IS NEARING ITS FINAL CHAPTER."

"Come along, Widdy." The stubby weapon strayed over the faces of Narthex's old antagonists. "You should not be in the presence of these gate-crashers. Just let me summon the Militia and we will have them taken away."

"You'll need a bigger barrel than *that*," muttered Sheldrake, "to keep *her* happy."

"He's right, you know," said Lord Tattersall, for once having heard his associate correctly.

"We'll see about that," said Narthex, discharging a quick burst of amber light into the flagstones. "We can settle this here and now as easily as tomorrow."

"Oh, posh," said Tattersall. "You couldn't possibly get away with physical violence in a place like this. Look at all the beastly Press around!"

"I doubt that he has the courage to try," said Tylyester.

"Children are more his style. This is the monster who impris-oned his own stepdaughter."

"He *what?*" gasped Lady Widdershins.

"Come *here*, Widdy," the Low Commissioner snapped.

"How *dare* you—you—"

"I only did it for her safety. Which *you* seemed unable to ensure."

"Her *safety*." Lady Widdershins advanced on him, oblivi-ous of the weapon in his trembling bony fingers.

"Stop!" cried Tattersall. "Stop, before he hurts you."

Lady Widdershins turned. "And *you*," she cried. "How can you *stand* there like a painted duck when *your own daughter* is involved?"

"My . . ." Tattersall blanched. "My . . . Do you mean—"

"I *do*," said Lady Widdershins.

"That's neither here nor there any longer," said Narthex, in a tone of wakening desperation.

"THE DAY IS WON," Thrull blearily crowed.

"Isn't *that* the truth," said Sheldrake, holding the Com-missioner's gaze. "Your charges against the Governor are nothing compared to *this*."

"That's not true," said Narthex, but his sharp chin slightly quivered.

"And *you*," said Tylyester, "are going to find yourself where *I* have just been."

Tattersall stepped forward. "Really, old boy," he said. "The time has come to do the honorable thing."

Narthex looked quickly around, like a man caught in an avalanche. His old enemy the Governor stood two paces away. Lady Widdershins glared hatefully from one side. Sheldrake leaned forward like a diminutive bull about to charge. Not like this, Narthex thought. It isn't going to end like this.

His fingers tightened around the gun. Like choosing from a menu . . . (the bony fingers tightened more) . . . start with Sheldrake; the others will be slower . . .

Paracelsus scooted across the patio before Narthex could add him to the list. The teeth that had punctured a sewer main buried themselves in the Low Commissioner's thigh. Narthex fired without a target, aiming only at the abstract locus of pain. He brought the gun down, clubbed the poodle. Paracelsus yelped and let go. Sheldrake lowered his head and charged.

"You beast!" screamed her ladyship. "You've hurt my poopykins!"

Narthex slithered aside; Sheldrake glanced off his shoulder. Realizing at last the hopelessness of his position, the Low Commissioner spun about and made a running leap from the patio. He plunged through an evergreen hedge into the low garden, where he gained the shelter of the clematis arbor leading down from Vesica's empty room.

"After him!" cried Tattersall, leading a disorganized charge. A number of guests, attracted by the commotion, wandered up to the patio and stood there smiling groggily. Lady Widdershins removed a silk scarf from the neck of an unconscious celebrant, dipped it in something she found bubbling in a glass, and dabbed it on her wounded poodle's forehead.

It began to rain.

Narthex reached the Gnat Walk between old rhododendrons, where it was as dark as the inside of a forest. He loosened his choker collar, dabbed at the blood running down his leg, struggled to catch up on his breathing. Whoever was pursuing him must have taken a wrong turn. A trace of confidence crept back, growing slowly stronger as though it were being fed in intravenously.

Things couldn't be *that* bad. They had gone too far to turn around completely. It might come down to who had more immediate access to the Press. . . .

"THE CITY IS OURS," Thrull assured him. "THE HOUR HAS COME."

Yes. The city. We only need to get ourselves out of here, away from Marshmain, back to the safety of our walk-up apartment. Where we can think.

But before he had taken a dozen steps, Narthex came to a halt, feeling as though his path had abruptly ended; as though the Gnat Walk went no farther than *here*. He raised his arms, felt nothing, no barrier, and shook his head. The blackness, the wildness of overgrowth, the air thick with smoke and sweat and dread—the air of unreality—must be getting to him. He blinked, wiping the rain away from his nearsighted eyes.

Something seemed to float into view ahead of him: something ghost-white, like a reflection of the Moon. In Narthex's overstrained imagination the reflection assumed the contours of another body, another walker lost in the darkness. Then it became a boy, a ghost-boy, stirring into existence from the shadows.

The Commissioner stopped. Not yet willing to be afraid.

"Hello, Narthex," said his stepdaughter's voice.

The voice had come from somewhere behind the boy—a dimmer, ill-defined ghost-shape in the trees.

"Vesica!" He took a great breath. Something rose within him that almost took the shape of happiness. "Oh, Vesica— you're safe! Thank God!"

"What god are you thanking?" she said.

The fear began. He couldn't see her, quite. Her evanescent form seemed to sway, to take on a variety of outlines not totally like a girl's, but not totally like any other. Only the boy in the foreground was distinct: long white limbs, patchwork clothes, two glowing dots of cloudless sky.

"Come here, Vesica. Come out where I can see you."

"Why?" she said. Her voice had shifted. It came from somewhere other than the half-seen, ever-changing shape; came at him from the darkness.

"Why, Narthex?" it insisted. "You never wanted to see me before."

This is a trick, he thought. This isn't my stepdaughter. This voice, calling me Narthex. This . . . It's a trick—a hallucination—something *he* has done.

"You!" he cried. He raised his gun at the ghost-white boy.

"Narthex," said the voice, the spectral voice of his stepdaughter. "Stop. Put that down."

He laughed. Or thought he laughed. Rain or tears dotted his spidersilk sleeve.

"But, Vesica," he said patiently. (If she *was* here, he wanted to explain to her; it was important that she understand.) "Don't you see? Don't you . . . See, I've *won* now. *We've* won. It's what—all these years—you know, back at the farm—and keeping you away, yes, from other children—and maybe it *wasn't* right, not all of it, but don't you see . . ."

"No," she said. "None of this is true. You're just making it up. Like a story, but it isn't really . . ."

"Stop it! You cannot speak to your father, your stepfather, this way."

"*Narthex*," said the voice, as full and as fluid as the air. "I'm not your stepdaughter any longer. I've been thinking it over, and I never was your stepdaughter—never really. I've thought it over. And I think I know what happened. How you did it."

"Vesica! But—"

"*Narthex*."

It was the boy now. The boy—Tamlin—whoever he was—stepped closer up the path. Up the Gnat Walk. It was very dark here. As dark as a forest. There were lights overhead, explosions. Or only thunder. Narthex waved his gun.

"Get away from me! Stay back! You—you're some kind of magician, aren't you? Not a boy. Some kind of, of devil! You've got Vesica under a spell."

"Put the gun down, Narthex," said the voice that wasn't his stepdaughter's, not his stepdaughter anymore.

"You've done this," he told the boy. "But I'll take care of you, *right now*. I've won, and no little puking brat is going to take it away from me."

The boy stepped closer. His eyes were visible; his slightly upturned nose; the ghosts of freckles on his cheeks.

Narthex shot him.

The thin amber stream shone through the blackness. It pierced the crowded air between the muzzle of the gun and the pit of Tamlin's stomach. The patchwork fabric parted; the beam entered his flesh through the diagonal white scar, his second navel, sign of a troubled birth. It slipped through skin, a wall of striated muscle, damp membranes, glands seething with adrenaline and bile, membranes and muscles and skin again, and once more patchwork clothes. Passed through all of them like the glass that covers a mirror.

Narthex gave a choking gasp.

Tamlin stood unmoving, his pale skin radiant and whole.

"You're not a real boy," Narthex accused him.

But Tamlin was a boy, even as he was something different. An angry vengeful boy, raising his hands.

A ghost raising its outgrowths of ectoplasm.

A monster raising its taloned paws.

The Presence, opening and closing like a mouth.

A mouth—Vesica's mouth—was open to cry, but there was no one to cry for. No one but herself. She stood alone in the Gnat Walk. A girl, once more only a girl. And her eyes were just normal eyes again, straining against the darkness.

Above her, zigzagging down from the sky, a sword of lightning the color of blood streaked toward the heart of the city. A thousand feet overhead it split like the tongue of a serpent. Its two halves spread like roots to curl themselves around the deathly gray towers. The topmasts disintegrated with the sound of a thousand amplifiers exploding. Maybe a thousand amplifiers *did* explode. Thrull's hologhost lingered for a long fraction of a second. His whining voice got out:

"THE GREAT DRY—"

And then it fell silent. Flames leapt from the towers into the air, and then the towers were falling, groaning down in an agony of severed steering cables. Their alloyed skeletons and insulated copper sinews broke apart and rained down in streams of electric-blue fire. From very far off, across the Sump, a collective wail of terror rose above the cheers of drunken partygoers, who shouted that this was the greatest Bull Roast *ever*.

Vesica was too horrified to breathe. Her retinas luminesced with images of destruction that lingered after her eyelids were closed, after she pressed her hands against them, after she drew herself into a bundle on the ground.

The ground seemed to embrace her. Its warm steady hug had the firmness of young muscles. It brushed her hair back from her face.

"Here, stand up."

A hand circled her wrist, helped her to rise. Tamlin stood smiling beside her.

Just Tamlin.

Just smiling—though his smile bore a weight of mortality that made it something other than a smile, or anyway other than the imperishable smile of a fourteen-year-old boy.

Well, Vesica would never wear the smile of just a girl again, either. Though that's all she was. A confused and frightened girl.

They were children but not just children anymore. And somewhere in the *not just*, as she now knew, lay the great difference between them.

"Come on," said Tamlin quietly. "It's time to go. Are you coming with me?"

"Where?" she said.

"I want to go back to the . . . to my father."

And Vesica, moving in to hold him, said,

"Oh, Tamlin—
    so do I."

Realities

Between them and the present flows a clear
stream shaded by great cottonwoods.
It's here that Ephraim tangles with
A KIND OF GOD HALF MAN HALF TALKING TREE
ICECAPPED PEATSHOD . . .
—JAMES MERRILL

Passiflora incarnata
Passion-flower

Vigorous and twining. Its brief flowering
is followed by fruits of exhilarating sweetness, which
ripen slowly and may be kept indefinitely.

Thirty-five

THE TWO WORLDS over-
lapped in Amy's laboratory. The present set of four-inch terra
cotta pots interpenetrated their own five-hundred-year-old
reflections. Of the two, the reflections were easier to believe
in; more persuasively *there*. And the plants they contained—
glowing, pale-green seedlings—were larger and brighter than
the downy-leaved oaklets Lorian had brought in from the
orchard; as if time's arrow were pointing backward, and
those ghostly ancestors had sprung from the duller stock of
their progeny.

Two factors made the illusion imprecise. Over the centuries the long lab tables had warped so badly that not even
Groby—not even groaning and shimming and counterweight-
ing—could bring the old wood into conformance with its
original contours. And Amy Hayata, strolling the aisles in no
discernible pattern, persisted in lifting the pots, examining
each seedling with fond attentiveness, then sitting them
down again *never* in the same places as before. Lorian traipsed
after her, adjusting their alignment, but the task was endless
and finally unrewarding. The two worlds would never coin-
cide. The divide was as impassable as the silence that stood
between Amy's unselfconscious monologue—notes to herself
or to some unmet spiritual heir—and Lorian's efforts to respond.

"What I really wonder," Amy said, "is how much of what I'm sending out there is getting through. All these years of it, and nothing. Or yeah, I know: a new rooting pattern and some extra toughness in the leaves, but not . . .

"Like writing the paper," she said more loudly—looking up, a new thought taking her away—"over and over, sending it out. And just like that, nothing. You have to ask yourself, is anybody listening? And why don't they send something back? Just . . . *anything*."

Lorian aimed a spray-bottle at the seedling she thought of as the Runt: short and homely, its leaves curled slightly under like ear-length hair. The mist descended. Each droplet made a lens that refocused the laser light of the projection. Around the Runt, the hologhost seemed to melt, to bleed a hundred colors into the air. For an instant, just there, the two worlds ran together.

Lorian shivered with the foreknowledge of what Amy was going to say, even before the botanist looked up from her momentary absorption. She, Amy, stared out through a window that had stood outside the field of the recording. The tree beyond it—a golden-leaved *robinia*, in Lorian's world—must not have been there then, or been much shorter, for Amy seemed to peer out over a great distance, northward toward the place where the North Star would be, if only it weren't full afternoon. If only.

Lorian bit her lip. She stopped her spraying. She opened her mouth as Amy opened hers. The little furrow on the botanist's brow was matched by a twitching simulacrum on the journalist's.

"I bet," said both of them, "I know what's going on."

Their phrasing was identical; the intonation differed insofar as Lorian could not reproduce, in her urban staccato, the wistful melody that wound through Amy's words.

"It's the field itself," Amy said, "I probably ought to think about. Not . . . Here I've been focusing on getting through to it—composing and recomposing the message—and I've never really concentrated on what it is I'm trying to get through *to*."

Lorian knew this all by heart. She had played it two dozen times since Groby found it.

Found it, pulled it down from the shelf without looking at it, put it in her hand.

This is the disk, he told her.

"No, that's not quite true," said Amy, speaking slowly. "The field . . . okay, I knew . . . but *me*, talking to *it* . . . I don't know, I guess I was waiting for an answer or something naïve like that. But it doesn't *work* that way."

Excited now. She walked to the desk where the matrix controller sat, still sits today, safely away from dirt and water; checked the dials. Are you getting this? her frown implored.

"It's okay," said Lorian. "Keep talking."

Amy would turn now—turned—and walk to the stool where Lorian was sitting. Lorian lingered, this once, before getting out of her way. The botanist, her reflection, her ghost, walked right up and sat on the stool with Lorian. *Through* Lorian; *in* Lorian. It felt, of course, like nothing. Just another part of the projection; a zone of differently modulated light. It was just barely warm enough to know it as something other than air—and when the sun was on you, not that.

But while this was true on some level, or most levels— that it wasn't Amy, nothing but light—Lorian managed to think that for one heart-stopping moment (if not in time then in another dimension, like the one where the meaning of a story lies) as the two of them shared the same uncushioned surface, laced together in their overlapping mind the same chain of words—in that moment or mood or story-land she and Amy fused together, became one dark-haired obsessive woman, shared one short and lonely sigh.

Because this is the disk. The final disk. The last words and breaths and pensive gestures of Amy Hayata. And if Groby had known this—if *only* he could have known, from small clues no one else would have noticed—then only Lorian could have truly understood. What this final disk meant.

"Hey," said Amy. Still alive, for how much longer? Another hour? Lorian tried to imitate her half-wry side-turning smile. Failed. "You know, I think in the next draft, I'm going to stick in a new appendix. On the Personality of the Field . . . or let's see. The Organizing Personality?

"Anyway.

"There would be this introductory part, this kind of long aside, where I talk about how systems people—group theorists and people like that—how they have this tendency to talk about their big software projects as though they were really creating artificial personalities. They say things like: Look, we've got as many cells in this system as you've got in your brain and ours work a little bit faster. And they mumble about synergy, and transcendence of categories, which is a concept that didn't appeal to them a couple of years ago. And then when they've built up momentum, they take this big huge leap and they say: Look—this thing can make jokes, and it can compose music, and it can write letters to your mother so that she can't tell it isn't you. And it can repair itself. And if we gave it the right hardware, it could reproduce itself with any variations you might like.

"So how can you say—they say—that it isn't alive? What makes you think it's any different than you?

"And of course no one but TV preachers has the nerve to disagree with them. Which is partly because they're all such loudmouthed good old boys and they all call each other by their first names and nobody wants to be left out of their barbecues.

"But *that's* a digression.

"The thing is—the point of the appendix—that if *their* systems are complex enough to be personified like that, then what about a system that's more complex than anything they can imagine? How about an ecosystem? How about the Carbon Bank Forest?

"So. Of course we're speaking a little bit metaphorically here. When we talk about personality. But it's, I think, a *good* metaphor.

"Careful now or they'll quit reading. The noosphere or, we'll just say, the forest, exhibits all the attributes of a thinking system. It has a capacity to keep records or, in other words, remember the past, and therefore can be said to learn. It's purposive—in the sense that it aims at more than survival—because it seeks to refine itself, to become . . . what's the word? More *perfect*. So there's no reason, with all this parallelism, that we have to think of the growth-field of the forest as just this featureless . . . this sort of empty database . . . like Rupert and those guys describe. The boys.

"We could really keep going with this metaphor; we *ought* to, and allow that the thing must have a . . . a set of, let's say, idiosyncratic attributes, that aren't logical really, but just grew or got organized out of the way history happened. Like, say, the great fires of the nineties. And the nature cults that built serpent mounds on the leys and did their worship rituals and otherwise screwed around with the energies. I mean, the field would record all that. It would respond to that kind of contact or impact in certain ways, and that would form part of its personality. And *especially* it would respond to efforts to—What am I trying to say?"

She strained. Then nodded.

"Right—to *imagine* it. Because that's the whole essence of the thing. Creating forms out of ideas. Taking this idea— say, *round-lobed leaf*—and bringing that into existence by means of morphogenetic creodes and gene libraries and transpositions. And all that.

"Only, I'm not sure I can explain this to someone that's trying to be objective. If they're not willing to do the program and see for themselves. I might end up saying, basically: If you know I'm right, you know I'm right.

"What I'd *like* to say—if this isn't overstepping my appendix—is that the field could just simply not avoid taking on the characteristics that were projected onto it. You'd have this elaborate feedback loop, where stuff would go in—starting with, maybe, *It's an old god with horns*—and the field would remember that, and play it back the next time some awareness came floating by. But the next awareness, if it came out of a different culture or something, would get the story a little garbled, and a modified story would be projected back and the channel would get rerouted, and dug a little deeper. Until finally you'd come to a pretty profound situation where the perceptions of a lot of observers—some of them astute and others less so—would have combined to build up a *very* resonant form. Like a story that's told over and over, or a song passed down around a million campfires, until it gets into something like its truest or closest-to-perfect configuration. Until it's a pretty close reflection of whatever subtle reality or creative impulse gave rise to it.

"Which is where *we* come in. With the field refined to this point, where it's got this personality that's been built up

and refined, so that it's *really close* to the truth of the situation, to reality, even if it *is* only a metaphor. It's—like I
said—a *good* metaphor. So good, we can take it as the closest
thing to truth that we can right now, with our particular kind
of intelligence, our associative brains, ever understand.

"God, you know?—I really believe this. I really think
this is *something*. I mean—" Turning: "What is it, honey?"

She looked away from Lorian. The eavesdropper strained
her ears. This time she could just hear, she thought, the little
footsteps patting down the ladder.

"Hey, slow down," Amy called. "What's the big hurry?
You don't want to fall and—"

"Mommy!" the small voice yelled. Loud, though just
inside the range of the direction-imaging microphones. Getting louder, racing toward the room. "Mommy! Mommy!"

"*Robin,*" the fond mother exclaimed. Her beautiful face
crossed with wonder and slight alarm. What could he be so
excited about, her eyes said.

Lorian stood on tiptoes, staring over a table. It always
happened so fast, she never thought to move to a better
position in the room.

Little Robin—the bright-eyed, impossible, eight-year-
old version of Tamlin—came dashing into the lab.

"*Mommy!*"

"Hey." (Kneeling, holding her arms out, preparing to
catch him.) "What's got *you* running like a rabbit?"

He hit the arms, bounced in them excitedly, was held
there.

God, it's uncanny, Lorian thought. The same eyes; the
same hair. The same boy, it's got to be. (But how can it?)

"It's"—Robin breathlessly announced—"some man!"

Amy's hand just perceptibly tightened around the boy's
arms and an instant later let go.

"There's a man outside!" he reiterated. "I could see him
from my room!"

Amy's facial muscles tensed. She caught his excited gaze
and held it carefully.

"Can you tell me what he looks like, honey? Is he
carrying anything?" She paused, watching his mind work.
Very gently she suggested: "A gun?"

He shook his head solemnly. Children can be *so* serious,

Lorian thought. A thing you didn't notice, if you didn't really look at them. Tamlin—Robin—said, "He's playing *music.*"

"Muse," was as close as she came to repeating it. Then she was standing up. "Show Mommy," she said, taking the boy's hand, "which way the man is."

Lorian thought, this time, she could hear the very faint strains of it. Not music, exactly, but something. Some other-than-normal sound. The harder she strained to hear it the more elusive it became—and then there were footsteps. Robin's bare feet moving across the lab, Amy's following, Groby's approaching up the hall. The irrational thought came to Lorian that the three of them would get stuck trying to squeeze together through the doorway.

"Men," she said aloud, "have the *worst* sense of timing."

"Oh, they do," said Amy. She shook her head and smiled back at the journalist, her spiritual heir, her only friend. The smile was sad and empathetic—but happy, happy, too. Joyful that her long isolation
was reaching
an end.

Thirty-six

"THEY'RE ALL HERE." Groby paused in the door of the lab, stood there moon-faced and uncertain, as though worried he might have interrupted some private interlude or rite. After all, Lorian never bothered *him* in the Bog Garden.

"They've all come back," he said after a moment.

Lorian was confused among other things by the feeling that she had forgotten something of tremendous significance.

"Who?" she said, half in irritation—like, it had better be somebody important. Then she understood whom *they all* could only mean, and stepped between the lab tables excitedly.

"How?" she said. "Where are they?"

Groby relaxed. His hulking bear shoulders came up and he pawed the clay-brown hair from his forehead. "I just saw them," he said, "from the meadow. They'll be landing any minute."

"You just—" Lorian began, but stopped herself short of *then how. . . .* She had been through all that with the Owl. There was no sense starting over again with Groby. She elected instead, as an experiment: "Oh, good. I've missed Vesica"—and found that somehow it worked, that she really could believe that Groby knew, and he would be right, and why had she ever doubted it? She said, "Do I have time to get the camera?"

Groby shook his head.

That quickly, they landed. Their aircraft was sleeker and quieter than any Lorian had encountered. It lowered stilts for itself, coming down to perch like a crane with its gray belly twelve feet or so above the herb beds that Groby had been tidying. Its exhaust stirred up an intense wafture of lavender and thyme, which grew sprawling across the hot sand beneath its ladder. Tattersall came down first, wearing a clean safari jacket and carrying a mug. His swimming-pool-blue eyes were glassy.

"Goodness," he said, peering around the compound, "what a disorienting flight."

"Oh, Tattersall!" exclaimed Lorian, running forward to embrace him, figuring formality could wait. "It's so good to see you! Did everything go all right?"

The Governor patted her back, shook Groby's hand, stretched his arm up the ladder.

"You may remember," he said, "Lady Widdershins."

It was not that great lady, however, who came next, but little Sheldrake.

"Place is a mess," he grumbled. "Those caretakers ought to be fired."

Groby and Lorian exchanged glances. Tattersall indulgently smiled. "Come along, Widdy," he urged from the bottom of the ladder.

The next thing down the ladder looked like a mound of self-propelled luggage. Knapsacks, hat boxes, garment bags: the contents of the airyacht's cargo hold disgorged themselves in a chaotic mass that thumped downward rung by rung. Reaching the ground, it became unbalanced, wobbled a moment, and collapsed on the aromatic herbs. Left standing in the middle of the heap, flushed an unbecoming pink with exertion, was the last person Lorian dreamed of finding there.

"Thrull!" she said, astonished.

The thin youth weakly nodded. "I'll pick it up!" he said hastily, as Groby bent to retrieve someone's expensive-looking bags. "I'll take care of everything. Don't worry."

Groby gave one of his wide, slow-ripening smiles. He

did not look as surprised as Lorian, or as surprised as Lorian would have liked. Stewing over this, she missed the epochal debarkation of the Chairperson of the Hardy Plant Society. Lady Widdershins, safely grounded, spent a few seconds adjusting her hat and her flying-shawl before rapping soundly upon the ladder and declaring:

"Whoever designed this device had no concept of the limitations of the human knee."

Groby bowed. "Your ladyship, welcome to Balance Act."

"And this," said Lord Tattersall, indicating a dark-robed figure that lurked like a shadow within the hatch, "is my old friend Ernest. That is, Professor Tylyester, the Dean of the Secret College. He's writing this paper, you see . . ."

"Where's Gerta?" interrupted Sheldrake, rubbing his stomach, as the Professor descended. "Where's the Owl?"

Lorian brought her eyes into a stern formation that said: Good question. She cast them in Groby's direction. Let *him* explain it.

The big man cleared his throat.

"Oh," he said offhandedly, "they, um . . . went away."

Sheldrake frowned. "What do you mean, 'went away'?"

The big man shrugged.

When it became evident that he was finished, that there was no more, Lord Tattersall said, "But surely . . . that is to say, where could they have gone? Do they plan to return? What did they *say*?"

Groby frowned, as though trying hard to grasp the point behind these difficult questions. After a period of no-speedier-than-usual consideration, he said, "I guess they thought it was time to be going."

"But . . . leaving Balance Act?" His lordship was nonplussed. "How could they . . . I mean to say, it seems a bit surprising—after all the work they've done, their attachment to the place and so forth—that they would just, *leave*. After all, they thought of themselves as caretakers."

That's right, thought Lorian. Keep squeezing him.

Groby thought a while longer, not quite so long this time, and nodded. "That's true," he admitted. "But they may have figured, you know, that Lorian and I would be here, and we could take care of the place. For the time being."

Tattersall looked from one of them to the other. Lorian

gave him a look by which she meant to convey the full measure of her feelings about all this. It either failed to, or Lord Tattersall had feelings of his own.

"Well," he said. "That does make a bit of sense, doesn't it? The two of you seem to be getting on quite well."

And Groby—preempting any of Lorian's objections—said, "Have you brought Tamlin? And Vesica?"

The boy and girl sat side by side at the table. Their knees lightly touched. On the polished wood before them, a handblown vase held a choir of white lilies and a solo red rose. The air carried a gentle, bittersweet melody from speakers across the room. Flute music. A musician, said Groby, had lived here once.

"Or anyway we found a lot of tapes. Some of them have singing on them. Do you remember the song that Gerta . . . oh, I guess you must. Well, that's on one of them, and some others."

The First Biotic Crusade had assembled for dinner after a separation of two months. Lady Widdershins was present, of course, as the representative of the Hardy Plant Society, and Tylyester as the leading authority on Amy Hayata. There was no doubt, however, that the dinner was a reunion of the Crusade, or that Lord Tattersall was in charge of it. He sat at the head of the table, very tall. Candlelight sparkled off his decorations. These had been pinned on his chest by nearly everyone after the Press conceived the idea that he had personally saved the city, if not the world. He objected that the world had not been saved at all; or at least, not until the Crusade was finished. The Press ignored him, as it had always done. It was fitting. He had always ignored the Press. He suffered fame and wealth in silence.

Vesica was extraordinarily proud of him.

She did not, however, show this. Her face revealed only a troubled blankness—like a flat expanse of water, hiding turbulent depths—identical to the expression on Tamlin's. The two of them, despite the regulation dining-table distance between them, seemed to huddle together, guarding voiceless secrets from the others, brooding over questions of identity and fate, ticking off each passing minute—each minute they had left to spend together—with hidden hands.

If their dining companions noticed this uneasiness, this air of apartness the young people shared (and they must have, for the polished table wasn't *that* long), then they chose, in the manner of which only true friends are capable, to take no notice. The reunion went on.

"Thrull," the Governor called, or rather mentioned. The youth was out of the kitchen like a cat.

"Yes, sir?" he panted, wiping his brow, smearing it with tomato sauce.

"We're finished with the soup now."

"Okay. I mean: yes, sir." He began clearing bowls away, stacking them daringly on one arm.

"I think we'll wait a few minutes," said Tattersall, "before the chicken. Just a bit more wine now, if you would."

"Yes, sir," said Thrull, lurching away with the soup bowls. "I'll only be a moment."

He was out the door again.

It was unbelievable.

"He was that way," Tattersall recollected, "when we found him. That was . . . How long ago was that, Sheldrake?"

"Day before yesterday."

"Ah. Quite. We had just flown up from Riverrun, and we had all these *poets* you see, traveling with us—friends of mine, in a way—and they all got a bit tipsy at the Hoar's Bed Inn and made up this rather outlandish scheme to recapture the manor."

"He's talking about his place at Deeping Lube," explained Sheldrake. "See, the last time we were there, there was this Pure Force flag flying from the catwalk, and somebody was shooting a power-cannon at us, and we barely made it to town alive."

Thrull reentered and topped off everyone's glass. He hovered expectantly.

"That will be all," Tattersall told him, "for just now. Why don't you get yourself something to eat?"

"Oh, no," the youth said quickly, as though an alarming suggestion had been made. "I'll wait for you to finish."

Faintly, his lordship smiled.

"Anyway," said Sheldrake, warming up to the story, "things were pretty much the same when we got back. Except the trees were bigger, growing in the streets and so forth. So we sat at the inn talking it over, and a bunch of these poets went out and, um, *found* these dirty old robes somewhere— you know, like the Pure Force always wears? So, they all get dressed up and head right on up the hill toward the manor, marching and carrying signs and all that. You couldn't have told them from the real thing. When all of a sudden, the power-cannon opens up on them. *Whoom.*" (His flat palm hit the table.) "Dirt flying everywhere. It's a good thing whoever was firing was a pretty awful shot, because the closest he came to hitting anything was, he blew up a wagon with some reporters in it. Or they claimed to be reporters, but they didn't have any credentials. Anyway. Lord Tattersall at this point tells the poets to hold still for a minute, he wants to think it over. And what happened next— I mean, you wouldn't believe it."

Tattersall, who was following this account with close attention (as they all were, even Vesica and Tamlin) raised his napkin to his lips and quietly coughed. The Crusaders looked up the table.

"It was purely," he said, "a matter of observation. The poor marksmanship. The choice of targets. The fact that at no time ever had we seen any signs of life there at the manor, other than the gun itself."

"What he did," said Sheldrake, "was, he said: 'You all stay here, I'm going up and put an end to this.' Just like that. And then he *really did.* I mean, he walked right up the hill, all by himself, and the power-cannon just sat there recharging or whatever they do, and when he got to the top he walked right in the front door just like he owned the place . . . I mean . . . and the next thing you know—"

"There was no one there," said Tattersall. "But Thrull. All alone. He was cowering in the master bedroom, where someone had set up a frightful array of electrical equipment. There were raster-screens by which he could aim the gun, and hologhost recorders, and airfax machines, and other things I could not begin to recognize. It was very impressive. Of course the bedroom was rather a mess. As soon as I entered he threw himself down on the floor in front of me, and he said . . . Well, I suppose that's a personal matter, really."

Sheldrake snorted. "The Governor's his idol now, is what it comes down to."

"Really, Sheldrake . . ."

The little man shook his head. "No, that's the truth. See, until now he's done everything Narthex"—a glance at Vesica—"everything he was told to. And you see where it got him. Ditched in Deeping Lube and forgotten, after he had made all these recordings and believed all these promises about him being the one to lead the Pure Force. For *weeks* he was there by himself like that. He didn't dare go out, because he knew the townspeople would kill him. But on the other hand he didn't dare let anybody in. Meanwhile he just sat around in his lordship's bedroom thumbing through all these family records, all these pictures of the Governor and his relatives—right back to the First Earl. I guess he'd never seen anything like them before. You know, people that didn't have any money—"

"*Sheldrake.*"

"Hey," said the little man, palms up, "I'm your accountant. But even so, they had this certain . . . quality about them. So by the time his lordship comes gallivanting up the hill like some kind of crazy white knight, little Thrull has pretty near fallen in love."

The Governor coughed, this time without the napkin. "I don't think," he said, "I would put it quite that way."

Sheldrake smiled nastily. "That's why *I* told it," he said.

Lady Widdershins dreamily nodded. She had put down, even considering the capacity conferred by her body-type, an extraordinary amount of wine. It was the first time she had taken alcohol since . . .

"Yes," she said, "I can believe that. I can quite believe it. There is something about them. Even *I* was not immune."

In what ought probably to be recorded as an act of misplaced gallantry, Tattersall kicked her swiftly under the table.

"It's true," she said, waving like a surrender flag a white-gloved arm. "It was the cause of my, ahem: Indiscretion."

Inasmuch as the fruit of her Indiscretion was sitting two places down the table, one might have thought the less said about this, the better. Vesica turned crimson on Lady Widdershins's behalf.

"Widdy," said Lord Tattersall, "perhaps you shouldn't—"

"*I* shouldn't!" she exclaimed. "I, who have borne this *ghastly* burden of guilt and shame for all these . . . these . . ."

"Fourteen," said Vesica.

"These fourteen years! While you, dear Tatty—and I do mean *dear* Tatty—have carried on in the bliss of ignorance living your life as you pleased. Unchained, as I was, to the yoke of a blackmailer."

The Governor pursed his lips. "Come now, Widdy," he said, glancing worriedly at Vesica, "I'm afraid you got into that yourself."

"I did!" she cried. "But only to protect *you*. I mean, how would it *appear*, for the Governor of All the Northern Territories . . ."

"You could have told me," he said—like a spectator pointing out, after the fact, the losing move in a knecht game. "And I would have married you."

Her ladyship raised a perfumed handkerchief to her nose, seemed on the verge of crying. It amounted only to a single sniff, as in distaste. "Married me," she pronounced antiseptically. "That is *precisely* what I was afraid of. Don't you see? I'm *much* too fond of you for that."

The Governor looked as though he wasn't entirely sure what to make of this. Her ladyship reached over and patted his hand.

"Do you remember," she said, "when you used to call me *Lunaria*? Your little money plant?"

"I remember," he said stiffly, "quite well. I am only thankful that *you* do."

"I have never," she said, smiling in remembrance, "been so insulted in my life. And the idea of getting *married*. Well! I have better things than *that* to occupy my time with."

Here she may possibly have winked across the table at the Governor; by candlelight, it was difficult to tell. Lorian, seeing that everyone else was blurting out whatever they felt like, said:

"So what happens now?"

Lord Tattersall looked at her as though grateful that someone else, anyone else, had spoken. "What happens," he repeated, investing this question with all due gravity. "What happens next, rather depends."

He glanced at Lady Widdershins, at Sheldrake, at Vesica. Very quickly at Tamlin. Back at Lorian again. He said, "Chiefly, it depends on the outcome of the Crusade. You see, we have given some thought—all of us—to occupying the home at Biggar's Neck. If it can be occupied. It is much nicer than Deeping Lube, one must admit, and much more suitable for bringing up a young lady. At the same time it is very much within the bounds of the Northern Territories, so there should be no objection to moving the seat of the governorship. Although Widdy—that is, Lady Widdershins—does not intend to *reside* there, on a permanent basis."

"Two weeks per season," her ladyship declared, with a firmness perhaps intended to effect cursory repairs to her image, "is positively all one could stand. *Not*," she emphasized, "that one does not love the place. But one is so badly needed, really, in the city."

She *did* wink at Tattersall now, Lorian was sure.

"And let us be frank," the great lady added, with a candid lowering of her gaze. "One is much too old to get started at this mothering business, isn't one? And far from sufficiently wholesome."

Vesica wore an expression that implied she didn't *need* mothering, but that was neither here nor there, apparently.

"I think we'll get along," said Lord Tattersall, "quite well. In any case, I have engaged a housekeeper."

"Mrs Blister," Sheldrake explained. "I hired her myself."

"So you see"—Tattersall held his hands out, fingers spread to encompass those present around the table—"everything is contingent. It all depends. Upon whether or not the Crusade is successful. Because if the forest, you see, continues to run amok, there is no sense even contemplating living here in the North. Or the South either, before long. Whereas—"

Groby looked up from where he had been very quietly, in apparent distraction, staring down at the table. He spoke up now in a way that suggested a large, methodical hand reaching out to take the lead of the conversation.

"No problem," he said.

Lorian nodded, as though she had been expecting this moment to come. "Listen to this," she said acerbically. "He thinks he's figured out what's the matter with the trees."

"Well, I guess so," said Groby. "It wasn't hard, really,

once the Owl showed me. . . . Of course, solving the problem—that's going to be a little different. But it shouldn't take long."

An air of expectancy, thought Vesica. That's what there was around the table. A kind of feeling that they all had together—even Tamlin now, showing some interest—as they waited for Groby to go on.

He looked around at them, his face round and flat and puzzled. "I've, um, prepared a report," he said slowly, as though unsure what they were waiting to hear. "But it's pretty complicated. I mean, it's simple really, but it's sort of long."

He paused. "Do you want to hear it?"

Yes, nodded everyone at the table, but—

"No," said Lord Tattersall. "That can wait until tomorrow.
                    Oh, Thrull—I believe
                         we are ready
                          to dine."

Thirty-seven

THE NORTH STAR barely penetrated the thin blue membrane of the sky when Tamlin and Vesica emerged from the loft that had once, long ago, been an eight-year-old's bedroom.

"Be *real* quiet through here," Tamlin whispered. "The beams creak and you can hear from down in the guest rooms." After five hundred years, they still did.

The boy and girl crept like ordinary teenagers sneaking away from home; not conspirators, carrying out their plot; not wood-sprites, returning before daybreak to the sanctuary of the forest. The machinery of the dome whispered behind them. Docile from wine and relief at being back again, safe at Balance Act, the Crusaders slept.

Tamlin led the way on long, spry legs. His strength and agility had returned. His patchwork pants and shirt—a gift of greater value than Vesica had known, stitched together from her very own baby clothes—were worn into conformity with the habitual bends and rhythms of the boy's body. Her handiwork didn't look so slipshod anymore. Time had put its gloss on things, made the strange juxtapositions snug. Vesica wondered if this morning would be the end of all that; if time, for her and Tamlin, would stop.

The northern air was so thick with life you almost had to

hold still to breathe it. During the night it had gained a special delicacy or sweetness, as though the stars were filling it with fragrant emanations that the scorch of sunlight, even the dispassionate glare of the Moon, would reduce to so many photons, then disperse. But the night was moonless. The firmament twirled between one cycle and the next, and many things were uncertain. In Riverrun, a precession of astrologers assembled near the poisoned wreck of the Observatory, straining for a whiff of the new day. In the blue mountains of the North, where everything had its beginnings, eagles patrolled the frontiers of the world, protecting it from the icy mysteries beyond.

The North Star did not seem far away, in that immanent moment; it hung at the very center of things, with both worlds—matter and numina, the heavens and the earth—spiraling around it. Like the calm center of a maelstrom, it did not move at all.

Tamlin and Vesica hurried through the compound, excitement growing inside them as the sky got bluer and the night air fell still at the approach of dawn. The herbs and flowers and carefully chosen trees inside the four-acre earthbound ark looked perfect and immortal. It might have been any year, any century, future or past. And that was the point of Balance Act, after all. To keep things just as they were. While humanity caught up, came to terms with them.

The limbs of the thrice-coppiced oaks stretched upward, like the arms of prisoners begging to be allowed to die. In their heavy shadows the boy turned; his face loomed up big and white before the girl behind him. She stopped.

"It's kind of a long walk," he said. "Should we take anything to eat?"

She remembered going hungry, the night she crept away from camp; the night she found Wild Turkey Pool all by herself, before she knew anything about the ghost-boy or the dragon path or the Silence. She remembered feeling light, clear-headed, barely material.

"That's okay," she said. "We're already gone now."

"The Report," recited Lord Tattersall, "of the Findings of the first Biotic Crusade, Together with a Recommendation for Future Action. If Any. Will we be able to edit this later on?"

"No problem," said Groby. His sausage-sized fingers manipulated the workings of the hologhost machine. It had been rewired in such a manner as to PLAY and RECORD at once. The electronic aspects of this were less challenging than the philosophical. It had taken half an hour, on this sluggish sun-bright morning, for Tattersall to grasp the idea of recording a recording; holding a mirror up to the distant mirror of the past.

"Very well," said the Governor. He glanced around the lab at the Crusaders. Their numbers were augmented by Lady Widdershins and Professor Tylyester, and diminished by the absence of Tamlin and Vesica, whom no one could find.

("Let them alone," Tattersall had commanded, when Sheldrake proposed a search for the missing youngsters. "They'll be all right."

While he may not have understood *everything*, he was fairly solid on the important points, and at any rate was still the Leader.)

"We will begin," he said, "with Lorian, who will inform us briefly of who Amy Hayata was and what she was doing here at Balance Act. We can call this part, Background. What do you think, Sheldrake?"

"It'll never sell," the little man muttered, "with a title like that."

"Start the hologhost," Lorian told Groby, then turned to face the rest of the Crusade. "The disk we're showing," she explained, "was the one left in the recorder when everything . . . stopped."

"Oh?" said Tattersall. "Did you find it in the machine?"

"No," said Groby, his finger poised over the PLAY button. "We didn't find it until the Owl showed me, um . . ." His ponderous mind made a new connection. "I guess somebody must have taken it out, for safekeeping."

"I wonder who?" said Lord Tattersall.

Groby frowned. One would have thought this question would have occurred to him already. Evidently not. Nor did it seem to matter, now that it had. He gave them his well-known shrug.

"Maybe the Owl, or somebody like that."

Somebody like the Owl?

Groby went on: "See, there have been people living

here, off and on. Or I don't know, maybe *on* and on. Kind of a tradition. Like the way a story—"

"But this *disk*," said Lorian, reclaiming the floor, "was the last one Amy—Doctor Hayata—made before whatever happened to her, happened. And it's pretty interesting. Her final thoughts and so forth. Of course, she didn't know they were final. But they *were*, is the point. Go ahead, Groby."

The sausage-sized finger pressed down. There was an electric sizzle; then a phantom laboratory sprang into existence beside the one generally regarded as real. Except for its pale-green prisoners, the projection was empty.

"Where is she?" whispered Professor Tylyester. One could sense his excitement at being about to meet, as it were, the object of his lifelong work.

Groby pushed another button and the hologhost began to flicker, fast-forwarding. "The machine was on a timing device. I guess so Amy didn't have to worry about forgetting it and missing something—"

Tylyester's expression, which grew suddenly reverential, shushed him. Amy Hayata had entered the lab. She strolled in her usual (wistful, pensive, dream-slow) way down the aisles, unmindful of her audience. It was, for her, somewhat later in the day. Maybe an hour before lunch. Soon she would be heating up a bowl of meatless stew.

"Good morning," she said.

"Who's she talking to?" Tylyester whispered worriedly.

"Sometimes," said Groby, "you get the feeling she's a little self-conscious in front of the recorder. Like she has to break the ice."

"*Shh.*"

". . . to be gained," Amy was saying, bending over a table, "or how much, I should say . . . by inducing further transpositions this summer. Although I'd like to step up production of Bowman-Birk inhibitors before the gypsy moths show up. And I'd like to turn *down* ethylene production in the leaves. There's already more of that blowing in than they can handle. Actually there're a million things I'd *like* to do. But I just—"

She froze; her image was streaked with interference. Groby's finger squashed the PAUSE button.

"I forgot to tell you," said Lorian. "Don't worry too much

about the technical parts. I mean, we can look them up if
you want, for the final report."

Tylyester cleared his throat. "It's not *that* technical, really. She is speaking here of relatively simple mechanisms
that plants employ, some plants, to preserve their internal
balance."

Lorian nodded. "Yeah, well. Let's hear a little bit more."

Groby pressed a button.

"—don't know," Amy finished. From the speakers came
sounds like footsteps and a distant, muffled clatter. Amy
looked up. She waited for half a minute, but the sounds did
not repeat.

"What was *that?*" said Lady Widdershins—rendered jittery by a hangover this morning.

"The trouble is," Amy went on, oblivious, "we can *do* all
these things, but we can't make the *trees* do them. Spontaneously, I mean. So ultimately it's no good. It's a problem of
volition, really—of will or choice or something. A forest
meets all the criteria for cognitive systems but that."

She sighed, and the Crusaders, sensing the depth of her
weariness, drew up on their stools and stretched their backs.

"Well," said Amy, "I suppose there's nothing we can do
about it. Evolution is either going to save them or it's not.
All the big jumps are preceded by some major challenge to
survival, so here it is. *Quercus robinia* or bust."

She turned away from her audience and retreated down
the illusory aisle.

PAUSE.

"I guess," said Lorian, "this would be a good time to say
a few things about Amy's work. To begin with, the forest
was different back then."

Professor Tylyester said, "What is this *Quercus robinia* she
talks about? An extinct species? She doesn't mention it in her
paper."

"A nonexistent one. At least, at that time. See, Amy was
trying—"

"Just tell him," suggested Groby, "it means Robin's oak."

"Oh, yeah." Lorian nodded. "That's right. She planned
to name the new species after Robin."

"And who," began Tylyester, but Lorian shook her head.

"You've got to see it to believe it. Take my word.

"Doctor Hayata," she said more formally, "lived at a time when the forest wasn't doing so well. Not like today. And her job, what she was doing here at Balance Act, was trying to figure out a way to make the forest able to overcome these various problems it had—heat and poison rain and so forth—and start to grow again. She decided to concentrate on one particular species, white oak—I think because it's a pretty grand-looking tree when it's healthy, but it was being hit pretty hard by the changes in the air. So she figured—I'm just guessing here—that if she could solve the problem for white oaks, the other species would be easier."

"She was trying, then," said Lady Widdershins, "to Improve the Line."

The term was new to Lorian. "I guess," she said, "at first. But at some point she decided the solution would have to be more . . . far reaching. By *this* time"—indicating the blurry image in the lab—"she was trying to create a brand-new kind of tree with a different strategy for survival. Let me read you something."

From a stack of papers she produced Amy's old notebook. "It's a quotation from someone she admired, called McClintock. 'There is little doubt'—I'm reading now—'that genomes of some if not all organisms are fragile and that drastic changes may occur at rapid rates. These can lead to new genomic organizations and modified controls of gene expression. Since the types of genome restructuring induced by such elements know few limits, their extensive release, followed by stabilization, could give rise to new species or even new genera.' " Lorian lowered the notebook. "She underlined the last part, and next to it she wrote Q. *robinia* with a couple of exclamation marks."

"If I may just interrupt," said the professor. "To put this in some sort of context. In Amy's day, you see, this sort of thinking was rather radical. It was generally considered that the genes one inherited—whether one was a scientist or an aardvark or a tree—these genes constituted a sort of script which one must follow, a role one was foreordained to play, with very slight allowance for improvisation as one went along. And what Hayata suggests—not just here, you see, but throughout the body of her work—is that the genetic script is not so rigid as that. She believed that the story told by the genes—and I am using her own imagery here—that this story is of a very special type, a story which is about many things *including itself*, and that the principal character of the story—which is to say, the organism itself—is free to a greater or lesser extent, according to its capabilities, to re-structure its role, rewrite the story, *from within*. You must see how that put her at odds with many of her colleagues."

Lorian listened to all of this impatiently. She turned to Tattersall, who was supposed to be in charge here, in a silent appeal for recognition.

The Governor, taking due note, tapped lightly on a lab table. "I think," he said carefully, "we can all appreciate that. Appreciate the originality of Doctor Hayata's work, that is to say. But what, in the event, went wrong? What has happened to the forest? *That's* what we need for our report."

"I should think," Lady Widdershins sniffed, "that we *know* well enough what *happened*. This endangered forest you all are speaking of, as though it were some pitiful child, has altogether *ravaged* our beautiful countryside. Just look at Biggar's Neck—if you can bear to. Your poor defenseless forest has simply *ruined* it, as it threatens to ruin everything else."

Lorian was prepared to take umbrage, on Amy's behalf, at the great lady's accusatory tone, but Groby spoke first and more calmly.

"That's not quite true," he said, in a shy and self-effacing way, as though whatever was untrue about it was probably his own fault. "The forest hasn't overgrown everything. At least, not yet. And ruining things isn't *all* it's doing."

"You will have difficulty," her ladyship sniffed, "convincing me of that."

Groby diffidently smiled. "Well," he said, as though this were a poor and ignorant suggestion, but the best he had to offer, "there's the compound here. It's hardly changed at all. Nor has the countryside around it. Despite five centuries having passed. And to me, that's at least as amazing as anything else.

"Besides that," he said, quickly enough to spare Lady Widdershins the stickiness of backing down, "there are things that the forest seems to be—sort of the opposite of destroy-ing them—actually *preserving*. Keeping alive, you could say, past their time. Just a little thing here and a little thing there. Orchids, for example. And old oaks. Even certain smells."

"Dittany-of-Crete," said Lorian (on cue; giving rise to a general suspicion that they had rehearsed this. Though they had not).

"*You* know," Groby continued: "things that don't make much sense by themselves, but maybe are part of some pattern."

"Are we straying," fretted Lord Tattersall, glancing at the recorder, "from our topic?"

"Oh, no," said Lorian. "We're finally getting back to it."

Groby fussed with the hologhost controls. "Let me see," he said, "if I can find the place . . ."

The hologhost flickered. Amy's form raced comically up the aisles and down; her voice chirped like a cricket, then dropped abruptly several octaves to its normal register. Her image slowed.

". . . wonder," she was saying, "is how much of what I'm sending out there is getting through. All these years of it, and nothing."

Groby PAUSED it. Lorian said:

"That's the thing right there. This *sending out*, and *getting through* . . . What she was doing was, like, jumping over these tiny little biological and chemical things that the Professor knows all about, that control the way the forest grows, and going right to the source. Right to—"

"The root," suggested Sheldrake.

"That's okay," said Lorian, unwilling to be interrupted again, much less amused, "as a way of speaking, but it's not exact. The thing Amy was going after was, like, the essence of the tree itself, its, um . . . 'organizing principle' was the phrase she used—the thing that makes it a tree, that gives it its identity. Because what she decided was, it isn't good enough to teach the tree how to, for instance, thicken its leaves. You've got to make the *tree* decide to thicken its leaves. Which means, in a way, that you've got to change not just the tree's little chemical processes and whatnot—but more like, its *attitude*. 'Inserting a new hierarchical loop in its self-description' was how she put it. I know it sounds kind of funny . . ."

"It sounds," said Lady Widdershins, "distinctly less than funny."

". . . but Amy talks about—this is later—she talks about how it's just a metaphor but a *good* metaphor. But you'll hear all that. Anyway, at the time she made this disk her work was going pretty well—very well, I guess—but she was getting more and more frustrated because she couldn't really, like she says, *get through*. She just couldn't figure out how to go from making the trees learn to do this and learn to do that, to making them learn how to *learn*. She could give them these defenses, these various biological weapons, but she couldn't make them really want to get out there and fight. Do you see what I mean?"

"Yes," said Tylyester.

"*No*," said Lady Widdershins.

"I wonder," said Lord Tattersall, "just for purposes of clarity, if it would be better if *Amy* could explain these things, herself."

Lorian looked helplessly at Groby, out of words. The big man shook his head. The July sun was well up in the sky, and perspiration had begun to trickle down his temples.

"She doesn't," he acknowledged, "just come right out and say it. But you have to figure, she wasn't talking to you and me. She didn't know—she couldn't, could she?—that we would ever be here, or what we would be like, or the things we would want to find out."

Lorian sadly nodded. "And we can't tell her."

"So what's the point?" said Sheldrake, glancing at his watch. "Did she ever get through to the damned forest, or didn't she?"

"Of course she did," said Lorian, as though surprised that anyone should ask.

Groby nodded, his thick brown hair lying in a heap on his forehead. "She got through, all right. Or I should say, *someone* did. The forest was gotten through to. There's no doubt about that."

"What do you mean," said Lady Widdershins, "*someone* did? If you mean someone besides this Hayata woman, then what are we bothering with *her* for?"

"Well . . ." Groby's finger massaged the PLAY button. "The problem is, we really don't know what happened here at Balance Act, do we? In the end. We can make some good guesses, but . . . On the other hand, we *do* know what's happened since. We know how the forest has been behaving."

"Like a little pissant," said Sheldrake.

Groby nodded. "I think that's putting it pretty well."

"It is?" The short man looked disappointed.

"Sure," said Groby. "Energetic, destructive—but destructive, you might say, in a creative way. And angry. Going after farms and villages and all. But at the same time, not *just* angry. In some ways it's protective—almost gentle. If you were to generalize the thing, you could say it acts pretty upset, but also sort of mixed-up."

Turning away, Groby rambled down the aisle toward where the shivery vision of Amy Hayata stood imprisoned in the past. He poked a finger into her insubstantial form.

"If *she*," he said, "had gotten through to the forest, in the sense that we're talking about, it's hard to believe the forest would be acting like this."

Lorian shook her head.

"No," said Groby. "But someone . . . Something got through to the forest, especially the oaks, and ever since . . ."

"Especially," said Lorian, "these last few months."

"Right. Especially then. It's been, what would you say? Having a tantrum?"

Tattersall frowned. He had not had occasion to learn very much about tantrums.

"Acting," Groby elaborated, "like some kind of kid."

"But whatever it's doing," said Lorian, keeping the record straight, "it isn't because Amy told it to."

Groby said, "That's right. Amy wouldn't have taught anyone to act like this. What I meant was, a kid that's out of control, that's, um, alienated and rebellious and so forth. Like a teenager, say, that something bad has been done to."

"You're getting at something," Sheldrake deduced. He turned to the Governor. "They're getting at something, but they won't spell it out."

Groby rumbled up the aisle. He showed, for the first time since anyone had known him, a hint of impatience. He said, "It's not so easy to spell out. There's so much we can never know. Things that we can only try to get close to, the way Amy had to get close to the truth by talking in metaphors.

"But you're right: we're getting at something." The sausage-sized finger came down. "Let's watch the rest of the disk. There's someone here you might recognize."

The two children climbed the black rocks along the hillside, guided as much by the faint tingling of the dragon path through their toes as by the faint gurgling of the waterfall. The sun was hot on their shoulders, and the hours of walking had left them thirsty and tired.

"It's funny," said Vesica. "It seems so different now."

"No," said Tamlin, a step ahead of her, shaking his head. "It's the same."

She supposed it was. Only she had changed, become a different person and yet, like Tamlin, remained herself. The different person that she was looked down on things—at Tamlin, at Wild Turkey Pool, at herself—from somewhere above. Yet the person that was still Vesica remained a part of it all, as fully engaged as ever. Her feet moved over the rocks with an easy intimacy. The sultry air moved in and out of her lungs as though the distinction between inside and out were insignificant. She walked beside Tamlin as if the two of them had always been together.

At the same time, she was afraid: of him, for him, of her growing knowledge of what he was. His hair hung down onto his patchwork shirt, long and sun-lightened like that of any fourteen-year-old boy, though Tamlin was not a normal boy and he was not fourteen years old. He was an illusion, she knew; but a *good* illusion. So good, she could not entirely abandon it. Real and make-believe, at once.

At the top of the hill a cleft in the rim of black rock admitted them to the circular pool of almost-motionless water. Their reflections, inches apart on its surface, shivered slightly, as if from excitement. Seeing her face there next to Tamlin's made Vesica realize she *was* excited; the excitement had been growing inside her all morning, but keeping still like the North Star in the sky. Now the sky was as blue and bright as Tamlin's eyes, and the excitement began to ascend her spine, causing her chest to tighten and her neck to glisten with sweat. She turned her head from the reflection and moved away.

"Here's where I put the orchid," she said. "That's where you were standing, when I first saw you."

Naked, she thought. White as a ghost.

Tamlin stepped around the pool, the other way. Black walls rose beside them. The sound of splashing water came from everywhere, though the small cataract that it came from was plainly visible against the western face.

"My mother," said Tamlin, "said the water comes all the way down from the mountains. That's why it's so cold, I guess. All that ice and snow. But somehow it gets underneath the ground, and stays underneath all the way to *there*, and then it comes out and starts the stream that goes down past the compound."

Vesica was a quarter-way around the pool now. She said, "Farther than that."

Tamlin faced her quizzically. She could see both him and his reflection: those long legs, shivering in the water. She said, "Farther than the compound, I mean. It connects up with other streams and goes all the way down to Deeping Lube, and then it turns into a river and goes—"

Tamlin shook his head. "It dries up," he said. "The trees are drinking it."

This seemed to please him. "Oh," said Vesica.

He told her, "I used to water my mother's orchids."

"Your mother," said Vesica steadily, "was Amy Hayata."

Tamlin looked down; his reflection looked up. For a moment, just a moment, he was a little boy again; one could imagine him coming here on summer mornings when the world was different, when there was time to swim and play and mark your height on boulders and smell the herbs on the porch outside the kitchen door. He must have seen this himself, in his reflection, for he looked up abruptly, at Vesica across the pool, and his eyes were older now.

"I've tried to remember that," he said. "But it comes in pieces. I've got little parts of it, like pictures you remember from a book—the kind that pop up?—but you forget the story." He took more steps, circling around toward the waterfall. "I know you're right, though. It's the only thing that makes sense."

Makes sense? thought Vesica. Well, it did and it didn't. It was true, and a fairy-tale.

Yes and no.

"God, it's hot," she said.

"I know."

"And my legs are all scratched." She sat on the warm rock beside the water, pulling up her jeans to inspect her shins.

"If you'd just followed me," said Tamlin, "like I told you to, it wouldn't have happened."

"Oh, yeah?" said Vesica. "Look at *you*."

Streaks of dirt and blood ran from his ankles to his knees. He had reached a place where the lip of the pool narrowed to an eight-inch downslope of damp rock. He pressed one hand against the wall: helpful in keeping his balance, possibly, but useless in preventing a slide into the water.

Vesica said, "I bet you're going to fall."

"No way." He took another step, now rapt with concentration. "I used to do this *all the time*. I remember."

Vesica smiled at him. The laborers' sons at Gravetye Farm had acted this way, showing off in front of her, and this bit of normalcy in the midst of so much strangeness reassured her; as though whatever weird things had happened to the world, it was still the world, still the place you ate and slept and laughed in. (Or was it?

Yes and no.)

"Look," she said. "Your feet are slipping."

They were, and Tamlin struggled—successfully, so far—to keep them on the rock. As one foot slid down toward the pool, he shifted his weight to the other, sidling a few inches farther along the rim. Both hands were now flat against the cliff-face, keeping his center of gravity as far in as possible.

"If you think this is so easy," he said through gritted teeth, "you try it."

Vesica grinned, enjoying her role as onlooker. "I didn't say it was easy. I'm just saying you can't do it."

He took a step. As he did, the foot still planted made a rapid slide for the water. One arm came free, throwing his weight sideways; he got the second foot down, wobbled, flexed his knees. (So much in command of his body now, Vesica observed. Not like at Riverrun.) And just when the danger was past—when he was firmly planted on the rock, and only another couple of feet away from the hollow behind the waterfall—something small and shiny came loose from the drawcord at his waist and entered the pool with a splash.

"Oh, *no!*" cried Tamlin.

From the sound of his voice, almost a shriek, Vesica knew it had been the double flute. Out of the water and in again. Somehow it figured.

"It's so *deep* here," the boy panted, staring into the dark water where the flute had disappeared.

His eyes came up to Vesica's, and the same thought crossed both minds in the same instant.

They dove with equal gracelessness: Vesica from a crouch, unwilling to take the time to stand up all the way; Tamlin from his slip-sliding position on the rim. The water was clear and unbelievably cold. Through it, they swam up white and fish-eyed to stare at each other, waving their hands crazily, then they went under.

They spiraled, corkscrewing down. The sun made wavy shafts of yellow-green that fell on the bottom and made it look close, deceptively close, and glinted off the tiny, tiny flute that nestled there. Vesica felt her hand grabbed and her body drawn toward Tamlin's. The boy was shaking his head. He pointed at the bottom, thrusting with his finger in stages: *down down down*, the gesture said. *Too far.* Reluctantly Vesica nodded.

They surfaced with a great splash that broke the shimmering mirror of the pool.

"I can't believe it!" moaned Tamlin, devouring air. "I can't believe I dropped it!"

Vesica nodded. They shared two hands and flapped at the water with the others. "It's all right," she said between breaths. "It's only . . . anyway, we know where it is."

"A lot of good—" he began, then slipped beneath the water. Not a very good swimmer, anymore. He came up sputtering. "Let's try it again."

"No," said Vesica. "Let's get out a minute, and think this over."

They pulled themselves onto the sun-warm rocks. For a minute they just sat there, shaking off the chill.

"I want the flute back," he said.

"I know, I know." She turned to look at him, at the

patchwork clothing plastered to his skin, then up the steep black walls. She said, "Maybe if we dove from up there, we could get deep enough."

Tamlin nodded, following her gaze. He stood up and chose a point to start climbing, but Vesica stopped him.

"Just a minute," she said. "If we're going to do this, we might as well do it right."

He frowned.

She stood before him. The excitement that had been rising up her spine reached her larynx, and she couldn't open her mouth to explain. She made an outward motion with her hands—as though setting him aside for a moment, pushing him away—then brought them to her neck and began unbuttoning her blouse.

Tamlin's eyes opened, too startled for the moment to turn away.

She got halfway down, just where her breasts would start to show, and figured out how to talk again. It was like breathing, only you had to take a gulp first.

"I don't know about you," she said, "but *I* can't swim with my clothes on. You don't . . . you can just wait here if you want to."

Great things, great energies, hung in the air. Tamlin's eyes flickered down and then up; he nodded.

"Okay," he said. Meaning: no big deal. He slipped the patchwork shirt off in a smooth, convincingly offhand motion.

So that was how they would play it: like just friends, like children a lot younger than they were. Like brother and sister. Vesica finished unbuttoning her blouse and let it slip to the rocks. Tamlin was waiting, letting her catch up. She unfastened her jeans; he took off his patchwork pants; she slid out of her underwear. The air touched them all over like a warm smooth cloth whose fibers were pure electricity.

The way they were playing it, each of them had to both look and not-look at the other's body. Otherwise, if they had ignored each other, it would have been like it mattered, which it couldn't, whereas if they had just stared openly it would have mattered a lot. So looking and not-looking, they helped each other up the rocky wall. Tamlin first. It was awkward but it was funny too. His back to her, his small furry sac hung between his thighs at Vesica's eye-level, and

she could only think that this was very gallant of him because their positions could have been reversed.

They reached the top. The forest sprawled hot and lazy
around them, seeming, in comparison to the way Vesica felt,
only half-awake, even half-alive.

"Okay," said Tamlin. His eyes shone at hers with special
brilliance, and hers shone back. They both breathed deeply,
and somewhere behind their uncertainty and embarrassment
were tremendous, ready-to-burst smiles. Because whatever
this was that they were doing here together, it was certainly
an adventure. He said, "Where do you think it is?"

Meaning the flute. She frowned. This was something
concrete to think about—and easy, too, for it required so
little of the vast new space that had opened inside her brain.
She pointed. He nodded.

He dove.

: slipping into the water: the water parting to admit him:
waves spreading in concentric rings from the point where the
boy's slender form had vanished: splashing against the rim:
droplets dotting the rocks where the fallen clothes lay: Vesica's toes hugging the warm black stone and her knees
trembling, not just themselves, but as part of the same
energetic circuit that began with Tamlin slipping into the
water, and ended with his face appearing, mouth open,
above it again.

"Did you get it?" she called down. Meaning the flute.

The head shook. White limbs, shortened by refraction,
treaded water beneath it.

"Get out of the way, then," said Vesica. "And let me
try."

Her own dive was less tidy than his, from lack of
experience. She entered the pool with the feeling that she
was taking a great piece of the sky down with her. Bubbles,
foam, blue-green water as clear as air were swirling before
her eyes as her legs kicked violently behind, driving her
lower. Once she was past the roiling surface, into the calm,
she saw the unmoving bottom as clearly as if it were *right
there*, touching-close, and the tiny silver flute twinkling at its
center like a star. It was just as so many things in her life had
been: beautiful, longed-for, unreachable. And for once in her
life the thought did not dishearten her. She turned back,

guarding her breath and the time that remained to her, and let irresistible forces take her back to the sunny world where she belonged.

Tamlin sat on the rocks, bare- and cross-legged, watching her swim to join him. She did so unhurriedly, resting from the dive. The water caressed her long, tan body. *Her* body, she thought. Not the alien, self-willed thing that had bathed in the manor at Biggar's Neck, with the squirrel watching. This one was part of her; she was living inside it; the two of them together crossed the pool and held a hand out to the boy beside the water.

The boy lifted her out. She sat wearily beside him.

"Well, I guess it doesn't matter," he said. "I mean, we tried to get it."

"Sure," said Vesica. They were staring at each other's eyes, not worrying about the rest, not worrying about anything. Their limbs were covered with goose-bumps, but they had left the chill somewhere behind. She said, "I mean, anyway, I took it out of the water in the first place, and now it's back again. Maybe it belongs there."

Tamlin nodded. The sun was bright on his hair, his slightly freckled face, his widening shoulders.

She took his hand from where it rested on one bare knee, raised it to her lips, and kissed it. A smile quivered across his face: uncertainty, gratitude, affection. She studied the hand more carefully; ran her fingers down his, around the large knuckles, over the back where the ant caravan began. She thought of how large and intricate a thing a boy was—all these limbs and joints and muscles, these places covered with hair or not, the ways he reacted when you touched them. Tamlin's breathing had deepened. She felt a surge of delight that matched his—matched the delight she felt in him—and thought how wonderful it was to be here with him, with all of him, with all the time in the world to plumb his boyish mysteries.

They maneuvered into a new position, facing each other. She raised a leg to let one of his slide beneath it, and ended up something like sitting on his lap. Only not that. Laps disappear when you stand up, as everyone knows, and now Vesica discovered that they disappear, too, when you take your clothes off. Where Tamlin's lap used to be was only an empty space framed by firm-muscled thighs that angled outward at forty-five degrees. Their insides were dusted with soft hairs that grew thicker as they approached the great enigma at their vertex. Vesica looked at the boy's face and found that it had reddened. His eyes fell—to her breasts, then to the place where her own lap would have been.

"Hey," she said.

He looked up. Hot-breathed, he murmured, "You're beautiful."

"So are you," she told him, matter-of-factly. Because he was, but that wasn't what right now concerned her. "But hey," she said, pointing, "what, um . . . I mean, is everything all right? Am I, like, too heavy on you or anything?"

Something had happened to Tamlin; something had changed. Not just *that*, not one thing, but everything at once. His large hands moved uncertainly around her, first touching, then grabbing her behind the shoulders, drawing her farther up the platform of his thighs. She wiggled a little, making it easier, and was surprised by how light and smooth and . . . and *exposed* her body felt.

They were playing it differently now. Not little kids anymore; not just friends; and *for sure* not brother and sister. Now it was like something she didn't know about: something that made her tremble. It wasn't fear—though there was a little of that. There was a little of a lot of things. She took one of his hands and brought it to her breast, pressed it down there, and laid her head back to think about the odd, rich, wonderful feeling that caused.

Tamlin made a noise, a sort of little groaning. She opened her eyes, worried that she was hurting him, and found his face right in front of hers. So of course she kissed him. And even that was different. More eager, like. His hand was still on her breast, squeezing, and his other arm was behind her, and because the kiss seemed urgently to require it she slid the rest of the way up his imaginary lap and pressed herself against his tautly muscled abdomen. At the same time she opened her mouth.

You never really thought about skin until something like this happened. There was skin *everywhere*, though. Inside of you and out. Tamlin's tongue explored the skin inside her lips, inside her cheeks; his chest expanded hotly against her small tingling nipples, hard as acorns but a lot different from when you go from a hot bath to a cold bedroom; his hands moved down her back and under her soft buttocks, cupping them, making them feel small and warm like a little girl's. He touched her everywhere, and everywhere he wasn't touching her right then she wanted him to. As though her skin, this new skin she had discovered, had started itching, all of it, inside and out. So she stretched her legs apart and curled them around him, pressing her whole body into his as tightly as she could, thinking in a vague and breathless way that this might help.

She looked down. She had trapped something in the mossy space at the crux of her legs—something she had studied before in the black-porticoed townhouse. It had looked big to her then, but that was nothing. Now it was long and flat and mushroom-capped, and looked decidedly dangerous. Tamlin rocked his narrow hips, rubbing it against her, and that must have been unbearable to him in the way that the inside-out itching was to Vesica, because he closed his eyes and groaned and pulled her closer.

"Does it hurt?" she asked him, not intending to sound coy but sounding that way.

Of course it didn't hurt. He didn't bother to answer. He moved his hand down into the very small space between their sweat-slick bodies, shoving the fat obstruction aside and twisting down further until he had wedged his hand into her damp velvet V.

She drew a rapid breath in. For an instant she felt something that was nearly panic. Only for an instant. For Tamlin, in his much-more-than-fourteen-year-old wisdom, had discovered, amid the whole expanse of her newly discovered body, that source of unease which most urgently, desperately, agonizingly required attention.

Quickly she brought her hands down to touch, to squeeze, to surround the single horn of her half-demon lover. While the half of him that was just a normal teenage boy stared back as amazed and thrilled and terrified as Vesica herself, and breathing harder.

And then.

Still clutching him, she raised herself a few inches onto her knees, then another few inches—high enough to straddle the large instrument for which the double flute had been lost—and then she pressed herself down on him.

Pressed Tamlin inside of her.

Pressed the most enticing, intimate, secret part of the boy deep and deeper and so deeply that it hurt, that she cried out but kept squeezing him and pressing him up and up, into her body.

The sun that shone on the naked children was a feeble thing beside the white electric fire that entered Vesica when Tamlin did; that streaked up through regions she hadn't known existed; that pierced all the barriers of what had been a smart and determined and plucky and, above all, *rational* young mind. Until there was nothing left of all that—nothing of rationality at all in that blinding thrust of pure sensation, pure awareness, pure *being alive* that swelled through Vesica's body and exploded like a power-cannon in her mind. And as the light of that explosion filled her cranium, as her reason fled through her ears and eyes and nostrils, the pure conscious light that remained looked out at Tamlin—

down, a few inches, at the boy that Tamlin had been, or that had been Tamlin—

finding there a reflection of itself, a soul stripped bare of sensibility. But not a perfect reflection. No:

For somewhere beyond that glowing moment, in dimensions less exalted, the girl was still there. Somewhere, she was still Vesica.

But the boy

was

(*Oh,* she cried)

not a boy but an ancient spirit

(*Tamlin*)

possessing her, filling her body

(*what's wrong*)

writhing through her mind in a dozen shapes, a hundred kinds of being

(*what's happening to you*)

grunting with violent, feral passion that tore the illusion of a fourteen-year-old boy apart like shreds of clothing

"Stop!" cried Vesica

glittering before her eyes like the shards of a broken

mirror: sun-gilded hair blue eyes white skin pale freckles firm just-widening chest bold virilia soft leg hairs muscled thighs: shattering:

and falling into a great five-hundred-year-deep emptiness: and the final part the mouth the flesh-pink lips open wide and: inaudibly shouting:

and Vesica's mouth finding it, covering it, silencing that cry
while her arms swept out
pushing the naked boy
into the water.

Thirty-eight

THE FOREST shuddered and became still.

Its boundaries stabilized.

Its five-hundred-year expansion ended in a moment. Less than a moment.

Unprecedented changes had occurred within its genome: a series of transpositions, recombining old patterns, old chromosomal threads, old story-lines, into startling new alignments. Now that was over.

The frantic, bright, disorderly moment of creation—of building new forms, new species, new realities—had passed. A plodding era of evolution would replace it.

The godlike work of the scientist, the magician, the artist, was done. The imaginary was transformed into the real; the word made matter; the idea given form. Now the engineer could settle down to tending it.

In Balance Act, the oaks that grew from thrice-coppiced stumps began to die. The power that had maintained them (and kept orchids alive in the treetops, fluids moving through the vascular tissue of the cedar wall, caretakers tending the grounds of the research station) was gone from the forest. It had been an odd sort of power, strident and chimerical, never entirely at home there. Now it had vanished, slipping through the trees with the stealth of a wandering *trouvère* (who hadn't meant to be around so long anyway, hadn't known what he was getting into) sneaking back to the roadway, his lifelong home, before dawn.

The forest remained. It was very old. The five-hundred-year stay of the visitor had been a short while by its standards—barely long enough to see it pass from childhood to adolescence. But such periods, however brief, can be epochally eventful. Great transformations can occur in the time between the beats of a heart; the breaths of a storyteller; the thrusts of a lover. The forest had changed; its character had altered, yet it abided in itself. It was still the forest, and it was not.

It was an adaptive, homeostatic, quasicognitive living system comprising hundreds of thousands of species, billions of residents, trillions of interactions, joined together in a network more complex than even the linkages within the human brain.

Or it was the Haunted Woods where the Great Dryad lived, and the Young Pucca. Fair Janet and Young Tamber Lane. Friendly giants, ax-bearing woodsmen, princesses disguised as farmgirls. Robin Goodfellow.

Or it was both of these things. A place on a topographical map, and a place in a storyteller's imagination.

Real and make-believe.

Yes and no.

But if a change had come over the forest, was there anyone to know? Did anyone have the instruments to measure it, the eyes attuned to let them see?

Groby opened his eyes in the Bog Garden, on the afternoon in July when the change might or might not have become apparent. He waited for Lorian, who sat beside him on the old bench, to finish her program, the silent ritual he had taught her. Several minutes passed.

Bluejays were skirmishing with mountain larks in the upper branches of a golden-leaved *Robinia*, the old cultivar called 'Frisia.' It must be some squabble over territory, though it looked to Groby like a dance. The mountain larks swooped

down and then retreated; the bluejays retained defensive
positions and held their ground. Peripheral branches changed
hands, but the contest, the dance, had reached a kind of
dynamic equilibrium. The issue might not be decided before
dark.

Groby realized that Lorian was looking at him. Her eyes
were wide and glassy, like Thrull's when he had been at the
devilhemp. She didn't seem ready to speak, quite yet, so
Groby began gently humming. An old tune, something written for a play. Incidental music. One of Amy's favorites.

"It's calmer," Lorian said after a verse or two. "Everything's gotten calmer."

Groby nodded. He began to whistle.

Lorian settled back, staring at the rusty metal that was
once, she and Groby were pretty sure, a piece of sculpture.
Did that make it a piece of sculpture still? Or was even art
only mortal—did it need to be renewed, its pieces recycled
after a while?

"It feels . . . better," she said.

"I think so," said Groby.

The sun was lower than when they had started, an hour
ago. Smells of cooking blew down from the dome. Carda-
mom, thought Groby. Fenugreek. A curry. That meant Lady
Widdershins in the kitchen, bossing Thrull around.

"I think," ventured Lorian, "Amy would be happy now."

Groby nodded. The words of the old song tripped just
short of his tongue-tip: You have but slumbered here, while
these visions did appear.

"Yes," said Lorian. "And no. She would have wanted to
see it."

Groby said, "Maybe she did."

Lorian smiled softly, as though something barely substantial had caressed her cheek. "Maybe she is."

—Really?

Yes and . . .

Naked, the boy and girl walked hand in hand along the
stream to the grotto where the ancient oak hunched like a
weary patriarch, hanging on. Vesica felt very much as though
she were walking in a dream. And as in a dream, it did not

occur to her to disbelieve the great manlike being who sat quietly there, among the boulders, where lines and numbers and a name had been etched a long, long time ago in the stone. The being was large, but in a way that would not have been easy to measure. A feeling of tremendous vitality emanated from him so strongly that Vesica could feel it like pressure against her bare skin. His eyes, which shone with their own light, radiated an immense dynamism, and an even greater calm.

The boy and girl drew near him.

"What is he?" whispered Vesica.

"Can you see him?" The boy looked at her in surprise. "He's my father."

"*No*," said the being. The Presence. His voice was gentle, melodic, like the music of a waterfall. Yet it was loud, too, and seemed to come from everywhere. From the rocks, the water, the trees.

"I am not your father," he said, his smile as bright and beguiling as a rainbow. "I was Tamlin's father—but you are no longer Tamlin. Try to remember now."

Vesica drew closer to the boy, sensing his confusion, squeezing his hand. Paradoxically perhaps, she did not feel confused herself, or in any way out of place here. Rather, she had a feeling of enormous clarity, as if something long hidden had finally become plain.

The boy hesitated. "I'm . . . my name is Robin."

The great being inclined his head to Vesica. "I have kept him for some few years, with me here in the forest."

"The long dream . . ." said Robin, as though from a distance.

The mysterious other smiled. "But forests age quite slowly. He became restless. And angry."

Robin nodded—slowly, his memories returning. The Presence stood, drew near the two children. As he moved, the forest seemed to wrap itself around him with swirling, chittering activity, though none of this was quite apprehensible to the ordinary senses. He peered down at Robin with an expression of unmistakable fondness.

"And you caused a bit of trouble, didn't you?" he said. "Well, perhaps that was your right. Perhaps it was necessary, for balance."

The ineffable Presence sighed.

"Spirit alone is not good enough for you, is it? For any of you. That is good, I think."

"You gave me a body again," said Robin, in a tone of wonderment.

"It is your body," the Presence said. "I could not give you that. I tried to help you fashion it, so that you could return, but . . ." He displayed his broad, hairy, claw-tipped hands. "I have not the touch for that. You needed other help than mine."

Vesica found herself staring at her own hands, studying their fine shape, their long fingers and delicate nails, as though she had never seen them before. Robin took them in his own and stared at her.

"You," he said. "You helped me."

"She did," the Presence agreed. "And others. Many others. Do not forget so quickly: all life is one on this world. I am part of you all."

Vesica stared at Robin. Then at the Presence, then at Robin again. "Is he . . . are you . . . really, human again? I mean, still . . ."

Unexpectedly, the great being threw his head back and gave forth a bellowing laugh. It was a startling sound, and Vesica felt as though she had heard it before—the sound of the sun coming up, spring awaking, flowers in the fullness of their bloom.

"He has always been human," the Presence declared. "Even when he was half tree. It was an awkward hybrid. But a vigorous one."

In one great palm he held a single acorn: small, brown, unremarkable. He said, "*Quercus robinia*. A gift to Nature, some years ago. Now Nature returns it."

He handed the acorn to Vesica, who accepted it uncertainly, and as soon as it touched her hand it became a flower, an orchid of indescribable color and delicateness. Its fragrance, so rare in orchids, filled her nostrils yet remained elusive, defying identification. Vesica strained for it, feeling that something wonderful was slipping away from her. She looked up to find that the mysterious being was receding into the distance. Before the ancient oak he paused.

"Goodbye, children."
"Father!" cried Robin.
And *Wait*, thought Vesica, *what happens next?*
—But the story
was done.